DOGTO

Whitney Logan, attorney-at-
Monica Fullbright shows up with a thousand dollar
retainer wanting to locate her missing housemaid, an
illegal immigrant named Carmen, Whitney takes the
job. She may not like playing sleuth, but she can't afford
to be picky. Enlisting the aid of Lupe Ramos, a chicana
prostitute who works the street below her office, she
soon finds out that Monica is not all she seems. And
when the two of them stumble on the housemaid's dead
body, they quickly find themselves on a fetid trail of
Latin politics, drug smuggling and misguided allegiances.
Nothing is as it seems in Dogtown.

SOULTOWN

Whitney Logan and Lupe have gone in different
directions, the only thing in common their shared dream
of a new start. But Whitney figures she owes Lupe
something, and agrees to help her reunite her with her
son, now living with Lupe's ex-boxer brother Hector and
his new girlfriend in Koreatown. When they show up to
get the boy, they find themselves in the midst of an
armed robbery. However, this is no simple operation, but
a complicated theft involving old Korean friends.
Whitney agrees to help, and soon finds that Hector's
girlfriend Kim and the old friends all have closely held
secrets that none of them are prepared to give up. Even
her alliance with Lupe is an uneasy one. Deception is
the order of the day in Soultown.

MERCEDES LAMBERT BIBLIOGRAPHY

El Niño (as by Douglas Anne Munson, Viking, 1990;
reprinted as Hostile Witness, Pinnacle, 1992)
Dogtown (Viking, 1991)
Soultown (Viking, 1996)
Ghosttown (Five Star, 2007)

DOGTOWN
SOULTOWN

TWO MYSTERIES BY
MERCEDES LAMBERT
INTRODUCTION BY KEN BRUEN

STARK
HOUSE

Stark House Press • Eureka California

DOGTOWN / SOULTOWN

Published by Stark House Press
2200 O Street
Eureka, CA 95501, USA
griffinskye3@sbcglobal.net
www.starkhousepress.com

Exclusive trade distribution by SCB Distributors, Gardena, CA.

DOGTOWN
Originally published by Viking and copyright © 1991 by Mercedes Lambert
Reprinted by permission of the Author's Estate.

SOULTOWN
Originally published by Viking and copyright © 1996
by Douglas Anne Munson
Reprinted by permission of the Author's Estate.

"Break My Heart in Smithereens" copyright © 2007 by Ken Bruen

"Mercedes Lambert" copyright 2007 © by Lucas Crown

ISBN-10: 1-933586-21-4
ISBN-13: 978-1-933586-21-2

Cover type set in Franklin Gothic. Text set in Figural and Dogma.
Cover design & book layout by Mark Shepard, home.comcast.net/~shepdesign

The publisher would like to thank Lucas Crown for his persistence and assistance in making this book happen.

First Stark House Press Edition: March 2008

0 9 8 7 6 5 4 3 2 1

BREAK MY HEART IN SMITHEREENS
The Work of Mercedes Lambert
by Ken Bruen

"I thought you had to be drunk to write, that's what all my heroes did."
Is there a more heartbreaking line ever uttered?
Douglas Ann Munson, aka Mercedes Lambert.
I weep for her, for the wondrous talent she never realized she had, for the lost potential, for the sheer waste of a vulnerable human soul.
Here was talent writ huge.
Dogtown and Soultown.................. just pure brilliant noir classics.
Look at this.
From SOULTOWN, she is listening to the oldies. Earth Angel, Only the Lonely and then goes

I'd started to wear makeup, and there was a line of black mascara smudged under my eyes.

I swore as I used spit to wipe off the mascara. It would fucking figure I'd nod after waiting all this time.

Tell me, isn't that a killer and that is only the first page?
Soultown is stone classic.
Here's the narrator.
Dressed in a tight red skirt and purple spandex bustier, LUPE RAMOS EMERGES FROM THE LA JAILHOUSE................. ready to begin the first day of her life.
Lupe is looking for her son.
And with her friend WHITNEY, they begin and yeah, it's not going to be pretty; with a sinking heart, they find among other items, a dead body and worse in the middle of an armed robbery.
The writing is so in your face............ you are truly there... you don't want to be........... who would, and you know it's going to get worse.

But the sheer quality of the writing, the lure of Lupe, you stay for the awful ride.
And on they go, into the very mouth of hell.
Defiant and mouthy all the way.
What's not to love.

You read SOULTOWN AND................. gasp.............. at the sheer cojones of this pure spirit of talent.

Then Dogtown......... **where it all started.**

What a Novel.

Whitney Logan, lawyer, vaguely successful, the rent is 2 months overdue but who's counting.

And she is soon involved with beloved Lupe, the attorney and the hooker, allied and instead of any resolution, they find.............. a dead body................ and to say all hell breaks loose is one of the great understatements.

And the cast of characters that come down the pike.............would restore your faith in the true underbelly of life in all it's sordid and touching humanity. Few writers could convey real empathy, true hard won compassion like Mercedes.

Both of these books are among the finest noir, the best mystery you'll ever read and move you to tears, laughter and the true sense like all her heroines has of................ bring it on.

They did.

And she did.

I don't have too many regrets, but never having met Mercedes is one of the big ones.

And second.............. that she never realized she was/is, one of the major players, not just in noir but in mystery.

She breaks my heart with her beautiful writing.

And smashes it with her life of not knowing.

These 2 books stand as witness to one of the truly greats.

I never knew her and I miss her so.

KEN BRUEN

DOGTOWN
A Whitney Logan Mystery

by Mercedes Lambert

To Referee Robert Leventer
Serve the People

"If it's that delicate," I said, "maybe you need a lady detective."
"Goodness, I didn't know there were any.... But I don't think a
lady detective would do at all. You see, Orrin was living in a very
tough neighborhood, Mr. Marlowe. "
—from *The Little Sister*, by Raymond Chandler

CHAPTER ONE

Harvey Kaplan looked like he'd been dead for twenty years. At least since Woodstock. I saw him standing at the top of the stairs screaming his head off, his face turning red. The last guy in Los Angeles with a ponytail, and he was having one hell of an argument with his guru. The skinny bearded little Indian was screaming too, waving his arms around, his white robe flapping like a loose spinnaker. It had been a long time since I'd seen Harvey on his feet. Usually he just sits in his office. Sometimes I hear him chanting or the tinkle of little bells. Mostly I smell pot and incense wafting out from under his door. I try to avoid Harvey Kaplan. He is my landlord, and right now I owe him $850.

I was tired, limping in my high heels, coming back from a disappointing day at the arraignment court on Bauchet Street. I had picked up only one case, a loony woman charged with creating a disturbance at an abortion clinic. She had snuck into the recovery area to shove plastic fetuses in the faces of women who were still crying and half drugged from the procedure.

The guru pushed past me, banging into my briefcase and muttering something about motherfuckers. I had enough on my mind what with worrying about where plastic fetuses came from.

Securing a smile of deliberate but vacant pleasantness, I made it up the stairs, sidestepped Harvey, who was still hyperventilating, and unlocked the old oak door to my office.

WHITNEY LOGAN
ATTORNEY AT LAW

It cost me thirty-five dollars to have that lettering done. Before my arrival eight months ago, there had been a bookkeeping service here. They had moved out fast, abandoning a scarred orangy pressed-wood desk and a battered black file cabinet. I gave the furniture a few coats of black paint and did the walls an off-white. The building had been constructed in 1936, solid and hopeful as a WPA project. The woodwork, which goes halfway up the walls, is all real; and, except for some rough spots where the former tenants had used brackets for bookshelves, it looks good. The glass light fixture in the ceiling is authentic. I've hung a couple of Dutch Masters reproductions from the art museum on the wall along with my law degree and certificate from the State Bar. Some pink cymbidiums made from silk are arranged in a black ceramic vase on top of the file cabinet. I sit here a lot and think how nice it all looks. That the bookkeeping service went out of business should have told me something.

The usual thing when you graduate from law school is to go to work for someone else, at least for a while. Become a public defender, or a city attorney, or join a firm. You get the regular paycheck, the group insurance policy, the paid vacation. I didn't do it that way. The legal aid office where I wanted to work had closed down because their funds were cut. There was a freeze on hiring at the PD's. Same thing at the ACLU. I didn't have a mentor or any connections; I've always been a loner. This meant I was reduced to following the want ads in the *Daily Journal*.

My first interview was at the real estate development department of a large investment company on Wilshire Boulevard. They were under pressure to hire a woman attorney, and all that seemed to matter was that I had a pleasant attitude and a big bust. Rows of women at typewriters were lined up like a sweatshop. The typewriters sounded like machine guns. I fidgeted through the interview and never went back.

My next job interview the senior partner took me to lunch, offered me a job and told me he'd have my office redecorated. As I was floating out, heady with my own success, he called after me to announce we would have to go to San Diego for the weekend to firm up the deal.

The last interview was near downtown at a place specializing in personal injury. I was led down a long corridor through an impressive law library. Pausing to examine a book, I smashed my hand into the wall. It turned out that only one wall was books; the rest had been painted to resemble sets of the Federal Reporter. The partner who interviewed me had decorated his work space like the Oval Office. While he studied my resume, I studied the room. Right-wing plaques and homilies carved from wood adorned the walls. There were lots of photos of him in the embrace of local fascists and guys who looked like insurance executives. An eagle with a twisted neck stood watch behind his desk. I saw him frown when he got to the part that said I was a member of the National Lawyers Guild. He gestured around the room and asked why a nice girl wanted to work in such a dirty business. He laughed when he said this. I got up. I couldn't think of a single reason why I would want to work for him.

Eight hundred and fifty dollars is two months' rent. I dropped the briefcase into one of the matching black vinyl chairs in front of my desk. Those chairs are empty most of the time. I want to be a good trial lawyer. Serve the people. Defend the Bill of Rights. The work I get is what I'm able to hustle from court appointments and a few phone calls from an ad in the yellow pages. I do misdemeanors, drunk driving, a preliminary hearing if I get lucky.

I wrestled open the sticky window behind my desk. The August heat rushed in. Despite the roar of traffic, I could hear Harvey pacing around me as I stared out. Hollywood Boulevard, Tinseltown, U.S.A. There's a drugstore on the corner, a Thai restaurant downstairs and a place across the street that rents porno videos in Spanish, Vietnamese and Armenian. I don't know what I expected when I hung my shingle out here. I wanted to protect the downtrodden and make a modest and honest living doing it. Twenty-five years old, right out of law school, and the only advice anyone had bothered to give me was from my mother, who told me to keep my subscription to *Town & Country* magazine. I had two good suits, a strand of opera length pearls, and Harvey Kaplan breathing down my neck.

"Look, Harvey, I just need till the end of the week," I heard myself saying. If things get real bad, I'll take a divorce or a custody case. I haven't done many of them. The money is good, but I hate the sniveling and whining that go along with it.

"Whitney, you're a nice lady. You got some good vibes, but I need to get paid. I'm giving you a terrific deal. The office. My library."

Harvey had a terrific library. Cal Reporter. Federal Reporter, Benders, Shepherds. Manny Washington, the process server who comes around sometimes to take papers for me, told me that Harvey used to be one number-one criminal lawyer. I don't know what happened to him. He hardly ever leaves the office now. He's gotten tied up with the guru people, and there's a small but steady stream in and out of his office of these pasty-faced aesthetes who wear wooden beads and beam like a good shit was the secret of life. Harvey does their wills, little accident cases, and helps divest them of their property, which they give to their "foundation." Manny Washington says it's too much drugs.

Oh, my folks would help me if I asked them for money. They live in Maryland, and all it would take would be a phone call. Every time I get an idea like that, I hate myself. And my father. He always told me I'd never make it through law school, that I didn't have the brains or the personality. I went through law school on a trust fund my grandaddy set up for me. It ended when I graduated, and I made it through the bar exam on what little I'd been able to save the last year. As soon as I passed the bar, it was "my daughter the lawyer" and you'd think he'd been there with me all along making cheese sandwiches and fixing coffee while I stayed up all night studying.

I turned to face Harvey. "The end of the week. I promise." I did not have a dime. If it cost a nickel to take a trip around the world, I couldn't get to Pasadena.

Harvey sighed, stroking his gray beard, studying me while considering this extravagant pledge. "Friday, then," he said finally as he closed the door behind himself.

I will say this for Harvey: he is no lech.

Two days later I was puzzling out a discovery motion on the abortion clinic case with a couple of Harvey's books propped in front of me and a half order of rice noodles from Sam's downstairs when there was a knock at the door. I bent under the desk to find my shoes. When I looked up, there was a good-looking brunette standing in the doorway.

"Whitney Logan?" she asked as I stumbled to my feet, turning my ankle slightly while shoving one foot into a shoe. "I thought you'd be a man."

"Nope. Sorry."

"I hope you're not too busy." Her voice rose, making it into a question. "I'm Monica Fullbright. I'm looking for a lawyer to help me with a little problem. A silly little thing." She shrugged to show just how silly it was and came across the room with her hand outstretched.

Monica Fullbright's hand was baby smooth and tapered with about thirty dollars of porcelain nails, which were painted an expensive, tasteful red. She was tall, slender and well dressed in a beige gabardine pantsuit and a silk designer scarf with a horsey motif knotted around her neck. It was hard to tell how old she was. Not more than forty. She had on a good-sized diamond ring but no wedding band. Whatever kind of problem she had certainly didn't look as if it was causing her any harm.

She gave a final firm pump to my hand before sinking gracefully into one of the chairs. Monica Fullbright smelled like money, and she sure didn't look like any of the hookers I saw down at Bauchet Street. She looked the way my mother wanted me to look, like one of the women from *Town & Country* magazine. Pure Hancock Park. The class part of LA, the old money before Beverly Hills. Charge accounts at the wine store, the dry cleaners and the hairdresser on Larchmont. I felt the way I do around my mother's friends when they come over to play bridge in their cashmere pullovers and expensive loafers. My arms feel too long for the sleeves of my shirt, which is buttoned too tightly around my neck. I feel twelve years old, gawky and unattractive, although I'm wearing a navy blue silk suit and a pair of black Charles Jourdan pumps. I felt a terrific urge to bustle around the office and clean up, but I had to content myself with moving the noodles out of the way, making room to place my elbows so I could lean toward her in a manner I hoped projected great confidentiality.

"I'd love to help if I can. What's the problem?" Maybe she was rich but took little things from nice stores. Maybe she hit someone's car in a parking lot. Whatever it was, I sure hoped it wasn't a divorce.

"Mind if I smoke?" She looked around for an ashtray without waiting for me to answer. It was hidden under a stack of index cards with notes about discovery. She lit the cigarette. "Well, I'm sure you'll think this is pretty ridiculous, but I've lost my housekeeper."

A missing maid? Did she think this was an employment agency? That I was going to get up and put on an apron?

"If a person's missing, all you need to do is file a report with the police." Missing-person reports are common knowledge. You don't have to be law review to figure it out. I tried to keep my voice neutral. Her helpless attitude really pushed my buttons. I've taken care of myself for years.

Monica Fullbright dropped her head slightly and shook it as though she were a schoolgirl being reprimanded. The expensive smell was Joy perfume.

"I didn't want to report it. She's illegal. I'm not sure what the rules are, but I know I'm supposed to pay a tax or something. I was afraid if I reported her missing one of us might get into trouble. I don't know what to do. Everyone hires these girls." Monica Fullbright raised her hand helplessly so that the big diamond winked across the desk at me.

I hate to hear women called "girls." Particularly by other women. Either Monica Fullbright was a lot older than she looked or I was supposed to sympathize with her about how hard it was to get good help. Other than that, I couldn't figure out what she wanted me to do. I could fill out a missing-person report, but then so could she. I must have had a pretty blank look on my face, because she kept talking fast at me.

"She's worked for me nearly three years. My kids are crazy about her. I know it would be easy to find someone else—those girls are a dime a dozen—but it's so hard when you've already taught them how you want things done."

She was probably paying a lousy eighty-five dollars a week and working the woman like a dog. Watching the refrigerator to see how much she ate.

"When I was divorced a couple of years ago, I had to go out and get a job. I'm the manager of Crystal's. Carmen gets the kids their dinner, takes care of them when they get home from school. I can't function without her."

You read all the time about these latchkey kids who come home to an empty house and have to lock themselves inside until their mothers get home. Sometimes a fire starts and they burn to death. But that only happens in the ghetto. It does not happen to women who are managers of one of the most exclusive clothing stores in Beverly Hills.

"Carmen's from Guatemala. Every year or so she goes down there to see her family."

"How, if she's not legal?" Wouldn't she know more about this since they had been living in the same house for years? Didn't they talk to each other?

Monica Fullbright banished the beginning of a frown. "I don't know how she does it. She has a Guatemalan passport she showed me. All I know is that two times before, she's gone and come back. I'm afraid something has happened to her this time."

"What is it you want me to do?" Did she want me to call the police? To bust down kitchen doors in Beverly Hills to find out if the woman had gone to work for someone else?

"Go to Immigration, find out if they've got her. There must be a way to bail people out."

I know nothing about immigration law. I never even took the class in law school. There could be a lot of business in this neighborhood, melting pot that it is, but I always assumed they went to people who had some connection with their community or at least spoke their language. I barely know enough Spanish to get a glass of water in a Mexican restaurant. It made me wonder why Monica Fullbright had really come to see me. I was about to ask her when she stubbed out her cigarette and pulled a Gucci wallet out of her purse. She laid ten crisp one hundred dollar bills on the desk.

"I'm afraid if I go down there to look for her they'll know I've been hiring her illegally. I don't want my ex-husband to find out she's gone because he'll give me hell about the kids being alone. He knows Carmen and he thinks she does a great job. If I don't get her back, he might take me to court to change custody. He's got a new girlfriend living with him now. Maybe he thinks she'd do a better job than I have. I don't know. I just don't want to have any problems. I told you you'd think it was silly." Monica Fullbright sighed and shook her head the naughty schoolgirl way again.

Damn it. Custody cases are ugly. The clients are always hysterical. But at the hundred dollars an hour I was going to charge, who's to complain? I opened my legal pad to a clean piece of yellow paper.

"How long has she been gone?"

By the time Monica Fullbright left half an hour later, the ashtray was overflowing and I had learned a lot about her. That she lived near the Rancho Tennis Club with her two children, Mikey, who was five, and Luke, who was almost seven. That her ex-husband was a hot-tempered TV producer with an Italian last name, and he was paying a grand a month in child support. Despite all the details she gave me about the household and the good-natured ministrations of the loyal Carmen, the only thing I managed to write down was the name—Carmen Luzano.

She had left LA on July 21 and was due back on the sixth of August. That was three days ago. I didn't bother to jot down the description Monica Fullbright gave me. Dark skin, five feet tall, shoulder-length black hair. It would be hard to guess how many women in this town fit that description. There had to be at least half a million of them. Mexico. Guatemala. Two hundred thousand at a conservative estimate had fled the bloody civil war in El Salvador.

After Monica Fullbright left, the air smelled like smoke and expensive perfume, and what I was left with was a feeling that was hard to grasp. It was the feeling that I had not been told the right story. Still, the money was on the desk, and it never hurts to learn something new. I glanced at the retainer agreement I had her sign. I sketched on the yellow pad for a few minutes before I realized that I had forgotten to ask for the one thing I needed if I was going to identify the woman at Immigration. A picture of Carmen Luzano.

Although I hurried down the stairs and out to the street, she was nowhere in sight. There was only the usual motley crew—an elderly black wino on the broken green bus stop bench, a bottle of Tokay in a paper bag trailing from his limp hand; two teenage Vietnamese boys on their way to the video arcades on Western; a hooker standing in the shade of a pepper tree on the corner. I have nothing against prostitution. It should be legalized. But not on my doorstep. Wasn't I having a hard enough time making a go of it without it looking like I was working out of a house of ill repute? The ridiculous day-trippers. Purple satin hot pants. Ankle strap shoes. Bad wigs. I'd seen this one before. She was young and latin, with long curly hair. She glanced my way without any apparent interest as I walked toward her.

"You been here long?" I asked her.

"You a cop?" Her gaze swept past me out into the street, where a line of cars was approaching from downtown.

"I was looking for a woman."

She readjusted the purse that swung from her right shoulder. "I'm not into that scene."

It had been a long time since I'd been to bed with anyone. Never with a woman. Nearly three months since I broke up with Ed Harrison, the monosyllabic commodities broker I met at a bar in the Marina. Once when I was a freshman in college I did wake up in the middle of the night in bed with one of my sorority sisters. It was after a big football game where we beat the University of Virginia. I was still drunk and didn't remember much that happened after we left the party at the Sigma Chi house. I'm sure nothing happened. Nevertheless, I could feel myself blushing and I could hear my voice getting frosty.

"Neither am I. I'm looking for a woman who just came out of the building. She must have come right past you. Nice-looking woman in a beige pantsuit."

Beige was obviously not in her vocabulary. She had on a black leather miniskirt, a screaming pink stretch top that bared her midriff, several large rhinestone bracelets and a pair of white go-go boots. I myself am the dress for success type. Gray suits, navy blue skirts, sensible shoes. I've never worried about looking like I was in corporate drag because I've got a nice face and great hair. My hair is blond and wavy, and I have it cut in a chin-length bob. Simply put, a look that says classic but contemporary. Her look said cheerleader gone bad.

What is that supposed to convey? That cheerleaders do it with everyone? To feed some fantasy that men have about doing it with nubile juveniles? Under other circumstances I would have wanted to know these things. We would probably have had a rewarding conversation on this subject. We could have gotten into some consciousness raising, but I just wanted to find Monica Fullbright and get to the bank.

"Did you see her or not?"

She shrugged, still watching the traffic.

"Sorry to take up your time. I can see you're real busy here." I turned on my heel and walked to the end of the block by the drugstore, where I looked up and down Wilton. Monica Fullbright wasn't anywhere. I was going to ask the drunk on the bus bench, but he was already asleep.

Traffic burned by, commuters impatient to get home after work. I decided to call it a day and head home myself. I still live in the same place I had while I was in law school. It's a hot stucco cube in Sherman Oaks, that part of the Valley squeezed between Ventura Boulevard and the Hollywood Hills. In August and September it's like being trapped in an oven. There's no air conditioning, and they've started to let kids move in.

I gave the hooker a wide berth on my return. Chewing her gum lazily, she watched me while pretending not to. No wonder I was getting such shitty cases, stuck in this hole, this low-budget Babylon. Next, I'd be getting some lunatic who wanted me to write a will in favor of his dog.

"Hey," she called after me. "It was a beat-up, old black Lincoln. VZF 194. You're really not very good at this, are you?"

I turned back to thank her, but she was already climbing into the cab of a little white pickup that had stopped at the curb.

CHAPTER TWO

Immigration and Naturalization Services have their offices downtown in
the Federal Building on Los Angeles Street. I found this out the next day
by calling information. Bounded on one side by Chinatown and on the
other by Little Tokyo, it's a cold steel structure, an unwelcoming fortress of
indeterminate age. No sense of history, no grandeur. No uplifted torch. It's
all bulletproof glass and warnings not to trespass on federal property.

I parked my old blue Datsun in the underground parking structure
across the street and walked through the plaza of the Children's Art Museum. It was hot. Even the kids were listless. Although I had just showered
at the gym, I was already feeling sticky and uncomfortable. The tinny com-
puterized music of Triforium, a giant electronic tower that sprays the city
with unwanted harmonies and flashes of colored lights, polluted the
already overburdened air. In front of the Federal Building a group of nuns
moved back and forth across the sidewalk in their weekly silent vigil
against the war in Central America. A mutated Frank Sinatra tune
groaned behind them.

INS is on the first floor. The line was stretched out nearly to the front
door when I joined it, even though it was barely nine in the morning.
Hundreds of people from every country in the world wove their way
through an anxious maze of ropes toward a distant row of officials behind
desks. Arabic, Spanish, all the Asian languages and their subdialects
bounded off the gray marble walls. There were old women haggling
among themselves, couples quietly holding hands and whispering, children pulling away from their parents and being pulled back. There were
many uneasy-looking Filipinos rummaging through their purses, bored
Arabs smoking elegantly and with disdain. There were even about thirty
women who looked like Carmen Luzano.

Or at least what I had come to imagine she looked like.

Short. Dark. Faint moustache above the upper lip. It was hard to tell. Particularly without a photograph. I had called Monica Fullbright twice the
night before, but there was never any answer, not even the ubiquitous
phone machine. I supposed she had taken her kids out to dinner when she
got home. She probably had a microwave but was too lazy to cook. Someday soon I want to have a microwave. A VCR. A car without terrifying
noises under the hood. I was staring vacantly into space, thinking about
how grateful Carmen Luzano would be when I restored her to her full-
service kitchen, when I heard someone call my name.

"Whitney. What it is."

It was Leo Hernandez. He was a year ahead of me in law school. A real skirt-chaser but a nice guy. Totally undeterred by the fact that he's married to a beautiful woman who supported him through law school by waiting tables.

We shook hands and exchanged hasty pecks on the cheek, mine a bit hastier than his.

"So, *qué pasa?* What's shaking?" he wanted to know. "A detention hearing?"

I started to explain, but he spotted a couple of his clients waiting for him on the other side of the room before I got to the part about Monica Fullbright. I thought he might get a laugh out of it. The sheer ridiculousness of it. The fallen ideals of law students. You start out thinking you'll save the world, and you end up trying to get papers for someone's maid.

"Check B-18 for detainees," he said as he hurried away. "Give me a call if you need anything. Anything at all." His smile hooked up into a happy leer as he disappeared into the crowd.

B-18. But for that hot tip, there's no telling how long it might have taken me to find room B-18, which was located outside the building, back by the rear parking lot and down an unmarked flight of stairs. A piece of white paper was stuck to the door, but it had come loose on one side and the wind blew it about so that reading the handwriting on it was nearly impossible. Parked outside was a small fleet of unmarked green vans. The same puke-green the cops use on their undercover Ford Fairlanes. A black man in a green uniform stood watch just inside the doorway of B-18. It was very clear this was a holding tank.

Compared to the first floor, the room was strangely empty and quiet. Most of the room was separated from the short hallway by iron bars and steel mesh. There was a desk inside this cage. A door to one side of the desk led to what I guessed was a cell. Several black vinyl chairs like the ones in my office were the only other furniture. This made it somewhat easier to understand what Monica Fullbright had been worried about. No matter how many times I've been to Sybil Brand Institute for Women, to County, to the custody tanks in the courthouse, every time I hear those sally port doors close behind me, I think of all the things I've done wrong and I'm afraid I'm not going to get out again.

Behind the desk sat an INS officer with enormous breasts barely buttoned into a green shirt. Three gold necklaces with crosses and hearts fell across her chest, a gold heart hitting the plastic name tag above her left nipple.

"Give me the blue form," she growled without looking up from the paperback romance she was reading. Its lurid cover was all throbbing ruffles and Gothic castles. These books are written by divorced men using noms de plume with exotic geographic references such as Margaret Deauville and Helen Saxony.

I had to trek back upstairs to find out what a blue form was while she was riding the high Jamaican seas with a ne'er-do-well named Osvaldo or in the embrace of a sad but mysterious English lieutenant.

"Give me the A number," she said as I pushed the representation-of-attorney form across the desk to her.

"I don't know any numbers. I know the person's name, country of origin and date I think she was crossing the border. I don't know anything else."

With her lips moving, the woman read another page before she slid off the stool to copy down the information I had. She was back almost immediately, seating herself and turning to the page she had marked in the book.

"She's not here. Check El Centro."

El Centro is about five miles from the Mexican border. It's a big detention center. I've seen pictures of it on television. They try to make it look good, like a junior high school, but it has guards and very high walls. El Centro is also where they hold people waiting to come up for hearings on requests for political asylum. Carmen Luzano was, from what Monica Fullbright had told me, a woman my age, ordinary in appearance. A simple woman. I imagined she had been terrified when detained, that she had cried out for her parents and worried about losing her job. As much as I disliked Monica Fullbright, Carmen Luzano stirred all the cockles of my liberal heart. It was a major effort to get the INS woman to give me the El Centro phone number. Newton's fifth law of physics. A body at rest tends to stay at rest. And ends up a federal employee.

Back again across the lobby of Immigration through the ever-swelling crowd, back to the far end of the lobby where the telephones were located. El Centro was busy for a long time. As I waited on hold, I imagined the joy and gratitude Carmen Luzano would feel when I sprung her from wherever they had her. She could reassemble her American dream, use remote controls and get pedicures from Vietnamese refugees on her days off. Leaning against the narrow simulated-wood partition that separated me from a man who was shouting something indistinct but angry into the phone, I wondered if I would be able to get the job done in the amount of time I had been paid for. The man bumped against the partition, hitting me in the shoulder. Phone booths are out. The corporate big boys have told us we can't be trusted. We carve up the walls, we etch dirty words on the coin-return box, we spill sticky drinks on the telephone directory and rip out the pages. Increasingly, I was annoyed with Monica Fullbright's petty and bourgeois needs. I wanted to get back to the office and do some real law work. She was going to pay for this. All of it. The phone calls, the standing in lines. While they kept me on hold, I wrestled my map book out of my briefcase and studied the freeways that lead south out of the city.

Glancing at my watch, I saw I could drive to El Centro, bill for expenses and be back by five. It all turned out to be unnecessary. El Centro didn't have her either.

What if I did find her? I wondered. What then? I headed for the law library up on First between Broadway and Hill, where all the city's efforts at landscaping end and there's only concrete and gum wrappers. As usual, I tried to avoid the panhandler with the gray hair and the military cap. In my mind I call him the Captain. He's there every day by the entrance to the library, his feet wrapped in rags and stuffed into filthy tennis shoes. He waves. In the cheery booming voice of Santa Claus, he says, "Have a nice day. God bless you"—unless you are a woman. Then he adds after you've passed, in a voice so low you think maybe you're imagining it, "Suck your pussy."

With half an hour of research, I had the concept of what I was supposed to do. There would be a hearing. My incisive cross examination would be valueless. I would lose because Carmen Luzano's housekeeping skills didn't qualify her for a preference and there were already 75,000 Mexicans ahead of her waiting to get into the country. Monica Fullbright would have to look for a new girl. Hiring a lawyer is not like getting your brakes fixed—you can't guarantee results—but still I don't like starting from the down position.

It seemed like a lot for Monica Fullbright to be putting herself through. Why was she so interested in this particular maid? Didn't her kids go to day-care centers? Didn't they belong to swim clubs and soccer teams? With a grand a month she could have had an English nanny and their dinners catered by Chasens. I was thinking about all this, trying to get a bead on Monica Fullbright, when I walked right past the Captain. And he got me.

"Eat shit and suffer severe coronary failure!" I yelled back. Not hysterical, but it was the best I could think of in my black rage.

It was hot. It was smoggy. I was probably the last woman left in town wearing panty hose when the temperature had soared over 95. I hiked over to a little place on Third I go to sometimes and ordered a couple of chicken tacos and a Tecate beer. An electrical fan sputtered sporadically. I didn't know what to do next. I could ask Leo Hernandez, but he would try to hit on me again. A waitress with a gold front tooth stood sleepily by the cash register, occasionally brushing a fly away. She was probably illegal. The people at the next table were probably illegal. I was searching for a needle in a haystack. This depressed me so much I ordered a guacamole and another beer while I tried to decide what to do. Finally, admitting I was at a standstill, I got up to use their phone. Leo Hernandez wasn't in, but his secretary turned out to be real chatty. She's the one who told me about the detention centers in Hollywood and Inglewood.

I wanted either to find the woman and do what I had been hired to do or to get back to more challenging work, like the muni court trial I had coming up. I was obligated to Monica Fullbright for only three more hours. That was how I decided to try Inglewood first, because it was the farthest. Actually nothing in Los Angeles is that far. If it's farther than a forty-minute drive, you don't need to know about it. It's a foreign world. The majority of the people in this city have no idea what is forty minutes away from them. Leo Hernandez, who was born in East LA, once told me he had not been to the west side of town until he went to buy his books for the first year of law school at UCLA.

Inglewood is only thirty minutes from downtown. It is the home of Hollywood Park racetrack and the Forum, where the usherettes are outfitted in orange-and-black gladiator costumes. The detention center is southwest of the city hall so that it lies almost directly under the flight path of jets landing at LAX. It looked like an abandoned Quonset hut hastily erected on a piece of property bordering the light industrial zone of Inglewood. A high metal fence surrounded the area. The silence was punctuated every couple of minutes by the whine of a jet descending into the city. I saw only one driveway in and out of the detention center. When I tried to drive in, an INS officer sitting outside a kiosk motioned me to back out and find parking on the street. He looked bored when I handed him my representation-of-attorney form. I gave him the same info I had given the woman downtown. Running a fat thumb down a ledger of green-and-white computer printout, he shook his head. I got back on the freeway. Later I found out Inglewood is used only for busts from the airport.

In Hollywood the detention center is on Orange Grove, one of those anonymous north-south streets, where the rental prices are high and sometimes two or more undocumented families crowd into the first apartment they have ever had with hot water and a garbage disposal. Although crime is high, it looks like a regular residential area. Freebase is everywhere. Kids stand on the street corners, whistling to get your attention and sell you the crack. The older homes are inhabited by little old ladies with blue hair and broken hips who take long strolls in aluminum walkers, pursing their lips at everything. There is no sign on the detention center, but you can't miss it; it's the only building on the block with a high metal fence around it. A group of boys played soccer on the worn-out lawn behind the locked gate.

I was admitted through an electronically controlled door into a shaded hedge that led into the interior of the building. The information center was housed in what had once been the manager's apartment. Wearily I gave the representation-of-attorney statement, now dog-eared in my sweaty grip, to the officer. While he checked his list, I examined the room.

The usual gray metal desks and chairs, a few posters of an overweight Smokey the Bear from the forestry service and some dirty ashtrays.

"There's a Lusano here, but she's from El Salvador. You want to see her?" asked the INS man.

He motioned me toward a bedroom that had been made into a waiting room.

Basically I've always been lucky. I passed the bar exam the first time. I got into the law school that was my first choice. I've never had to have braces on my teeth, I've never had a serious illness and I've never been injured in an automobile accident. I have won a Panasonic stereo in a drawing at a department store. This might have explained the disappointment I felt when the woman first appeared.

She was an Indian. About four ten, frail as a bird. Her face was heavily wrinkled, and she stared back at me impassively when she was brought into the bedroom-cum-waiting area. She was sixty if she was a day. I couldn't imagine her making the long trip through Mexico, running across the open fields at San Ysidro, lying in the bed of a truck as it pulled into Los Angeles in the hours before dawn. Now they had her locked up like a criminal.

Most of my clients are guilty. It's all a matter of degree, of intent. The old woman looked at me without blinking. I couldn't think of anything to say.

"*Viva, viva,*" I told her finally. They were the only Spanish words I knew.

CHAPTER THREE

Crystal's is the opposite end of the scale. Located across town on Rodeo Drive, it is the perfect Beverly Hills boutique—slick, expensive and theatrical. Baby palm trees in terra-cotta pots flank the doorway. A parking valet in a red-and-black monkey suit stands attentively to the side, periodically checking the terra-cotta pots for offending gum wrappers or discarded cigarette butts. He leaps to attention when a Rolls-Royce pulls to the curb. He is conversant with the rich in three languages.

The doorman made a laconic half bow as I walked through the beveled glass door to look for Monica Fullbright and get some more information from her about Carmen Luzano and her disappearance. Wasn't it just possible Carmen Luzano had decided to stay in Guatemala? Had Monica Fullbright considered that?

Top-of-the-line designer couture collections are displayed like artwork against stark white walls edged in black marble. The ceiling is at least twenty feet high. Track lighting shines down from industrial steel beams highlighting mannequins casually draped with layers of exquisitely expensive Italian sportswear. An espresso bar with an enormous copper coffee machine sits in the middle of the room.

Long-legged salesgirls floated across the black marble floor with sultry deadpan expressions, eyes fixed at a spot slightly above my head as though they were on runways. A woman who was vaguely familiar to me from television was sitting at the bar having a glass of champagne while her bill was being totaled. The paparazzi hover outside the door of Crystal's when the lunch crowd has broken up at the Bistro Garden to catch those half-candid, half-contrived photos that appear on three color tabloids at the checkout stand of the market. The bored and besotted stagger into the bright sunlit afternoon with their purchases.

"Something I might show you?" purred a tall, slim redhead who appeared silently at my elbow.

"I'd like to see Monica Fullbright."

The redhead looked puzzled. "Is she New York? We don't carry her. How about one of these fabulous Leonardo shirts? We just got them in. We're the only one in town who has them." She dangled the shirt in front of me. "Sensational, isn't it?"

"Monica Fullbright, the manager."

Quizzically she looked around the room. Her cheekbones were high, her cheeks dramatically sunken. It takes at least a hundred and fifty dollars of cocaine a week to maintain that sculptured look.

"You want to see the manager? Have a seat over there." She pointed at the bar and disappeared.

Two more gorgeous salesgirls on a break were draped over the end of the bar. The one closer to me had her back turned and a mane of long, rich brown hair thrown over one shoulder. She was leaning forward, a thin white cotton skirt pulled tight against her perfect ass.

"Come on down and see me tonight," she was coaxing. "It's a lot of fun. Then we'll go get a drink or something to eat."

I sat there for a good five minutes listening to her describe her job moonlighting as a mud wrestler over on Western. I realized I had sidled practically into the middle of their conversation when a smoky voice with an English accent brought me back to the purpose of my visit.

"I am the manager. May I help you?"

I slid off the stool. It definitely was not Monica Fullbright. The woman standing before me was blond. An aging Vegas showgirl with legs up to her neck. She must have been a regular in the toughest aerobics workout in town, because even under twenty pounds of imported cashmere she looked slim. She must have been sweltering in that outfit, but she gave me a beautiful smile. I wondered if she could tell I wasn't going to buy anything.

"I came to see Monica Fullbright."

The woman studied me without replying, quickly assessing my shoes and clothes. I was glad I was always willing to pay top dollar for good shoes. She immediately dismissed my inexpensive white suit but took another peek at my navy Bruno Magli shoes.

"I'm with the Angel City Credit Agency. We're doing an investigation in connection with a loan application." I lied with such alacrity I was astonished. I consider myself very honest.

"We do not give out our customer list nor any information about our customers."

"I was told she was the manager."

"Who told you that?" she demanded in a voice like gravel.

Monica Fullbright had told me she was the manager. Granted, I don't get out much, but there's only one Crystal's. It occurred to me that all my instincts about her had been correct. That there was something innately fraudulent about her story. I didn't want the woman to see the confusion I was experiencing.

"On the loan application, she listed this as her job."

"She's not the manager," the woman snapped. "Never has been. I've been here three years and I never heard of her."

The woman was angry, but I decided to press on. She listened to the description I gave her. She even pursed her lips slightly while thinking about this so that tiny lines formed above her mouth and the lipstick seeped in like an unattractive road map.

"No, she's never worked here."

"Well, we certainly can't be approving a loan in that case." I tried to chuckle knowledgeably as if I'd had this experience many times before and wasn't really surprised. "People do these things all the time. That's why we have to go around and ask questions. Thanks for talking to me." I wanted to get out of there before she could ask me anything. I backed toward the door. Picking up one of Crystal's charge applications from a Baccarat bowl, I waved and hurried out.

I didn't look back until I got to the car, which I had parked a couple of blocks away in the residential area known as the Flats.

Were the hundred-dollar bills Monica Fullbright had given me as phony as the story about her job? Harvey had taken them from me gladly when I paid the rent. I was up to nearly eight hours of work for her and I wasn't going to do any more. I'd refund the rest of her money. If I had to. On Doheny, across from the little park that divides Beverly Hills from the west end of Boys' Town, I pulled into a gas station to call her and tell her that. I didn't trust her and I didn't like being lied to. Two teenage boy whores lounged in the shade of the building drinking cokes and swapping stories. I tried a couple of pay phones before I found one that worked. My call was picked up on the second ring.

"Hi. I'm not in now. Leave your number, and I'll call back." Monica Fullbright had recorded this message with some jazz playing in the background. The saxophone was cool and mellow, but it did nothing to smooth me out. The message I left didn't mention Crystal's. I just told her it was important for her to call me back.

I hung up feeling dissatisfied and cheated. I wanted to get rid of her right then and there. I wanted to go to her house and tell her off. Her file was in my briefcase. I got back in the car and took out my map book for the second time that day. She had told me she lived on Valdivia Street in Rancho Park. I thumbed quickly through the index. No Valdivia. I went more slowly. Still no Valdivia. I checked the file again; that was the address she had given me. I threw the map book into the backseat. The bitch. Why had she lied to me about her address? What was she up to? Tapping my fingers impatiently on the steering wheel, I wondered how long I'd have to wait before she called me again. I watched a woman on the opposite side of the street carry a bag of groceries up a flight of white stairs to the second floor of an apartment with purple bougainvillea cascading from the roof; she fumbled with a key before she got the door open. How could I find Monica Fullbright? I slumped unhappily down in the seat to think about this. In the movies the hero went to a contact at the phone company or the DMV and got the information.

That's when I remembered Lisa. I did not let myself think of this ordinarily. I'd met her in a disco right after I got admitted to the bar. A lesbian disco. I don't know why I went there. I'd never been there before and I never went back. She bought me a few drinks, I bought her a few drinks. Then she asked me to dance. I freaked out and went home. Alone. She called my office a few times after that. I did a DUI for her when I was just getting started. She worked for the phone company. Reluctantly I got out of the car and started to call Lisa but decided it was better to go in person to ask a favor. I got back in the car hoping she wouldn't try to hit on me again or that she wasn't too angry to tell me what I needed to know.

Her office is on Wilshire near MacArthur Park, where the city starts to look like the tropics. There are a few views in downtown LA where you get the sense the whole thing has been hacked out of the jungle and concrete thrown on top of it. She was on a break when I arrived. After I used the house phone to talk to her, they cleared me through security and sent me up to an employee lounge where she was drinking a coke and eating orange-colored crackers with peanut-butter filling. Lisa's a supervisor and a union shop steward. She'd been worried about the drunk-driving incident coming up at her job; I'd gotten it thrown out on a *Trombetta* motion. I figured I was in pretty good with her.

"It's a little late to be coming around to collect that dance," she said before I had the chance to explain myself.

"I need a favor."

"Sorry, girl, I'm taken. Got a new sweetheart."

"Congratulations. Look, I'm serious. I'm here on business. I need you to look up an address for me."

"I'm on break for another seven minutes. Sure you don't want a coke?" She took her feet off the chair opposite her.

I sat down.

She looked away from me and lowered her voice. "Jesus. You really are indiscreet. Where did you learn this shit? The movies? You know what could happen to me for doing this?" she growled in a whisper like an angry bulldog.

"I'm sorry. I didn't want to come...."

"I didn't say I'd do it."

"I'm desperate. I got to find this woman."

"It's an affair of the heart then?" She looked disappointed. Lisa is heavy. Masculine. I can tell she had bad skin when she was younger.

"No." I told her about Monica Fullbright.

Sucking the rest of her Coke out of the plastic cup, she ground up the remaining ice cubes, then nodded a couple of times as she examined me. "Ok, give it to me."

I scribbled Monica Fullbright's phone number on the back of one of my business cards.

I sat alone in the employee lounge watching the palm trees dance around the edge of MacArthur Park lake. In the center of the lake a fountain shoots straight up like a geyser. No design factor. No bent sculpture. No curvature or flowing water. The water shoots straight up in the air and pounds back down. They rent paddleboats from a ramshackle shed covered with graffiti. No standing in the boat. Don't go near the fountain. The lake was full of paddleboats with little Salvadorean and Mexican kids trying to get as close to the fountain as possible.

Lisa came back in. She had stopped somewhere to recomb her hair. "Call me if you change your mind."

"Sure. Definite. Thanks a lot." I stood up to shake hands with her. She pressed a small piece of paper into my hand.

I waited till I was outside to open it. There was an address in Culver City.

Culver City is a narrow strip of land between the dry concrete channel of the LA riverbed and Venice Boulevard. It's the home of MGM Studios and a sizable community of Hare Krishnas who live in apartment buildings surrounding their main temple. The temple is across the street from the Michael Jackson Burn Center of Brotman Memorial Hospital, a gift the singer was apparently moved to make after having part of his scalp blown away during the filming of a soft-drink commercial. Other than that, Culver City is Anyplace, U.S.A., with self-service gas stations, shops selling croissant sandwiches and a couple of restaurants with bad Mexican food.

The residential parts of Culver City are rather dismal shoebox apartment houses inhabited by people who stick plastic flamingos in their front yards and blue and green Hollywood lights in the bushes.

Monica Fullbright's true address was on Allison Street in the back unit of a decaying set of bungalows. An old lady in an orange plaid housedress and a gold pair of rundown-at-the-heel mules with marabou feathers on the toes was watering a strip of camellia bushes. A rheumy-eyed little poodle lay apathetically on the side of the driveway with its tongue hanging out.

I quickly invented a name for myself and a story to tell the woman, but she wasn't interested in me. She didn't even see me. All of her concentration was focused on the hose, the stream of water and the snails and dog shit she was flooding in the pools forming beneath the camellia bushes. She looked like the kind of woman who was used to minding her own business. I strode purposefully but quietly behind her to the back of the property.

The bungalow blinds were drawn. I knocked on the door and waited. I knocked again, but no one answered. I put my hand on the doorknob and jiggled it. It was locked, of course. For a minute I thought of sticking my business card under the door but decided I didn't want Monica Fullbright to know yet that I knew where she lived. I decided to go to the gym.

Gold's Gym in Venice is the bodybuilding mecca of the Western world.

Located two blocks from the beach in a semi-industrial area that is now populated by the lofts of successful artists, design firms and the extremely prestigious Chiat/Day ad agency, it is a former warehouse. There are 47,000 square feet of Nautilus, Icarian and Eagle machines and enough free weights to give one to every man, woman and child in Belize. At any given time there will be several hundred serious bodybuilders pumping iron to some jacked-up bass-heavy rock and roll while examining themselves in the floor-to-ceiling mirrors that cover all the walls.

I hurried in to get out of my suit and into my workout clothes and to see if Rodney was there. I don't know Rodney's last name. Somehow we've never gotten around to last names. He and I been knowing each other, as they say, for about two months. We've never made a serious commitment to each other, but whenever we are both there Rodney will spend some time training with me or spotting for me. Freud said, "The body is the ego."

On my way in, I glanced over to the juice bar to see if Rodney was there having one of his strawberry protein drinks, which had a strange chemical smell, or some wheatgrass, which he claims is good for toning the muscles and releasing toxins. Although there is a serious amount of steroid use here, releasing toxins is a hot topic. I like that about the gym. Conversation is limited to what you ate, how you shit it out and your muscles. I didn't see Rodney and went upstairs to the women's locker room and changed into a black bandeau top, black tights cut off at the knee and a pair of red high-tops. When I first started, I wore a baggy sweatsuit, but Rodney told me muscle is an aspect of feminine gender and that I should get clothes like the other women wore so I could watch my body as it changed.

When I was in law school, I started training at the UCLA gym as a way of handling stress. I started again just a few months ago. With my gloves and belt I hurried back downstairs. It was a leg day. I put on my black gloves and spent a few minutes stretching before looking at the weights. I went to one of the squat racks and broke down the weights that were already there. Whoever had been there before me had been squatting three hundred and fifty pounds. Weightlifting is a lot like life, and the lessons are much more apparent from the beginning. Breaking down three hundred and fifty pounds and storing the excess weights means you have to do just one thing at a time. I left a hundred pounds on the bar, wrapped a small white towel around the center of the bar and fastened my black support belt around my waist.

It's still a lot of weight for me although Rodney says I should be able to squat my own weight by now. I wanted a spotter. I looked around but didn't see anyone I knew. Squats hit the quadriceps femoris muscle group, also known as the front thighs. I stared at the bar and concentrated my energy on it. This is part of my self-realization.

"Approach the bar like a lion."

I heard Rodney's voice and looked up to see him in the mirror. Not quite six feet tall, black guy with a buzz cut. Rodney is a former Marine and former member of the Chicago Police Department, probably in his midthirties. That's as much as I know about him except that he has won the Mr. South Bay Contest and some other local contest I don't remember the name of. I have not yet been able to figure out what Rodney does besides work out, and the subject has never come up. That's how it is here: conversation is strictly limited to the body. I ducked under the bar, then straightened partially so that it rested across the back of my neck and my shoulders. I felt the weight settle on me. I stood the rest of the way so that the bar cleared the rack.

Rodney pushed a block of wood a couple of inches high behind my heels, and I backed up onto it. "Ok, baby, set often. Now and then. Set of ten. You know I'd do it for you if I could."

I squatted to parallel. By the eighth rep I was breathing like a horse and my face was contorted in an ugly way.

"...ten."

I put the bar back on the rack and grinned at Rodney. He grinned back and put another seven and a half pounds on each side of the bar. "Ok, ok, let's not be standing around. Pyramid. Five. No jive. Five."

The increase of weight was staggering. I barely got the bar back on the rack.

Rodney added another ten pounds to the bar. "Three. You not me for three."

My knees sagged, and I thought I was going to drop it. I got to parallel. I saw myself in the mirror. It was the first time I'd squatted my body weight. I pushed up, then did it two more times. I put the Olympic bar back on the rack and hid my face on the towel feeling close to tears.

"Wasn't no doubt in my military mind," cackled Rodney. He poked me in the stomach as he turned away. "Don't forget those abs."

It was very late in the afternoon before Monica Fullbright did call. I found I had spent a lot more time thinking about her than my rabid right-to-lifer whose, muni court trial for assault and battery was less than two weeks away. One of the things that I had learned so far from practicing criminal law is that only the guilty ones bother to call you very often. I was up to four calls a day from Mrs. Peterson, the "civil rights protester," as she called herself. Most of these calls were to read to me from the alarming and strangely punctuated religious tracts she carried with her. Lots of exclamation points. Lots of Armageddon.

The phone rang while I was on line one with Mrs. Peterson. Monica Fullbright sounded winded, short of breath. I thought about the way she had smoked cigarette after cigarette here in my office. Tapping the cigarette to the ashtray two times, nails perfectly manicured, the hand holding the cigarette slightly clenched.

"I went to Crystal's. They said you don't work there."

She answered quickly, "That's what I told my ex-husband. I wanted to be ready in case this turns into a full-scale custody battle. I wanted him to think that I was working in a real good place. You know how it is with guys in the industry."

This is a town of pathological liars. Everyone is making a deal. The boulevard is paved with stars and percentage points. Box Office Boffo. Even my gynecologist has *Variety* in her office.

"Ok, I understand, but don't try to horse me around. You hired me—that means I'm on your side." I decided I wasn't going to tell her I knew she had lied to me about where she lived. I was trying to think of how to tell her I wasn't going to work for her anymore.

"Of course. I know it was unnecessary. I'm sorry. I told you, this whole situation about the kids has me so upset. I know I'm probably behaving foolishly."

Did she actually have any children? Monica Fullbright might be a knockout, but she was also really an airhead. Anything she told me was a privileged communication. I couldn't tell anybody even if I wanted to. Didn't she know this from watching television? There were only two reasons she would have to lie to me: one, it was simple habit, or two, there was something about her story she didn't want me to know. My imagination began to race; she was a white slaver, a runaway heiress, on the dodge from the law....

Why was I wasting my time with her? I asked myself. Let her find another errand girl. If I could do a good job on the Peterson trial, it would help me get some more work out of Division 39. I've done only three jury trials so far—two possessions and a solicitation for prostitution—but I have a 2-and-1 record. You do a good job, the judge remembers, the city attorney remembers.

All that rapport helps. Then they want to work with you again. I was sure it was more important for me to get ready for my voir dire than get wrapped up in the hassles of Monica Fullbright's failed marriage and acrimonious ex. If in fact there was any truth to that story. I could refer her over to Leo Hernandez, who would probably give me a kickback, which the bar wants us to call a referral fee.

"I haven't come up with anything on your Carmen Luzano. I think you're wasting your time with me. Let me give you the name of a friend of mine who specializes in immigration law." I didn't want to mention the return of the unused portion of her retainer fee. Unless she said something about it first.

"She called me," Monica Fullbright interrupted. "She's here in Los Angeles."

My heart sank. Now I felt obligated to finish the job. Aren't we like doctors? Don't we have professional duties whether or not we like our clients? "Great. Let's make an appointment. Bring her in, and we'll get her status clarified." I wondered if she understood this meant the case was a deadbang loser. My pen hovered above my nearly empty calendar.

"No," Monica Fullbright said hurriedly. "She's afraid. She thinks someone from Immigration is following her and they're going to grab her. That's why she waited to call. She wants you to go to her so you can explain about the papers and the hearing."

I should drive somewhere to get her? Weren't they prosecuting people in Texas for transporting aliens and providing sanctuary?

"I told her you'd be there this afternoon. She's waiting for you." Monica Fullbright said in the voice she probably used when she wanted new jewelry, "I understand this is going to cost more for your time."

She was right about that. "It's my usual. A hundred dollars an hour."

"I can pay it."

Could she? It wasn't much of an apartment she lived in. She had signed a retainer agreement with me. I was going to have to develop a form so they'd have to provide me with some information, like a driver's license, in the event they tried to skip out on my bill. A quick credit check, whatever they run in order to accept Visa and MasterCard. They hadn't taught us this in school. She better not bitch when she got my bill.

Although the street name she gave me was familiar, I looked it up to be sure. A business area downtown. I checked my hair, turned on the answering machine and locked up the office. I was nearly down the stairs before I remembered that they speak Spanish in Guatemala.

The hooker was by the pepper tree, as usual. Hollywood Boulevard late in the afternoon, the constant line of traffic, an argument erupting into a fight in front of the camera store across the street. A couple more hookers—black ones in purple lame and wigs like the Supremes—stalked the corner. That afternoon she was a blonde. She was wearing a red knit minidress with black fishnet hose and a pair of black sandals. The "chase me, catch me, fuck me" kind, with clear-plastic heels. She was picking at her cuticles.

"Hi."

She looked up suspiciously.

"Do you speak Spanish?"

"Do cops eat doughnuts?" She gnawed on her finger until it began to bleed, then spat the offending piece of skin on the sidewalk.

"How much do you charge for your time?"

She put her hand on her hip and lifted her chin to take a better look at me. "Just your time. That's all I'm interested in. I need to hire an interpreter. How much do you charge?"

"You tell me."

She'd been arrested. All the girls I talked to at jail used that line.

"No, you tell me."

"Thirty-five for a straight fuck or a blowjob. It goes up from there. Where's the guy? I need to see him before I decide." Her voice was childish and breathless. I hadn't noticed that before. She had painted a black beauty mark above the left side of her mouth. "If you're heat, this is entrapment," she pouted. "It'll never stick."

I'm five eight in my heels. She was at least four inches shorter and a lot lighter. She looked like a kid.

"You've been in jail, haven't you?"

She shrugged. "Once."

"This is a real job. No sex. Fifty bucks. All you have to do is come with me and translate what I say." I didn't know if this was enough to offer, but it was the best I could do.

She thought this over for a few seconds while she watched the traffic. "You want me to talk dirty, is that it? Ok, fifty bucks and I'll tell you about a guy who fucked me with a champagne bottle. Let's go sit down in the coffee shop." She turned on her clear-plastic heels and started to walk.

"No, you don't have to tell me anything. I'm a lawyer and I just need someone who can translate for me while I'm talking to a woman from Guatemala. I'll pay you. Now, do you want it or not?"

Another line of cars approached from the east and went past us without slowing. The last of the cars sped out of sight toward West Hollywood.

"I got to be back by nine," she said finally.

We were already in my car and I was trying to get the air conditioning to work before she spoke again.

"Where we going?"

I handed her the paper on which I had written the address. I told her about Carmen Luzano. Leaving out the part about Crystal's and the thousand dollars.

She glanced at the address, then folded the paper. "Sounds like bullshit to me."

"What do you mean?" Obviously she had no concept of what life was like west of La Cienega.

"There's a million crummy offices downtown with guys who do immigrations. *Trámites.* You don't even have to be a lawyer. They're like notaries. Very official-looking rubber stamps. Very latin. If this Carmen wanted papers, she'd go to one of them."

"She's scared," I argued. "She needs the lady she works for to take care of it for her. She's probably not very bright." I bit my tongue. What the hell did I care what the hooker thought? I was paying her. Under other circumstances I would have called the interpreters' office at the court building and gotten a referral to someone certified, someone qualified.

"What's your name?" I asked, resolving to make our time together as painless as possible.

She crossed her arms in front of her chest and stared out the window without looking at me. "Lupe."

"So, what country are you from?" I asked, making a last-ditch effort to communicate with her.

"East LA," she snapped.

After that there was silence as I drove over to Wilshire Boulevard and turned left, heading for downtown. Near Western is the building that houses the Office of the British Consulate. When I was in law school, I demonstrated in front of it in solidarity with the IRA hunger strikers in British prisons. I hadn't had that thought for a long time. Bobby Sands, dead for at least two years.

"You're an Aquarius," she guessed.

She couldn't possibly believe in that crap, could she? I didn't say anything. I wondered how she knew I was an Aquarius.

"Look, look! Isn't it beautiful? Norma Talmadge's husband bought it for her," she cried, excitedly pointing out the window at an old pink-and-white building on the corner.

"The silent-screen star?"

She nodded. "This was the most fashionable area in the early part of the century. Everybody stayed at the Ambassador." She rattled off a list of stars: Marion Davies, Charlie Chaplin, Joan Crawford . Then in a low, reverent voice she whispered, "Marilyn Monroe went to modeling school at the Ambassador."

So that was it. The wig. The beauty mark. The whispered voice. She must have thought she was the reincarnation of poor Norma Jean. This time I looked out the window, not wanting to talk but acutely aware of a static rubbing sound like crickets as she crossed and recrossed her legs.

"Get into the other lane, then turn right," she told me after I had driven a couple of miles east. Although she seemed to know the area, she unfolded the paper and checked the address again. Then she looked at me as though measuring me for something, double-checking me on the story I'd given her about needing an interpreter.

I slowed down and did as she said, swinging the car onto Main Street. We were on the western edge of the garment district.

"There it is," she announced, pointing out the window again.

The building we were looking for was eleven stories of brick shaped like a U and hung with a series of orange-and-brown-striped awnings that sagged over the sidewalk. A flophouse called the Hotel Vogue was next door, and the rest of the block appeared to be businesses that either sold or repaired sewing machines. Two oriental tailors and a mini-market occupied the ground floor. A row of open windows on the second floor revealed a sweatshop with a group of hunched-over Mexican women in black listening to Spanish rock and roll. I couldn't tell what else was upstairs. It could be hotel rooms, stores, wholesalers, more sweatshops or offices.

I pulled into a lot behind the theater across the street. The theater was real old Hollywood, with Greco-Roman columns someone had thought to update—improve, if you will—with red, yellow, green and blue neon. This was once a beautiful city. Now no one seems to care about its preservation.

Lupe got out of the car to wander around the closed ticket booth, inspecting what was left of the ornate carving. A man at the edge of a crowd waiting for a bus detached himself from the group to sidle up and whisper in her ear.

I had shoved some money into the hand of the parking attendant and now I hurried up to Lupe and touched her on the back of the elbow to get her moving.

"Hey, let's go."

"What do you think? I'm going to turn a trick right here?" Lupe snapped.

"No, I didn't say that. But we have to hurry. The woman's waiting for us, and I'm sure we both have other things we want to do this evening."

A fire escape snaked up the right side of the building. It made the place look like a seedy East Coast tenement. From the construction, the general air of neglect, I guessed it to be forty to fifty years old. That is an old building for Los Angeles. The lobby was ocher-painted stone. Two stairways flanked a bank of elevators. A guard was on duty, but his back was turned and he was trying to make time with a pretty woman in her early twenties who was waiting for an elevator. He didn't notice us.

With the paper on which the address was written clutched in her hand, Lupe was already halfway up the stairs.

"You got terrible handwriting," she said. "Look at the way it's all jammed into the right side of the paper and the way your loops are all crooked. You know what that means?"

It means I must be out of my mind to be rattling around this old building with some birdbrained harlot who thinks she's a movie star. And a dead one at that. I was slightly out of breath by the time we got to the third floor and my legs felt like they were on fire from the squats I'd done that morning. The hall was deserted.

"Here's 320!" Lupe called out.

"Be quiet." I knocked on the door. The sound echoed down the hall. From somewhere else came the hum of sewing machines. No one answered the door.

"I thought you said she was waiting," Lupe said rather smugly, jiggling the door now.

I knocked again, louder. "She is."

"*Somos amigos. Abre la puerta,*" Lupe called, twisting the knob and leaning into the room as the door swung open.

The room was empty down to its yellow walls. A broken fluorescent tube of light in the ceiling blinked on and off. A kicked-in gray metal wastebasket was on its side in the middle of the floor. Beside it a woman lay stretched out as if she were crawling. The windows were closed and it smelled like gardenias.

I have never seen a dead person except for Kevin O'Rourke's mother. She died of cancer when we were in the tenth grade. There was a rosary at St. Margaret's, and they put her on display in an open casket. Someone had dressed her in a frilly navy dress and a pair of red earrings. Her hair looked very stiff. Kevin O'Rourke stopped dating my friend Jacquie Dill shortly after that. He eventually left school and transferred to a seminary.

"She's dead," Lupe decided as she strode past me. She put both hands under the woman's right shoulder and turned her over so I could see for myself.

The woman's arm hit the floor with a thump. Her hair was black. Her skin was dark. Bright pink lipstick was smeared across her full lips and her chin. An old thin scar above one eyebrow cut almost to her scalp. Her eyes looked as if dying had surprised her and it had hurt. A lot. Her black dress with white polka dots was caught up around her waist, and her torn black bikini underpants dangled uselessly from one hip.

"Carmen?" I put out one hand as I walked toward her, as though I could help her up or shake her awake.

"Junkie. Must have o.d.'d." Lupe knelt beside the body. She pointed to a needle on the floor between the woman's hand and the wastebasket.

Was I going to have to call the police? Did I have to tell them about Monica Fullbright? "What do we do now?" I must have said aloud.

"Get a drink." Lupe pulled the woman's skirt down, covering her nakedness.

CHAPTER FOUR

The place looked more like the bowling alley on the *Titanic* than a cocktail lounge. From the far end of the room came the click of a sporadically hit pool ball, the sound of one guy passing time. I picked my way carefully across the dark water-soaked carpeting and around a couple of broken pinball machines that blocked the way to the bar. Three red baby spotlights suspended among the exposed wires on the ceiling shone down, making the fat man behind the bar look like a braised maraschino. The toothpick in his mouth snapped to attention as Lupe climbed onto the barstool, her red knit miniskirt riding dangerously close to that which is referred to by the poets as "the mound of Venus."

"Martini, straight up. Double olives. Two of them," she said, laying her purse on the bar and settling herself without seeming to notice his oily leer.

I didn't think she was old enough to drink. But since I met Monica Fullbright, all of my perceptions had seemed questionable. The jukebox had blown a speaker, or along with everything else I was losing my hearing. The sound was cranked up as high as it could go, but it kept fading in and out. Bobby Darin was singing "Mack the Knife." He sounded like a pygmy who was being strangled. My hands were sweating.

Behind us five Mexican cowboys with big hats were crowded into a booth next to the cigarette machine. I noticed the machine had a padlock on it. We were only a couple of blocks from the bus station. The cowboys howled like coyotes at Lupe's legs. Lupe didn't seem to notice, even when the cowboy on the end of the booth fell off the black banquette. None of the cowboys had even looked at my legs, and I have very nice legs. Over the cash register hung a tattered Dodgers' schedule and a large red sign announcing the management's intent to arbitrarily refuse service. I found myself pushing my fingers through my hair as I died to collect myself. I felt like I'd run a 10K instead of walking half a block.

"I can't believe it. She's dead," I repeated to Lupe, leaning toward her, my mouth pressed against her ear.

There were more animal sounds from the banquette. It was the third time in less than fifteen minutes that I had made this statement to her.

"Dead as a mackerel. Hey, shaken not stirred," she said to the bartender.

"Of course, ladies." He turned his back to us, and there was a violent sound of metal hitting glass before he laid a spoon down on the counter and turned to us with his wet red smile.

I dried my hands on the little napkin printed with dirty limericks and pictures of naked women that the fat man slapped in front of me.

"Oh, for crying out loud, calm down. Drink your drink. Here's looking at you. Here's looking at you, kid," Lupe said in a throaty voice, lifting her glass and giving the mirror a left profile. Casting her eyes demurely downward, she raised her eyebrows slightly as she studied the effect in the reflection of this Lauren Bacall impersonation.

"I am calm. Very calm. I just need to figure out what to tell the police about why I was there." I crumbled the napkin and dropped it on the bar. My job is to protect my client. And I don't like the police much, anyway.

"You want me to call the police? I'm not scared. I called the cops when my cousin Beto o.d.'d."

"No. I'm on my way to the phone right now. I was just practicing in my mind what I'm going to say. Like what time it was when we were there." I looked down at my watch. Seven fifteen. Less than an hour and a half since I'd left the office.

Lupe drained her glass, watching me without saying anything, waiting for something. She sucked the last olive out of the drink. "The cops are going to be real excited about a dead hooker."

"What are you talking about?"

Lupe tossed the matchbook in front of me. It was black with red lettering. Blossom Club.

"Blossom Club." She pushed the matches closer to me. "This was on the floor when I rolled her over. It's a new club downtown. Dime-a-dance place."

What would Carmen Luzano be doing in a place like that when she had a good job with Monica Fullbright? That didn't figure. I didn't even know those places still existed.

"I don't know who that girl is we found, but she's not the Guatemalan you told me about," said Lupe, cutting in on my thoughts.

"Of course she is. How can you tell what nationality someone is just by looking at them?"

"Her teeth were in real good shape. Unnaturally good shape. Caps, I think. She had a vaccination scar on her arm, and the insides of her legs were shaved. Those latin girls let it grow, like jungles. I say she's an American, a chicana."

I swirled the empty martini glass in my hand. "It's pretty hard to believe that some complete stranger would just happen to wander into the same room where I'm supposed to meet Carmen Luzano and then die."

"Suit yourself. I'm only telling what I seen," Lupe said, still angry, picking up her glass again. The cowboys lurched into a drunken version of "Rancho Grande" and were shouting to be heard over Bobby Darin.

Impartially I tried to let this information sink in. The din of ragged voices was starting to give me a headache, and the cheap gin was eating at my empty stomach. It would save a lot of trouble if the dead woman were some random interloper. But now that Lupe had thrown down the gaunt-let, I had to prove the dead woman was Carmen Luzano. And I owed it to my client. It wasn't just that Monica Fullbright had bought my time; it was more than that. Whenever I think of turning my back on something I've begun, I hear that old familiar refrain of my father: "Quitters never win and winners never quit." I heard it now and deep in my gut recognized it. It was the strange and probably unhealthy combination of feelings that I have had all of my life; a feeling of duty, of responsibility, and the belief that there is some one perfect act I can perform to win Daddy's love.

The door to 320 hadn't been locked. Maybe Lupe was right. Maybe it was just a neighborhood shooting gallery.

I slid a ten to the fat man. "I'll go back to have another look at her," I announced to Lupe. She was on her feet and behind me although I didn't ask her to come and I didn't want her with me.

By the time we got back to the building, the sun had dropped behind the skyscrapers to the west so that a purple sci-fi glow softened the stone exterior. There is a natural but theatrical order to things here in Los Angeles. The cinematographer's golden patina of afternoon. Then the pink or orange sunset made glorious by smog. Purple. Fade to black. In the parking lot where I'd left my car next to the movie theater, a film crew was beginning to set up a ring of tungsten lamps, framing a shot. That happens here, the conversion of street corners to sets. A certain unreality of location, an uncertainty of time.

All the doors were locked except the one at the far south of the building. A straight-back chair was pulled close to the door. The security guard I'd seen earlier wasn't there, but he'd probably only gone to the can or across the street to pick up some tacos. I hurried inside, gesturing for Lupe to stay out on the sidewalk where she was. She pulled her attention away from the crew across the street.

"It's only television," she said, shrugging, then she slipped through the door after me.

I'd tried to make it clear I didn't want her on my tail, but I didn't want to waste time arguing with her. I ran up the stairs on tiptoes so I would-n't make any noise. Lupe must have taken off her sandals, because I didn't hear anything except the sound of our breathing until we got to the third floor. Nearby the elevator rumbled to a stop. I began to imagine being taken into Division 82 through the back door, the end of my brilliant career. Was it breaking and entering if one door downstairs was unlocked? The elevator doors opened. I pushed myself flat against the wall of the stairwell, pinning Lupe beside me with one arm. We looked at each other sideways like people edging around a ledge. I could feel her breasts rising and falling under my arm. The elevator doors closed.

"Stay on the stairs. Keep an eye out." I pulled my arm away quickly, embarrassed. If anyone did come along, she was smart enough to say she worked in the building, that she had worked late, that she was on her way to meet her boyfriend.

The lights hadn't come on yet, but the pink sunset was oozing in through a window at the far end of the hall. Someone had placed a package outside the office belonging to a button supplier. The door to 320 was closed just as I had left it. It was still unlocked. I felt the knob turn easily in my hand. It was one of those proverbial moments when your life passes in front of your eyes. I saw myself jumping off the roof at Melanie Hemmingway's house on a dare when I was eight, swimming past the end of the pier at Wocala Beach in the dark, joyriding in a stolen car with Maxie Lewis when I was sixteen, the car accident when I was a freshman in college and the girl in the front seat went through the window. I would never be here if I didn't hate my father. I'd be home, safely married to a guy with group insurance and monogrammed shirt cuffs. I didn't want to see the dead woman in the torn underpants, but I stepped into the room.

The neon was still blinking. The walls were still yellow, the trashcan still upended.

But the room was empty.

Why had I never wondered if there had been sharks in the ocean at Wocala Beach? Or how high the roof I'd jumped off was? My heart pounded. Had someone seen me this evening when I discovered the dead woman? Clearly someone didn't want her death known. But I had seen it. And so had Lupe.

Slowly I walked back out of the room through the open door down to the end of the hall. I stood staring numbly into the fading pink line of the horizon. The window looked out over an alley separating the building from an equally dismal row of sweatshops fifty yards away. It was postnuclear—the gutted buildings, the alley empty except for a trio of stalking cats. A number of chutes jutted out from the building and ran down to green metal dumpsters. The dumpsters were probably full of rats.

I decided I didn't want to find out what other horrible things they might have in them.

CHAPTER FIVE

"How can she be gone?" demanded Lupe when I got back to where she was waiting and told her what I had seen.

Dazed, I shrugged and started down the stairs to get out of the building. "Don't know," I mumbled.

"Didn't you look for her? She couldn't have walked out on her own."

"Let's go." I tried to step around her.

Lupe planted herself in front of me and glared up at me. "Wait a sec, didn't you haul me down here so you could do a job? Find some broad. And now you're not even going to look for her? You did take someone's money to do this, didn't you?"

"You said it wasn't the same woman, so why should I—"

"*Exactamente.* You don't know if it was the same woman or not. Shouldn't you find out? That's what you got paid for. You think I put myself out on the street, take someone's money and then say, 'Oh, I don't know if I want to do this or not.' "

"It's not the same."

"Isn't it? You took money from a trick, a client, whatever you people call them. Fucking lawyers. Biggest crooks around." Lupe shook her head. "Well, you might try to jack her, but not me. You still owe me fifty bucks."

I turned and went back up the stairs. I did owe Monica Fullbright something. I searched the room again. I looked in the alley. I opened the dumpsters. Lupe sauntered after me, not saying anything.

"That's it? That's all you're going to do?" She put her hands on her hips when I had lifted the cover of the last garbage can.

"Yeah. What the fuck else do you think I should do?" I dropped the lid of the dumpster loudly.

"Go to the Blossom Club. Ask who she was."

All the way down Figueroa I asked myself what I was getting into. Yes, why was I doing this? Because I felt obligated to Monica Fullbright? Something about my childhood has made me believe that whenever something goes wrong it's my fault. It could be a drought in Ethiopia, a flood in Peru, and it's my fault. And I should do something to fix it. I'd already worked past the number of hours Monica Fullbright had paid me for. Now I was moving fast into territory I knew nothing about. I'm not talking Figueroa Street, a major north-south transection named after one of the original Spanish land grant dons and commemorated in the Christmas Parade down Hollywood Boulevard by stylized banditos on palominos weighted down with fifteen hundred pounds of silver saddle trappings and embroidered charm hats. I'm talking about bodies that moved and women who died with their legs splayed.

Lupe stirred restlessly in her seat. It was only a few blocks to where we were going. I had tried to give her cab fare, to tell her to go home, to leave me alone, but she wouldn't. Her insistence was almost savage. At first I had thought she was scared because she believed the dead woman was a prostitute. Maybe the woman's death reminded her of the brutality and danger of her own life on the streets. Maybe the woman reminded her of a friend. The more I watched Lupe in her silence, I realized she wasn't scared, she was angry.

Just up ahead on top of a tall, ugly old building that looks like a Masonic Lodge is an ocean liner. Los Angeles is a very strange place, a city where illuminated ships can float through the night sky, where the entire meaning of life can be reduced to twenty-five words and it is called high concept. We passed the Variety Arts Center, a vaudeville preservation hall and repository of one of the great collections of black-and-white glamour photos of the forties. Or so Lupe told me.

The Blossom was on the south end of Olive.

"Look at that." She pointed out the open passenger window into the dark at a large, nearly deserted parking lot we were passing. "Know what that is?"

I shook my head.

"The first movie studio in LA. Dude named Selig rented an old mansion that was there and did a movie called *In the Sultan's Power*. About 1909. I never seen it. Director got shot to death a few years later right in front of the studio. And what does it look like now? Just another old parking lot."

A warm night breeze blew in, rustling some loose papers lying among files on the back seat. Lupe slumped back into silence and stared moodily out the window.

Parking the car behind the dance club, I hesitated, then started nervously to check my hair again in the rearview mirror. But I caught my hand as it was reaching to turn the mirror toward me. I wasn't going to let her see that I felt foolish or confused.

I got out of the car and looked at the Blossom. "Can we just walk in? Do they let women in these places?"

Lupe shrugged. "Not really. They don't want B girls and hookers hanging around trying to crash the scene. You're going to have to give the guy at the door some money."

They couldn't possibly think I'm a hooker, I started to protest to her, but she was already moving and I had to hurry after her as she approached the door to the club. She smiled at the young Korean who was manning the door and squeezed his arm. I couldn't hear what she was saying, but he smiled back at her and laughed with surprisingly yellow teeth for a guy so young. Lupe stepped past him into the club. I started to follow her, but he stopped me. I pulled ten dollars out of my purse uncertainly and held it toward him. He shook his head. I extracted two fives and added them to the ten. He took it, flashed me the yellow teeth, and let go of my arm.

Inside, the Blossom was surprisingly trendy and neon. There was absolutely nothing reminiscent of blossoms or flowers. I had expected murals of cherry trees or at least a few potted plants. The bar was outlined by fuchsia light tubes, and the walls were painted a light gray. A sound system played anonymous white dance music. The place was packed with prosperous-looking Korean businessmen in dark blue suits and imported ties. There were no Mexican or Central American customers. All of the women I saw on the dance floor were oriental.

"This doesn't look very promising," I snapped at Lupe.

"Yeah, well, you figure it out. I'll be in the bathroom."

Sighing, I turned to make my way to the bar. None of the men I passed at the tables along the way looked at me with more than a second's flash of interest. I threw my chest out and told myself it didn't bother me. All of the stools along the bar were occupied by oriental women in slinky dresses and by overfed businessmen. I saw the only empty table, away from the dance floor, and headed for it. As I seated myself, I looked out across the dance floor and saw one thin black woman dancing. So they did hire women who were not oriental. Then I saw a latina with an older gentleman shaking herself in a quickstepping but fluid motion. During the next two numbers I studied all the women.

"You like something from the bar?"

I looked up at the waitress who stood beside the table. She was short and curvy, with long black hair and a short black dress.

"Two martinis."

She turned away.

"Miss?"

She turned back with an artificially patient look and readjusted the drink tray with empty glasses that she held in her left hand.

"Can you tell me if there's a woman named Carmen working here?"

"Carmen? No Carmen. Two martinis, yes?" She started to turn away again.

"Any Mexican women?"

"Only Mexican girl, Maria." She pointed out onto the dance floor to the latina I had already seen. "Here the men like Korean girl. Japanese girl." She gave me a look that said I was wasting her time and hurried away.

"That was very nicely handled," said Lupe, who reappeared at that moment and took the chair opposite mine. "Good thing you're not planning on becoming a detective. But I think she's telling you the truth. I took a quick walk around and didn't see anybody latina. Let's get out of here."

"I just ordered a couple of drinks," I fumed, not wanting her criticisms. It was her idea we come here. She had insisted on it and pushed me into it.

"I don't want another one."

"Well, I do and I just ordered them, so we're going to sit here and drink them."

Lupe crossed her arms and looked back out across the dance floor. Her foot tapped impatiently on the gray tile beneath her. "I can't believe I used to be into this scene. It's pathetic. I hate talking to these bozos."

"Aren't these women more like courtesans than prostitutes? Aren't they supplying more than just a sexual service?" I prodded.

"Oh yeah, they're all marriage and family counselors. I bet more than 99 percent of these guys here are married. Where'd you come from, a turnip truck?"

The necessity of a snappy comeback was eliminated by the waitress setting two martinis in front of us.

"No olives? You didn't ask for olives?" Lupe looked at me and shook her head in disapproving disbelief. "A fucking turnip truck." She lifted the glass to her lips and drained it in three swallows.

My hand shook as I reached for the glass in front of me. I drank the martini in two gulps. I thought I was going to fall over sideways when the first wave of gin hit my stomach, but I didn't let anything show on my face. If I had to go up against her, she would see that there was nothing she could do better than I could. I left my last ten on the table and rose, slightly woozy, from my seat. Then I led the way majestically to the car.

"So, you used to work in a dance hall? That's how you know so much about it?" I asked as I unlocked the car door for her. I couldn't stop myself from needling her.

"Latin place. Not racist like this joint. I don't know how that one latina we saw in there got hired. Hey, that's it," she said, snapping her fingers. "That Carmen, or whatever you say her name was, was probably working at one of the latin joints and she came over here thinking she could make more money but she got the door slammed in her face. I bet she worked at that trap, the Club Tropical, where I used to work. That's where all the girls start out."

"Where is it? I'll go check it out," I said eagerly.

"The Club Tropical." She gave it an accent and smiled at me. "You can't go there. You're a *gabacha* and you don't know your way around."

"I do, too."

"Don't be ridiculous. Just drive." Without looking at me, she fastened her seat belt.

I slammed the car door shut and got in on the driver side, mumbling under my breath at her.

"Down to Pico," she ordered.

The streets were full of latinos standing in front of apartment buildings, drinking beer, making love against their cars. Vendors sold tacos. It was like a small village but in the very center of the city. Lupe's directions were cursory, and we headed west of downtown.

"Won't you at least share your vast experience with me and tell me what this place is like?" Even I didn't like the tone of my voice.

She didn't snap back at me but instead, as if there was something important on her mind, replied rather absently, "I worked there a week and a half maybe six, eight months ago. It's full of part-time hookers and women who are looking for husbands. Women who are hard up and don't know where else to go. Lots of the men are *mojados*, wetbacks, but the owners try to make sure all the women are legal. They have enough hassles with vice poking around they don't want *la migra* coming down, too. It was run by a guy named Jimmy Olvidado. They call him the Pirate because he's got a big moustache and a bad leg."

As I slowed the car near our destination, Lupe pulled out her cosmetic bag from her purse. "You should put on some makeup."

I glanced sideways, watching her redo her mouth and add several layers of eye shadow to her already black eyes. My idea of makeup is mascara. Maybe some cherry-flavored lip gloss for a big date. She patted the blond wig carefully into place before snapping the compact shut. But now, here we were parked outside a dark box with a flashing sign that said Club Tropical.

"Let me have some of that stuff." I put four shades of purple around my eyes, bright pink on my cheeks, and rubbed some luminescent crimson across my mouth. I took off my suit jacket, hung it carefully behind me, unbuttoned my white silk blouse to where my bra began to show and ratted my hair up with my fingers. Lupe was looking at me with interest, or maybe it was just amusement; I thought she was about to make some crack, but all she did was mumble, "I gotta make a call," and head for a phone booth outside a little market further down the block.

I hastened after her.

"Don't you get scared walking around at night?" I asked, looking up and down the street as I stood near the phone. This was another one of those phone booths with the door ripped off.

"No. I got more things to worry about," she said as she dialed. "Anyone can get killed on her way home. Your car can go off the road. Freeway shooters. Anyone can get killed by some weirdo who gets off on that stuff. There's all kinds of creeps. No, I just got to worry about incurable diseases and assholes who try to put out cigarettes on my tits."

Suddenly I felt like a clown. I wished I could rub the ridiculous makeup off my face. That I had never put it on. It was all the things I hate about being weak, about having people think I'm vulnerable just because I'm a woman. "Why are you doing this? Why don't you get a regular job?"

"And do what? Maybe I could get lucky and be a meter reader for the gas company?"

"I don't know. You could be a receptionist. You could go to school..."

"Oh yeah, maybe I could become a brain surgeon in my spare time. Maybe... *Oye*, Mom." She turned her back to me so I couldn't hear well.

"Did Joey go to sleep all right tonight?" Then to make sure I didn't catch any more, she switched to Spanish.

"Who's Joey'?" I asked when she hung up the phone. "Your brother?"

"You're too much, you know that? You're used to poking your nose into everyone's business. You think life's just like walking into a holding tank and getting some complete stranger to tell you every terrible thing he's ever done so you can concoct some defense. 'Ohhh, she was poor. She was from a broken home.' All that bullshit. I bet you think you're a liberal or some kind of red, too."

Actually I'm a "declines to state" because I don't want to get a lot of junk mail, but I didn't bother to tell her that. I just went and stood by the curb with my hands in my pockets. The only cars I saw were far in the distance, and it was still except for the whoosh of the Harbor Freeway, which was a couple of blocks away.

"Sorry. Guess I am a little shook up tonight," she said after a long silence to my back. "Joey's my baby. My mom's taking care of him. I'm twenty-one years old. From East LA. Here's a picture of my boyfriend, Alfredo Gomez. Anything else you want to know?" She extracted a wallet from her purse, and from it she then removed a black-and-white photograph encased in plastic, which she shoved in my face.

Lupe and a man stood side by side with their arms around each other. I took a quick glance at the handsome latino. He had a big smile and beautiful dark eyes, but he was about three inches shorter than Lupe. "Forget it. You don't owe me anything. I'm not the cops. Or your pimp." I turned with irritation toward the car.

Lupe grabbed me angrily by the arm and spun me toward her. "I've never had no pimp," she exploded. I pulled my arm away from her to walk back toward our destination.

Men had been entering the Club Tropical. Usually alone. Older men in cheap suits, thin handkerchiefs tucked into breast pockets. Occasionally a pair of young latinos with polished boots and brilliantined hair. The slightly hesitating walk of the newly arrived, the illegal. The hesitation but without looking back.

At least that's the way I felt when I walked in. It was dark. There was actually a red light in the entrance. A big Samoan bouncer stood at the bottom of a flight of stairs that led up to the dance hall from which music was pounding and lights flashing. It must have been one of the last places in town still using strobe lights. It was like having an acid flashback except this wasn't a college frat party with boys dressed up in togas made out of bedsheets.

Something like an earthquake made the floor shake, but it was only the big Samoan moving to block the stairway.

"We're here for jobs," I heard myself saying. "Heard they were hiring."

"Ad said we could start tonight," Lupe added, placing one delicate brown hand on the railing. Her scent enveloped me. It was Arpege. My mother used to wear Arpege. I hadn't thought of that in years.

"Upstairs. Mr. Olvidado's office. First one on the left," the bouncer told us in a surprisingly soft, melodic voice.

Jimmy Olvidado's office was furnished in cheap blond Swedish modern, the kind that was popular all across America in the late fifties. A long, low table with a turquoise blue ceramic ashtray and lots of cigarette scars stood in front of a couch of beige-and-blue nubby fabric. Jimmy Olvidado was slumped on one end of the couch with his feet up on the table in front of him, a black telephone balanced on his paunchy belly. His head was cocked, pressing the telephone against his shoulder, and he was telling someone off in Spanish. He had a moustache the size of a shower curtain.

He looked at our legs and our tits. If he had ever seen Lupe before, he didn't show it.

"Good evening, ladies. Nice to have you with us. You going to be starting this evening? Good," he said before either one of us could speak. "You ever done this before?"

I nodded my head yes. Lupe shook her head no.

"All right, fine. We got a nice place here. No dating the customers. Work as many nights a week as you want. It's thirty cents a minute; clock in and out. Tips are yours. See Ruth next door. She'll get you fixed up with your time cards."

Ruth, a very tall black woman, looked at our driver's licenses and Social Security cards without much interest, as though she expected them to be phony. I noticed that Lupe's full name was Guadalupe Virginia Ramos. Then Ruth led us to the throbbing beast. The dance floor looked like a Mexican wedding. Men on one side of the room, women on the other. In the center of the floor a half-dozen couples were going through the motions to a loud, bass-amplified boogie. The men did awkward two-steps, trying to fit their natural rhythms and exuberant Latin forms to the disco beat. The women gyrated wildly, arms flung above their heads, legs apart, pelvises swinging. Occasionally they would look in the direction of the man they were dancing with to give large, toothy smiles.

"I know that one," said Lupe, indicating a tall, undulating redhead with a mass of shoulder-length curls and a formfitting blue-sequined minidress. "I think her name's Linda Campos."

"You stick with her then, and I'll see if I can find someone to talk with." None of the women wanted to talk. They were all busy licking their lips and running silent account books in their heads, but at last I found a pudgy black woman seated alone near the corner of the room. I took the chair next to her and pulled it a little closer.

"How you doing? This is my first night. I'm so nervous. To the max. Have you worked here long?" I noticed I sounded like the shoplifter from the Valley I represented in Van Nuys a couple of months ago, but I kept chattering on.

Eventually she turned to me, her eyes half closed, obscured by a row of golden beads that tied her hair off in braids, and said, "Chill out, girl. You want to start slow, finish big." She had a throaty growl for a laugh and the kind of bad breath associated with PCP usage.

"How are the tips here? The woman who told me about this place said that she was making some good money. Twenty-five dollars a night," I guessed.

"Who told you that?" sneered my companion. "Twenty-five dollars is nothing. Twenty-five dollars is when you let them suck on your neck like vampires. The real money is in the television room, if you can stand it. Let them get their hands up under the dress close enough to your pussy so they can feel the heat coming off it. Another good one is you get them to take you out to breakfast, then you can tell them about your sick mother or whatever your trip is. Course, whether you go to bed with 'em is up to you." She smiled broadly, apparently happy in the contemplation of her own financial security.

I pulled the chair a bit closer.

"The woman I was talking about—oh damn it, what was her name? It was just on the tip of my tongue. Carmen. I think her name was Carmen."

The woman glanced away from the dance floor and toward me. "Don't no Carmen work here," she snapped knowingly.

"Yes, yes. You know her. She's about my size, maybe a little shorter. I don't know if she's Mexican or what, but she was sort of dark skinned. Pretty good looking, and she had a scar up here by her eyebrow. I'm sure she told me her name was Carmen."

"You be talking about Cathy, and she ain't so good looking."

"Cathy?" I echoed.

The woman spread her big hands on her knees and leaned toward me to sneer. "I know her because we both be in the bathroom at the same time the night she started and we both fixing up our makeup. I saw she lifted up her bangs and had this big ugly 'ol scar on her forehead that she put some makeup over and powdered real careful."

"That's her. Of course. Cathy. How silly of me. I just met her recently. I don't know her that well. Seems like a nice lady."

"Seemed full of shit to me," she snorted again.

I wondered how to play this. I didn't want to seem too interested, but I couldn't stop myself from blurting out my next question: "Did she say something to you?"

"Humph," the woman snorted again and gestured dismissively with her big hands. "She be telling me about how she wasn't going to be here long. She's gonna be the star in some play up in Hollywood. That's what everybody says, that they're not going to be here long." The woman laughed, her breath all over my face.

In the most profound sense, that is certainly true. We are just here for the short run. Some shorter than others, I thought, recalling again the awful sprawled body of the dead woman and the frozen pain on her face.

"She was an actress," I said to keep the conversation moving.

"That's what they all say."

"Did she tell you when this play is going to be or where?"

The woman shrugged with disinterest while watching the dance floor. "I don't know. I wasn't listening. Dropping all those names like I'm supposed t'be impressed. Shit."

It was then I saw a very short man standing in front of me, bowing slightly from the waist, a white handkerchief pressed into the hand he offered me. Four songs later he left me, and I started to look for Lupe.

Finally I spotted her leaning against the wall smoking a cigarette by a soft-drink machine. She looked bored. The woman in the blue microdot dress stood by her side, oblivious to her, swaying to the music and hungrily scouting the dance floor.

"I didn't know you smoked."

"I used to." She ground it out angrily against the wall, scattering little red sparks.

"Find out anything?" I whispered with a nod toward the redhead.

Lupe shook her head. "A few new girls, but no Carmen. This used to be a hot spot for Mexican men working downtown. Now it's full of Cubans. Filipinos. Looks like Jimmy's moving up in the world, pulling a crowd with a little more money...."

"Seems like a swell place. How come you quit?"

"I got tired of being groped for buffalo heads, know what I mean?" She dropped her dance card on the floor and headed for the door.

Outside kids were still playing on the corner. Mothers sat on sagging porches with radios turned up. Rock and roll and latin dance music and the continuous sound from the freeway. Lupe stared for a moment at some small boys kicking a soccer ball back and forth.

I wondered how old Joey was.

"Let's make it quick. I got to get going. I got a living to make," she announced suddenly in a cold, flat voice as if I had dragged her along to the Club Tropical against her will.

I hadn't asked her to go anywhere with me. I had told her I wanted to go alone, and she had insisted on coming. I didn't feel like arguing with her anymore and I didn't know why she was angry. Was it because she had identified with the dead woman, or was she angry because she thought I was slow and chickenshit? I didn't ask. We got into the car and headed toward Hollywood.

Another Friday night in Hollywood. The moon hanging in the sky like a badly lit three-D postcard. Bright lights. Action. Motorcycle freaks. Punk rockers on acid. A small Salvation Army band. Half a dozen chicano car clubs. Several adults in skimpy clothing made of lurex raced by on roller skates. Tourists from Iowa stumbling down the street, studying the bronze stars of their favorite actors and actresses embedded in the pavement. I've read they charge the actor $3500 for the cost of installing the star. I started to ask Lupe if she knew this but decided to just keep my mouth shut.

I pulled up in front of my office but didn't turn off the engine.

"You were right, Lupe. She was there at the Club Tropical and she was an American. I'm pretty sure I can find out about her now. Thanks. Can I give you a check?" I asked, fumbling in my purse.

"Do I look like a bank? You think I got my pussy insured by the FDIC? I want cash. I'll be by your office for it."

The car door slammed shut, and she was gone, striding toward the corner smoothing her skirt around her hips and straightening her wig.

I went home and sat in my sweatbox in the Valley with a pint of bourbon and a bowl of ice. I plugged in a cheap Japanese fan and let it blow my thoughts around awhile. The last thing I remember before falling on my bed was calling Monica Fullbright to tell her answering machine that Carmen Luzano had failed to keep the appointment. Then I had the kind of dreams where big black birds try to pluck your eyes out and you wake up with the sheet knotted around you like a vine.

CHAPTER SIX

It was all I could do to fry an egg in the morning. The egg stared up at me accusingly. I threw it in the sink. It was hot in the apartment. I made rye toast, which was dry and stuck in my throat. My head hurt. I had an enormous hangover, so I stumbled around the kitchen banging cabinets while I made coffee, the real kind with chicory in it. It's the only thing that's still Southern about me. Also, one of the few things that work on this kind of hangover. The only gratitude I could muster that morning was that in fleeing my family, I had been able to escape the curse of one of those bad Southern accents. I had managed to leave mine at the Arizona state line.

I put the coffeepot on the table in the dining room, got the newspapers, sat on the stained gold carpet the landlord refuses to replace and started to look for a play starring the dead woman. There are a lot of Equity waiver places in town, so I figured I could find her—if she was an actress and if she was in a play. Using all four of the papers—the *Times*, the *Examiner* and the two local freebies that run kinky-sex ads and all the alternative-entertainment listings—I made my own list. By the time I finished, it was nearly noon. There were forty-one theaters, not including a church doing a production of *Pygmalion*. Three of the theaters had all-male casts, one on Crenshaw was called the Black Ensemble and most of the rest seemed to be doing tired sitcoms about infidelity on Midwestern college campuses. Again I wondered who this woman called Cathy or Carmen was. After what I'd seen, it was hard to imagine her as a fresh-scrubbed coed. Eleven of the theaters were actually in Hollywood, and only two had shows opening that weekend.

Usually by this time on Saturday I've been to the gym already and am at Sunset Beach, laid out and tanning after swimming a mile. The only thought on my mind most Saturday afternoons is which park to go to to find a game of tennis. This morning, however, nauseous and hung over, I was trying to sort out the complex reasons why I felt the need to find out who the dead woman was. I pulled on my black tights, a sky-blue T-shirt and the red high-tops, and got in the car to go to Venice. No matter what's going on in my life, I lift weights.

True, I'd taken money to do a job I seemed incapable of doing, but hadn't I worked to the best of my ability and billed fairly? True, my crazy family made me feel like I had to be a hero to get any kind of acceptance, but hadn't I left them on the other side of the United States? My head ached more as I thought about Lupe's anger, then, without wanting to think about it, the violence that had been committed against the woman in the loft.

There wasn't a cloud in sight. Birds of paradise, orange trees and stubby pines lined the street. Sprinklers pumped water onto the emerald lawns. Mexican gardeners trimmed ivy. In the distance was heard the persistent drone of a leaf blower. Such are the charms of Sherman Oaks.

True, I continued my conversation with myself, I had felt myself to be a victim of sexual discrimination when I was looking for a job. But hadn't I managed to create work for myself? Wasn't I lucky I'd been able to go to law school? Wasn't the law all that could protect us from violence? Then I understood it did not need to be as complicated as I was trying to make it. Not psychologically intricate. It was simple, I realized as I pulled onto the freeway.

I did not trust Monica Fullbright. Whatever she knew, I wanted to know.

It was an upper-body day. I don't think a woman can ever be as cut as a man, so my goal today is to delay the effect of gravity on my tits for as long as possible. This means decline flyes, incline dumbbell presses, decline dumbbell presses. Life is down to the basic elements here: I just want to have incredible pecs.

Rodney was by the Olympic barbells and looking like he was training for high intensity. He wore a black cut-out T-shirt that read Totally Awesome, a pair of bright-yellow cheetah-print mid-calf tights and a red-and-black silk bandanna like a skullcap. A guy called Payaso was spotting him as he bench-pressed three hundred pounds. I saw the veins in his arms popping, and he glistened with sweat. I stopped to watch. The spotter bent over him as though not convinced that Rodney could make the weight. Rodney pumped the weight three times and put it back in the rack as easily as taking a pie from the oven. He got up and wiped the sweat off the bench he had been lying on.

"Pecs today, am I right?" he grunted at me.

I nodded and took a pair of twenty-pound weights from a rack.

Rodney picked up a pair of twenty-five-pound ones. "Stress has to increase progressively," he said, handing them to me and ignoring my doubtful look.

I lay back on the incline and bent my knees slightly to keep my back against the board. I pulled the weights into my armpits, then pushed up. Rodney made me do three sets of fifteen and had to help me with the last three of each set. I moved over to a decline bench and lay down, placing my knees over the elevated pad and securing my feet under the grips to do flyes. While the pectoralis major muscle has a single point of origin under the deltoid, it fans across the chest to insert at several points all down the sternum. You need to work the muscles from different angles for total development. I closed my eyes and took a deep breath as Rodney handed me the weights. The first step in developing an incredible body is to create a strong image of the kind of body you want. I saw myself tall and lithe, with breasts like a Valkyrie's. I opened my eyes, and the weights sagged toward the floor. I felt Rodney's hands near my elbows and smelled the great sweat of him. A rough moan escaped my throat as I struggled with the weight.

"You're an animal. Train through it!" he growled.

I would never let Rodney see me cry and I didn't for the next hour.

Upstairs, after a shower, I pulled on a pair of white cotton slacks, a white tank top and a pair of teal blue Maude Frizon sandals, and set out for Hollywood hoping the air conditioner in the car was going to work for a change.

Near the Hollywood Bowl, I exited the freeway on Barham, then drove down onto Highland. Tour buses clogged the right lane, and Japanese tourists hurried through the crosswalk with their cameras already out and snapping away at the white fountain at the entrance to the Bowl. Traffic slowed even more as it funneled toward the Boulevard, a long line of cars fighting to make the turn west toward the Chinese Theater and its famous courtyard full of the concrete handprints and footprints of the stars. Al Jolson's knees, Betty Grable's legs, Trigger's hoof and Jimmy Durante's nose. Even I went there when I first moved here. Even I have a snapshot of me placing my hand in Marilyn's handprint.

I stayed to the left to avoid the Boulevard and swung onto Franklin. My back was sweating against the old vinyl upholstery of the car although the sun was broken by a canopy of tall magnolia trees. Greasy-looking white blossoms littered the road. Red-and-yellow Spanish-revival apartments loomed above the street. From an open window came the sound of a guitarist and his drummer racing a beat ahead of him through their own speed-induced version of "Purple Haze."

The yellow legal pad on which I had written the addresses of the theaters I was going to check out fluttered slightly on the seat next to me. I decided to go to the one on Las Palmas first. It was hard to find a place to park, I got panhandled three times and there was nobody at the theatre. Exasperated, I pulled my damp tank top away from my back. I thought of having a glass of iced tea and waiting to see if anyone appeared at the theatre who might be able to answer my questions, but the fast-food place nearby was full of junkies and a peculiar deep-fat-and-vomit smell. Checking the next address on the list, I climbed back into the car.

A picture of the dead woman was in a window at the second theater.

It was a standard head shot. Her hair was longer. Someone semiprofessional had done her makeup, and there was a heavy line of black above her eyes. The Galaxy Theater was on a side street in east Hollywood, squeezed between an Arab bakery and a tabernacle church. It was less than fourteen blocks from my office. The photo was in a very large glass display case to the left of the entrance, as though the theater itself had once been a store. The door was open, and a man in a plaid shirt was sweeping the floor. I went in. It was hot and stuffy. On the other side of the red velvet curtain that hung in the doorway I could hear voices.

"Nice ficus," I said to the man sweeping the floor.

He smiled in reply and stopped pushing the broom. "You come to get tickets for the show tonight?"

"Yes. I think someone I know is in the show. Cathy."

"Which one? We got two. Vega or O'Brien?"

"Vega." At least that was the name on her photo.

"Sorry. She's out of the show," he said curtly and resumed sweeping a little harder.

"Out?" No lie. She was out for good. "Why is she out of the show?"

He stopped again and wiped at his forehead with the back of his hand. "Didn't show up for the opening last night."

"I can't believe it," I exclaimed in an unnaturally high voice that I hoped made me sound surprised. "She talked about it all the time. She was so excited. Did she get sick?"

He shrugged. "Don't know. She didn't even bother to call."

"How unprofessional." I sounded even more fey. "What on earth did you do?"

"Steve was furious. Especially after the way she begged for the part. Fortunately, it wasn't much of a part, and one of the other girls was able to fill in."

I clasped my hands together in a beseeching manner and frowned because it was the only way I could think of to convey that I felt upset. "This really worries me. Something must have happened to her. Don't you think so?" Then I waited.

He swept a pile of dust and lint between us. "Nope. She was a flake. I think she was scared. Had the jitters."

So she went downtown to cop. That made a certain amount of sense. It could have explained the short and apparently unhappy life of Cathy Vega, but it did not explain Carmen Luzano. What was the connection between them? The two women must have known each other. Was it Carmen I was supposed to be helping, involved somehow in the death of the one who called herself Cathy Vega? Didn't *vega* mean "star"? As in Las Vegas. I made a mental note to ask Lupe the next time I saw her.

"I should talk to Steve," I announced, glancing past the man's shoulder to the entrance to the theater. "He must be worried, too. Is he here?"

Almost on cue I heard a man's voice on the other side of the curtain, which I slipped through.

"Goddamn it to hell, honey, pick up your feet. You're a beautiful woman on her way to meet her lover, not an elephant on the way to the burial grounds."

The blonde he was talking to seemed to have frozen to a spot near an imaginary door. She was beautiful and young. A petulant look was working its way across her face.

"Steve," she whined, "I was doing it like you told me before."

Around the stage were a man, two more women and a woman sitting on a folding metal chair with a script in her lap. One of the women fidgeted slightly with either impatience or boredom.

"Right." He sighed after a moment with a great deal of control in his voice. He clapped his hands, stepping from where he was standing in front of the first row of chairs and into the center of the stage. "We're going to take it again from the part where Diana finds the note and hurries out to meet you, Jim. Diana, get on your mark."

With great deliberation, the blonde studied the floor, then moved six inches to her left.

He turned toward me. He was ruggedly handsome, like a cowboy in a cigarette ad. About five ten, 160 pounds, dark curly hair with some gray at the temples. Tan. The kind of guy who comes from New York and complains there isn't any real theater in LA. Who has himself paged at the Polo Lounge. A ladies' man. He gave me a nice warm smile, but his eyes narrowed in annoyance at my interruption.

"Yes?" He used a voice that made this question sound like an open invitation—Lunch? Drinks? Your place or mine?—without really caring what the answer was.

I returned his smile as I stepped forward. "I came to see you about Cathy Vega."

He did look annoyed.

"Lola Flier. I'm casting assistant at Mylar Productions," I said, holding my hand out to him and wondering where these names came from. It would be Freudian and too expensive to find out. "We've been hearing some very exciting things about you and your productions."

There were shuffling sounds and as much excited murmuring as can be made by four people.

"We just finished a run-through of a scene from the show we opened last night. Practice makes perfect, right kids?" Steve gestured magnanimously at his players.

There was a chorus of well-rehearsed laughter from the stage.

None of the papers had bothered to review the show.

"Please, go right ahead. Don't let me interrupt." I started to take a seat on one of the folding chairs in the second row.

"No, we're breaking now. Seven o'clock, everybody. Diana, get us some coffee, will you?"

The blonde pouted and started to say something but clumped off the stage after the others.

"Mylar Productions? I don't believe I've heard of it," he said with a trace of tentativeness.

"Really?" I parried. "We're a subsidiary of Gulf-Western." You learn these kinds of phrases by just watching the evening news out here in LA, but it seemed to convince him.

"Cathy," he purred, ready to be helpful now. "Yes, Cathy. A raw talent. A beautiful girl, but presentation, style—she got it right here in the workshop."

I'll bet she got it right here. Working under her director.

I smiled encouragingly. "We're looking for a look that's exotic."

He nodded to indicate he understood the subtext. "Ethnic. Sure. That's Cathy. Real little Mexican spitfire."

"Of course, we'll want to see her bio, credits, all of that. We're looking at some other women now, trying to see as many as possible, to tell you the truth. I understand she's got quite a good part in this current show."

The blonde, who was bearing down on us with two miniature Styrofoam cups, laughed. "Actually she only had two lines, but she must have had terrible stage fright because she didn't even show up last night."

He glared at her.

"She will be here tonight, won't she?" I asked, disappointment written all over my face.

"Absolutely," he said without a trace of conviction. "I talked to her last night after the performance. Just a little stomach flu."

"When was that?" I asked.

"Yeah, when was that?" echoed the blonde, giving him a look that would have driven a weaker man to his knees.

"What a group, huh? Beautiful, aren't they? These kids. The way they work together, the camaraderie."

The blonde slopped the coffee on him and left.

I drank the tepid instant as fast as I could. Cathy Vega had been dead long before the curtain went up. I wondered if he knew she was dead or if he was just a compulsive liar.

Steve handed me two tickets for the evening performance.

"Let me have your card," he called as I hurried out.

The blonde was outside, twirling her car keys with annoyance. "Too bad about Cathy," she sneered. "Guess she couldn't handle a part that called for keeping her clothes on."

CHAPTER SEVEN

This was the place, if you were a singing nun or a yodeling teddy bear who was new in town. Foxy Elite was busy on Saturday afternoon. An unhappy-looking fat woman was squeezed into a chair behind a desk that was too small for her. I had pumped the blonde into telling me the name of Cathy Vega's agent by promising I would take some of her photos for the files of Mylar Productions.

"I'm tired of jumping out of the goddamn plastic cake with icing on my tits. I'm a dancer," complained a woman who was limping up and down the small reception area.

"Cake calls—the worst," agreed an almost beautiful young man with carefully colored blond hair. "Look at this," he said, pointing to a bruise near his temple. "I almost knocked myself cold the last time."

The other people in the room turned magazine pages, apparently waiting for some higher calling.

The phone rang. The fat woman mumbled into the receiver, made notes on a pad, then swiveled toward the group as she hung up.

"You, Louise. We need a bondage nurse out to mid-Wilshire."

One of the women dropped a magazine on a small table beside her and got up, stretching.

It had been going on like that for fifteen minutes since I arrived. Tap-dancing valentines, a midget in a clown suit, a scantily dressed body-builder, two very young boys with leather and bad skin, and a hard-edged black hooker who looked like Jimi Hendrix. A creep wearing a motorcycle cap like Marlon Brando in *The Wild One* kept staring at my naked toes. Foxy Elite was in the corner suite on the second floor of a piss-yellow building on Cahuenga, two blocks from Vine at the intersection of Selma. It was the kind of block with lots of neon cocktail signs that don't work and an auto-body shop with a big hungry dog in a fenced yard. What made this block distinctly, quintessentially Hollywood were the number of custom-photo labs doing posters and album covers.

The bondage nurse jostled my knees on her way to the door.

I was waiting for Bob Alton, the agent. He represented theatrical, voice-over, juvenile and modeling. I knew this because I had picked a copy of *Hollywood Print* out of a rack of bookie sheets and postcards at the local newsstand.

"Am I going to be able to see Mr. Alton soon?" I asked.

The two boys with bad skin smirked at each other.

I had already declined to fill out an agency application form and had flipped through the tattered movie magazines.

"Did I tell you I was here about Cathy Vega?" I waited for this to make an impression, since Cathy Vega seemed to be the only one of their stable with a legit career.

The receptionist toyed with a pink bonbon from a box in front of her before popping it into her mouth. A second and third followed before the interminable chewing was interrupted by the buzz of the intercom.

"You may go in now," she said, licking her fingers.

Bob Alton was posed behind a desk littered with folders and black-and-white photos. The blinds were half drawn. The lighting was careful. There were a couple of Warhol prints on the wall. A Pomeranian with a red bow on top of its head growled mechanically and immediately went back to sleep on a somewhat soiled white sofa.

"Good to see you," he said, partially extending his arm so I had to lean across the desk to shake hands with him. He had on mascara.

"An honor." A once-in-a-lifetime. Where else in Hollywood could you see an agent without an appointment?

He leaned back, elbows on the arms of his chair, fingertips pressed together in front of his chest, in an attitude of relaxed attention. He was wearing a pale pink silk shirt. His hair brushing his collar was dyed brown and frosted in front. Whatever age he was pretending to be, he was at least fifteen years older.

"What can I do for you?"

In this town that means fuck you. Keep it simple, I said to myself, the bare details. I told him my real name, gave him one of my business cards and said I was looking for Cathy Vega. "I think she may be in trouble." I made a flourishing hand gesture encompassing the room, meaning big trouble, all of you.

"No, no, no, no. It can't be. If there was trouble, I'd know about it. This isn't just a business. We're family, me and my *artistes*. "

He actually said that last word. I imagined him being fatherly with the bad skin twins.

"What kind of trouble?" he asked, having completed the formalities.

"She was doing a play...."

Surprised, he looked blank for a millisecond, then cunning, then back to blank. He could not have been a very good card player. "A play? Yes, we had one under discussion...."

"She didn't show up last night for the opening. She had such a great part. Big."

"You're a lawyer, right? Did she have a contract?" He picked up a pen and started to doodle some numbers.

"I don't think so. It was with an acting workshop."

He dropped the pen. "So it's not breach of contract. What is it?"

"I didn't mean to upset you. It's very simple. She was a witness to an accident. I need to get a statement from her, but she seems to have disappeared. I wondered if something had happened to her. I thought you could tell me if she was around."

"Don't they usually send investigators?"

I giggled girlishly. "That's the usual, but I'm a new lawyer and I'm just starting out. I don't have the money to hire investigators like the big insurance companies do." I fished my state bar card out of my wallet and held it in front of him as though it were my proudest possession in the world, giggling all the while like an adolescent.

He waved the card away. "She's around. I just sent her on a job yesterday."

"What kind of job?"

He searched among the disarray on his desk and located a file. "Modeling. Cathy Vega. I helped her pick out that name."

"What's her real name?"

He shrugged. "Something Mexican. I don't remember. Nobody ever made it with their real name. That's what counts in this business: flexibility. You know, Dean Martin, Dino Corsetti. Tony Curtis, Bernie Schwartz. Marilyn Monroe, Norma Jean Baker."

As I nodded at Bob Alton, the Pomeranian let go of some loud and very unpleasant gas. "What kind of modeling?"

"Swimsuits for a manufacturing company downtown. She's going to represent a new line called Bahia de Angeles." He pronounced it badly. "I don't think that name works—too long. Guess that's why they wanted a Mexican. When he called, he asked for her."

I tried not to look excited. "Who?"

"Mambo—now that works for me. Short, punchy, easy to remember." He picked up the pencil again and made a note that seemed to satisfy him.

"Who asked for her?" I repeated, leaning forward in the uncomfortable fake Eames chair in which I was seated.

"Guy named Rudy."

"Downtown?" I asked, sinking back in the chair. "I went down there yesterday, and no one was there."

He scowled at the folder. "He said they'd be shooting all day. Seven hundred and fifty dollars for the day. That's what I understood. Guy spoke English pretty good, not too much of an accent."

"They must have just used her for a test shot and let her go. They're probably testing a lot of women."

"They could have done that by seeing her portfolio. He told me they wanted her for the job."

I could see he was thinking that she'd gone behind his back to cut him out of his ten percent.

"I can't believe it. It's a dog-eat-dog world. I helped her pick out that name," he complained. The Pomeranian stirred in its sleep, feet twitching in an atrophied rabbit-chasing dream.

"Now, if you'll excuse me." He was already punching a phone number written on a scrap paper in the folder.

From where I stood I was able to read an address on the inside cover of the folder. I couldn't see the phone number because his hand lay across it. I've always been able to read upside down. One of my many small talents. I got up and made like I was headed for the door. It didn't look as though he knew she was dead.

"Say," he called after me in a snake oil voice. "Have you ever thought of doing some modeling?"

My grandmother once told me I was lucky to be able to go to law school since I wasn't pretty enough to be a stewardess. I turned back, but before I could be a smartass, he was talking on the phone. He asked for Rudy a couple of times, then hung up.

"I'll be damned," he mumbled, crumbling the paper on which the phone number was written. "It's a Pioneer Chicken place."

I closed his door behind myself on the way out. The receptionist had replaced the top on the box of chocolates and was sitting with her fat hands folded on top of a worn-out back issue of *The Star:* NINE-YEAR-OLD GIVES BIRTH TO QUINTUPLETS FROM OUTER SPACE. She looked bored. The bad skin twins were still there and a couple of new per-oxided young men with tight jeans had joined them. There was an air of nervous expectation like in a bar the hour before it closes.

"Psst," the receptionist hissed sotto voce at me as I was walking past her desk.

I stopped suspiciously. Was she, like Bob Alton, going to try to sign me up for a modeling course? A thousand bucks. Ten sessions. Learn to put on makeup and walk like you've got something up your butt.

"Cathy was here just a couple of days ago." She smirked knowingly, like she was glad to be one up on her boss.

"Oh." Was it acting lessons? I'd have to read *A Doll's House* with the creep in the motorcycle cap?

"Cathy told me"—now the receptionist smiled beneficently at me, apparently most pleased with herself that she had this information—"that she's busy over at a workshop on Carlos Avenue near Gower with some other girls. Singers and dancers. They're putting together a revue. I think she's going to leave Mr. Alton." She seemed very satisfied by this possible turn of events.

I replaced the grimace on my face with something pleasant and nodded as though I knew how to keep a secret.

"When you see her, tell her I got another agent for her. A real one." She lowered her voice even more. "I'm leaving here, too. Haven't told him yet." She jerked her head in the direction of the closed door of the office I had just left. "At a real talent agency." She wrinkled her nose as she glared over at the bodybuilders. "Give her this card and tell her I'll be there as of the first of the month. She should call me then." She edged open the thin center drawer of her desk, palmed a card from a stack and looked around the room before she passed it covertly to me.

The card was thin and cheap. You could see daylight through it. La Belle Artistic Entertainment, it read. I stuck it in my pocket. "You think she's over at this workshop? Could I find her there today?"

She nodded. "She said she's there rehearsing every day."

Of course Cathy wouldn't be there, but I might find someone who could tell me about her. I drove over to Carlos Avenue, which runs parallel to Hollywood Boulevard between Bronson and Gower. Although I parked the car and walked up and down the block several times, I didn't see anything resembling a theater or rehearsal hall. There were just a few badly maintained apartment buildings and near Gower a large parking lot. Was this another of the parking lots that had once been something else? A studio? A famous mansion? The site of some terrible crime? Did history just vanish?

CHAPTER EIGHT

The address I had memorized from Bob Alton's file was a sagging four story Spanish style apartment with a red-tile roof in the Central American refugee camp that has sprung up around Cherokee and Yucca. There was a cactus on a balcony of the third floor, and someone else had glass wind chimes that tinkled above the din of traffic. A pregnant teenage girl sprawled against the car in front of mine, spitting on the sidewalk. Paint was peeling off window frames around open windows. The windows on the ground floor all had bars over them. I stopped. What was I doing? I felt peculiar. My stomach hurt. I didn't belong here. Yes, a woman was dead, but it was not my responsibility. Why did I need to be the one to find out what had happened? Everything I'd been told so far had turned out to be a lie. I turned back toward the car.

As soon as I had done that, I knew what the sickness in my gut was. Like when I was a kid and my dad got drunk. The same cold nauseous feeling I had for six weeks when I was studying for the bar exam. I was afraid.

I made myself walk up red tiled stairs into a courtyard with palm trees and flowering bushes. It was the old Hollywood glamor, but the tile around the empty fountain was carved with gang names and filthy words.

I didn't expect to find her name on the mailbox, but it was there. Vega. Number 9. There was another name below it scratched out. Doors were flung open because of the heat. A few Salvadorean families were gathered around a plastic wading pool, men drinking beer and women yelling at the kids splashing in the water. In front of apartment 5 three musician pasty dudes stood swigging some nasty-looking swamp water from jelly jars. A ghetto blaster was pounding the ground with predictable three chord Satan revery.

Number 9 was the last unit on the left. I knocked on the door. I kept knocking until it suddenly opened.

"Fucking heavy-metal freaks." The woman who answered the door scratched herself sleepily through a torn hot-pink babydoll nightie. She had mascara all over her face. Her hair, dyed blue-black, stood out stiffly. Another Midwestern sweetheart who'd come to be discovered.

"I want to see Cathy."

"Not here." The woman started to close the door in my face. I surprised myself by putting my hand on the door and pushing back. It was getting to be a drag being the bearer of bad news, particularly that in which no one was interested.

"I hope you know where to find her, because I think she's dead."

The woman staggered backward until she fell into a chair beside a shaky chrome dinette table.

I took this to mean come in. The furniture was broken. On the floor lay a teddy bear looking like he'd been mugged at knife point. I closed the door, walked over and sat down at the table, which was littered with cassette tapes, a stack of fliers for a rock club called Acid House, a bag with the sick looking remains of some Mexican takeout food and a few white tablets the size of pencil erasers with crosses etched on them. Street speed.

"Dead," the woman repeated in a sleepy voice. "That's heavy. I thought she was over at her boyfriend's."

"How long has she been gone?"

She pulled the nightie around her body as though she had just realized she was naked. "You a friend of hers? She had some weird friends, but I don't remember you."

"I'm a friend." I realized that I almost felt this lie was true, unlike all the others I had told so far that day. I was beginning to feel Cathy Vega was someone I had known, and the memory of her in the torn underpants wouldn't leave me alone. "Tell me how long she's been gone."

She tilted her chin defiantly at me. "You might be a cop."

"No, if I was a cop, I'd want to know where you got these amphetamines." I picked up one of the tabs from the table, then dropped it so it bounced onto the floor.

Apparently what I had said made sense to her, because instead of arguing she sighed deeply and shuffled around in a pile of flyers until she found a small manila packet. She opened the packet and tapped white powder onto the table. Picking up a razor blade, she started chopping coke as though I weren't there. She snatched a straw out of the sack of Mexican food, stuck it in her nose and took two hard hits. "Hmmm, that's better." She wiped at her nose with the back of her hand. "Couple weeks ago, I don't know. Around the time we were going to do a gig at the Scream."

The same time Carmen Luzano had left town.

"You two in a band together?" The receptionist at the agent's had said singers and dancers.

She laughed. "Cathy couldn't carry a tune in a bucket. Just me. Moral Standards, ever heard of it?"

I shook my head.

"Before that I was in Bad Pussy."

I shook my head again. "What about Cathy? Was she working lately?"

With both hands the woman pushed her stiff hair back from her face and then leaned suspiciously toward me. With the black circles around her eyes, she reminded me of a lunatic raccoon. "Working? What's that got to do with it? Why are you asking all these questions? I thought you said she was dead."

"She is."

The woman pushed aside the sack of food with annoyance. "I don't believe you. What happened? Was she in an accident?"

"She o.d.'d with a spike in her arm."

"No way!" the roommate exploded, pounding one pale hand with broken lavender-painted nails on the table for emphasis. "She didn't shoot drugs."

"I saw her. I was at a loft downtown last night. She was dead. There was a hypodermic needle lying next to her. I went out to get help. When I came back she was gone."

The roommate roared dismissively. "What were you on? She probably just passed out for a while. Maybe she went home with some guy."

"You saying she didn't use drugs?"

"A little grass. Diet pills. That's all."

"Diet pills?" I poked at the speed again.

The woman yawned and rubbed her eyes. "She was always trying to lose weight. So, she used speed sometimes. Big deal. She stuck her finger down her throat sometimes, too. That was pretty gross. I heard her in the bathroom. She was tired of just being sent out for parts as someone's maid. She thought she had to really be a fox to break into the business, on account of being Mexican."

I paused a few seconds as though concurring before pressing on. "Cathy must have thought she was pretty good looking. She was modeling."

"Modeling? Is that what she told you? She never told me about modeling! Maybe that's what she called that weird telegram service."

"She was in a play," I countered.

"Yeah, she was all worked up about that. I think she was really in love with that acting coach of hers. He banged her a few times, and all she got out of it was a crummy walk-on part."

"He wasn't her boyfriend? She said he was."

"No way. She's got some dude who's a bus driver. He doesn't come around much anymore, but when he does he's always pissed off. When she didn't come home after a couple of days, I figured they were making up."

A greasy orange stain was spreading across the table where she had moved the bag of food. I moved my hand away from it. "What's the name of the boyfriend?"

"Hey, you said you're a friend of hers. You ought to know all this shit."

I shrugged. "I just met her recently. At the acting workshop, but I had to drop out 'cause I didn't have enough money for it. Then I saw her at the party last night and I got kinda worried about her. Ok? So, who's her boyfriend?"

"Pete something. Mexican name."

"Where can I find him?" Maybe he would know something.

"I'm gonna make some herb tea. You want some?" She got up; I followed her into the kitchen. She put some water into an old coffeepot and picked a chipped cup with yellow ducks on it from the sink. "Sure you don't want some? I got chamomile, raspberry and orange sunset."

I shook my head and repeated, "You don't know where I can find her boyfriend?"

"Look, I've only known her four months myself. But I knew her real good." She gave me a smug glance that said I'm a much better friend than you are. "I was looking for a place to stay after I split from Derek. He was the bass player for Bad Pussy, right? Man, he turned out to be a freaky geek, always trying to hit me."

"Nope, don't know him. Sorry."

She lit the burner of the stove with a match. While she was waiting for the water to boil, she took a massive quantity of vitamins, washing them down with Hawaiian Punch that had been left out on the counter. "I liked Cathy right away. She was real intense, know what I mean? She knew Shakespeare. All that shit. I met her at the laundromat."

"Here in Hollywood?"

She nodded as she poured the sizzling-hot water into the cup and stuck a tea bag in it. "Cathy's got it covered. She said she's not going to end up just a bit player. She even got some new head shots for her portfolio." The woman went into the living room, and I ambled after her.

"At the workshop Steve said we should all get new photos. Can I see Cathy's?"

She put the cup down on the dinette table next to the dirty glasses. "I don't know...."

"Come on, what's the harm? I just want to see how they turned out."

I followed the woman into the bedroom. There was a queen-sized bed and mattress thrown on the floor. Piles of clothing were strewn about. The closet looked like it had exploded. The window was covered with tinfoil to make the room dark. She bent over to pick up a cardboard box under the window. She had a rose tattoo on her butt.

"That's JoJo," she said about the lump in the bed. "He's the bass player in Moral Standards."

"I've heard of him," I mumbled, trailing her back into the living room.

"This is Cathy's work stuff. We didn't get a desk yet. We're still redecorating." She placed the box on a couch with a broken leg that was propped up with a stack of bricks.

The first thing in the box was the same photo I had seen in the display window at Steven Morris's workshop. "These look great, but when did she get them? She told me she was hurting for money and she was going to have to wait."

"Within the last month or so. Yeah, I guess she had to hustle around to get the money for them. Cathy didn't want a straight gig or a day job. She had to be able to go to auditions. I don't really know how she was getting money, but she told me she'd done some work and gotten five thousand dollars."

Working in a dance hall? I wondered to myself. That was a lot of dances. A lot of heavy petting. Was it the truth? She hadn't told the truth about the revue she said she was rehearsing on Carlos Avenue. The photographer's name was on the back of the photo. Rudy Sancerre, with an address on Third near Vermont. Sancerre, like a bottle of bad wine. Rudy. Same name as the man who had called Cathy's agent for the modeling job in the loft downtown.

"I want this photo, ok?" The top of my pecs ached, and I felt like she wasn't listening to me.

"I don't know. She just got them. They're expensive."

Then I did something I've seen only in the movies. I peeled out some money and laid it on the table. The effect was spoiled a little because I had only two dollars.

"I guess you can have it."

I was already busy looking through the rest of the contents of the box. An old issue of *Variety* had Steven Morris's name circled in red. There was a small worn-out pair of ballet slippers, a program from a high-school play in Kansas City and a lot of little scraps of paper with names and phone numbers that you collect in bars. I didn't think I'd be able to get them out of the apartment without a hassle, so I left them. There were some surprising photos showing Cathy Vega plump and naked. I managed to slide one of these under the photo I already had. At the bottom of the box was a ream of yellow fliers with an awkwardly executed flag drawn on it. I had enough Latin in high school to figure out what "TIERRA Y LIBERTAD: Partido de Revolución de Guatemala" meant, but it didn't help me figure out what Cathy Vega was doing with it.

I pointed at the stack of fliers. "What's this?"

"I never saw it before. Must be some show she was in."

"Was she interested in politics?" I wondered aloud.

"You mean like a Republican or something? I don't know. When I first met her, she used to talk about war in Central America, stuff like that. Like a sixties Vietnam thing. But hey, that's cool. The Byrds, Moby Grape, Jefferson Airplane. Those are cool sounds. Me and JoJo, we're putting some psychedelic licks into our mix."

I took one of the fliers. It seemed to mean something, because there were so many of them.

"Was her boyfriend from Guatemala?" I asked. The synapses in my brain were starting to connect Cathy Vega and Carmen Luzano. Two women, approximately the same age, the same appearance, leave town or disappear on the same day. One's dead, the other missing. "Did she have any friends from Guatemala'?"

"The only person I ever met was Pete, who I told you about. It's kinda weird, 'cause she used to get a lot of phone calls from different people, but nobody ever came over. You're the first one of her girlfriends I met. One of them's been calling a lot lately. I thought you were her, but you're not. She's more of a soprano, plus she don't have that kind of Southern accent like you do."

The woman leaned over and turned on a telephone message machine that was perched on top of a stereo speaker.

"... I gotta go to Guitar City this afternoon."

"... Lucy, it's Amber. I gotta borrow that black velvet blouse of yours, ok?"

"Calling to see if you're back yet. Can't wait to see you."

Damn. I knew that voice myself. It was Monica Fullbright.

"You never saw that woman with Cathy?"

The roommate yawned again and shrugged. There was a crashing noise from the next room as if JoJo had fallen out of bed, a lamp hitting the floor and then the gurgle of the toilet flushing. She rolled one of the white tabs around the top of the table with her finger.

"Hey, man, we got to get going. We got a sound check. You seem cool. I'd put you on the guest list, but we already got too many," she said, handing me one of the fliers from the table to add to my collection.

I didn't feel cool. I felt hot, agitated. What was with Monica Fullbright? Why was she lying to me? I got up.

"Hey, if you see Cathy, tell her we're late on the rent. I need some of that bread from her."

The metal freaks were still shuffling heavily around their stoop as I left Cathy Vega's apartment. The Salvadoreans had gone inside, leaving doors flung open and the air a babble of television noises. Out over the Pacific the sky was purple and pink. It made me thirsty. I wanted to call Monica Fullbright from some place with refrigerated air and lots of ice cubes.

A young couple was courting on the hood of my car, so I left it where it was and walked down Cherokee toward Hollywood Boulevard. There was a bar a few doors before the Boulevard. I went in. Lava lamps and blowfish with light bulbs stuffed in their bellies made the room glow yellow. Several large carved tiki gods guarded the bar where I seated myself.

"Welcome to hell," said the bartender, a giant albino negro in a dress and cowboy hat, as he moved toward me. "What can I do you?"

"Southern Comfort and water. Rocks."

He had it in front of me almost before I had finished saying what I want-

ed. I took several long sips while I looked around the room. At the end of
the bar a drunk was talking to his glass. A tea party of tough guys in
designer jeans and muscle T's was telling loud, dirty jokes at a table on the
other side of the room. The record on the jukebox ended; a slow song started. A couple of very buff and peroxided bodybuilders glided out of the dark
to dance, glued together in slow motion. A latin guy about my age came
in, sat a few stools away and ordered a beer, which the bartender gave him.

"You working here long?" I asked the bartender as I slid him one of my
business cards, which he studied for a second.

"I'm White Hunter. Nice to meet you. I'm here most of the time. Have
been for about six months."

"Ever seen this woman? Ever see her in here with anyone?" I showed
him the head shot of Cathy Vega. The guy with the beer glanced over at
me, then down at the photograph.

The bartender picked up the photo, tilting it toward the light as he
examined it. He dropped it back down on the bar. "Never seen her. I love
this town. It's all like the movies. Cops. Robbers. You a detective? I love the
schmooz."

"Hey, man, get me another beer," the latin guy interrupted. He stared at
me, although he was speaking to the bartender.

"Where's the phone?" I asked.

The bartender pointed past an angry-looking tiki.

I dialed Monica Fullbright's number, which I now knew by heart. It rang
twice before the recorded message clicked on. There was her voice again,
promising she couldn't wait to see me.

"I got your girl for you," I said.

"Tell me where she is," Monica Fullbright cut in on the message I was
leaving. She sounded like she'd just been given a big surprise party or she
had a snout full of coke. She must have been lying by the phone, waiting
for it to ring.

My hand gripped the phone tighter. "Not so fast. She wants you to come
see me."

"No. I can't. She knows where to meet me, what to do."

"Monica." It was the first time I had called her by her first name. I wanted
her to know I wasn't impressed, no matter who she wanted me to think she
was. "Monica, this ain't no fooling around. I'm going to be at Happy Times
Lanes at Vermont and Olympic in an hour. We'll talk then." I hung up fast.

There was another Southern Comfort waiting for me at the bar. The bartender dropped a fresh ice cube into it so that it overflowed on the imita-
tion mahogany counter.

"From the gentleman." He nodded in the direction of the latin, who
glanced quickly at me, then away.

This does not happen to me often, strange men wanting to buy me drinks. The last had been Ed Harrison, and it still made me feel queasy to think how that had ended. This man was of medium build, but his forearms, which were propped on the bar, were enormous and muscular. I wanted to get a better look at him, but he was partially turned away from me. As if reading my mind, he swiveled suddenly to face me.

"You like to party, girlie?"

There was a deep vertical crease between his eyes, the kind you get from liver damage. He did not look like he was in the mood for fun. All around it was a pretty weird bar, and nothing about it made me feel inclined to linger. As I gathered my things, I took another quick peek at the photos of Cathy, comparing the head shot with the one in which she was naked. They had been taken at approximately the same time, I decided, since her hair was the same length and style in both. I looked up and saw the latin guy staring at the picture in which Cathy was naked. His eyes flickered up to mine. Hastily I stuck the photos in my purse. Naked, there was nothing erotic, only a sad vulnerability. That must be why I was feeling obsessed with her. Whoever she was, she had come to LA with dreams like mine. To be free and make it in the big city. But the city was full of bad characters and quick to punish.

Now she was dead.

Could I be chewed up, spit out, empty and wasted as easily as she had been? More and more I felt I had to find out who she was and what had happened to her. After dropping a couple of dollars onto the bar, I found my car keys at the bottom of my purse. I made a point of not looking at the latin, who now watched me hungrily. What did he want? Sex? To rob me?

"Thanks for everything. It's been great. *Hasta luego.*" I was out the door.

Even though there were lots of other people on the street, I knew without turning around that he was following me. He was back there, a good seventy paces, ambling along, hands shoved in the pockets of his pants. I walked faster, sidestepping an old lady with a ratty little dog on a leash and slipping through a crowd of kids clustered around a guy from Michoacán who was selling popsicles from a rickety pushcart painted red and green. The young lovers, who were still locked in an awkward embrace, jumped off my car when I got in and started the engine.

Koreatown, where the bowling alley is located, is so big now it has its own exit marked on the freeway, but I decided to take the surface streets. On the corner a couple of black hip-hop boys had set up their box and were shaking and breaking and doing the Roger Rabbit to a tape of Run DMC. It was only after being caught in the slow traffic of gawkers on the Boulevard, past the theaters, past my office, the oriental markets, the used-car lots, as I was making the right turn onto Vermont, that I saw the old green Volkswagen rushing to make the turn after me. It pulled up close behind me, nudging my bumper. I looked in the rearview mirror.

It was the guy from the bar.

I floored my car into the turn, but before I got more than two blocks, I caught another red light and he pulled up to my bumper again. I looked into the mirror, but all I could see this time was the lower portion of his face, the mouth set in a hard line. Accelerating away, I got far enough in front of him so I could see his license, which I scribbled on the back of an old parking ticket. I was glad he was enough of a good citizen to have a front plate. This is a tough town to meet someone. Although I hadn't been on a date since the last dismal roll in the hay at a dingy motel on Ventura Boulevard with Ed Harrison, the commodities broker, this all looked a little intense for my taste. Ed always wanted to know why I wouldn't let him come to my apartment. The fact was, I didn't want him to sleep in my bed.

I made a brazen left turn across oncoming traffic and pulled into the parking lot of the bowling alley, making for a space as close to the front door as possible.

He pulled in a few spaces to my left. He was on me before I got to the door of the bowling alley, grabbing my arm just above the elbow, hard enough for his fingers to make white spots on my tan.

"Hey, honey, you shouldn't have run off. I want to talk to you," he rasped in my ear.

I'd guessed his height right in the bar, but he was heavier and stronger than I expected.

"I'm busy. Get lost." I wrenched my arm away from him.

"Calm down, baby. I'll bet you'd like to get high. Come with me. I'll get you anything you want."

"I told you no." He blocked my way to the door.

"Cocaine, baby? How about that?"

"Fuck off."

"Snort some coke, take off your clothes, take some pictures. That's what you like, isn't it?"

"I don't know why you're bothering me, but there's going to be big trouble if you don't get out of here right now." Then, if that didn't sound tough enough, I slapped him.

He rubbed his cheek. "I saw the photo you have. I saw you looking at it. I know what you're into."

A couple of giggling teenage Korean girls came out the door and walked between us, a blast of icy air rushing out.

He took a step toward me as though he would follow me inside, but more teenage girls came streaming out the door, separating us.

"You fucking dyke," he snarled over the heads of the schoolgirls. "We'll see each other again."

"I can hardly wait."

Then I went into the Happy Times Lanes and found the ladies' room. I washed my face, examining it as I dried it with a scratchy paper towel. I didn't like that he'd called me a dyke. It was, I guessed, a generic epithet, like cunt. I put on some lipstick. My breathing began to return to normal. My life had gotten strange since I met Monica Fullbright.

I went out and took a seat at a small table in the bar that was between the shoe rental and a room of video games. The video games sounded like atomic bombs. This was exactly why I had chosen the bowling alley. I wanted a private place for the chat I was going to have with Monica Fullbright, yet one that was public with enough background noise to give her trouble if she was trying to tape our conversation. The bar was nearly full, and a cable channel was running the races from Del Mar.

The waitress, a tall Korean in a beaded angora sweater, came over. I ordered a Mai Tai. Back at the bar I saw her place a glass under a dispenser on top of a metal plate with a computer keyboard. She hit a few panels, and fruit juice poured into the glass. The machine made a mean Mai Tai.

I didn't have to wait long before Monica Fullbright came in. She was wearing a white skirt, a black cotton pullover and a gold bracelet that might have been real. For a moment she stood in the doorway to the bar, blinking and disoriented, pushing a pair of heavy black sunglasses to the top of her head. Her hair was tied back in a ponytail by a silk scarf. She looked like Jackie 0 on the back of Aristotle's yacht. When she saw me, she smiled, gliding forward with that purposeful hip-rolling stride models have.

"I'm sorry it's been so hard to get hold of me lately. I've been so busy." She smiled more as she sat down across from me and put her purse on the table between us.

I picked her purse up—a Louis Vuitton. Real or fake? I shook it and placed it on the other chair at our table. That should take care of any tape recorder. "Can it, Monica. You've been jerking me around long enough. I want to know what this is about."

"Really? I don't know what this is about or why you asked me to come here. You asked me, remember?" Monica Fullbright frowned at the purse, then took a cigarette from it. She lit the cigarette and blew the smoke away from me.

"I could be in trouble, Monica. I think you could be, too, so why don't you just come clean with me and I'll try to figure it out. All right?"

"I'm not in any trouble. What are you talking about? I hired you to do a simple job; find someone for me and take care of her immigration papers.

You call me and tell me you've done it. What's the problem? Just tell me where the girl is, and if I owe you any more money, you can give me a bill."

"Yeah, I found Carmen for you." I got the head shot of Cathy Vega from my purse and dropped it on the table between us. "Of course, she doesn't look this good now. She's dead."

Monica started to reach for the photo but then pulled her hand back so it rested on the edge of the table. She stared at the photo and blinked a few times, something pulling the corner of her mouth. "I'm sorry to hear that, of course, but I don't know who this woman is."

I pushed the photo closer to her. "She o.d'd in a loft downtown, but she wasn't alone. Somebody fucked her either before or after she died. I don't know. I can't tell. I'd have to have the guys at the police forensic lab tell me."

"It's not Carmen." Monica Fullbright tapped her cigarette against the ashtray several times although it didn't need it. "It s not Carmen," she repeated.

"Of course it's not Carmen. There isn't any Carmen. It's an actress named Cathy Vega. Or something. Who knows what her name was before it was Cathy Vega? Does this look familiar?" I took out the nude photo of Cathy Vega and dropped it on the table.

She looked away.

"I know you know her."

Monica Fullbright played with the bracelet on her left wrist, watching it as she turned it. "I'm telling you for the last time, I don't know anything you're talking about. Now, if you'll excuse me." She started to stand up but I put my hand on her forearm and pushed down.

"What's the game? Porno? Prostitution? S and M? Somebody lined up a phony photo shoot and sent Cathy downtown. Somebody knew what would happen. You've been trying to set me up, use me for a bird dog. I don't care what you're into, but I'm not going to let you pull me in on it to take a tumble. Either tell me what you know or you'll talk to the police."

By this time I was talking to Monica Fullbright's back and she was halfway to the door, my voice muffled by the sound of strikes and spares and oriental laughter.

CHAPTER NINE

I had the machine get me another Mai Tai.

Then I sat watching the ice melt in the sticky bottom of the glass, sickly sweet rum and canned fruit juices turning brown, while I tried to figure out what to do.

Why didn't I just go to the police like I had threatened Monica Full-bright? Because now I was afraid of what she had involved me in. She had hired me to look for a Guatemalan woman named Carmen Luzano. I had-n't been able to find her, so Monica Fullbright conveniently told me where she was. I went there. A dead woman was on the floor. I'm no expert, but she must have been dead awhile, because her arm was getting rigid. The sound with which it had hit the floor when Lupe turned her over still made me sick. The dead woman was not Carmen Luzano. She was an actress named Cathy Vega. Although Monica Fullbright knew Cathy Vega, she said she didn't. Monica Fullbright had called Cathy and left a message saying she wanted to see her.

Cathy Vega had died under very bad circumstances. Monica Fullbright had killed her, I guessed, and was trying to use me for an alibi. If I report-ed my suspicions—and that's all they could be without a body for the police to examine—they would put the screws to me with the attorney-client privilege. Fuck up my career. Prove my father right. I might even be an accessory after the fact.

At last I peeled myself out of the chair and went to get my car. It was dark outside but still hot. Bluish lights cast a shaky pall on everything like a black and white negative. The parking lot was half full. Traffic was solid on Vermont. Koreans in expensive clothes and big cars. Black and latin families shoved in junked station wagons or scorched pickup trucks on the way to markets to spend their crummy paychecks. My car was where I had parked it but was listing to the left. A flat front tire. I changed it, getting grease all over my white pants. At the gas station, they told me they could-n't fix it. The tire was history. It had a deep stab wound in it. Like an ice pick.

I looked around the gas station. I didn't want to go home. The man who had followed me was out to get me. I didn't want him to know where I lived. Had Monica Fullbright sent him after me? Was he looking for Cathy Vega? I could go to the club Cathy Vega's roommate was at, catch the first set and try to get lost among the black leather doomies who liked to flaunt their pale, wasted night selves at the Scream, but I wanted to be some-where where it would be easier to watch for the man. He must have picked me up originally when I left Cathy's apartment building. Until I had time to run his license and find out who he was, I didn't want to see him again. With blue paper towels I rubbed angrily at the black stains on my pants, but all it did was smear them more. There was a spot of grease on my Maude Frizon sandals. Finally I decided to go back to the office. There was no point in trying to hide that from my latin tail if he'd been hired by Monica Fullbright. And at least I could catch up on some work I'd been ignoring.

The front door was locked, but there was a light on upstairs in Harvey Kaplan's office. As if I had arrived safely at the proverbial port in a storm, I felt a tremendous sense of relief. I could talk to Harvey. Why not Harvey? The good daddy I'd never had. Everyone getting started in the business needed a mentor, a godfather. Why not Harvey Kaplan? We'd had some fairly decent conversations. He'd given me a few pointers on my first prelim—a rather uninspired and sloppy grand theft by a poor *vato* who lived on Berendo near the freeways. He'd hotwired an old orange Toyota, then nodded out at the wheel behind some Mexican horse in the entrance to the alley, just west of New Hampshire and north of Washington. I'd already forgotten his name. He was bound over and was on his way to two years in Chino. That's the way it is. They go to state prison, and we go to lunch. Manny Washington said Harvey Kaplan had been an ace.

I heard music as I went up the stairs in the dark. Harvey's door was closed. I knocked softly. Pushing the door, I peeked in. Harvey was laid out on the couch snoring, his mouth open, a cloud of pot smoke thick as the haze in the beginning of June. Harvey's leg twitched like a dog with a bad dream. There was an embroidered afghan on the arm of the couch; I laid it over him. Before I left, I turned off his radio. The all-oldies station in Pasadena was playing the Beatles and Simon and Garfunkel. Coo coo ca choo.

The paperwork on Mrs. Peterson's motion was still spread across the top of my desk along with Harvey's book I'd been using. I turned on the desk lamp, opened the book and started to work. I was down to the part where I had to think of a reason why Mrs. Peterson's First Amendment rights assumed priority over the safety of the women in the abortion clinic when a small stone came flying in the window, landing on the desk.

I snapped off the lamp and hit the floor. Another small rock came sailing through the window. I crawled over to the wall beside the window and peered out. In the circle of light beneath the streetlight was Lupe Ramos in another one of her goofy getups: this time a pair of purple toreador pants, silver high heels and a yellow halter top. I think she thought she was Rita Hayworth in some postmodern *Blood and Sand*.

"Hey you, Whitney, Whitney. Come here."

"Shh, what the hell are you doing?" Was she going to drive me crazy about the fifty bucks I owed her? I was almost broke again, the way I'd been laying out money today on drinks and bad leads.

"I'm in trouble."

"Go away. I'm busy."

"Come down here."

"I'm working." I started to turn away from the window. "Remember the fifty bucks you owe me," she said, raising her voice so that a couple coming out of Sam's downstairs looked up to see who she was talking to.

I went downstairs. "What's the problem? Cops run you in again?"

She tossed her long black hair nervously back over her shoulders. "My brother's looking for me. He's gonna kill me."

"What?" I moved closer to the pepper tree and away from the street lamp.

"I told my mom I was a cocktail waitress—"

"A cocktail waitress?" I laughed. "That's a new name for it."

"Yeah, a cocktail waitress. What do you think? I'm gonna tell my mom I get paid to screw illegal aliens? I told her I was a cocktail waitress. In a nice place in Hollywood. Like Ciro's or Mocambo. A beautiful place where all the stars hang out. But there ain't been places or stars like that for thirty years. No Marilyn or Lana. Or Rita." She sighed as she adjusted the strap of her halter top. "Anyhow, my mom believed it, but my brother, well, I guess someone must have seen me on the street and told him."

I glanced away from her and looked around the street, feeling embarrassed. So we did have something in common after all. I never voluntarily tell my folks anything. But did she believe the city was so small he could find her? Why didn't she move to a different street corner? I thought she wanted to know if I had seen him. "What's he look like?"

"Hector Ramos? 'Manos' Ramos? You never heard of him?"

I shook my head.

"Light welterweight. Two-time contender for All City?"

I shook my head again.

"Well, it don't matter. He's washed up. Over the hill. A few too many blows to the head, know what I mean? But he can still kick my butt."

"Yeah?" I said, growing wary.

"I have to get off the street tonight. Take me home with you, and I'll forget about the *plata* you owe me."

"I can't do that! Why don't you call your boyfriend? What's his name? Alfredo?"

"He'd find me at Alfredo's. Come on. I'll be gone in the morning." Lupe put her hands together prayerlike just below her full red lips. Linda Darnell in the chapel before the last fateful bullfight.

"No...." I hesitated, wondering how much Lupe knew or suspected about what I was involved in.

Defiantly she flicked one hand out at me. "Afraid I've got cooties?"

"No, I have something to do."

She stepped toward me. "What is it? I'll help you. No charge."

I didn't need her help. Or want it. But I did feel guilty imagining she'd already been seen with me and now was in as much danger.

"The dead woman we found..." I faltered.

"Are you still carrying on about that? That's life on the streets. Tell your client she was at the Club Tropical and let it go. What's it to you, anyway? You didn't care that she was a hooker."

"...I don't think she died accidentally...."

"*¡Que mala suerte!*" she swore, stamping her foot. "I knew I should have stuck with blowjobs. I wondered why there was no spoon next to her to cook her smack."

My silence must have made her even more nervous, because she began to pace the sidewalk. A gray car slowed down and honked at Lupe, but she didn't look up.

"Who did it? You think they know about me?" She stopped pacing and put her hands on her hips.

I had trouble meeting her gaze and keeping my voice up. "I don't know. A man followed me today."

"Followed you! What about me?" she asked furiously. "You got me into this. You have to take me with you."

"I said not to worry. I'll figure it out. I know what to do." Did this have as hollow a ring to her ears as it did to mine?

"What? What are you going to do?" she demanded.

I had screwed up. I had taken her downtown. I didn't want her in my way and I didn't want to feel responsible for her. "I need time to decide if you can stay at my place," I hedged.

"Okay, but let's get off the street whether we go to your crib or not." She glanced nervously around. One of the black working girls on the opposite side of the street—the one who looked like Diana Ross on steroids—waved at her. Lupe waved back, looking distracted. "What's your plan?"

It felt dark under the pepper tree. Protected. Darker than a womb.

"So, what are you gonna do? You ain't said yet. I don't think you got a plan," she prodded impatiently.

"I do," I snapped defensively. I did not.

"Good." She folded her arms across her chest. "Then I'll go with you. I'm very observant. Besides, what are you going to do next time you need to speak Spanish? You *gabachas* are in the minority here now, you know."

"All right, come along," I said, exhaling in defeat. "But I'll do all the talking, understand?"

Lupe's car, an old red Fiat with the passenger door painted primer gray, was a couple of blocks away on Wilton. Birds of paradise grew around the doors of an old red brick apartment building we walked past. A yellow dog ran across the street and was chased noisily by a couple of Mexican kids. She unlocked the car doors, got in and started it up. For the next several blocks Lupe lapsed into silence, for which I was grateful. Where were we going? I had told her I had a plan. We couldn't just drive around all night. Although it was getting late, it was still in the mid-eighties. The breeze on my face was hot and smelled like lemon grass. I ran my hand over the grease stain on my pant leg and wondered whether I should tell Lupe anything about Cathy Vega. The streets of Hollywood were full of the flotsam and jetsam of the Third World, teenage girls who had gotten themselves up to look like MTV sluts and many other happy dreamers. We could, I decided finally, drive by Rudy Sancerre's and see what kind of place it was.

I was just about to tell her this and explain what I had learned about Cathy Vega when suddenly Lupe began reciting about Jesus Christ.

Alarmed, I looked sideways at her.

"It's from *The Robe*. The same book Lauren Bacall used to read out loud from to improve her voice. She used to drive up to Mulholland and read it out loud. That's how she got that great voice."

I turned away. What had I gotten myself into?

Rudy Sancerre's place was called Flamingo Photo. It was on Third near Western, a small gray building with the bars in the windows painted pink. A large neon sign with the street number hung over the top of the studio, but everything was dark inside and the front windows were blacked out with heavy construction paper. An alley on the west side of the building separated it from a Mongolian barbecue joint, and to the east was another photographer's studio with wedding pictures and immigration photos in the window. Flamingo Photo was bordered in crab orchard stone, something that you don't see much out here but that was popular in the neighborhood where I grew up. Twice I told Lupe to drive around the block while I looked at the studio, figuring out my plan of attack.

Finally I had her turn into the alley. Right behind the studio was a small parking lot he shared with the businesses on Western. There was an oriental massage parlor with a bright light above the door and a Mexican pool hall with its door open, *ranchero* cowboy music with guitars mixed up too high spilling into the night. Lupe pulled into an empty space near his door. The parking lot was dark except for the halo of light above the massage parlor. Lupe's face was in the darkness. As she pulled up the parking brake, her hand brushed against mine. Her hair smelled like lanolin. A heavier layer of perfume with a rose base made me feel dizzy for an instant.

I got out to look around. A narrow sidewalk ran along the back of the buildings that fronted Third and was divided from the parking lot by a tall wire fence. A sagging metal gate with a length of rusted chain and a pad-lock held it shut. Rudy Sancerre had a lot of little plants on shelves around his back door. Succulents with fat leaves splitting open, parched ferns. A gnarled rubber plant in a pot arched by the door. I walked around to the front of the building and knocked on the door. While I waited, I examined the photos in the window of the other studio. A decal of crossed Ameri-can and Cuban flags was pasted on the window. No one answered, so I went back to the parking lot.

Lupe had gotten out of the car and was dancing by herself, doing a funky *cha-cha* to the cowboy music. I hoped nobody from the bar saw her; I did-n't want the parking lot to fill up with cowboys.

"*¡Que buena la vida! Los Bukis,* my favorite band. It's great to be alive," sang Lupe, dancing over to me.

"Yeah, I vote we stay that way. "What had I expected to find here in the middle of the night?

The song ended and another began. "Ay, *Los Caminantes me matan,*" said Lupe, swaying to the music. "This is great, but why are we here?"

I whispered that I had learned of Rudy Sancerre when I found one of Cathy Vega's photos.

"Then we should look around," Lupe said.

I snapped my fingers. "Great idea. Oh damn, I left my X-ray specs in my other purse. Let's get out of here." I would do this in a more conventional way: I would call Rudy Sancerre and set up an appointment.

"We could look through that window," Lupe said, pointing to one next to the door. "Come on, I'll help you up so you can climb over." She posi-tioned herself near the fence, putting her hands together to give me a leg up.

"Are you out of your mind? Why don't *you* climb over the fence?"

"I have to be careful. I have a kid to take care of. Maybe you're the only one they're following."

"He. Not they. There's only one person following me."

"You are such a whiner. Maybe you're afraid."

The next thing I knew, I was halfway up the fence and about to put one leg over the top when I heard a car pull into the alley. I let go of the top of the fence, a piece of wire cutting my left hand, and dropped to the ground just as the car pulled into the space in front of Rudy Sancerre's door.

"Hey, you, what are you doing there?" The man who jumped out of the beat-up old BMW sounded coked up, nervous. He had a high, skinny voice, like Minnie Mouse on gas.

I felt like a doe caught in his headlights. I had landed off balance, one hand on the ground like a break-dancer.

"You, girl, get up, get away from there now." He reached back into his car, watching me while feeling around by the side of the driver's seat.

Slowly I got to my feet. I put my hands in the air.

I was surprised to see him pull out a bottle of champagne instead of a gun.

He was short—only about five feet tall—and round. His hair started below his ears and crept down his neck in stringy brown strands. He was about thirty. He wore cowboy boots with high heels.

"My friend, she was just, yes, she was just looking for her contact lens. You know how they fall out of your eye sometimes," Lupe cooed breathlessly, walking toward us with her hips twitching. The air around us got hotter.

The man stared at her. Dazed, he reached back into his car and took out a camera bag and a medium-priced Nikon.

By this time I was next to him, towering over him. "Actually, to tell you the truth, I came by on the off chance of meeting you, Mr. Sancerre. I know it's awfully late, seems a little crazy—"

"Are you from one of the credit agencies? I've told you people a million times, a million fucking times—"

"We're not from a credit agency. I came to see you about some photo work," I said.

"Why didn't you say so?"

"I have to go the bathroom," interrupted Lupe. "Can I use yours?" She gave him a promise-filled pout.

He unlocked the gate and gestured toward the door. He fumbled for an instant, feeling for a light switch inside the back door. When he got the lights on, we stepped inside. Flamingo Photo was one large room with light gray walls and a ceiling twenty feet high. To the right of the door was a bathroom with a sink that dripped. To the left was an alcove with two mirrored walls, a built-in dressing table and a small stool. The room opened out. There were built-in orange wood counters with some cooking utensils piled on them, stacks of correspondence including an envelope with the stamped return address of the Beverly Hills Municipal Court and proof sheets. Piles of large brown manilla envelopes, slides and discarded film boxes. A shaky ladder propped against the wall of a shoebox-sized enclosed space led up to a loft sleeping area. The guy was living in the place. Nothing was up to code, and he was sleeping on top of his darkroom. He had a refrigerator, an old gas stove and four chairs. At the far end of the room were some light stands, a tripod and a couple of light packs.

Lupe posed in the doorway, a hand on her hip, before entering the room with her bewitching gyrating strut. Her silver high heels shone brightly against the warm brown of her skin, and the room seemed to tilt slightly.

The man bustled around, sweeping piles of magazines and papers off the chairs for us. He took three mismatched glasses from one of his cupboards and popped open the champagne, which gushed out onto the concrete floor. Giggling politely, Lupe and I held our glasses out. This seemed to make him happy. It reminded me of that old toast that goes "Champagne for our friends—pain for our sham friends." The stuff tasted like it could take the paint off the walls.

"Cheers," he said, clinking glasses with us.

"I saw some of your work and I wanted to find out about it, Mr. Sancerre," I said.

"Thank you. This is delicious, Mr. Sancerre." Closing her eyes, Lupe gave an ecstatic wiggle that made her breasts shimmy.

"Call me Rudy," he said, pouring himself another glass. He had his feet up on the table.

"You do a lot of head shots?" I asked.

"Lots. I love show business. Love the people. Show business is my life. Is that what you're here for? Got a special; four shots for $89."

"We're not actresses," Lupe said in her best Marilyn voice, applying special emphasis to the word *actresses.*

He leered back at her. "Thank God. Those people drive me nuts. Do you know how hard it is to collect a fucking $89 sometimes with all that bullshit?"

I took out the head shot of Cathy Vega. "This is some of your work, isn't it, Rudy?"

He took the photo from me and nodded. "Sure. Great lighting. A cut above the competition."

I took this to mean he did advertising work when he could get it. Three hundred, five hundred, a thousand bucks a day to light computers and cans of hair spray. Make them look interesting. I looked around the studio. He wasn't getting many of those jobs.

"It's very artistic, Mr. Sancerre," Lupe purred.

"Top quality," I chimed in. "Absolutely. Rudy, do you remember the woman in the photo?"

"A real dog. Ooops—friend of yours?"

"Sort of," I said. "I was really struck by the composition." It was a standard full-face head shot. I tried to think of some more positive things to say about the picture but couldn't. "I guess you get a lot of business this way—word of mouth. Is that how she got to you, or did you already know her?"

"What's with all the questions?" he replied with irritation, setting down his glass.

"Yeah," Lupe breathed. "What's with all the questions? This is Saturday night. We want to have fun, don't we, Mr. Sancerre?"

I glared at Lupe, but she didn't seem to notice me.

"I've never met a photographer before. I was just curious," I said, still trying to catch Lupe's eye, but she was busy giving Rudy Sancerre an inviting look while running her finger lightly around the rim of her glass.

"Ad in the trades. I think that's where she came from. I don't really remember. She didn't have a portfolio, not a professional one." Nearly wet with drool, Rudy gaped back at Lupe.

"You remember her? I'm sure you're real busy." I looked around the studio again: there was absolutely no indication that he had worked at all lately.

"Yeah, I remember her. How about some sounds, girls? I forgot your names. Sorry. I'm great on faces, lousy on names."

"Whitney."

"Great name. Is it real?"

"Lupe."

"Great to meet you. Hey, Lupe, how about you turn on the FM up there? Get some cool jazz sounds going."

He watched Lupe's ass move across the room and as she stretched up to a shelf to turn on the radio. All-night jazz station. 'Trane blues-shift kind of music.

Snapping his fingers, nodding his head in time to the music, he seemed to relax. "Ok, great. Now it sounds like we got a party going."

"So what about this woman, Cathy Vega?" I asked.

"Yeah, how do you do that?" asked Lupe, picking up the head shot he had dropped onto the table next to his glass of champagne. "She looks great. I'd like to have some nice pictures."

"I did that shot right here in the studio about eight weeks ago." He sprang out of his director's chair and went over to Lupe. Taking her by the hand, he led her into the middle of the studio, where a dark gray backdrop was hanging from the ceiling.

"Stand right there. Looking sexy just like you do. Perfect." He turned on a light that was placed there and adjusted it so it illuminated the left side of her face. He moved another light until it was slightly behind and to the right of her.

"What about Cathy Vega?" I repeated.

"Same kind of setup. Glamour lighting. Give them some nice shadows. Great eyes, Lupe." He walked back over to the table and picked up a polaroid camera. He shot off one picture. "Makeup's a big part of it. You want real good pictures, Lupe, we'll get a professional makeup artist in here for you. Make you more beautiful than you already are."

I glanced over at Lupe. She was practically purring.

"Cathy Vega do her own makeup?" I asked, fighting to stay in the conversation and keep his attention.

He was only half listening to me because he was counting under his breath. "... eighty-eight, eighty-nine, ninety. Ok, there it is. How's it look?" he asked, walking over to show the Polaroid to Lupe.

Lupe took the picture from him. She looked pleased.

"See, you've got it. The look, Lupe. You ever thought about being a model?"

"Cathy Vega do some modeling? You line up modeling jobs?" I asked, interrupting.

"Her?" he hooted. "Cathy? Vega? Not likely. Didn't have the body for it. Okay, Lupe let's have another one. Give me some pout." He pulled one of Lupe's halter straps down and caressed her shoulder for a second as though he were making a final adjustment to her costume before clicking off another shot. "Usually the product people pick out their own models. But I can help a girl get started. Make her a nice portfolio. Maybe introduce her to someone if I think they'd like her."

"I always thought I was too short to model," said Lupe, still examining the polaroid.

"You never arranged a modeling job downtown for Cathy Vega?" I prodded.

"You're gorgeous, sweetheart. Gorgeous." He examined with satisfaction the second polaroid as he peeled the cover off it.

I looked at Lupe. She was pretty. Her skin had started to glow. I didn't know if it was his lighting or some excitement that had taken over.

"Here you go, sweetheart." He picked up his glass of champagne as he handed the polaroid to Lupe. "Downtown? No, not hardly. Look, I'm sorry if she was a friend of yours, but she was a dog. Totally ordinary looking, no cheekbones, no neck. She couldn't get a job modeling trash bags. I don't know who the hell she thought she was kidding. How was she going to get any movie or TV gigs?" He took the polaroid from Lupe's hand and dropped it along with the other one onto a wooden counter I was leaning against. "Let's have one more, Lupe. Look to the left. Lots of attitude. Stick your boobies out. That's good."

I took the other photograph, the nude one of Cathy Vega, from my purse. Incongruously she was sprawled against a painted backdrop of palm trees. I glanced around the studio. In a corner were a lot of backdrops rolled up and leaning against the wall. Black, light, blue, pale pink, red.

"Rudy, is this one of your pictures?" I held it out to him.

He was still counting and didn't look up immediately when I spoke to him.

"She really looks a lot better with her clothes off," he said when he did glance at it. "I didn't realize that."

"You didn't take this picture?"

"Is that the kind of picture you'd like?" More interest in me flickered in his beady, coked-up eyes than he had demonstrated so far. "How about you, Lupe, you want some pictures like that?"

Lupe stared blank-faced at the photo for a second. She looked confused, and her eyes met mine. She pulled her halter strap up on her shoulder.

"You never did any nude pictures with her?" I asked.

"Her?" scoffed Rudy. "She was a goody-two-shoes type. At least she pretended to be. A real professional virgin. Probably saving it all for the casting couch, for someone who could do something for her."

So he'd tried to hit on her and she put him off. This was certainly different from what I would have guessed about her. The type my father used to call round heels. With a push-button forehead. He used to say things like that. Why buy a cow when milk was so cheap?

"She was a real whiner. Not a trooper like our little Lupe here. And she bored the shit out of me talking about politics. I mean, we try to get a party attitude going here so people can relax, look natural. But no, she wants to talk about Central America and discrimination."

"Guatemala?" I guessed and wondered whether to take the flier out of my purse and show it to him.

"Where? I don't know; they all sort of run together in my mind south of Acapulco. She was carrying on about not getting any work because of the politics at the studio. I don't know what she was talking about. She wasn't getting any work because she was a pain in the butt. I just turned up the music and stopped listening."

I looked at the photo of Cathy Vega again; sprawled against the backdrop, her eyes half closed, her back arched, her legs spread open. It reminded me of the way I'd seen her in the loft.

"So who takes these pictures?" I asked. "Looks pretty professional to me."

"Lots of guys. Anyone with a hundred bucks for a Japanese camera. Or a girl like her. Excuse me a second." He went into the bathroom and partially closed the door. We heard two snorts before he reemerged, smiling and a little flushed.

"Allergy problem." He tapped his nose with one finger. "Now, Lupe, let's get some more pictures. You're looking hot. Whitney, you come over here and get in the picture, too. Let's have the two of you girls together." He walked toward Lupe and pulled her shoulder strap down again.

"I don't take my clothes off. And I don't do lesbo stuff." She bristled, walking away from the lights.

"Touchy, touchy. Can't be like that if you want to make it in this town." He certainly had a way with women, I could see that. Guy probably couldn't get laid if he was passing out pardons at Sybil Brand.

"Was this taken in a studio or in someone's home?" I asked pointedly, ignoring his perverted intent. I could imagine what he thought he could get the two of us to do for his picture.

He took the picture from me and looked at it for a while. I couldn't tell if he was thinking about my question or just staring at Cathy Vega's snatch.

"Studio," he said finally. "You can tell by the lighting. It's set high. The guy would need to have a place with high ceilings like this. He was probably using a strobe pack, too. See, you can tell by the shadowing."I

I glanced down to the opposite end of the studio, where there were two black strobe packs.

Lupe brushed past him to the table, where she picked up her glass. He hurried to fill it for her and tried to get her to look at him.

"How do you get these pictures developed? You send them to a regular lab?"

"There are a few labs who do this kind of kiss-the-pink stuff, but it's mostly underground. You have to know who they are. Guy must have had his own darkroom or access to a darkroom. Probably did the printing himself. You want to see my darkroom?" He walked toward the cubicle built against the east wall.

I stayed where I was. The last thing I wanted was to get into a small enclosed space with Rudy Sancerre. I stared down at the counter I was leaning against. It was littered with polaroids. I looked at the ones of Lupe, pretending to examine them again, wondering how to get us out of there. Whether or not Rudy Sancerre was getting any action, he certainly knew a lot of women. There were blondes, brunettes, an exotic oriental beauty with unnaturally thick hair curling to her waist. The idea of him inspecting them and sniffing them like a dog made me sick, but I was fascinated. I kept shuffling through the piles of polaroids.

I was surprised to hear Lupe say she wanted to see the darkroom. I glanced over, but she didn't see me. Lupe was like the women in the photos I was looking at. Ambitious but a little naive, starting to get hard and shopworn around the edges before they reached their midtwenties. The innocent girl, but with the look in the eye that says fuck me harder. No wonder Lupe's brother was looking for her.

They were mostly the standard head-shot setup. It was interesting how empty most of the women looked, as if something had already been taken from them, something burned out of them. Most of the women, if not actually good looking, managed to convey an empty, almost pathetic eagerness to please that molded their features into conventional friezes. I thought about the pictures of Cathy Vega. There was something slightly different from the others, something that looked alive about her in the photo. It was the inability to really fit the mold, although the desire to do so was clearly there in the hairdo, the makeup. Something about the picture of Cathy Vega showed she was playing a part even as she was being photographed. She must have been a very bad actress.

"What's that?" I heard Lupe ask.

"That's the developing solution," Rudy Sancerre said. He sounded like a guide at Disneyland; part patience, part artificial cheer. He sounded like Mr. Peepers with a hard-on. I half expected the door to the darkroom to swing shut and the red light above the door to go on.

"This stuff really stinks," she said.

"Then we put it in the tray with the wash solution."

I went back to looking at the photographs. It sounded as if he were keeping his hands to himself. There was a gorgeous redhead with a frizzy halo, like a soiled Botticelli angel in black lingerie. There were several shots of a tall black woman with her hair braided.

"Now, Lupe, I'll show you how we print a photograph. Just close the door and..."

"I take mine to Fotomat."

There was a blonde who looked like a farm girl who had come to town to get into car commercials. Huge smile, enormous teeth. A brunette in a tiny Brazilian bikini and... I realized I didn't hear Rudy's voice anymore. I started to go over to the darkroom to check on him, but then I heard Lupe say something about not wanting any. I went back to examining the photos. There, in the middle of the pile, maybe three quarters of the way down, was something that jolted me.

A polaroid of Monica Fullbright.

She had a pair of glasses pushed down on her nose and her hair pinned up in a ponytail with some of it falling about her shoulders. It was her! Was she posing as a schoolgirl, or had he simply caught her in an unguarded moment?

"Hey, Rudy, who's this?" I asked, walking into the darkroom. I caught him in mid-toke, a tiny gold spoon to his nose, a small amber vial clutched in one hand. Lupe didn't say anything. He snorted and put the spoon back in his pocket. I was surprised he didn't have it hanging on a gold chain around his neck.

"Oh, that's just the girl who does makeup for me sometimes. If you decide you want to come back and get some pictures, just let me know and I'll line her up. I'll give you a good price, but since you aren't actresses, I can't give you the $89 special."

"I get more than that for a blowjob," said Lupe. She slammed the back door on her way out. I heard the Fiat misfire, then start up.

CHAPTER TEN

I ran out of Rudy Sancerre's studio expecting to see Lupe driving away. She was waiting for me. I had her take me back to where I had left my car, then follow me down the Ventura Freeway to my apartment. There was a fat, nearly full moon in the distance, hanging over Pacoima. I did not feel like playing the willing, gracious hostess. There would be no putting out of the little fingertip towels. No tiny pink hand soaps shaped like seashells and scented with L'Air du Temps.

It was nearly midnight. Still no answer at Monica Fullbright's when I called there. Angrily I slammed the phone back onto the receiver. It was obvious she didn't want to talk to me. I forgot to ask Lupe if she had eaten, and she didn't mention it. I handed her a couple of sheets from the hall closet and gave her one of the pillows from my bed. She spread them on the couch. I would have to go back to Rudy Sancerre's soon, without Lupe, to find out what he knew about Monica Fullbright.

As I turned down the hall to go to my room, I surprised myself by blurting out, "Why'd you go into the darkroom with him?"

I thought she smiled. "To give you time to look around the rest of the studio."

Somehow that made me feel better, and I went to bed.

On Sunday we were both restless and didn't know what to do. I disappeared for a couple of hours, saying I had to do laundry. Mostly I wanted to be by myself, so I went to the gym although it wasn't one of my regular days.

I decided to make it a leg day. You can't have too many leg days. I wanted to squat again. I was still a little sore from the other day, but soreness is a positive factor. A certain amount of pain can feel good. I loaded a hundred pounds on the bar, strapped on my belt and put on my gloves. I looked around for Rodney but didn't see him. I wondered whether I should try it on my own. I examined myself in the mirror. Your body defines much of your social reality.

The weight rested on my shoulders, and I adjusted the bar across the back of my neck. Rigid and frowning, my face stared back at me from the mirror behind the squat rack. I exhaled deeply. There's a tendency to hold your breath when you're working with weights, as though you have to save that energy, have some reserve. I have to keep remembering to breathe. I glanced around the room looking for Rodney again, then stared into the mirror again, studying the arrangement of my body. During intense training you have to use your mind like a muscle. I remembered what I wanted, what I've always wanted since I was a kid: to be strong. I saw myself squatting the hundred pounds. Then I did it. I put the bar back on the rack after three sets.

I added another fifteen pounds and focused myself in the mirror again. I like to sweat and I was wet. I like to look in the mirror. My hands wrapped around the bar, and I wondered if I was supposed to pyramid or if I should go for more reps. I decided to go for the reps and did three sets of ten. I was shaky and panicky by the time I got the bar on the rack after the third set. Taking the towel off the bar, I wiped my face. I put another ten pounds on the bar as Rodney had done, closed my eyes for an instant and leaned my head on the bar like I was praying.

"Fear of pain is a serious weakness in a person," I heard Rodney say.

When I came back in the middle of the afternoon with the Sunday paper, she was on the couch with, I was surprised to see, a volume of Jane Austen from my bookshelf. I thought I would be uncomfortable with Lupe in my apartment, but she had a way of being quiet and keeping to herself that suited me fine.

"I'm hungry," she announced, dropping *Pride and Prejudice* on the floor. She was still in the toreador pants and halter top. Barefoot.

There was no food in the apartment. I would have to take her out somewhere.

"Let's go," she said.

"You're supposed to be in hiding, remember?" I grumbled without looking up from the crossword I was working.

"I gotta eat, don't I? Everyone's gotta eat."

"Okay, let's go," I said, but not as reluctantly as I sounded. I unfolded my legs, got out of the chair next to the window and stretched.

"Like this? I can't go out like this," she complained. "Don't you have something that would fit me?"

The black Raiders jersey I loaned her was enormous, hanging nearly to her knees and off one shoulder. She slipped the silver high heels on again. Payless Shoe Store brand, I noticed. All man-made materials. Without makeup she looked seventeen or eighteen. People stared at us as we walked over to the deli on Ventura Boulevard.

Lupe had an orange juice, a bagel with lox and cream cheese, extra onions, and a side order of buckwheat pancakes with real maple syrup. I was hungry, too. I couldn't remember when I'd last eaten. I ate quickly without talking, without looking at her except for a few furtive glances. Finishing my eggs Benedict, I looked around for the waitress to bring me some more coffee. Lupe didn't drink coffee. Bad for the skin, she said. She cited Gloria Swanson. The waitress came by our booth with the coffeepot, and Lupe asked for an order of rye toast, dry, with orange marmalade and strawberry jam. When the waitress brought it, Lupe carefully spread one slice with marmalade, the other with jam.

"I always save the strawberry for last."

I didn't know what to talk to her about. She told me some funny stories about her brother when they were growing up. She gave me the complete biographies of Jean Harlow, Lana Turner (actually discovered not at Schwab's but at an ice cream shop across from Hollywood High) and Carole Lombard. Another silence fell upon us.

"You're thinking of giving up," she said out of nowhere. "I can tell. You're not going to finish this."

"Finish what?" I looked around at the empty plates scattered between us.

"Finding out who Cathy Vega really was."

I stared guiltily into my coffee cup. *Quitters never win and winners never quit.* That fucking voice of my father in my head. Yes, I had thought of it. "You're wrong. I wasn't thinking of giving up."

"You're afraid."

"No, I'm not."

"Yeah, you are. 'Cause you don't know how to make it on the streets. That's probably why you went to law school. So you wouldn't have to get a real job."

"I went to law school so I could help people," I said angrily. That sounded so foolish, so unconvincing.

Lupe stood up from the table with a big grin on her face. "You been a big help to society so far. What's your record, get three drunk drivers back out on the street again? Here's your chance to do the right thing, something that really has to do with justice and equal rights, and you're sitting on your behind."

"Equal rights?" I mouthed stupidly at her.

"Goddamn right. Until there's equal rights for hookers, whores, prostitutes, whatever you want to call us, no women are equal." Lupe laid a ten-dollar bill on the table and gestured at the waitress as she walked toward the door. "That's for you, honey." She turned back to me. "Let's go to the movies."

"The movies? We're in hiding, can't you remember that?"

"What do you think we should do, sit around and stare at each other all afternoon? Besides, it's Sunday and the movies are my church."

"There's a preseason football game on TV. Raiders and San Francisco." I protested, but she just laughed and sauntered ahead of me with that hip-swinging walk.

We walked down the street to one of the mini malls that are spreading across the city like an ugly lesion, had an argument about what to see and finally settled, after much insistence by Lupe, upon a cop thriller.

"Maybe you can pick up some pointers from it." Lupe said she didn't have much cash with her and she asked me to pay for the tickets. Then she asked me to get her some popcorn and a diet coke. A weekend father gaped at her, ignoring his son, who was pulling on his arm. Even in the baggy T-shirt, her breasts were impossible to ignore.

"Some chocolate-covered raisins, too," she said as the guy behind the counter was ringing up the popcorn.

I ripped another couple of bucks out of my wallet. It was one of the movie theaters decorated in gray and red and intended to be classy, but the floors were sticky and littered with Milk Dud boxes. The movie was loud and violent, badly directed, badly acted. There were lots of explosions. Lupe watched contentedly. I closed my eyes to think my own thoughts. She was right, of course. Until all women are equal... I'm going to get whoever killed Cathy Vega, I vowed against the background of squealing tires and gunshots. And I would do it without Lupe. Thank you. How long did she think she could stay with me? I had to make it clear to her that tonight was her last night. No exceptions. Lupe stirred slightly at my side; she had put on more of the perfume with the rose base.

It was a slow day but not unpleasant, I had to admit. We spent some more time around the apartment and went out for a pizza at night.

Monday I had to go to Department 117 on the eleventh floor of the criminal courts building to do an arraignment and trial setting on a possession of heroin for sale. It was something I was handling for an old guy named Burt Schaefer while he was in Hawaii. I did the prelim, and when the guy was bound over, Burt told me to go ahead and get the case ready for trial. Burt's been practicing twenty-five years, running himself ragged racing from court to court trying to pick up appointments, always booking more work than he can possibly handle. I've been lucky to get in on his informal overflow list. I don't know how he gets away with it. He's got peptic ulcers, high blood pressure, and he's at least sixty pounds overweight. He wears a chain across his fat stomach with rabbits' feet and things that are supposed to look like Phi Beta Kappa keys dangling from it.

Burt himself was in court when I arrived. He was sunburned, pieces of charred skin hanging from his jowls. I was glad to see him. He owed me a couple of hundred bucks and he was always good for cash.

"How's it going, kid?" Burt always calls me kid, but I've noticed he looks at my tits a lot.

Picking up my transcript copy from the counsel table, I took a seat next to Burt in one of the chairs shoved against the partition that divides the counsel table from the peanut gallery. Burt was having a schmooze with the court reporter, who was knitting and nodding intermittently in his direction.

"So, you're going to trial, kid?" he cracked.

"Yeah. I thought I did a good prelim but..." There's nothing like seeing your errors in writing, the objections you should have made, a time you should have moved, a time you should have kept still. It's like trying to learn kick-boxing or karate from watching a videotape.

"They're all guilty until you prove 'em innocent. Don't let anyone tell you it's any other way." Burt roared at his own joke.

I got my cash and moved away from Burt. He is bad for my idealism, and I didn't have time to sit around. I had to find out who the man was who was following me. I put on some lipstick and fluffed my bob before I sashayed across the courtroom. The bailiff in 117 is called Radar. He's short, got a head shaped like a dish and eyes in the back of his head.

"Radar, I need a favor. I need you to run a DMV on this license number," I said, unfolding the old parking ticket with my scribbled writing and pushing it in front of him.

"Not supposed to," he said without looking up from the gun magazine he was reading.

"I had a little accident over the weekend. A fender bender. I got to find out if this guy was honest about the information he gave me. He said he didn't have a driver's license with him."

"Okay, give it to me," he said with a sigh. There's a real sense of them against us around here even if we're on different sides: prosecution, defense, it's still us against the rest of the world.

After giving the ticket to Radar, I had him let me into the lockup. I heard the click of my Charles Jourdan black high heels across the concrete floor and the deep sound of men's voices. Doesn't matter how many or how few guys are in there, as soon as you call for your client and start to talk to him, there will be some guy who gets up and goes over to take a piss in front of you. I have seen every kind of dick—every shape, length, width, horses' dongs and things that look like pretzels—pee out thin yellow streams in county facilities.

I assumed my usual position: shoulder against the bars, back to the pisser, hands in suit pockets. Herbert "Sly" Evans was waiting for me. He smirked at the pisser and the other guys in the cell. It was a mystery to me what Sly had to smirk about. He was going down for at least four years.

"Yo, Miss Logan, what's happening? Lookin' good today." Sly Evans is a criminal. He's got a sheet as long as the proverbial arm. The stereotypical product of a broken home, a Watts matriarchy of fundamentalist churches and laundry hanging in backyards of stubby grass and broken bottles. Sly Evans likes to wear suits and gold chains. He has a pierced ear from which usually dangles a heavy knot of gold chain; but it is now empty and slightly scabby from where he's been picking at it. He's growing out a conk, and his hair is tied in a tiny ponytail at the back of his neck.

"My old lady here? She give you some money for me?"

Sly Evans is the kind of guy who hits women, hangs out in the back of liquor store parking lots.

"No, your old lady's not here. I haven't heard from her."

Sly scratched his chest above the top button of his blue county overalls. Around his neck hung a stringy white pouch with money and cigarettes. They make these by ripping up their socks. County overalls don't have pockets. Sly is torn between the belief that I will flash my gams at the DA or go to bed with the judge so that his case will be dismissed and the belief that I am as green as snot and he is going to eat a big one because of my incompetence.

"Sly, I'm talking to the DA. I'm trying to get them to offer you two years." I imagine state prison to be like a small Midwestern college campus with walls around it. Folsom is supposed to have an incredible weight room. They have world-class boxers. Suddenly I had an unpleasant thought about Lupe's brother, "Manos" Ramos, chasing me but I pushed it out of my mind. I was getting jumpy as a cat.

"Man, I'm innocent. I am not doing no two years. I am not doing no time. I want you to talk to the judge today about getting me out of here or an OR. You tell him I got me a job waiting for me."

What kind of job? I was about to ask, but Sly was quicker than I was. "I got a cousin who got a cab. He's gonna let me drive it part-time."

Sly Evans was picked up in a motel room on Hollywood Boulevard with a skinny weasel named Lamar Johnson and seven balloons of heroin. Here is Sly's story: He and his buddy are walking down the street when these two girls come up to them and say, "Hey, baby, you want to party?" Because they are no fools, they jump on this, wrapping their arms around the girls' waists, and off they go to this crummy motel setup where the girls already have keys to the room. Everyone starts to make themselves comfortable amid much hahas when one of the girls says, "Hey, sweetie, let's run over to the liquor store to pick up some C.C. and wine coolers so we can party down the right way." The next thing they know, the broads are gone and the police is knocking in the door. The shit has to belong to the whores, right? It's their room.

The first time I heard this story, I thought I saw possibility in it. Sly develops a trembly voice when telling this story, amazed and hurt. It is impossible to keep your eyes off Sly Evans when he talks. His front tooth has a filling shaped like a marijuana leaf with a diamond in the center of it.

"I don't know nothing 'bout no shit," Sly keeps telling me. I remember the first time I interviewed him over at the glass house. He told me heroin is not a happening drug. He is indignant that I as his lawyer do not seem to understand this. It was not news to me. Everyone is using cocaine now. Teenagers, school kids, housewives. That is what a Republican administration is doing to this country. No one's eating any better or going to school or job-training programs, but now they have cocaine in the ghetto. Rock cocaine. Crack. Pellets the size of peas that will kill you. Cut with PCP sometimes, held together with baking soda or whatever's handy. The government and organized crime together.

Sly tells me the only ones dealing smack are the fucking Mexicans. He presents this as a defense.

I wondered what Cathy Vega was sticking in her arm. I asked Sly what drug can be used without heating it to make it liquid.

"Oh, momma," Sly moaned. He was in pain. He was convinced now that I was stupid, that I would not be able to find my way from one side of the courtroom to the other if we went to trial.

"They don't teach us this stuff in law school, Mr. Evans."

He vacillated between pride that I turned to him as a teacher and fear of what I would look like in front of a jury. Finally pride won out. Sly Evans has beaten the system on numerous occasions with PDs as young as me.

"Cocaine. It is water-soluble. Do you dig? You take a spoon of water, put in your cocaine, soak it up with a piece of cotton and fill your needle from the cotton. Understand? Cocaine—not crack. Crack, it do not dissolve. That's why the boys can hide it in their mouths."

I heard the other men laughing as I walked away.

Radar slipped me a piece of paper as I came out of the lockup. "Here. And you better pay that parking ticket."

I started to thank him, but he brushed me away. I unfolded it as I arraigned Sly and set our trial dates.

The Volkswagen belonged to one Peter David Manzo, who lived on Almira in East LA. Cathy's roommate told me Cathy had a boyfriend named Pete. I wanted Radar to get more for me, but I could tell from his eyes that I had used up my last favor with him.

I know a lot of bailiffs. I seem to project a certain wholesomeness that appeals to law-and-order types, the guys who go to rifle ranges and want to invite me to go waterskiing at Lake Elsinore in their RVs. I stopped by 131 to see the bailiff. I had to buy three candy bars his son's Little League team was selling before he would feed my information into the computer.

While he was on the phone, I wondered what to do about finding Monica Fullbright. How could I make her tell me what was going on? Monica Fullbright was not who she said she was. Nobody in this town is. The guy who cleans your pool is an actor. The girl behind the counter at the hamburger stand is a musician. Everyone else is writing a screenplay. Twenty percent of the population is illegal and pretending they're not here. The entire city is a Greyhound bus station.

"This guy a friend of yours?" asked the bailiff as he finished the phone call with the computer.

"New friend," I replied.

"I would have thought you could have done a lot better than this.

I got out my pen and the little black notebook I carry in my purse.

"Shoot."

"Got an arrest in '86—breaking and entering, dropped. Another arrest in '86—breaking and entering with a conviction. Two arrests for under the influence of an opiate in... Jeez, there's a lot of these, sure you want it all? Guy's a junkie. He's out on parole right now."

So that was the kind of crowd Cathy Vega had run with. Drug users. The roommate had been wrong. Or lying. She sat right there in their apartment and swore Cathy Vega didn't do drugs. She had enough reason to lie. She didn't know who I was and she probably didn't believe Cathy was dead. Thought Cathy was shacked up or strung out somewhere. It looked like Cathy Vega was just a junkie who'd been killed. And for a while I had thought she was a woman like me. Monica Fullbright had me running around like a crazy person. For what? What was it Monica wanted?

I went back to the office. I was through being lied to. I was mad at myself that I'd blown things all out of proportion. Like I'd been on the edge of hysteria. I had to take care of my own business. I had been running around trying to he a Girl Scout. I am not a Girl Scout, I am a lawyer. UCLA cum laude. I needed to sit down, be quiet and do my work. I was through chasing for Monica Fullbright, and I was through inventing stories to explain the death of Cathy Vega. She was a junkie. Plain and simple. The Peterson trial was less than a week away. At the office, mail was stacked up waiting for me. Bills. Lots of bills. I needed to do some work I'd get paid for. Harvey Kaplan walked in on me while I was sorting them.

"Were you here the other night?" he asked without looking me in the eye. He was rumpled. He was still wearing the same plaid shirt and jeans I had seen him asleep in, but had added a baseball cap, with his ponytail sticking out the back.

"Just for a little while." I threw the DWP bill for my apartment into the trash. They would wait another month.

"Were you expecting someone? There was a guy by here a while ago, trying to snoop around your office. A bruiser. Black T-shirt. Eyes sort of crossed. Definitely a carnivore."

"About twenty-five?" I thought immediately of the man following me.

"Older than that. Closer to thirty. Nose smashed against the left side of his face."

It had to be Lupe Ramos's brother. How had he found me? Had Lupe gone out on the streets? Had she gone home yet? Did she tell him about me?

Harvey was scratching at a bead bracelet he wears around his wrist. There are weird talismans from Katmandu and the Himalayas hanging all over him. He always has on at least two necklaces, tantric scapulars with people wrapped around each other like snakes.

"Harvey, have you done any cocaine cases?"

"Have I done any cocaine cases?" he said, swallowing the last word and looking dreamy, almost wistful, thinking of his past. "Sure. You think they invented it after I stopped doing criminal law?"

"Well, I wanted to know—"

"Always get your money up front. Never trust a junkie with money. That's the only part you need to remember—never trust a junkie with money. Particularly *your* money." Harvey stopped scratching to glance at the bills on the desk.

"Harvey, there's something very strange about my new client." A mysterious brunette hires me, a complete novice in the field of immigration law, to find Carmen Luzano, her missing maid, in the maze of red tape that is INS. Only there is no Guatemalan maid. Instead, there is a chicana actress named Cathy Vega; Lupe said she was a hooker. Cathy Vega shows up dead at a place Monica Fullbright tells me to go to, then tells me she doesn't know any Cathy Vega. I find out from Cathy's roommate and from Rudy Sancerre that Monica did know Cathy. Men start to follow me. Monica Fullbright had dragged me into something both illegal and dangerous. Nobody will tell me the truth about anything. But I didn't want to tell the whole story to Harvey. "She's lying to me about something, Harvey. Now I can't find her."

"Did she pay you yet?"

"Crisp hundred-dollar bills. The ones I gave you. I got the feeling she's mixed up with drugs. A guy's been following me. Not the one you saw, another one."

Harvey looked thoughtful. "Could be drugs. Sounds like your client's a small fish. Know what I mean about the food chain?" Harvey was looking past me—that is, he was looking at me, but like he wasn't seeing me.

What the hell was I beating my gums with Harvey Kaplan for? He was fried as usual. Delusional.

"You need the source. Always go to the source if you want to know..." He started to mutter to himself in Hindi or whatever language his guru group uses. He fingered the wooden beads around his neck. "You paid the phone company yet?"

"I'm going to do that today."

"If you got a problem, you need to take it to a higher authority," he repeated.

"God?" I hoped I wasn't in for one of Harvey's dreary and incomprehensible harangues about the innumerable and strangely named deities he chanted to.

"The cops, Whitney," he replied, sitting on the edge of my desk and picking up the half-finished motion for Mrs. Peterson's case, which he studied for a moment. "I can tell there's something more bothering you. You've been edgy and distracted lately. You haven't been able to do your work. Go to the cops before you're in over your head."

"Thanks, Harvey, but I'm not over my head. No problem. Now, excuse me, I got work to do." I don't like cops. I don't like authority figures. Harvey couldn't help me; he wouldn't understand.

Harvey hesitated as though there was something more he wanted to tell me, but then dropped my papers back on the desk and stood up. "Sure. Me, too. If you're here at night, turn out the lights when you leave, all right?"

I sat down at the desk and stared at the volume of Wests I had been using on the abortion clinic case. I stared at it for a long time. The blue binding, the gold leaf print. Soothing self-contained colors, the idea that everything you need to know is in a book. You just need to know how to use the index. When I felt calm enough, I turned on my phone machine to check my messages.

The only person who had called was my father. The sound of his voice irritates me. I turned the machine off and pulled out a bottle of bourbon I keep in the bottom drawer of the desk. I poured an inch into my glass, then turned the machine back on. It was the same as all his other phone calls. He sounded about three sheets to the wind. Why didn't I get a real job? When was I going to get married? He wanted to be a grandfather.

I pushed the machine to rewind. Like Carmen Luzano, like Cathy Vega, like Lupe, I have a hidden life. My father has no idea who I am. I finished the bourbon in one gulp. I poured another one. I've always told myself I'd never drink. I'd seen him do enough of that. The photos of Cathy Vega were still in my purse. I put them on the desk in front of me. She had good skin, a strong, nearly square jaw. Her penetrating eyes stared back at me, mocking and defiant.

"Damn you, Cathy Vega." I tipped my glass to her. "I'm going to find out who you are and what happened to you. No one's ever going to hurt me or use me like they did you. Or Lupe. Nobody's going to mess with Lupe, not while I'm around."

CHAPTER ELEVEN

I set the glass down abruptly. I was starting to feel like a big sister to Lupe. From my purse I extracted the folded flier that said Revolución de Guatemala. I smoothed it out. No address, no phone number. I pulled the phone directory from the bottom drawer of the desk. Where to look? Under Justice? Under Political Associations—radical? There were no listings under the letter G. I called information. They didn't have any listing, either. I folded the flier back up and put it in my purse again along with the photos of Cathy Vega. Then I took out my map book and looked for Pete Manzo's street in East LA. I guessed he might be working, so I decided not to head over there until around five and to go to the gym to work off some of my excess energy instead. Although I looked out the window many times for Lupe, she never appeared. I wondered if her brother had found her.

It was my upper-body day. I spent some time stretching. I didn't see Rodney, and when I asked at the front desk for him, they told me I'd missed him by about half an hour. I decided to work on my triceps and biceps. I took a set of ten-pound weights for dumbbell kickbacks. It's a good idea to do a couple of sets using the lighter weight. I bent over a black vinyl bench with one hand on the bench to steady myself and watched myself in the mirror as I brought the weight up behind me to parallel with the ground.

I glanced over at the guy next to me working his biceps. He was black and only about five foot seven but around two fifteen of solid mass. Twenty-two inch arms. I watched to see what he was doing.

It seemed to be working for him. I finished my set and got up to do what he was doing. He took a seventy pound weight. I took a fifteen. He leaned over an incline, placing his arm against the upright bench. I noticed he was wearing a pair of blue-and-black zebra-stripe tights. Animal prints are very big at this gym.

I lifted my weight carefully, focusing on the weight as it moved up and down. It was never my intention to either imitate or compete with men. Nothing could interest me less.

I braced my elbow against my inner thigh. He was gone when I looked up. In the locker room I stripped off my sweaty clothes and examined myself in the full length mirror. Tits small but firm, abdomen flatter than a couple months ago, not much meat on my rib cage, the beginning of an indentation in my thigh just above my knee. Biceps small but no flab. I flexed my biceps and struck a pose. Evolution is not a myth, and women have a greater tolerance for pain than men.

It was nearly three-thirty and time to go out to Pete Manzo's so I got back on the freeway headed east and back to the Boulevard near my office.

I took Hollywood Boulevard to where it converges with Sunset a little east of Vermont, then down Sunset into downtown and over to First Street, up across the bridge to Boyle Heights. You pass through a million neighborhoods demarcated by graffiti and the changing languages of signs above stores. Armenian, Thai, Spanish, Japanese. Back to Spanish. Around the beginning of the century Boyle Heights was where the wealthy Jews lived in big Victorian houses. Italians, too. There was an Italian community then, long since disappeared. The first thing you see when you come across the bridge is a housing project called Aliso Gardens. Two-story buildings, parched grass, kids who look like they don't get anything to eat except macaroni and chicken necks.

High wispy clouds stretched out to the east of the city. I followed First Street to Evergreen, where I checked the map again and turned left past a cemetery. His house was a yellow bungalow with bougainvillea. I drove by it twice, then parked twenty yards away behind a pickup truck on the same side of the street and turned off the engine.

Surveillance work is not like it is in the movies. It is hot. It is boring. At the end of an hour I was busting for a pee. Two little kids kept coming up to the passenger window to ask me what I was doing. One asked me for fifty cents to get some ice cream.

Behind me the street sloped up to the north where City Terrace hangs over the 10 Freeway. The top of the hills had been leveled. Sybil Brand is up there in the trees. It was a lower working class barrio where women grew yellow roses in their front yards and the men rebuilt cars in driveways. Pete Manzo's house was surrounded by a black wrought-iron fence, matching bars across the windows. A woman went out the back door, and I slouched down in the seat, watching her hang laundry across a line stretched the width of the backyard. She was in her late fifties or early sixties, with graying hair cut short. It was the kind of neighborhood where men lived with their mothers, brought home their paychecks and drank too much.

Seven, then seven thirty came and went. I turned the radio on and listened to the news on KPFK, the alternative radio station, which I like because of its progressive orientation. There was more fighting in Lebanon and another insurgence into Nicaragua by the Honduras-based contras. Then I fiddled with the dial until I found a baseball game in Spanish just so the sound would keep me company. By eight o'clock it seemed everyone in the neighborhood had arrived home and turned on the game. Baseball is one of the only sports I don't like. I don't think it would be interesting unless they played it with a live grenade. But there were cheers from inside the houses whenever Fernando came out to pitch. The car seat

was sticky where I had tried earlier to pee into an empty diet 7-Up can. It
was nearly nine and almost dark when the Volkswagen came toward me.
I scrunched down in the seat and watched. Near the end of the block a
family had brought canvas lawn chairs out to their front yard and were listening to the game. A ball from their yard rolled into the street. Rather
than stopping to see if a child ran out, the Volkswagen swerved. The car
slowed down in front of the yellow house, downshifting into the driveway.
The guy who had been following me got out. He was wearing a blue
Dodgers cap. Slamming the car door behind him, he went inside without
looking around.

Another fifteen minutes passed with me slumped in the seat staring into
the dark before he came out again. Of course, I had thought of going up to
knock on his door, but I wanted to catch him off guard, off his own turf. I
had a hunch he wouldn't stay home with Mom. When he came out, it was
like a film running backward. He got in the car, slamming the door and
gunning the Volkswagen out of the driveway. I let him get halfway down
the block before I started my car and pulled from behind the truck to follow him. He rolled into the intersection just past the stop sign at the end
of the block. Naturally he was the kind of bad driver who drove without
using his turn indicator. I was creeping along behind him, but he didn't
seem to notice because his head was bobbing up and down like he had the
radio on. I hung back until he turned left on First. A line of three cars cut
him off from me as he sped west back toward downtown. Accelerating, I
was able to keep the green top of his car in sight. Suddenly he took a sharp
right into a narrow street and disappeared.

I slowed way down and made the turn onto the street carefully. The air
was sweet with night blooming jasmine. The east side of the street was
residential; big old cars were parked on either side so that passage was
tight. The west side of the street was a large three-story stucco building
with a big parking lot behind it. The green Volkswagen was gone. I could
see he hadn't had time to hit the other side of the little valley. It all looks
flat from downtown, but there are a surprising number of small hills. The
graffiti confirmed that I was in Happy Valley gang territory. As I drove
into the parking lot, which was full, I saw the Volkswagen again over in
the second row of cars, moving slowly, looking for a place to park. A Mexican family got out of an old Plymouth sedan, the woman straightening
the red dress of her chubby little girl and yelling at the boy, who started to
run in front of my car.

She jerked the boy back by the arm. After smacking him on the butt, she
led her family toward the stucco building, on which were painted the
words "El Mercado" in big letters. My quarry moved farther toward the
edge of the lot, still looking for a parking space. Suddenly a pink-and-black

Chrysler backed out in front of me without looking. I slammed on the brakes and threw my car into reverse. When I looked up the Volkswagen was at the far end of the lot and going out a driveway that exited on the same street I had followed it down.

The Volkswagen disappeared again.

I pointed my car toward the same driveway, but before I got there, I saw the guy with the blue baseball cap strolling down the sidewalk toward the building. I turned my head away so he wouldn't see me. He had his hands in the pockets of his khaki pants. He was whistling a happy tune.

By the time I found a parking space at the end of the block, he was gone. The street was dark with overhanging palm trees. As I walked up the grade toward the parking lot and the stucco building, it was quiet except for the sound of rats scurrying across telephone lines. I cut through the lot, which was illuminated by a ring of lights around the top of the building. As I got closer, I heard mariachi music.

The entrance to the building was covered with multicolored makeshift awnings and crowded with stalls. Women were selling mangos on popsicle sticks, baby clothes, enamel cooking pots and whistles cut from gourds. Babies were crying. Children yelling. Voices were raised in Spanish, and there was laughter. A man tried to sell me a giant black sombrero with "Mexico" scrawled on it in silver glitter.

I pushed my way through the crowd. The narrow corridor extended inside past more stalls with herbs, videocassettes, shoes, belts and a strange assortment of candles in the shapes of women. Then the corridor widened, continuing past a butcher shop with sheeps' heads and unidentifiable piles of animal innards. A line of people stood waiting by a big black noisy machine stamping out tortillas. The tortillas hurtled down a conveyor belt toward eager hands.

The room opened to its full size. There was a supermarket with several checkout stands. A bookstore. A little studio for passport photos. No sign of the man I was following. It was at this time that I realized I was the only tall blonde in the place. The only blonde. I wondered if this would make surveillance more difficult. I wondered if it was too late to go back to buy the sombrero.

The music was deafening. I glanced up to where it was coming from. A balcony overlooked the entire shopping area. At the end of the tortilla line was a flight of stairs; I hurried up them. I smelled cilantro, onion and garlic. On the upper level of the building were at least half a dozen large food stalls with seating. Each food stall had a stage with mariachis competing for the strolling crowds. The place was packed with families, groups of guys getting drunk and crying in their beer about *mi ranchito,* couples on dates kissing and feeling at the long tables. The waitresses were busy taking orders and pushing through the crowds with plates of *carnitas* balanced on their arms. I mingled and kept looking for the guy with the blue baseball cap. I finally caught up with him in front of a place called *Luz de Jalisco.*

Pete Manzo was drinking orange soda out of a bottle while examining a display of seafood stews behind a glass counter. Finally he got a waitress's attention and told her what he wanted. He found a chair at the end of a table and sat down.

I watched him for a few more minutes while he waited for the food. He lit a cigarette, smoked about half of it with his eyes closed, his foot tapping off time to the music. He woke up when the waitress put a bowl of something in front of him, and he ate quickly. I was about to walk over to ask him who the hell he was and why he had followed me when a man came up to him and tapped him on the shoulder.

This man was what can only be described as a mean-looking motherfucker. He was about thirty-five. Muscles on top of muscles burst out of his cut-out T-shirt. A mosaic of black jailhouse tattoos covered his arms. He was balding and had a red bandanna wrapped around his forehead. Pete Manzo didn't look surprised to see him, but he didn't look real happy either. They went through a fairly elaborate soul handshake that involved wrist grasping and heavy horizontal motion. The man looked for a chair, but there wasn't one. Pete Manzo kept eating and looking at the mariachis while the man talked into his ear. The man was talking softly, then louder, starting to get annoyed, but Pete Manzo kept shaking his head no. Finally Pete Manzo said something real fast, crumbling his napkin into the bowl of stew and pushing his chair back.

I tried to stay close to the railing so I could follow him, but the crowd between us swelled as the band lurched into an energetic rendition of *"Guadalajara"* and fat ladies danced in the aisle. I saw him hurrying down the stairs I had come up. I launched myself through the crowd by pushing an old lady.

"Excuso, excuso. "

I slipped on the stairs in my high heels. It was the same cat-and-mouse game. He hadn't seen me yet, but he must have been worried about whatever it was the muscleman had said to him. By the time I got to the ground floor, he was disappearing down the narrow corridor like the white rabbit into Wonderland.

Out in the parking lot the scene was quiet. No one arriving, no one leaving. No green VW. I cut diagonally through the parking lot, heading for the driveway closest to where I had left my car. The striking of a match and then the laughter of four teenage boys smoking dope in an old Chevy startled me as I walked past them. The street too was deserted. I heard an engine start up in the distance and hurried on thinking it was the Volkswagen, but it was only an old coupe that chugged past me, its lights shining up the hill toward First Street.

I had lost him.

I didn't know what to do but get in the car and go back to his house to wait for him. In the distance I heard *norteño* music. I was getting my keys out of my purse when I was grabbed from behind, two strong hands locking onto my upper arms close to the elbows.

I stomped down hard with my right foot, catching the heel of my black Charles Jourdan pump in the toes of a tennis shoe. There was a little groan; he sounded more surprised than hurt. I looked over my shoulder. It was the man in the blue baseball cap.

"Let go of me." I struggled to get my arms free.

He pulled harder, trying to jerk me off balance. I picked up my right foot again, angling the heel down as hard as I could into his shin. I felt the heel scrape against bone.

This time it hurt him. He said, "Fuck goddamnit," and nearly let go of me.

I managed to wrench my right hand free and rummaged wildly in my purse for a little can of mace I keep with me.

"Why are you following me? What's in there?" he asked, shaking me and grabbing for the purse.

"You followed me first! Want me to scream?" My arm burned where he was holding it, and I tried again to pull away from him. I thought by this time some of the people in the houses would come out to see what was happening. The porch light went off at the house we were standing in front of.

"Tell me why you're following me," he repeated, shaking me harder, his nails starting to dig into me.

"No! You tell me." I had to keep the purse away from him and twisted to try to keep it out of his grasp.

"You know where Cathy is." He tried to slap me, but I was twisting away from him and the blow hit me in the shoulder.

I bent forward suddenly, then back, throwing my right shoulder against him as hard as I could. I felt a surge of power like I feel when I'm lifting weights. He stumbled sideways as I pulled away from his arms. I fought for the purse. In the bottom of it I felt the can of mace and got my hand around it. He stuck a foot between my legs, and I fell on top of him. I was straddling him awkwardly, my skirt hiked up.

With a quick motion he tried to rise up and grab for my throat to pull me down. He smelled like garlic.

"I got mace!" I squirted the air to the side of his face. Acid fumes exploded.

Clutching his face, he let go of me. "I can't see!" he cried.

"Why'd you follow me?"

He coughed and couldn't stop. I felt him shaking under me.

"I'll spray you good unless you answer my questions. Now, you going to talk, or you want to go blind?" I jiggled the can in my hand. It sounded like it had ball bearings in it.

"Been looking for Cathy... saw you comin' outta her... could find her if I followed you...."

I'd gotten the mace illegally, without taking the special three-hour training program. "You're Pete Manzo, right?"

"How'd you know?" he sputtered.

"I'm psychic."

"Why do you want to know about Cathy?" He had stopped thrashing around, but he kept grinding his fists into his eyes and was still breathing with difficulty.

"Your parole officer couldn't make it; he sent me to check on you, make sure things were ok with you."

"Bullshit."

"Your PO's named George Stephens. He's over on Valley Boulevard. I want to know about Cathy, or there are going to be cops on your fucking tail every minute of the day and night. You're not going to have time to do anything but pee into glass bottles."

"You got nothing on me," he whined. Another racking cough escaped from him.

"I know Cathy's your girlfriend. You want to see her. Tell me. Maybe I can talk her into it. Otherwise I tell George you were selling drugs to that guy at dinner." Did he know Cathy was dead?

He took his hands away from his eyes to squint at me. "She told you? About me?"

I nodded. "Yeah, she told me about you. So come on, what's it going to be? More mace, or I fix you up with Cathy?" I put my finger back on the black nozzle of the mace can. "I need some details. My finger's getting itchy."

"Met her... couple years ago... together 'most a year. I got locked up. When I get back... eight months ago... she's different... gone Hollywood." He tried to clear his throat and he spit into the grass.

"Yeah, I met her agent."

"That pimp! She wasn't getting no work... she got *loca*."

"She started hooking." I guessed.

"No!" He jerked under me. Did he know about her job at Club Tropical?

"She slept with her acting coach," I said, egging him on.

"No!" he shouted. "She wasn't really like that... just crazy 'bout making it big, having her own TV show... for all the brown kids. Make 'em proud to be *raza.*"

I felt stupid sitting on top of him, straddling his groin. I was tired of being yanked around. I played with the nozzle of the can. I held it over his face. Who knows what they put in mace? It's flammable. It probably causes cancer. "Why don't we cut the crap here before I have to spray you again?"

"*Chingao,* you don't understand nothin'. Nothin' 'bout being oppressed. Last time she worked she was an extra in a fucking tortilla chip commercial. They had her hair braided, dancing around with some faggot in a serape."

"Look, we both saw the nudie shots. What do you think she was doing, auditioning to model tampons?"

I wasn't fast enough. I saw it coming but couldn't move. His fist connected with the lower right side of my jaw. I felt like I'd been struck by lightning. I let him have it with the mace. A mist of bad chemicals rose up, mingling with the odor of a nearby eucalyptus tree and roses. I nearly emptied the can in his face. We were both coughing like crazy by now

"Never saw that picture... till... the bar the other day. I'll kill her." He gagged and turned away, tears and spit running down his face.

So that was his story. He was watching her apartment waiting for her when I wandered into the picture. He decided to follow me to find out what I knew about her. How long had he been trying to find her? Had he been at the loft downtown? I didn't believe a thing he said.

"When was the last time you saw her?" I wheezed. I felt dizzy.

"Couple weeks... said she was going outta town... been lookin'... thought she had another guy."

"Did she?"

"Don't know... don't know where she goes... what she does... different since she moved to Hollywood."

"You don't know who she's been hanging out with lately?"

Another coughing spasm shook him. "Said I wouldn't understand... politics or something."

"Where'd she go?"

He didn't answer.

"She went to Guatemala," I prompted.

"*¡Mexico!*" he insisted. "Said so."

"What for? Work? A vacation?"

"People like us don't go on vacations," he said bitterly. "Maybe she was fucking her way to Ensenada. The bitch."

I punched him in the groin. Because I felt like it. For lying to me. For dogging me around. Because he had hurt my arm and nearly shattered my jaw, because he had scared me, because I had rolled in a pile of dog shit and my skirt was ruined. Mostly because I felt like it. "Stop lying. She went there for drugs." I rolled off him and onto the ground.

Moaning, he tried to pull his legs toward his body. It was a moment before he could speak. "No! She don't do nothin' with drugs."

Grabbing him by his shirt collar, I jerked his tear-stained face toward me. "I saw her with a spike in her arm just a few days ago."

He slumped on the ground when I let go of him. "Didn't know how to use one... saw me stick myself... went crazy. Never let her see me again." He shook his head in disbelief. "You can't just stick a needle in your arm. You're a bad mechanic, miss the vein, end up with bruises size of lemons all over your arm."

"She left you, didn't she?" I pushed myself to my feet and stood wobbly and breathing hard.

"...girl used to love me...."

My eyes were watering, and he was blurry. I looked down at him, and felt half crazy with the desire to kick him in the nuts one more time. But I didn't. "Then you ended up in jail again."

He was crying.

Either he was lying to me or there was a lot he didn't know about his former girlfriend. I felt sick all of a sudden. Dizzy.

"Pete, I hope you told me the truth. Don't make me do something I don't want to do." I didn't know exactly what I meant by that, but I knew I meant it.

He got to his feet, brushing his pants off, moving slowly, and we both walked to our cars in silence.

I don't remember much of the drive home. The streets were nearly empty. Deserted auto-body shops and used tire places stood silent. I didn't really know where I was, but I kept the skyscrapers of downtown in front of me so that I was heading west. I curved down Brooklyn onto Mission, then I found the freeway.

I felt like a truck had hit me. My legs were shaky and tired where I'd been gripping Pete Manzo like a runaway horse. My jaw was throbbing. My right hand was sore, bruised a little. Maybe I had hit him. My mind wouldn't stop racing, reviewing what had happened. I had been followed by a man. In time-honored tradition I followed the man. At first I had thought he was sent by Monica Fullbright. Or that he was after Monica Fullbright and using me. He was a junkie—unreliable by definition. Erratic. Probably dangerous. I had gone too far. I couldn't trust him to be gentle with me if he found me again.

I crawled up the stairs to the sweatbox apartment. It was dark. The door was closed, but the big window in the living room was open. I hadn't left it that way. I held my purse tighter to my chest and got the mace out again.

The can was almost empty. I threw the door open so hard it bounced against the wall.

"I was wondering when you'd get back." Lupe was curled up on the couch in the dark. The TV was on with the sound off.

I charged into the living room feeling territorial. "What are you doing here?"

"You look messed up. What's that shit all over your skirt?"

"I am messed up. I just had a run-in with Cathy Vega's boyfriend, the one in the VW who was following me. He's a junkie and a drug dealer. I'm beat. I need a bath. I need you out of here."

"Rough day, huh?"

"What are you doing here?" This is called the broken-record technique. It's supposed to get answers to questions.

"Want me to get you a drink? There's some beers in the refrigerator."

"Of course there are some beers in the refrigerator. They're my beers. This is my house. What are you doing here? You were supposed to be gone this morning."

Lupe uncurled from the couch and glided barefoot across the spotted gold carpet. She shut the front door, double-bolting it. "There's no reason to shout. These walls are paper-thin. You want the neighbors to hear you? God knows, I had to listen to them arguing all afternoon. He got fired, you know."

"The guy next door? The fat one with the long hair?"

Lupe shrugged. "I guess so. I didn't see him. I just heard them screaming at each other."

I put the mace back in the purse, which I dropped on the floor. "What about you? Aren't you working anymore?"

She didn't say anything. She looked at the TV, where two men were scuffling silently on a cliff. Eventually one of them fell over the edge, and she looked back at me. "I had the feeling my brother was still looking for me, particularly since I didn't go home last night."

"Good guess. He was at my office today."

"Oh Christ, I'm sorry. I didn't think he'd find you." She sat back down on the couch and began cracking her knuckles nervously. "Did you eat yet?" she asked. "I could make you an omelet."

"There isn't any food in the house." I sighed, rubbing my right shoulder and dropping into a chair across from the couch.

"I went to the store and bought a few things. I make the eggs with guacamole. You can have some tortillas. You'll feel better." She got up and headed for the kitchen, obviously glad to have something to do.

"What about your boy?" I said in the dark. "Don't you have to go home to take care of him?"

Lupe stopped in the doorway between the living room and the kitchen. She was outlined by the opaque white light coming from a street lamp. She turned to face me, but I couldn't see her face clearly.

"My mom's taking care of him for me."

"Did your brother tell your mother what you've been doing?" There are a lot of low things in the world, but you keep your parents out of it. At least that's the way I do it. None of my personal life gets to my father. Zip.

"I don't know. It would kill her. I thought I could pull it off. Make some money and get out."

"That's probably what Cathy Vega thought, too." I wished I hadn't said that. We stared across the darkness at each other.

"Let me have a couple tortillas with that," I said finally, more for a way of ending the silence than because I was really hungry. I picked up my purse, pushed myself up from the chair and headed for the shower.

I stood under the hot water letting it beat down on me. It seemed like a long time since law school. I was thinking about Pete Manzo, feeling an ache in my side, which I had pulled while we were tussling out there on some street I didn't even know the name of in East LA. I couldn't believe no one had come out to see what was happening, that no one had called the cops. I was thinking I gotta get the bastards before they get me, when the shower door swung open. Lupe handed me a bottle of beer. Then she leaned in and kissed me on the cheek.

CHAPTER TWELVE

I woke up. My shoulder felt like an elephant had stepped on it during the night. I spent a few moments feeling for all of my limbs before I opened my eyes. A bruise that looked like a map of Tennessee was spreading across my rib cage. I hadn't been so beat up since I played soccer in college. Slowly I got out of bed. I was stiff all over. I glanced at the neglected weight bench and barbells in the corner; I had thought I was in good shape. A blue seersucker suit just back from the cleaner's was in the closet, and I put it on with a white linen blouse. I am probably the last woman in Los Angeles who wears spectator pumps; I have them in navy and white, black and white and brown and white. Bally. Today I slipped into the brown and white pair. Out of habit I put on the opera length pearls.

I went into the bathroom. The right side of my jaw was pale purple where Pete Manzo had punched me. I got out my makeup and covered it with beige foundation. Then I powdered it with translucent raw silk loose powder, just like *Town & Country* says you should. I cranked open the louvered frosted-glass window above the toilet to look outside. It was hot and sunny already, and I wasn't going to let another day get by without finding Monica Fullbright.

Lupe was still asleep on the couch. Her clothes were neatly folded in a pile on the floor next to her, a pair of black g-string panties on top. One brown calf had kicked free of the sheets. I tiptoed past her to get the phone and carried it into the kitchen. Leaning against the wall, I dialed the number I had dialed so many times before and waited for it to ring. Monica Fullbright's phone rang twice, then a pleasant recorded female voice announced that it had been disconnected. I called back. It was disconnected.

This would mean another trip out to her rattrap duplex to try to find her. I wondered when she'd most likely be there. Morning? Afternoon? I should probably go to the office first, see if any of the courts had called me. Frustrated, I opened the refrigerator although I wasn't really hungry. There was a small dish with tinfoil covering it. I peeled back the foil. Lupe's guacamole. There was orange juice Lupe must have bought. I had to tell her to leave. A bottle of Stoly was hidden in the freezer. Putting the phone down on the counter, I wrestled out the ice tray.

"What time is it?" Lupe stood in the doorway pulling on a T-shirt, the dark place between her legs visible.

Looking away, I poured some Stoly into a glass. "About six. I'm leaving now. You have to go this morning. Today. Not *mañana*. Understand?"

The sun streamed into the kitchen window, throwing a chunk of light onto the yellow linoleum floor.

"No problem. I'll leave. Where are you going?"

"To find the bitch who sent me off on this wild goose chase, settle up with her, then I'm coming back here. Alone. To my apartment. And I'm going to take my time getting drunk."

"You'll be careful, won't you?" She looked at me beseechingly.

I turned slightly so she wouldn't see my jaw. "I promise to stay away from sharp ice cubes." My voice sounded fresh, smart. Why did I feel like a kid around her? I was older than she was. I was doing a better job of surviving the mean streets than she was. Wasn't I?

"I'll come with you."

"No, you won't. Go home. I'll take care of this myself. These people aren't interested in you. Just me."

Lupe stepped into the chunk of daylight. "That guy last night, that was an accident, some bad luck, *la vida loca.* A brokenhearted Romeo. He's not the one you have to worry about. I don't think it's that stupid shit Rudy either. I don't know who it is or how many of them, but if you're right, if it's about drugs, *pués,* those people kill people."

"Great, thanks." Did she think that thought hadn't crossed my mind? I threw more ice cubes into the glass.

"I'll leave this afternoon so you don't have to worry about my brother." Lupe adjusted the oversized T-shirt that was falling off her shoulders.

"I'm not worried about your brother. I haven't done anything to him."

"He'll think we're together."

"So?" I poured orange juice into the glass.

"That we're lovers."

Orange juice spilled onto the counter. "Lovers?" I laughed.

She took the bottle of Stoly from where it was standing next to my right hand and put it back in the freezer. With a sponge, she wiped up the spilt juice.

"That's ridiculous. I'm straight. Aren't you?" I'm not sure how loud I said it, because she didn't say anything in reply.

Instead she walked over to where the phone was sitting on the counter and dialed a number. The T-shirt I had loaned her drooped off one shoulder again.

"Is Alfredo there?" she asked into the receiver. They must have put her on hold, because she looked over at me and said, "Tow truck operator."

The birds outside punctuated the uncomfortable silence that continued between us.

"¿Alfredo?" she cooed into the telephone after a minute.

"¿*Como estas, mí amor?* Look, honey, what time are you going to get off work? Okay. Good. I'll meet you tonight at eight. Yes. The usual place. Yes. Okay. Good-bye, *mi amor.*" As she hung up, she gave me a superior smile.

Myself, I was in such a hurry to get away from her I didn't say good-bye. I went to the gym. There's nothing better when you have things on your mind. It is not possible to lift heavy weights and worry at the same time. It was a leg day. As I was stretching, I decided that I would work my glutes and hips. Although I am a typical mesomorph, a firm fanny is possible. I started stepups on a bench and did two hundred with ten-pound weights in my hands.

"Behind every great behind is a great mind," I heard Rodney say as I was sweating and shaking through the last twenty-five step-ups. I glanced down off the bench at him. He was wearing yellow-and-black leopard skin tights and a black Raiders ballcap.

I asked him what I should do next.

"A couple deadlifts for your back, then clean and jerk to get legs and arms." He pointed over to the rack of barbells near the end of the room, where the immense former warehouse door was open to the sun. I followed him over there. He told me he thought I was ready for fifty pounds. I didn't know if I was or not, but I took it from the rack. I closed my eyes and envisioned myself bringing the weight from the floor to my waist and then hoisting it above my head. The human nervous system cannot tell the difference between a real and an imagined experience.

"What happened? You hit yourself in the face with one of the weights?" Rodney asked.

I didn't answer but planted myself on a wooden block with my feet together for the deadlifts and took a grip on the bar with one hand curled up and the other curled down. I exhaled forcefully and began. The yoga people say that all human energy originates in the spine—the kundalini energy, they call it. I would never let on to Harvey that I know about this, but as I bent and lifted with the weight, I felt the energy rising along my spine.

Rodney clapped his hands. "Clean and jerk. Time to work."

I put the weight down and got off the block. Rodney nearly always spoke in rhyme. I changed my grip so that both hands were curled down. Pulling the weight to my waist as in the deadlift was no problem, but the weight wavered for an instant at the top of my chest. My ribs ached from my encounter with Pete Manzo.

"Drive," said Rodney. "Drive it up. Make me sweat."

The weight rose above my head. I looked at myself in the mirror with the weight aloft. The body is a symbol. Rodney stayed close to me while I completed the reps, then two more sets.

"Looking good, like you should." Considering that egos tend to run rampant in bodybuilding gyms, Rodney was an extremely decent guy. I replaced the barbell in the rack.

"Hey, Rodney. How come everyone here is wearing animal-print work-out clothes?"

He looked around the gym for a moment. "We are animals. We have hearts and lungs and blood and flesh and fur and teeth and claws." Very profound, Rodney is.

Once I had finished with the weights, I started to worry again about the work piling up on my desk, about the motion I needed to finish for Mrs. Peterson's abortion clinic case. That I wasn't getting any work from the courts. Most of all I was worried Monica Fullbright had slipped through my fingers. I drove to the office. The answering machine's red light blinked ominously. I must be the only lawyer in LA without a car phone. Without even a decent answering machine that could be operated by remote beeper. Two messages were from Mrs. Peterson, screaming at me for not returning her calls. There were a couple of clicks meaning some-one had called and hung up. A message from the printer said I still owed $37 for my last order of stationery. There was another click, and I was about to turn the machine off when I heard a muffled woman's voice.

"...get off the case...."

It was Monica Fullbright. She sounded fucked up out of her head, like she'd swallowed half her teeth.

I rewound the message and played it a few more times. I couldn't extract much more meaning from her words. I understood she was telling me I was fired.

"...leave me alone...."

That was funny. Did she think I was going to send her a bill for last night? What was I going to bill her for? Conferring with a witness? I snapped off the machine. I tried to work on the motion spread out on the desk, but the print kept jumping in front of my eyes. I tried rearranging the books and papers in front of me. Finally I got up and started to pace around the office. When I'd done the equivalent of two *k*s, I realized I had to get out of there.

Harvey was in his office drafting a will.

"Hey, man, how you doing?" I asked, peering around his door.

Harvey looked up as though I was speaking a foreign language. I wished he could help me. I wished he could tell me what to do about Monica Full-bright and her strange games.

"You see anybody suspicious around here last night, Harvey?"

"No. He put down his thick black fountain pen carefully, as though he might forget where he had placed it. "Watch your parking meters."

I was out of my mind if I thought there was anything he could do. I never even knew if he was talking with me or if he simply had old songs from the sixties running through his head all the time. I turned to go back to my office to get my briefcase.

"Whitney, you want to tell me what's going on? Word is that this building is staked out."

"Who said so?"

Harvey picked up the pen again and placed it at the top of his desk blotter. Apparently satisfied with this arrangement, he stared up at me. "I heard it on the street."

"How could you hear it on the streets? You never leave this place." The concrete must be talking to everybody in town but me.

"Somebody is watching this building. My aura is disturbed. I can feel it."

Harvey should stop smoking so much grass.

It was at least a hundred out. That's what happens in August. The smog traps the heat like a pressure cooker. You can feel the pavement starting to crack and everyone along with it. As I drove down Hollywood Boulevard heading east for the arraignment courts at Bauchet Street, I switched on the radio. It was already set on KPFK listener-sponsored radio for the progressive news. I like the alterative music you can't hear on any other station. I was hoping the next program would be one of the World Beat shows that play lots of African music and reggae. The local news was just ending.

"...at the Federal Building a coalition of groups representing the people of El Salvador, Honduras and Guatemala are gathering this morning to protest the latest shipment of military aid.... '

Guatemala! Maybe I could find someone from the group whose fliers Cathy Vega had been squirreling in her bedroom. My car sped up, making a right around the dogleg of Olvera Street, past La Placita Church toward Spring.

A noisy crowd was gathered outside the Federal Building. Besides the usual silent nuns, there were men and women in business suits, some college students and a few old people. They were in an elongated circle stretching the length of the entrance to the building, marching, shouting and carrying signs. There were at least a hundred and fifty, maybe two hundred people. I scanned rapidly, looking for posters about Guatemala, but I was still too far away to be able to read them. I parked in the underground and hurried back to see what was happening. This was larger than the usual weekly vigils.

I crossed the street to get closer. A placard reading "Our Taxes Are Death for Central America" was hoisted aloft by an old woman in a black dress. Many of the demonstrators carried single red roses and wore black armbands. I felt excited. It had been a long time since I'd been at a demo. The last one was before I opened my office. *"Apoyamos la lucha del pueblo salvadoreño,"* read another placard. "U.S. out of Honduras." I moved quickly through a crowd of bystanders and county employees on their way to lunch. That's when I saw the sign about Guatemala. I fished in my purse for the leaflet from Cathy Vega's apartment. Both had the same symbol of a circle with two red lines drawn through it. *"Partido de Libertad,* " it said in red letters. This sign was carried by a white guy about my age with red hair. Several more of these signs were carried around the circle.

A loud contingent of latino counterdemonstrators stood at the edge of the sidewalk shouting in an effort to drown out the chants of the protesters. If I hadn't been running for my own life, I would have joined in.

"El pueblo unido..."

"Communists..."

"Jamás será vencido."

"Communist bastards..."

The counterdemonstrators surged forward. An older man wearing heavy glasses with green-tinted lenses tried to grab the arm of a young man with a sign reading, "Nicaragua—No Contra Aid—Stop the Killing." The young man stumbled slightly as he was pulled off balance; he gripped his sign more tightly. Another man standing by the old man took the old man by the arm, speaking to him rapidly in Spanish and pulling him away from the demonstration. A brief argument punctuated by arm waving ensued between the two counterdemonstrators.

"Gusanos. Gusanos," shouted the demonstrators.

"What's that mean?" I asked a woman wearing a "No Intervention" button standing near me.

"Worms. *Gusanos* means 'worms.' These are the Cubans. The anti-Castro fanatics."

"Gusanos. " I joined in. *"Gusanos.* "

There were about fifteen of the Cubans. Mostly men in their late fifties or early sixties. Many of them dressed in black slacks and the traditional white *guayabera* shirt with short sleeves. They were wearing sunglasses, which did little to disguise the hate twisting their faces. The man who had pulled his compatriot off the young demonstrator stood near me, silent now. He was about my height, paunchy, light skinned. His naturally wavy hair starting to recede in a widow's peak. Although he had restrained his friend, he himself was enraged. He looked over at me as though he might take a step toward me. I had been staring. I crossed the street to the side of the demonstrators.

I collected a lot of paper and signed a few petitions before I located a woman handing out *Partido de Libertad* fliers. I was willing to bet my last dollar she had known Cathy Vega. She was pleasant looking, with very Indian features, a mole next to her nose and long straight hair to the middle of her back. She wore flat shoes and a baggy multicolored flowered dress with thin black straps. When I walked up to her and asked for a flier, I thought she seemed vaguely startled.

"What's this about?" I asked her.

"We are against foreign intervention in Guatemala and the rest of Central America. We want the American people to know what is happening in our country."

I imagined her saying the same words to Cathy Vega. She was a person who looked right at you when she talked. Her voice was musical and strongly accented. She talked like a grade school teacher. Continuing to study me in a direct way, she didn't disguise the suspicion she felt.

Maybe she had seen me standing by the Cubans. Maybe she thought I was CIA. FBI. This had been in the news lately, the infiltration of a Salvadorean solidarity group by government agents. "You're from Guatemala?" I asked, persisting.

"Yes." She started to say something more, but she was interrupted by a man's voice speaking Spanish. I don't know what he said, but his voice sounded angry.

I turned to see who was talking. The man moved in and stood next to the woman. He was a classic latin dreamboat in black pointed shoes, black slacks and a fresh white shirt. He nodded at me, smiling, modulating his voice. Words I didn't know flew between them. I knew he was talking about me. A few more sentences were exchanged before the woman spoke to me again.

"Tonight we're having a screening of a video about Guatemala," she said.

A screening. Do they call it a screening anywhere besides Hollywood? Or were they having screenings all over the Third World?

Before I could reply, she said, "I am Emma Garcia. Please. Come if you can. It's at seven o'clock. The address is on here." She handed me a different-colored flier and tried to smile. "You will be my guest."

They couldn't keep me away. I wanted to know what Cathy Vega had been doing with them.

The man pulled himself up straighter and inclined slightly toward me in the merest hint of a bow. "Yes. Please. Come tonight." He urged in a strongly accented and somewhat seductive tone. Against the backdrop of the granite building and public space, he was not only handsome but imposing. He stepped away and was gone into the crowd as quickly as he had appeared.

Emma Garcia looked annoyed as she moved away from me to hand out more leaflets. I wondered if she was angry at me or him. For a few more minutes I watched her passing out her fliers as she worked her way through the crowd. Near the south end of the building she stopped suddenly and gave another woman her stack of paper. I saw her hurry down the gray stone stairs to the sidewalk and head east. I felt the man continuing to watch me from where he had stopped at the edge of the crowd, dividing his attention between me and the still boisterous Cubans, who had pulled themselves into a ragged circle and were picketing with their own signs. The Cuban who had prevented the altercation removed a camera from a black bag he was carrying and took a couple of hurried shots of the demonstrating crowd. I turned and moved away as he pointed the camera at me. Some of the demonstrators stopped, posed, waved, threw him a peace sign or the finger. A news crew leaning on a yellow van sent someone out for some cokes. The nuns kept moving, saying their silent rosaries.

I waited until I got to Bauchet Street to call Lupe. True, I had told her to get out of the apartment, but I was hoping as I dialed my number she'd still be there. The phone rang and rang. Why wasn't she there? Had she gone out to work? Had she already gone to meet her boyfriend Eduardo Gomez or whatever his name was? I needed her help in translating for me. I had to know what the Guatemalans were saying.

"Hello." The Marilyn voice sounded tentative. Did she think I was checking up on her? That I was going to yell at her?

"Lupe, you still there? Meet me tonight at seven. I have to go to a meeting and I don't know if it's going to be in English or Spanish."

"I need to work. I work, remember?"

"You have to help me. When you wanted to stay at my place, you said you'd help me. You can work later."

"Later! That's when the freaks come out. I only do commuters."

"I wouldn't have called you unless I had to."

There was a brief silence. "What's this about?"

The pay phone was just outside the door to Division 20. A young chicana, twenty or twenty-one, with a black eye, came out of the courtroom crying. She'd probably been there to see a boyfriend who had battered her while he was drunk. A pimp wearing yellow shoes and a black linen suit lit a clove cigarette and looked impatiently at his fake Rolex. I drew closer to the phone. "I met some people I think Cathy Vega was involved with. I have to find out what they know about her."

"¡Hijo! You insist on playing detective. Don't you think you're being excessively macho about this?"

I gave her the address, which I read from the flier. "Lupe, when we get there, pretend like you don't know me. And wear some regular clothes."

She slammed down the phone. The dial tone was a sad sound.

Things were at a standstill in Division 39. I wanted to sit down. My ribs hurt. I took out my old Elizabeth Arden compact (the choice of Southern girls everywhere) and powdered my face again. The judge was back in chambers yakking about golf with a couple of his cronies. The bailiff leaned back in her chair painting her nails a toxic vermillion. There were two missouts who were coming in on the noon bus, but some other scavenger had already arranged to pick up their cases. Who was I trying to kid? Trying to work was a dodge I was using. I knew that. I had to get off my butt and find Monica Fullbright. Not only was I worried about her, I was shook up about Lupe, about her g-string panties, about her kiss, about even the way she had of looking at me.

It was time to drive back to Culver City to look for Monica Fullhright. Heading past the plaza at Olvera Street, I saw the adobe church and many Latinos lining up to go in. I glanced at my watch; a little after two. Surely not time for mass. Then I remembered I'd heard they had a free immigration counseling service. That made me think of Carmen Luzano. Everything made me think of Carmen Luzano. Was there a real Carmen Luzano, or was she solely the invention of Monica Fullbright?

Traffic was light on the freeway except for cars slowing to gawk at a Jeep Cherokee that had hit the center divider sometime earlier in the morning. A new Fela Anikulapo Kuti record came on the radio. Jamming high life. I turned up the volume and fiddled with the bass. At Venice Boulevard I got off the freeway and headed west toward Lorimar Studios, the biggest building in Culver City. On Allison Street I saw the same old lady on her knees working in the yard that I had seen on my first trip to Monica Fullbright's apartment. I snapped off the radio, cut the engine and parked several houses away. I put on my suit jacket and took my briefcase off the backseat of the car so I would look like I had a legitimate purpose. Maybe I only looked like an Amway saleswoman with a bruise on her jaw. The old lady was bent over a sick-looking purple plant, poking at it with a trowel, and I was able to hurry down the driveway to the back duplex.

I knocked and waited a second. Then I took a credit card out of my wallet and tried to slip the lock. This is much harder than it looks. I bent the card in two trying to push it through the door. I got my Neiman-Marcus card out and sawed away at the door. Eventually I heard it click open.

The beige couch was turned over in the middle of the room. A stereo had been thrown on the floor; jazz records were scattered about. Two potted plants had been knocked over on the carpeting and there were piles of dirt. A bookshelf had been pulled down, and a trail of Danielle Steele books led to the next room. The place had been turned upside down by someone in a hurry and without a strong respect for private property. I didn't hear anything, so I went in, closing the door behind me. Scrawled on the far wall in big dripping red letters was the same word that had been written on the Guatemalan fliers and placards: *PATRIA*. I picked my way across the room and used the credit card to touch one of the letters. It was only red paint. Thank God.

Immediately to the side of the small living room was the bedroom. The closet doors were flung open, and clothes were torn and thrown across the room. The bed hadn't been slept in. PATRIA was scrawled on the wall above the bed, and whoever had painted it there had dribbled red paint and made part of a footprint on the bedspread.

The Guatemalans had found Monica Fullbright before I did!

Obviously I couldn't tell if anything had been taken, but I got the feeling that the person or persons who had done this had done it more to frighten than to find anything. There was nothing in the bathroom to indicate what had happened. A tube of toothpaste neatly squeezed from the bottom up lay to the side of the sink. I opened the mirrored cabinet. An overwhelming array of cosmetics and lotions were lined up according to size, products by the same cosmetics company neatly side by side. There was a prescription for Tylenol with codeine. It was nearly empty.

At the back of the duplex was a surprisingly large kitchen with a wooden dining table in the middle of the room. All of the cabinet doors were thrown open. Monica Fullbright owned only a few mismatched dishes, a couple of pans. On the table were a bottle of cheap scotch, a razor blade and a glass of water. I licked my finger and ran it lightly across the razor blade; I put my finger on my tongue. Cocaine. I wondered if Monica Fullbright had been home when her apartment was destroyed. I wondered where she was now. I took a dishcloth, went back and wiped off everything I had touched.

The old lady was still standing in the front yard, watering again. She didn't look up until I was standing almost in front of her. Up close I could see she was at least eighty. I asked her to turn off the hose to talk to me. I had to repeat myself several times. She hadn't seen Monica for two days. She said this without much interest, as though Monica Fullbright was frequently gone. Without mentioning anything about the condition of the duplex, I managed to learn that the old lady was hard of hearing and that she drove to Gardena nearly every night to play poker.

I turned my car toward downtown. Why did the Guatemalans tear up her apartment? Monica Fullbright was in over her head, and whatever Cathy Vega had been doing had backfired on both of them. Cathy Vega was Carmen Luzano. That is who Monica Fullbright had sent me out to find. A Guatemalan woman named Carmen Luzano. If I was going to figure out what they were involved in, I was going to have to figure out why Cathy Vega had become Carmen Luzano.

And I was pissed off someone had gotten to Monica Fullbright before I had.

CHAPTER THIRTEEN

The quickest way back downtown through rush-hour traffic is Washington to La Brea up where the Parisian jazz club used to be. The club was leveled about a year ago. Although I'm not a hard core jazz fan, I used to like to go there sometimes to drink bourbon and feel real cool. I would spray myself with My Sin from the dispenser in the ladies' room which also sold little packets of Spanish fly. Now it's a post office. On three corners are gas stations and the hookers stand in the shade. Would Lupe go back out on the street today? One of the black girls was Lupe's age. She lit a cigarette and stared impassively back at me.

South, La Brea goes through the crack battlefields where drive-by shootings are frequent and teenage boys carry beepers and Uzis. North, La Brea passes abstracted Moorish arches and the buildings are a blur of faded pink and gray stone to the mecca of Hollywood. A somber, isolated innocence pervades this part of town. Nobody walks on the street. The people you do see waiting at bus stops are limp, melting in the sun. Traffic slows down. Everyone moves like a catatonic.

Who, I wondered, knew that Cathy Vega was Carmen Luzano? Were they the same person? Her former boyfriend Pete Manzo didn't know; at least he hadn't said anything that made me think so. Her agent, Bob Alton, didn't seem to know and probably wouldn't care. Her acting coach, with whom she had a brief and rather tasteless affair, didn't seem to know. Something about this idea got me thinking. Cathy Vega wanted to be a star. Even Pete had to admit she'd do anything to advance her career. She expected to get a big part in a play. Granted, it was only a workshop production, but she thought she'd be noticed. Maybe she actually believed she'd be discovered like the wacky story Lupe told me about Lana Turner. Cathy Vega thought talent scouts and casting directors would see her, but she had been passed over for a walk-on part. Maybe she was never really in the running for any of the good showcase parts. She'd been hanging around Hollywood for a couple of years without any apparent success. Becoming Carmen Luzano was playing a part, possibly a full-time part, but for what purpose?

Past Sixth Street the traffic slows even more. It's Hebrew schools, art galleries, design centers, then lighting companies and more of the ubiquitous photo labs. Rudy Sancerre—where did he figure into all of this? If he was the person who introduced Monica Fullbright to Cathy Vega, then he had to have a pretty good idea what they were involved in. My first thought was that they were dealing cocaine. I'd seen Rudy. I'd seen Monica's setup in her apartment but it didn't quite make sense. The coke in LA was all coming in from Colombia via Miami or through the Jamaican posses. Monica and Cathy could be penny-ante dealers, but why would Cathy, or Carmen, go to Mexico? Or Guatemala? If in fact she had gone to either of those places. I couldn't remember ever hearing of any drug coming in from Guatemala. The major export was what? Coffee, I guessed. But if it was Mexico Cathy Vega had gone to, it was heroin. Mexico is the largest supplier of heroin to the U.S. At least since the end of the Vietnam War and the CIA's departure from the Golden Triangle.

But hadn't Cathy Vega died while shooting cocaine in the loft? Why would she get involved with heroin? Granted, her boyfriend had a history of heroin use but she had left him. There exists on the part of cocaine users a certain snobbishness toward junkies. There are proprieties. Levels of social stratification based on one's drug choice.

Maybe she and Monica liked to speedball. It seemed like a lot of trouble for them to go to for the relatively small amount of heroin that would be necessary for their personal consumption. Besides, Monica Fullbright wouldn't have spent a grand on my services for a small amount of heroin. Speedballs. Of course. It was so Hollywood. Spending tons of money to get the feeling of going up and down at the same time. Just like the fucking studio execs who drove around in 450 SLs and wore Levi's 501s they'd ripped holes in. Distressed leather. Monica and Cathy were going to sell it. That had to be it. Did either of the women have a record for sales? The next time I went to the court building, I would have to check into that.

I headed for Third to see Rudy Sancerre again. Punk clothing stores and fifties furniture places gave way to the surge of Central American commerce. Did Rudy know Monica was missing? Perhaps she had told him where she was going. That was assuming she had gone somewhere rather than being kidnapped by the Guatemalans who ransacked her apartment.

I left my car down the block in the dirty parking lot behind a Pioneer Chicken so it wouldn't be seen. As I walked to Flamingo Photo, I considered the fact that the Rudy who had called Cathy Vega's agent had left, instead of his real phone number, that of a Pioneer Chicken place. How was Rudy involved with Monica and Cathy? Flamingo Photo's front door was wide open because it had no air conditioning. Was he more dangerous than I had originally guessed? It was too late to worry about that now, I decided as I stepped into the studio. At the opposite end of the room Rudy bent over a counter with a light box.

I knocked on the door.

He looked up from the negatives he had been examining. His yellow T-shirt advertised a Mexican restaurant in Montebello. Was he chicano? I wondered. His name didn't sound like it to me. His distinctive speech pattern—could it be called an accent? The agent had been sure the Rudy who called to hire Cathy Vega as a model had an accent. When Rudy looked at me, his eyes didn't register that I was a person he had met.

"Remember me from the other night?"

"Sure, sure. Never forget a face. Part of the business."

He probably remembered Lupe's ass much better than my face.

"I'd like to get in touch with Monica Fullbright."

"Who? Monica Fullbright? You mean Monica Farley?"

So she'd given me a phony name. Was I surprised? Only that her first name was real. Maybe she'd had a sudden failure of imagination on the way up the stairs to my office. "Yeah, your makeup artist."

He put down the red grease pencil he'd been using to mark the negatives. "You thinking of getting some pictures done?"

"Thinking about it," I replied evenly. "You can get her?"

"I could make you look great. Soft lighting, that's the key." He turned off the light box and hastened to pull a chair from the table for me.

I didn't sit down. "How about Monica?"

"The makeup? Don't worry. It'll be fabulous."

"When's the last time you saw her?"

"I don't know. I haven't talked to her for a couple of days, but it's no problem. Let's make an appointment. I'll get her." He started pacing around excitedly. "I'll make you some great pictures with my Hasselblad, but I'll need fifty bucks up front for the film and all."

A quick survey around the room told me there was no Hasselblad. Maybe he did have one once. Maybe he pawned it when things weren't going well, the way musicians pawned their instruments. His coke habit must have been costing him plenty. Maybe that's why there wasn't more furniture in the studio. Or photographic equipment. Maybe he himself was dealing coke to supplement his income as a photographer.

"Monica's gone, Rudy. You knew that, didn't you?" Why couldn't they be involved in something simple, like pornography? Straightforward beaver shots. It could be German shepherds, and I wouldn't care. But drugs, that was bad news. Certainly more people die each year from drug-related causes than from pornography. I didn't want him to know I was scared. My hand brushed against my skirt. I stood up straighter.

"Some very messy people rearranged your friend Monica's apartment for her. The kind of people who express themselves artistically with semiautomatic weapons." I made this up to shake him.

For the first time he looked as if what I was saying was penetrating his consciousness. Now we were starting to get into the reality therapy mode.

"Who are you?" he snarled, looking anxiously about the room. Was he looking for something to protect himself with? Did he have a gun? "What's this about?"

"You tell me. "

A car with a loose muffler rattled by, breaking the silence as he stared cagily at me.

"Cathy Vega's dead," I continued. "She died downtown at a place her agent says was a modeling job you set up for her. Now Monica's missing. Looks to me like a drug deal gone sour and somebody's pissed off."

He chewed his lower lip a bit and shoved his hands in his pockets to hide his nervousness. "Dead! Modeling job! I don't know what you're talking about."

"You don't? Call Monica. Ask her."

The seconds ticked by. He didn't move, and it infuriated me.

My adrenaline started to pump like crazy. Out of control. Like the last time I saw Ed Harrison. The scene in the motel when he called me frigid and a freak. I had felt all the blood pounding in my head and I thought that I might kill him. That's how I felt again. "Call her or I'll..."

He crossed his arms and smirked at me. "You'll what, bitch?"

I threw myself at him, pushing him off balance and into the wall. "I'll kick the shit out of you! You'll piss sitting down for the rest of your life!"

"Are you crazy or what?" He laughed in a phony way, as if saying he knew we were just fooling around, but he rubbed his shoulder and moved away from me. Angrily he stalked over to the phone, but with a smile plastered on his face like he was playing along with a little joke of mine. Rudy Sancerre was a short man who was used to trying to con his way through life by playing the clown. I could see how much hostility he really had in him. All the abuse and taunts heaped upon him when he was growing up. The bullies who beat him up. Rudy picked up the phone, dialed and heard the disconnect message. Frowning, he slammed the phone down and glanced at me uncertainly, not disarmingly but schizy, like he didn't know what he might do next.

I stared back at him without blinking but just as uncertainly. Many short men have been megalomaniacs. Or serial killers. Napoleon. Wasn't Hitler only about five feet tall? Yes, Rudy could be a stone-cold killer. No one can put up with the shit of being a midget. It's going to bubble out of them sooner or later. Was Rudy the one who called Cathy Vega downtown? Did he know the Guatemalans? Was he Monica's partner in the drug business? Had they bumped Cathy Vega off after the deal to get rid of her? A thousand questions raced through my mind. "So, where's Monica?"

In apparent shock he crumbled onto the stool next to the counter. It was like the scene at the end of the *Wizard of Oz* when Dorothy pulls back the curtain and sees the Wizard is only a little man. I feel this sometimes when I look at my father.

"Jesus fucking Christ," muttered Rudy.

"He's not going to help you."

"I'm not talking without a lawyer," Rudy announced churlishly, looking not at me but at the invisible thread he began to pull at on the knee of his jeans.

"I am a lawyer. I'm not a cop. Monica hired me to help her."

He looked up suspiciously. "You? A lawyer? What's your name? Where's your office? What did Monica tell you?" His words tumbled out; his eyes darted around the room.

Coke makes people paranoid. The first law of paranoia: whatever you think is happening, there's more going on. But then, if he was involved with Monica Fullbright, he had good reason to be paranoid.

I gave him one of my business cards, which he studied closely as he felt the engraving with his fingertip. The engraving seemed to assure him that I was a real lawyer. "Let's talk about Monica and Cathy."

He put one of his little feminine hands up to me. "Shh. Pipe down, will you? Somebody's in the darkroom."

"Who?" I asked, my voice jumping into the upper registers.

"Take it easy. It's just a buddy of mine who I rent the darkroom to sometimes, but I don't want him to hear us." He examined my card again before putting it in the back pocket of his jeans. Rudy motioned me toward the front door, where the traffic would absorb the sound of our conversation. Satisfied with this arrangement, he perched on the windowsill by the doorway.

"If there's going to be trouble, will you be able to cut a deal for me?" he wanted to know.

"The police aren't involved. Yet. Before she disappeared, Monica hired me to prevent the cops from being called." I quickly described to him the words painted on the dripping red walls and the torn-up clothing I had seen in her apartment earlier in the afternoon.

He drummed his fingers nervously on the windowsill as he thought about this. "All right," he said finally. "I'll tell you what I know. It's not much. And I don't know anything about Cathy Vega. I swear, nothing about Cathy Vega."

"Go on. If you want to help Monica." And keep your own skinny butt out of jail.

"I've known Monica for maybe five years. Actually, I knew her husband, her ex-husband. Cool guy, Dave. Saxophone player. Man, we used to have some kickin' jams in here in the old days." He sighed, flicking his hand in the direction of a conga drum in the far corner of the room. "I play the drums a little."

I nodded encouragingly, but without interest.

"Dave and Monica had this on-again off-again thing since I've known them. He's a chipper."

"A chipper?" I interrupted. This word has always annoyed me. It sounds like it means something good. Chipper. Bright. Vibrant. A good name for a dog.

"Ok, ok. He's a junkie. Been in and out of clinics, jail a couple times...."

Did they know Pete Manzo? Was he involved in this after all?

"Monica was always trying to get him straight. They break up, they get back together. Break up, get back together. That's her thing; she needed him."

"She bought drugs for him?" I cut in, wondering if this was where she had gained her experience in dealing.

"No! She wanted him to get clean and make lots of money."

They sounded an unlikely couple. He wanted to get down. She wanted upward mobility. It sounded extremely dysfunctional. Rudy dug a bent cigarette from the pocket of his T-shirt and offered it to me. I shook my head and waited for him to light it.

"Go on," I ordered.

"Dave could make good money if he could keep it together. Did a couple albums, but he just kept fucking up. Couldn't stay off the shit."

I nodded again to keep him going. "How about Monica? What's she do?"

Rudy Sancerre inhaled deeply and blew out three perfect French smoke rings. "Calls herself an actress. She's great with makeup, knows how to shop, how to put clothes together so she looks like a million bucks even when she doesn't have enough for a cup of coffee. But besides makeup for me once in a while, I don't actually know what she does."

"Hooking? Call girl stuff?" I pressed, trying to work out the various combinations that might have brought Monica Fullbright and Cathy Vega together and made them consorts.

He shrugged. "Could be. I always wondered where she got the bread to pay for the rehab clinics."

Rudy told me Dave got out of the last place Monica picked out for him and that he played around for a while doing the club scene. That must have taken some promoting on her part, I guessed, because the way Rudy described it, everyone in town knew about Dave's problem. The club gigs were going well, so the record company he'd been with picked him up for another album. As soon as he got into the studio, though, he started to fall apart again and the record company threatened to sue him for breach of contract.

"What's his name?" I wondered if I'd ever heard of him. Maybe someone I'd seen years ago at the Parisian Room. The name Rudy told me didn't mean a thing to me, but I filed it away in the back of my mind. Maybe in her panic Monica had gone back to him.

Taking another drag off his cigarette, Rudy Sancerre fell silent and shook his head as if remembering Dave made him unhappy.

"Come on, come on," I snapped. "Let's have all of it, or you're all going to end up in the toilet."

Rudy sighed loudly, and his foot, over which he seemed to have no control, tapped at the floor. "What I've told you, this is all about six months ago. He gave her most of the advance the record company gave him and he split to New York." That was the last Rudy had heard of him, except for some stuff through the grapevine. None of it good. Monica got involved with some young guy who said he was a record producer. With big ideas on how they could make a fortune. She figured she knew the record business, so she could control him. Then the kid split on her.

So far it all sounded believable. There are a lot of bad men.

"That's it. I got some makeup jobs for her, like I told you. She sold clothes for a while...."

But not at Crystal's. Did she lie to her friends? Did he actually know anything about her? "Don't jerk me—that's not the whole story. Give it to me, or you may have to tell the cops." I edged closer to him just to keep the pressure on.

"After the guy dumped her, couple of months ago, she started to get frantic, wanting money, saying she was over the hill. So..." He squirmed in his seat on the windowsill and let his voice trail off. He threw the cigarette butt out into the street.

An old woman coming down the sidewalk pushing a shopping cart with clothes, some pots, everything she owned, stopped and scooped up the butt. A pair of tennis shoes were tied to the handle of the cart. I've always been afraid I would end up on the streets. UCLA. Cum laude. All of that. That no matter what I do, unless I have some guy like my father, I will fail and end up a bag lady.

I adjusted my purse across my chest, straightening the leather strap, which was already straight. "You don't want to tell me? Fine, I gave you your chance." I stepped past him toward the door.

"No, no. I'm getting there. Hold on." Sweat started to form on his upper lip.

I crossed my arms and looked down at him.

"She decided to go for it, put together some money and make a score. Then sell the shit. I told her it was crazy. I told her to forget it, but you know what she said?"

Shrugging, I waited for him to deliver the one great line, the epiphany that would explain it all to me.

" 'Everybody's got to start somewhere.' "

I imagined Monica counting her pennies as she planned her career as a

drug czar. Not tipping at the Vietnamese places on Fairfax, where a man-
icure costs five bucks. Shopping the designer resale places in Pasadena for
that faux Ralph Lauren outfit she'd worn to my office. Buying the generic
brand scotch I'd seen in her kitchen.

"She wouldn't listen to me, she wouldn't leave me alone," he said hurriedly, running the words together. "I ended up telling her about some
people I knew in Mexico."

"Baja?"

"No." He flicked his hand dismissively. "Real Mexico. Michoacán."

"What was she going to do there?" I tried to imagine Monica Fullbright
in Mexico making the deal. Her designer sunglasses. The jaunty silk scarf.
I just couldn't quite picture it.

He swallowed uncomfortably, talking more to the floor than to me. "She
said she had around five grand." He looked up quickly, an innocent expression plastered on his puss. "Don't ask me where she got it. I'm not in on
this. I don't know how she was going to get it back up here to LA or even
what she thought she'd do with it when she got it here." Then he sighed
as though confessing this had relieved him of a bad conscience. Maybe he
actually believed that I could save him.

The heat from outside was unrelenting although it was late afternoon by
now. A bus stopped across the street. A woman, then another, and another, all latina, wearing cheap shoes and looking lost, got off the bus. They
were all illegal. One unfolded a scrap of paper, stared at it as though memorizing an address, her lips forming an unfamiliar name, then shoved it
into her bag before turning away. Each of the women paused briefly, with
uncertainty, then was lost in the crowd of shoppers.

"I don't know how she was going to get it back up to LA."

It was at that moment I knew who Carmen Luzano was. A mule. She
was supposed to make the deal, then bring the heroin from Mexico to Los
Angeles. She could cross illegally into the United States alone, maybe with
a *coyote*. Perhaps with a group of Central American refugees. It would be
a lot safer than trying to fly smack into the U.S. If she was caught in a
group, there would be sufficient confusion for her to drop the heroin.
Risky, but still a much better idea than trying to make it through customs
at LAX and past the trained dogs with a bag of H in her vagina. But something had gone wrong.

"How did Cathy Vega get involved in this?" I asked, not wanting him to
see my excitement.

"I already told you. I don't know about her. All I know is that Vega came
here for some photos and Monica did the makeup. That's it. They didn't
know each other before. As far as I knew, they never saw each other again
after that day."

"Are you sure?"

Before he could answer, the door of the darkroom swung open. A man in black slacks and a white shirt stepped out unrolling his sleeves and buttoning his cuffs.

"Hey, bro," Rudy called to him. "You done already?"

The man turned in our direction. He adjusted his black-framed glasses, setting them higher on the bridge of his nose. It was the Cuban I had seen earlier that same day at the demonstration. The one who had stopped his friend from attacking the young protester. The one who had glowered at me. The one who had been taking photos of the demonstrators.

"Hey, Armando, come here. This is a friend of Monica's."

The Cuban strode toward us with a sheaf of black-and-white photos clutched in one hand.

Did he recognize me?

"Armando's got the studio next to mine," Rudy our ever-cordial host explained, throwing one arm around the Cuban and pulling him closer to us.

I remembered the decal of the crossed American and Cuban flags stuck on the window of the place next door. I put my hand out to the man. Reluctantly he took it and gave it one weak, damp shake.

"Haven't I seen you somewhere before?" I asked.

"Have you?" he returned, not taking his eyes from mine. His voice was husky, flat, accented.

"Outside the Federal Building this morning at a demonstration about Central America."

"*Caramba*, Armando," Rudy exclaimed, dropping his arm and drawing back to look at his friend with concern. "You didn't go to one of those demonstrations again, did you? You know they just get you all upset. Your doctor told you you're not supposed to get worked up like that."

"Are those the photos you took this morning?" I asked, unable to make my voice sweet or wily.

He didn't answer. Although he made no move to show me the photos he held in his hand, I could see they were pictures of the crowd in front of the Federal Building. I wondered if I was in any of his pictures.

"May I?" I extended my hand toward him. His hand with the photos dangled at his side. He didn't want to show them to me.

"Yeah, let's see what you got there. More of those radicals and freakos?" Rudy leaned past me and took the pictures from the Cuban's hand.

Rudy studied the first photo quickly. "You try some of that new Fuji film I told you about? It's got great resolution, doesn't it?"

In the photo I saw the west steps of the Federal Building. I recognized several of the people I had seen at the demonstration.

Rudy flipped to the second photo. "Hey, that's you," he said, turning to me and pointing out a woman standing at the edge of the crowd.

I looked. It was me. My blue-and-white pinstriped seersucker suit looked baggy on me. My hair was blowing in the wind. I was staring almost directly into the camera, a frown making me look older. Around me were the demonstrators. A newsman was caught walking past me with a cup of coffee in his hand.

"You were using that new 125 telephoto, weren't you?" Rudy flipped quickly through the rest of the photos, stopping only to tap the picture of a short, dark-haired woman. "Whoo, look at the *chichis* on that little *ruca*. Oops, sorry," he said to me.

"Why did you take these pictures? What do you do with them?" I asked the Cuban. My face felt flushed. I couldn't suppress the anger I felt.

"Armando freelances them to some of the newspapers. Don't you, Armando?" Rudy interjected.

The Cuban nodded.

"I didn't want my picture taken," I snapped. "I'd like to have the one you took of me."

"When you are in a public place, you consent to have your picture taken," he replied coolly.

I couldn't argue the law with him on that one. He was right.

"Didn't you say you sold one to the *Times* of that demonstration back in June when that singer—what's his name—got arrested at one of those sit-ins at the Federal Building?"

"I sold two. One was on the front page," the Cuban answered.

"I don't blame you," said Rudy, going back to the photograph of me. "Look at those lines around your eyes. When I do your photos, I'm going to light you so none of that shows. Give her her picture, Armando."

The Cuban retrieved the photos from Rudy. He clenched his jaw angrily but recovered quickly, smiled and said, "Certainly. A lady does not wish to be seen in an unfavorable light. Or setting. I will make a print for you."

"Don't go to that trouble, just give me the negative."

"It's no trouble."

"I want the negative."

"It is my property," he insisted.

Was he going to try to sell it? It didn't look like a very dramatic or news-worthy image to me. Had he ever taken a picture of Cathy Vega? Maybe she had been at the demonstration in June. What did he do with the rest of the photos? Keep a file of them? Did he keep track of who came to the demonstrations for some reason? I did look terrible in the picture.

"When can I get it? Today?"

"I will give it to Rudy for you. It will be ready tomorrow or the next day.

Call Rudy." The Cuban bowed slightly, making his way to the door without bothering to look at me again. Of course, he had recognized me from the first moment.

"Later, man. You know you can use the studio anytime," Rudy called after him.

The door closed behind the Cuban.

"Great guy, huh?" Rudy asked enthusiastically.

"Lovely," I responded sullenly, feeling paranoid. "How long was he in the darkroom?"

"About forty minutes or so. Don't worry. He didn't hear us. He comes over and rents my place if I'm not using it."

That must be often, I thought.

"You known him long?"

"Almost eight months. He already had his studio when I got here. He's a nice guy. Does mostly weddings."

"Weddings?" I repeated. "So why's he so interested in those photos of the demonstrations? What's he do with them?"

"Makes dart boards. Hey, that's a joke. You got to shoot a lot of film to sell one picture. That's how this business works."

"I think he does something with them," I fumed.

"He's sort of eccentric but he's a good guy. He left Cuba about twenty years ago. He was married then, and had a little girl. He planned their escape for nearly a year. He had a Volkswagen, and every weekend he'd take his family down to the beach to camp in the same spot. He became known as a regular guy who loved to fish. People got used to seeing him and his family there. But really he was studying the tides and learning navigation. He made his Volkswagen into a boat—at least something that would float. One night when he had it all planned and knew the currents, he got his wife and little girl into the boat he'd made. The wife and the child drowned. He made it. Got picked up by a fishing boat. I'm not sure how long he's been in LA."

So he had probably been the low end of bourgeoisie in Cuba. I wondered if he'd got any money out of the country. Not much, I guessed, or he wouldn't have a crummy place like Rudy's. I wondered if he lived in his studio also.

"Armando's just a lonely guy, and he hates Castro, hates the communists. He goes out all the time with a group of other Cubans to protest."

So he had probably seen Cathy Vega at a demonstration. "What's the name of his group?"

"I don't know. It's mostly old guys like him. Some people say it's like an army, that they buy guns and train with them so they can invade Cuba someday, but I don't think they do anything but stand around and yell slogans."

I looked at my watch. It was nearly six. I left Rudy, telling him I'd be back in a day or so. I made him promise to call me if the cops came around to question him. Of course I knew they wouldn't but I hoped the implied threat would encourage him to contact me if he heard from Monica.

The sun was almost directly behind the Pioneer Chicken, making it glow pink and orange. Everyone in the street spoke Spanish. It could have been Buenos Aires or Lima, Santiago or San Salvador. But it was Lost Angeles, and I knew that just as Lost Angeles is on the edge of a precariously shifting continental shelf, I was on the edge of something unknown and dangerous.

CHAPTER FOURTEEN

Western Avenue, one of the city's major arteries, stretches from the port in San Pedro up to where it curves into the base of the Hollywood Hills. I left Rudy Sancerre's heading up Western a couple of miles toward Sunset to where my map book told me Casa Guatemala was located. Porno theaters, porno bookstores, the kinds of places that sell funny rubbers and blow-up dolls—that's Western. There are a few bad bars, a wig store, some latin markets and a disproportionate number of shoe-repair shops. I cruised on Hollywood Boulevard past my office. My windows were closed. Everything looked all right. I saw the curtains blowing in Harvey's office. About half a block east stood the heavily shuttered Falcon Studios, legendary home of swashbucklers Douglas Fairbanks Jr., and Errol Flynn. I had never paid much attention to it. Most of Hollywood is paved-over dreams and palaces that have become storefronts. Lupe could, I was sure, tell me more about its history. Would she show up to meet me or had she gone home to her baby? Was she out working or had her brother caught up with her? Guadalupe Virginia Ramos, I said aloud, trying to pronounce her name correctly and capture all the tropical essence, the Santa Ana wind sound.

Casa Guatemala was a small concrete building on the north side of Sunset. A medical clinic with barred windows stood to the side. A broken chain-link fence separated an auto body repair shop from its neighbor. I was early. The woman at the demo had told me seven. It was nearly forty minutes before the meeting was scheduled to begin. I drove around the block a few times getting a sense of the neighborhood and looking for Lupe's old Fiat. I parked my car facing down the hill on Micheltorena Street.

There was a Cuban restaurant on the corner almost directly across the street from Casa Guatemala, so I decided to go in to wait. A couple old guys sat in the back drinking espresso and squabbling in Spanish about something in the newspaper spread on the table between them. I took the table closest to the door and next to a window where I could see the street. An ancient royal palm with a thick brown trunk carved with hieroglyphics partially obscured the view. A waitress appeared from the kitchen, where a television was turned to a soap opera with a lot of hysterical crying. To have something to do, I ordered a plate of roast pork with fried bananas, black beans and rice. It tasted good. I couldn't remember if I had eaten that day. I asked for a beer and tried to put my thoughts in order as I drank it. The Guatemalans had either kidnapped Monica Fullbright or scared her away. I would have to be careful. It could be easy to vanish as Monica Fullbright had, as Cathy Vega had, without any trace, and perhaps no one would look for me. My family was far away.

I stared across the street, watching the front of Casa Guatemala without any idea what I was looking for. There were no windows and the door was closed. As I was pushing the last of the beans around on the plate, a dark-haired woman came out, walked a few doors away, returning almost immediately with a loaf of bread. I couldn't see her that well, but she didn't seem to be the woman who had talked to me downtown that morning.

It didn't look as if they were expecting much of a crowd at Casa Guatemala. No visible sign of activity around the building hinted that anything would happen there that night. Finally, about twenty minutes after the meeting was supposed to have begun, people began arriving. I waited until two men and then a couple in their early twenties went inside Casa Guatemala before I got up from the table. As I was waiting for my change, I saw Lupe coming down the opposite side of the street from the east in a pale pink dress. My first impulse was to rush out and wave to her, but I held back. The waitress, apparently distracted by whatever was happening on the soap opera, dropped my glass as she took it from the table, and it broke into a million pieces. I stepped over the broken glass and strolled outside. I was standing in front of the restaurant watching Lupe walk in my direction when my attention was caught by a sudden movement, a gleam of light that came from above me, somewhere over my right shoulder.

Light glittered from the roof of the next building, a three-story brick apartment with wrought-iron balconies and fire escapes. A man was on his stomach with a gun barrel trained on Lupe. The barrel followed her as she approached.

When I was about eight years old visiting my grandaddy one summer in Tennessee, some friends of his took me fishing with them on the Obed River. They had their daughter, who was about my age, with them. I think her name was Beverly. She was sitting fishing next to me with her legs dangling in the water when a cottonmouth moccasin swam up alongside her chubby tanned calf. For one long moment I looked at the snake, knowing it was poisonous, without saying anything to the girl because I didn't know what to do. Only daddies could protect us and save us. Quietly and slowly I got up and went to get her father. That's the polite little girl I was, the one who waited for daddies to fix things.

"Lupe!" I screamed.

She glanced across the street without acknowledgment. At the sound of my voice, the man jumped up, moving away from the edge of the roof. Lupe kept walking and went inside Casa Guatemala without looking at me again. I ran over to the apartment building. The door was partially open, and I pushed my way in. There was a central staircase and I ran up to the second floor. It was deserted. Somewhere down the hall I could hear children in one of the back apartments. I hurried up the last flight of stairs to the top floor. I could smell dinners cooking. Onions boiling, fried meat. Cilantro. A ladder led up to the roof. I climbed it with my heart pounding, not tired or out of shape, but scared.

I pushed the trapdoor in the ceiling above the ladder. It stuck for an instant, then flopped open into the persimmon blaze of sunset. I was able to climb out on the roof. There were beer cans, a couple of broken dolls, a sagging laundry line, television antennas and some discarded rubbers. Another ladder hung over the side at the rear of the building. I saw a man in black pants and a white shirt running down the alley. He disappeared behind another building, and I didn't see him again. Winded, I walked back over to the ledge in the front of the building, where I had first seen him.

It had a perfect view of Casa Guatemala and another small structure on the same piece of property. There were two large windows on the side of the Casa. Not only had the gunman been able to watch the front of the building and the street, but he could see what was going on inside. He must have had a high-powered rifle. Had I actually been crazy enough to run after a man with a gun? I stood catching my breath and contemplating the view when something glinted in the last fiery outburst before the sun sank into the Pacific. I bent down. It was the lens cap of a Leica camera.

By the time I had dusted myself off, reapplied my lipstick and wiped a scuff mark off my spectator pumps, the party was in full swing at Casa Guatemala. About fifteen people, including the woman who had invited me, were mingling and smoking. Voices rose and fell. The woman was standing near the door greeting people as they came in. The room was a storefront with a lot of mismatched folding chairs, posters on the walls and a table with literature spread out on it and a punchbowl. A television monitor had been placed in front of the rows of chairs.

"Glad you could come." The woman who had been passing out leaflets at the demonstration took my hand, shaking it a few times. Her skin was warm and soft. I felt her strength and confidence. She could be a courageous friend or a dangerous enemy.

Lupe was on the opposite side of the room talking to a guy with red hair. I had seen him carrying a sign at the demonstration that morning. They had their heads bent together and she was saying something that made him laugh. I felt a stab in my belly like indigestion. She looked up at that moment and glanced at me briefly as though she didn't know me before resuming her conversation. He laughed again as she spoke.

"I'm Emma Garcia," the woman said, letting go of my hand. "We have a very good video tonight on the living conditions and organizing efforts in and around Zacapa. We're very lucky to have this video. It was just shot in the last month and has been brought into this country to familiarize people with what the true situation is in our country."

"I'm interested in knowing the truth," I said, trying to read more in her Indian face, but I couldn't.

"We are lucky to have so much support from our friends because we take a great risk in bringing these videos. I welcome you as our friend."

"I first heard about your organization through a friend of mine."

She brushed her heavy hair away from her face with a hand bare of jewelry.

"Good." She smiled evasively, I thought, and she looked around the room.

"A Guatemalan woman named Carmen Luzano."

She pulled her attention back to me. "There are more than 200,000 Guatemalans in Los Angeles now." She wasn't smiling anymore.

"I thought you would know her."

"No." Emma Garcia folded her arms across her chest.

"I'm positive she mentioned—"

"The only thing that is positive is the historical inevitability of the peoples' will," a heavily accented voice interrupted. It was the man from this morning. The handsome one with the charming smile. Like a shoe salesman's. We nodded at each other in recognition. He wore a white shirt and a pair of black slacks. *"Esta en su casa. "*

The man on the roof had worn a white shirt and black slacks. Were they the same person? I told the man standing in front of me my name, and he told me his. Tony Guerrero. He was in his late twenties and too good looking. He had not been in the room when I arrived. Was he the man with the accent who had called Cathy's agent? If Emma Garcia had been nervous, he was cool as ice.

"I was just saying that I knew a woman named Carmen Luzano. That's how I found out about you."

He frowned slightly at me as though giving this some real consideration.

"Maybe you knew her as Cathy Vega."

"I don't understand. My English is not that good."

I wondered if Cathy Vega and he had been lovers.

"This woman I'm talking about, she disappeared."

"Ah yes," he sighed. "This happens. In our country many times, people disappear. A man is walking down the street, a car pulls up, two men in dark suits jump out and drag him away. The man is never seen again. A woman goes to the market in the morning to buy milk for her baby. She never comes back. The only thing found is a broken bottle on the sidewalk."

"You don't know her?" It was hot in the room and starting to get smoky.

"What?" He smiled. "Do you think that people disappear here? In your country? This great land of freedom?"

Emma Garcia placed her hand on his arm in an attempt to get him to stop talking. "It is time we should be starting our show. I will go tell Tommy." With a brief nod toward me she hurried away and over to the red-haired man Lupe was still talking with.

"No," I said to him, "to tell the truth, I hadn't thought about people disappearing. Not until recently." It wasn't until I'd seen Cathy Vega's body that I started to think about people dying. I always thought about dying as cancer, something long and protracted. Of course, there was the occasional sudden head-on automobile crash on the Fourth of July. But not people dying. Getting killed. Not people my age. Not people I knew.

"You're lucky. I have lost many friends. I have seen many people die. In my country," he added.

"So you're saying she wasn't part of your group?" His shirt was immaculate, perfectly fitted. The whitest white.

"Yes, that is what I am saying. Excuse me, the movie will start now." "Raul," he called to a man who was standing by the door. The man lumbered over to us.

"Raul, this is Miss Logan. Our guest, our friend. Please see to her if there is anything she needs." He said this in his charmingly accented English, then added several sentences in Spanish that sounded more urgent. Tony Guerrero gave me a beautiful smile and left me with the man.

Raul didn't talk much. He couldn't speak English, but he stuck to my side. He was short, dark, Indian. He looked like he'd seen enough people die that now he didn't much care if he had to die, too. He handed me a paper cup with a sticky red punch I didn't want. I stood there drinking it, watching Lupe across the room and wondering how Cathy Vega had fit into this group.

"I'm going over there," I announced to Raul, who didn't respond. "Over there, where that nice-looking young lady is standing. The one with the pink dress. I'm sure you'd like to meet her. I'll introduce you, but remember, I saw her first."

Raul followed me across the room as if he were glued to me. This was the kind of guy Lupe did tricks with. Silent, recently arrived, first paycheck. "Just relax, Raul. I'll do the talking here. "

Lupe spoke rapidly in Spanish to Raul. He smiled. Tommy Hutchings was smiling. They were all smiling. She said something else and they all laughed. Lupe gave me a gracious hostess smile that said we don't know each other.

"I'm going to start the video now," the red-haired man said to Lupe. "Maybe we can talk some more later on."

Lupe gave him a promising smile, and he turned away looking happy and pleased with himself.

"What kind of place is this?" I whispered, stepping closer to her.

"Stop acting like you know me," she hissed under her breath.

"I'm not acting like I know you. I don't know you. I don't even know you had any regular clothes."

"Of course I have regular clothes."

"You look nice."

"Thank you. It's Grace Kelly. *Dial M for Murder.* You can't stand here and talk to me. It looks suspicious."

"All right, all right. I just wanted to make sure you're on the job."

"Of course I'm on the job. I'm the one who's been trying to keep you on the job. Make sure you finish what you start." Lupe turned from me and asked Raul something. Her eyelashes fluttered. He looked around as though checking to see where Tony Guerrero was before crossing the room to get a glass of the sticky punch for her.

"Tommy, the red-haired guy," whispered Lupe. "He's an electrician who works at a studio. He must be the one who met Cathy Vega and brought her here. That's all I've found out so far."

"Didn't you ask him if he knew her?"

"Of course not. I'm subtle."

Maybe she was going to meet him again. I felt the knot in my stomach again. Chairs scraped across the floor. Someone coughed. People were taking seats. The lights went out, but twilight seeped in around the edges of the window, which was visible from the roof across the street. Tony Guerrero got up, his face like carved mahogany in the near dark, and said something in Spanish. Then he explained it in flawless English.

"What you are going to see is all true." He paused, allowing some late arrivals to find seats.

Raul came back with the punch, and Lupe took him by the arm, leaning into him as she thanked him. She sat down in the last row, motioning for Raul to sit next to her. I took the seat on the aisle.

The video began, black and white, no sound. Little kids with balloon bellies, close-up pictures of flies crawling on old people's faces, barbed wire, a burned corpse. A pregnant woman who had been stabbed repeatedly in the abdomen. Raul was transfixed, staring at the screen, his jaw clenched.

I closed my eyes. Tony Guerrero was providing a narrative in Spanish, his voice rising excitedly. I imagined Cathy Vega sitting here on this same hard metal folding chair watching one of these movies. Cathy Vega, who couldn't get a job in white Hollywood making larger connections between her life and the images up on the screen. Cathy Vega, who spoke Spanish, identifying with the urgency of Tony Guerrero's words. And she couldn't have failed to notice how handsome he was. Cathy Vega, who tried to save one homeboy from heroin. Who tried to get out of the barrio and up on the silver screen. Resorting to trying to sleep her way somewhere with credits and residuals. Passed over for a skinny blonde with a flat chest and whiny voice after the acting coach promised her, Cathy Vega, Cathy Star, the lead in his production. After she loved him, fucked him, sucked his cock, believing it because she wanted to believe it, because she had to believe it. There are a lot of ways to get even in Dogtown.

When I opened my eyes, Tony Guerrero was still standing to the side of the screen narrating the flickering images. All the energy in the room was directed toward the screen and his voice. There wasn't even the usual nervous cough or the shuffling of feet. I glanced sideways again at Raul, who was still staring straight ahead as though he were hypnotized. Lupe's profile turned toward me slightly, and I thought she shook her head at me. To my left was an open doorway with a hall that led to the back of the building.

"Bathroom," I mumbled at Raul's left cheek as I got up. He looked at me uncertainly.

"Baño," I repeated, nodding my head yes for emphasis. I got up from the chair and went for the doorway without waiting for his reply.

The first door was in fact the bathroom. I went in and locked the door to give myself a minute to think. There had to be some clue here in Casa Guatemala that would explain what was happening, something that would explain their involvement with Cathy Vega, but I didn't know what I was looking for. In the mirror over the rust-stained sink I saw myself. I looked beat. In the harsh light, wrinkles I'd never noticed before stood out across my forehead, around my eyes. I looked like I hadn't slept for days. There was a black smudge on my collar. A line of purple across my jaw. I splashed cold water on my face and wondered, as I blotted my face with paper towels, how long the video would last.

I left the water running. Closing the bathroom door quietly behind me, I went further down the hall. I could still hear Tony Guerrero's voice. It was dark. Just a bare bulb in the ceiling. There was another door on the right side of the hall. I opened it. It was the office. Minimally furnished. It had a desk, a phone, a lot of posters, some stacks of colored paper and a beat-up mimeograph machine. A heap of fliers like the one I had been handed earlier in the day lay on the floor. I opened the top drawer of the desk. A half-dozen plastic pens and some chewed-on pencils rolled around. There was a deck of playing cards with bent edges, one and a half sticks of gum and some loose paper clips. In the movies this is when the hero finds a stack of love letters, a deed, a will, a signed confession.

A cockroach darted from one side of the drawer to the other.

The second drawer held boxes of staples. A worn paperback Spanish-English dictionary and other small office supplies. In the bottom drawer lay a receipt book. All the entries were in Spanish. None of the recorded figures were large. Nothing over twenty-five dollars. It all seemed to be for things like *estampillas*.

Then I heard footsteps in the hallway. Someone knocked on the bathroom door, waited, then knocked again. I closed the receipt book in a hurry. The footsteps went back toward the main room. They were careful here. Nothing incriminating. It was bare; it was spare. As I was putting the book back where I found it, I saw a matchbook jammed in a corner. I pulled it out. Printed in red and green, it was from a motel called El Nido in the border town of Mexicali. Maybe that was the border Cathy Vega had come through. I put it in my suit pocket.

The main room was still dark and silent except for Guerrero's voice, which had lost none of its strength or urgency. At the end of the hall was the outline of another door, which I assumed had to lead to the backyard visible from the roof of the building across the street. I had also noticed that a small boxy structure stood behind Casa Guatemala. That had to be where they kept the good stuff. A bomb factory. A secret press.

As noiselessly as I could, I opened that door. It was almost completely dark outside now. The back lot deadened against a hill covered with ivy. At the top of the hill, a hundred feet or so above the yard, stood an apartment building. I heard radios and the laughter of children. I slipped out into the dark. The lot was covered with cracked asphalt as though it had once been the parking lot when the building was a business. The box seemed a recent addition, quickly built of cinder blocks with a tin roof.

An old motorcycle, a Honda, stood in the middle of the lot with an oil leak spreading under its tank. A few pots of tired geraniums lined a tall fence that enclosed the lot. The smell of eucalyptus and jasmine blew across the yard. The whine of cars from Sunset sounded distant, but maybe that was because the blood was starting to pound in my head.

The shed door was padlocked. A new padlock. I pulled at it once, but it wouldn't give. Next to the door was a window, but it was covered by a heavy dark curtain. Checking on the west side of the building, I saw the same fabric in the window of that wall. I pushed myself into the shadows and crept toward the back of the shed. It was the same rudimentary layout, a window in the center of the wall. I moved slowly along the back wall, inching toward that window. I could hear my breathing jagged, almost breathless—as I tried not to make any noise in my high heels, the metal tips hitting the asphalt.

Something brushed against the back of my legs. I looked down. It was a black cat. The cat rubbed against me again, meowing. I nudged it with my foot but it kept rubbing on me. The same heavy material hung in the back window, but the window was cracked open a couple of inches. I leaned forward to the window, the cat tangling itself between my feet.

"Scram!" I hissed, kicking at it.

I pushed the window up and pulled the curtain material back.

There in the room, illuminated by flickering white candles, was Cathy Vega. She was laid out on a platform covered with a red and black flag. Someone had dressed her in camouflage pants and shirt. Her hair had been brushed down, but it still stood out around her head, making her features look small. Her face was bare. It was the only time I had ever seen her without makeup. A scarf of red and black was knotted around her neck, and the room smelled. It had that same rotten gardenia odor I had smelled when I had seen her in the loft downtown. It seemed a long time ago. More than a few days. Centuries ago. And the smell was getting worse.

Cathy Vega was barefoot. All of my thoughts were lost in the candlelight. I could not remember if people got buried with shoes on or not. I don't know how long I stood there that way, transfixed by her naked feet. She had on red nail polish.

Something hard pushed into the base of my spine, bringing me back to Los Angeles.

"Is that a gun, or are you just excited to see me?" I said to the air. I have always wanted the opportunity for this kind of quick repartee.

An arm reached past me and jerked the curtain closed, enveloping us in the night. It was a woman's arm. I started to turn my head to look, but the something hard quickly moved up to the back of my head.

"Back up slow."

I recognized the voice as Emma Garcia's. I turned to look over my left shoulder, to talk to her. I saw Raul standing there, the same big, silent Indian eyes, and then I was falling and it was very, very dark.

CHAPTER FIFTEEN

Things were fuzzy around the edges, like a bad black and white photograph. A million years had passed. A lump the size of an eggplant had sprouted on the side of my head. I tried to swallow, but my mouth was dry. Someone had turned on a bright overhead light and there was a bad smell in the room. Feeling sick to my stomach, I pushed myself to my knees.

"Yes, we knew Cathy. Why deny it?"

I struggled to lift my head. Emma Garcia was leaning against the opposite wall, with Cathy Vega stretched out on the bier between us.

"Yeah, why bother?" I said, feeling my teeth with my tongue. My words sounded slurred. "Your credibility would be shot all to hell with me. I hate those kinds of disappointments."

Tony Guerrero stood over me holding a gun. He scratched his thigh with it nervously while watching me. Black slacks. White shirt. The man on the roof. The man who killed Cathy Vega? I looked around the room. Raul had Lupe by the arm. The defiant tilt of her chin might have fooled the others, but I was familiar enough with her painted eyes to see she was scared.

"Cathy came to us on one of our film nights, like tonight." Emma Garcia had a nice frame. I wondered why she hid it under the shapeless matronly dress. Part of the revolutionary process, I guessed.

"I bet she kept coming back. There's a real warm sense of welcome here. I like that." I tried to push myself up but I fell over.

"Whitney!" Lupe cried out as if she were telling me not to drive too fast or not to climb on the couch.

When had the Guatemalans discovered that she knew me? When Guerrero had been up on the roof and seen her walking down Sunset, had he known she was coming to meet me? Had he told the others we were together? I should never have told Lupe to meet me here. I should never have called her. It was bad enough I had taken her downtown with me in the beginning. An awful thought crossed my mind. What if they had been at the loft and seen her with me then? Winking at her, I pulled myself into a cross-legged sit with my skirt nearly up to my waist.

"How did Cathy Vega first come here?" I asked Emma. She had a thin mouth. I bet she could be mean.

"One of our contacts—"

"¡Callate!" Tony Guerrero threatened.

Emma Garcia lashed out at him in Spanish. She seemed to grow taller. They argued for a moment. Her voice grew louder and louder. She pointed down at Cathy Vega. Raul looked uncertain for an instant, then nodded almost imperceptibly when Tony Guerrero began to speak again. Another fast exchange ensued between Emma Garcia and Tony Guerrero.

"Who's in charge here?" Lupe interrupted impatiently.

Guerrero shot her an arrogant look before finishing his address to Emma Garcia, during which he switched to English so I could understand. He sounded as if he had learned English from records. The book of my aunt it is on the refrigerator. "Okay, tell her if you want. We will make sure they are not going to talk. This I swear on my life!"

"Us? Not going to talk? What does that mean? You going to kill us too?" I asked.

"¿Vas a matarnos?" echoed Lupe.

Raul looked at her with disappointment, as though he wasn't going to be able to have one of her special blowjobs.

"Like you killed Cathy?" I threw at Tony Guerrero.

"You think we killed her?" he said, exploding in disbelief.

Before I could answer him, Emma Garcia spoke again. She clearly wanted to prove to us, if not him, that she was *El Jefe*. "One of our contacts in the community talked to her, got her interested, then brought her here."

"She was always open, always growing," Tony Guerrero added, jerking the gun in my direction for emphasis. "She was a good *compañera*."

"Look, I don't want to be smart with you because my head hurts and I can see you people are not fucking around, but I don't think this is a good way for you to go about getting new members."

"She sought us out, she wanted to be with us," Tony Guerrero maintained. He dropped the gun back down to his side as though he had been caught in an awkward pose.

"Us, not you. Remember that, *Antonio*," Emma Garcia interjected with a sneer.

"She believed in social justice, in the people," Tony Guerrero insisted. He would look great on a poster. Fierce, dedicated, the intense eyes. I'm sure he was not unaware of this.

"What did she do here?" Lupe wanted to know.

Emma Garcia shrugged as she continued to glare at Tony Guerrero. "Not much. Little things. Handing out fliers, running the mimeograph machine, then painting slogans on walls at night."

"The more she did, the more she wanted to do," countered Guerrero.

I could imagine that was true. I'd seen what passed for an agent's office. Cathy Vega had been sent out on one too many calls, one too many singing telegrams as Carmen Miranda.

"So, Tony, what happened to her?" I asked.

"We decided to test her," Emma Garcia said hurriedly, answering for him. She did not look me in the eye when she said this, instead fixing him with a cold glare.

"Rough test! Do a lot of people fail it?" I tried to gesture toward Cathy Vega, but I needed both hands on the ground to keep upright.

Emma Garcia ignored this, but Raul seemed to use it as an opportunity to pull Lupe a little closer to him.

"She proved to us she was a good *compañera*, " Tony Guerrero said, addressing himself more to Emma Garcia than to me. "We decided, as a group, it was time to send her to Mexico to pick something up for us."

From the nervous way he emphasized "group," I guessed it had been his idea she go. And I was sure he had been in love with her. "To pick up what?"

"The video you saw tonight," said Emma Garcia a little too quickly. She stepped forward slightly, and the baggy dress swirled around her calves.

"No." I decided to throw out some bait. See what came to the surface. "It wasn't the video. It was drugs."

"*¿Drogas?*" Raul repeated in amazement.

"Drugs!" Emma Garcia retorted angrily, but Tony Guerrero raised his hand and again told her to shut up.

"Drugs? Please tell us about these drugs," he said in his most cordial shoe salesman tones.

What did they know? My brain was not working fast enough. How were they connected to Monica Fullbright? She must have gone against them, and they trashed her crib. Kidnapped her. Did they have her in another room here? "Why should I tell you?" Let them think I knew more than I did.

"For Christ's sake, stop beating around the bush or they'll think you're with the CIA," Lupe demanded.

"The CIA?" I laughed, but I was angry. I demonstrated against the war in Vietnam, against Three Mile Island, against aid to the contras. "Do you think I'm with the CIA?"

"How should I know?" Lupe replied. "I didn't even vote in the last election."

Tony Guerrero gestured impatiently. Raul said something in a low voice to Lupe and she fell silent.

"Cathy Vega had five thousand bucks with her when she left for Mexico. Do you expect me to believe that was to buy the video?" That was it: toss out my best card and see if there were any takers.

There was a long enough silence to tell me they didn't know about the money.

"What was she going to do with five thousand dollars?" I pushed. "Seems like just the right amount to buy half a k of bad brown Mexican smack."

"We have nothing to do with drugs here," argued Tony Guerrero.

"We gave her that money, but it wasn't for drugs," countered Emma Garcia.

They looked at each other in confusion. He didn't trust her any more than she trusted him.

"Whoever sent her to Mexico with that money knows how she died," I said.

"Bad idea using a junkie courier!" exclaimed Lupe. "I'm really surprised at you. Didn't you know she'd use the drugs herself? That's elementary. It's rule number one—don't get high on your own supply."

Angrily Tony Guerrero walked over to Cathy's body, knelt and untied the scarf around her neck. "You think there would be a black and blue mark like that if she just overdose?" He lifted her hair. An ugly dark mottled line about four or five inches long ran horizontal across the nape of her neck.

Someone had chopped her hard with a blunt object. I doubted a hand alone could have left such a bruise. Who was that strong? I looked up at Raul. She was probably out cold by the time her panties were ripped off and he... The needle could have been placed by her to make it look like an overdose. I felt sick to my stomach again.

He retied the scarf carefully and smoothed her hair several times before placing her head down.

Tony Guerrero had been sleeping with her. What did Emma Garcia think about that?

"So, who killed her?" I asked in a voice I hoped betrayed none of my confusion or fear.

"You! You fucking *imperialista!*" shouted Tony Guerrero.

"Me?" I screamed back at him. "You think I killed her?"

He waved the gun in my face. "One of you two. We saw you downtown."

"*¿Tu?*" Emma Garcia spat at him. "You weren't there. It was me and Raul who went downtown to meet her and told you we saw them there. We don't know where you were." Then she started rattling at him in Spanish again, but I understood *puto*.

Tony Guerrero must have killed her. That's why he hadn't gone downtown with them. He had been there ahead of them. Was it a crime of passion? Or was it cold and premeditated? An affair of the heart or political? They wouldn't go to the police. They probably had a revolutionary tribunal to deal with him.

"Who do you think killed your *compañera?* Was it Tony?" I goaded Emma Garcia because I wanted her to lose control, to bust him, to lash out at him, to get him away from me and the gun out of my face.

All she did, though, was give him a poisonous look. "We don't know. Certain subversive, reactionary forces."

"Monica Fullbright?"

They looked at me blankly.

"The woman whose apartment you trashed?" I offered.

Tony Guerrero pursed his lips as he studied Emma, wondering what this was about.

My head was throbbing. There were two Tony Guerreros. "Admit it," I said to him. "Cathy Vega was in the middle of a heroin deal you told her to set up, and it got botched."

"Botched? What is 'botched'?"

"Fucked up. *Chingado,*" explained Lupe.

Did she think we were at the United Nations? I glared at her. I wanted her to shut up and not draw attention to herself. I wanted them to forget she was with me.

"When was the last time you saw her?" I asked, pushing at Guerrero.

Emma Garcia locked eyes with him again for a second. There was hatred in her eyes. Things were certainly far from smooth here. "Yes, when?"

He couldn't help striking a pose and giving a great profile.

"The day before she went to Mexico," he admitted.

Emma Garcia snorted in disgust when he said this. Probably something else he had lied to her about. Was she still in love with him? "We sent someone to meet her, but she didn't show up. Our man waited a day for her in Mexicali."

At the El Nido Motel. The book of matches I had found in the desk. I wondered if they had searched me while I was unconscious. Suddenly I felt cold and violated.

"Later, when she got back to LA, she called us," continued Emma Garcia, ignoring Guerrero. "She wouldn't say where she was or why she'd been late at the border. She said she'd explain everything in person. I picked the video up from *a panadería* on Pico where she said she'd leave it for me. Then we didn't hear from her again until the day she died."

"What time?" I wondered how Cathy Vega had spent her last day.

"Noon. She told us where she was going to be working in the afternoon and to send someone to meet her. She sounded upset. When Raul and I got there, she was already dead. And that's when we saw the two of you for the first time."

No wonder they were suspicious of us. Fair enough. Cathy Vega had made some very unwise moves. Between ripping Monica Fullbright off, something about a badly planned heroin deal and a group of desperate politicos, somebody had knocked her off.

"If you didn't kill her, why were you there?" challenged Guerrero.

My head hurt. It was obvious they weren't going to tell me any more. "I didn't even know her. I was hired to find Cathy Vega, only I was told she was a Guatemalan named Carmen Luzano. I dragged in and out of Immigration looking for her. Finally I got a phone call telling me where to find Carmen Luzano, but when I got there Carmen was Cathy and she was dead.

"I've been chased, I've been hit on the head and my client's disappeared. That's everything I know except for the name of my client, and I'm not giving you that. So do what you want, but leave my friend out of this. She knows less than I do."

I got to my feet. Damned if I was going to let them hit me while I was down. "Come on, Lupe, let's book." I stared defiantly at Emma Garcia, then at Tony Guerrero. "Make your move, 'cause we're leaving."

Emma Garcia started toward me but fell back when she saw the others weren't going to help her. Tony Guerrero said something in Spanish to Raul, who immediately let go of Lupe. Rubbing her arm, she moved toward the doorway.

I had to step around Cathy Vega's legs to get to the door. Who was she? A martyr? A con?

"When this is all over," Lupe said, stopping in the doorway and turning back toward Emma and Tony, "I'll come back to help you. I don't like to see people going hungry. I got a little boy myself."

Lupe and I moved out into the night. We didn't talk as we walked past the body shop and liquor store to where Lupe had left her car. Los Angeles. Everything was different than it seemed. Salsa music poured out of an apartment across the street, and a man and woman danced in the open window. I told Lupe to meet me at the office. Without answering, she started her car. Would I be able to depend on her?

When I was fifteen and had asked my best friend, Tina Marks, to help me run away, she had told my parents. I watched Lupe take off down the hill toward Sunset, then throw a right heading back to Hollywood. Outside an apartment building I hid in the shadows, waiting to see if anyone came out of Casa Guatemala to follow us. After fifteen minutes I decided no one was going to. They probably already knew where to find me. I had a killer headache. Walking up the hill past the Cuban restaurant to here I'd parked my car, I felt weak. I got in, rolled down the window, puked on the side of the car and then eased away from the curb.

Punks. Streetwalkers. Palms shimmering in neon. All-night markets carved with foreign words. Everything was a blur. It was a quiet Monday night on the Boulevard. Quietly simmering, on edge. The way the city seems to get premenstrual before the *Santa Anas* start. By the time I got to the office, I was nearly screaming with pain. I made it up the stairs by hanging on to the railing and pulling myself up like a dead weight.

I came to fast when I hit the landing outside my office door.

WHITNEY LOGAN
ATTORNEY AT LAW

It was dark inside, but I could hear Lope's voice saying something in Spanish, then the sound of something bumping against the desk or chairs, feet stumbling. They had followed us! They must have left Casa Guatemala while I was walking Lupe to her car. They'd been searching my office to find out who my client was.

I crept toward the door as quietly as I could, but whoever was inside probably couldn't hear me because Lope's voice was getting louder and louder. I put my hand on the doorknob and was twisting it oh so slow and careful when I heard a crack, flesh hitting, flesh.

I jumped the door as hard as I could and landed inside. There were two silhouettes against the window: Lupe and a big man who was holding her.

Raul had followed us!

"Stop it right there!" I yelled and hit the light switch with my left hand.

The guy with the bullet head and no neck could only be Lupe's brother, Hector "Manos" Ramos.

"Hey, dude, what's going on here?" I asked foolishly. A red splotch was spreading across Lupe's right cheek.

"*Pinchi* muffdiver," he growled in reply, stepping toward me.

"I beg your pardon!" Where did he get this idea?

"You're the fuckin' dyke what's been messing with my sister." He turned and smacked Lupe across the mouth for emphasis.

"Don't do that again. This is my office," I added as an afterthought. "You're trespassing."

He grinned a big, stupid grin. "What are you gonna do about it?"

"I'm going to tell you one more time to stop it or else

"You stupid *hijo de puta!*" Lupe screamed at him. "I can do whatever I want."

Terrified, I gave her a look that meant stop! But either she didn't see me or she didn't care.

"You cannot do whatever you want. You cannot be no whore. You cannot be no dyke. You're a mother. You got a little boy at home. You're gonna go home now and you're gonna take care of business or I'm gonna kill you and I'm gonna kick your girlfriend's fuckin' butt."

"How about a drink? Maybe we could talk about this," I said.

Growling, he lurched toward me. Lupe jumped on his back, throttling him around the throat. He shook her like a dog shakes water. She scraped the side of the desk but clung to him, biting him about the ears. He lunged for the doorway where I was standing. I was glad I was an only child.

"Hector, I thought you were in training. Is this what you do, beat up on women?"

He pushed toward me, flinging Lupe from his back. She hit the floor. Picking herself up, she tried to throw herself between us. I caught her by the arm, jerking her off balance and toward me. Grabbing the edge of the tall bookshelf that stood next to the door, I pulled on it with everything I had. My entire set of unpaid-for Bender's California Criminal Defense Practice came tumbling down on Hector's head. It didn't stop him, but it slowed him down. Black's Law Dictionary, the hardbound edition, caught his right forearm as he raised it to swing at me.

"¡*Vamanos!*" I screamed at Lupe, but she was already halfway down the hall to the stairs.

The oak bookshelf smashed Hector in the chest, and they both went down. I didn't spend any time looking back to see how he was, but I heard him cussing and moaning, then the bookcase being thrown aside as I made it to the stairs.

A bleary-eyed Harvey Kaplan opened the door of his dark office to peer out into the hallway.

"Lock up after me!" I shouted, racing past him.

I hit the sidewalk running. Lupe was there outside the front door, panting, wild-eyed, swinging her car keys in one hand. Taking me by the wrist, she ran away from the Boulevard, dragging me with her toward her car. She opened the door and got in. She gunned the motor.

Then I did something I've always wanted to do. I jumped over the passenger door, tumbling into the car seat.

"Hit it, girl!" I yelled.

CHAPTER SIXTEEN

We shot into traffic. Lupe pulled a fast U in front of an oncoming diesel Mercedes.

"Where to?" she shouted over the honking horn and squealing brakes of the Mercedes.

"Mexico."

¡Mexico! Hector's gonna calm down. You don't understand. He gets like this all the time. Nervous 'cause he's got a fight coming up. And he's not getting laid."

"A few days before she was killed, Cathy Vega was in Mexicali at a motel called..." I felt in my suit pocket for the matches I had found at Casa Guatemala. They were gone. Had the Guatemalans frisked me while I was out cold? I felt ashamed to think of strangers touching me. "Did they search me while...?"

"I told them you weren't packing and to keep their hands off you, but..."

"Thanks." I thought of the strangers who touched Lupe, the men. It made me sick. I didn't want to look at her. "Did they find anything?"

She nodded. "Yeah, but I couldn't see what it was."

So they knew I knew about Mexicali. I stared straight ahead. On the left was Edgemont Hospital, a private mental institution where the county had tried to place a former client, Eloise Himes, after she had hacked up the living room of her apartment with a machete. Next to it was a run down two-story house the color of dog poo with a sagging door and broken windows. Farther up ahead the night was illuminated by the klieg lights of another supermarket opening.

"The video ended five minutes after you got up," Lupe continued. "Before the lights came back on, I saw the woman you'd been talking with go down the hall after you."

"Emma Garcia," I explained. "She's the leader."

Lupe swung into the left lane to get around a van and pushed the gas again. "I thought Tony Guerrero was the leader."

"There's a power struggle going on between them. I wish I knew what it was about. Who's aligned with who."

Lupe nodded in agreement. "Raul went after Emma. I thought I'd be able to snoop around without him stuck to me, but Tommy Hutchings, the red-haired one, came right over to talk to me again. The next thing I knew, they were hustling me to the back of the place and I saw them carrying you into the shed."

"Did they say anything before I came to?"

"No. It was spooky. We all just stood there looking at you and Cathy

Vega. I didn't know then they thought we killed her."

I massaged my neck with care. It hurt like a mother. "If you had to pick one of them, who would you say did it?"

"Emma." Lupe glanced over at me. "She's hard as stone. A *veterana.* "

"It's Guerrero." I told her about the man in the black slacks and white shirt who had been on the roof across from Casa Guatemala. Hesitating, I wondered whether to tell her he had had a gun trained on her, ready to blow her away as she walked down the street to meet me. It had to be Tony Guerrero. This explained his tardy arrival at Casa Guatemala for the video presentation. He guessed I would come to the meeting, perhaps even guessed I would bring Lupe with me. I couldn't get over it. The whole time we were there, they had known we knew each other. "He had a gun." I decided to omit the rest.

"*¡Hijole!*"

"Come on, Lupe, don't you see? That's why we have to go to Mexico. If I can figure out what she was doing there or who she met, I'll know who killed her."

"And we'll know who's after us. Dammit." She pounded the steering wheel. "It's just like the gangs. Those crazy *cholos* don't care who gets in the way. Step on their turf, and you're dead."

"Exactly. The place in Mexicali was called..." I couldn't pronounce the name, but I could see it. Red lettering on a black background. "N-i-d-o," I spelled.

Lupe laughed. "Sounds cozy. *El Nido.* The Nest. More class than those dumps I work on Hollywood Boulevard."

"We going south or not?"

Lupe chewed her lip. "I was going to go get my little boy today."

"You can't take him with us. It might be..." I didn't want to scare her off. Besides, if it was so dangerous, why did I want to rush down there? For the same reason I ran after the man with the gun. For the same reason I'd been trying to find Monica Fullbright after I knew she had set me up.

Because I refuse to be afraid of shadows and things that go bump in the night. My dad's older brother was killed in a head-on collision when my dad was young, and since then my old man's always been sort of afraid of driving. His brother was drunk and plowed straight into a semi. I'd rather hit the semi than be scared every day.

"I just want to see him for a minute. He doesn't know where I am. He's only a baby."

"Your relatives are taking good care of him. You can call him in the morning," I said, sighing impatiently. It would take only a day to go to Mexicali. We rolled without speaking past art deco facades that had been reduced to sloppily painted barbershops and one hour photo labs.

"If anything should happen to him..."

"Nothing's going to happen to him," I said, cutting her off. "You should have thought of this a long time ago. Before you started hooking. Before you dropped out of school. Before you got knocked up. So don't pull a Loretta Young on me now." I turned away. It was none of my business. Why did it make me so mad? Were they purely political sputterings on my part? Out of the corner of my eye I saw Lupe chewing her lip some more. I didn't know if she was angry or trying not to cry.

"I'm not the Farmer's Daughter," she snapped. "I'm a lot cooler than that."

Junkies stood in pools of yellow light outside the bad bars on Western. In silence Lupe drove down Santa Monica Boulevard and onto the ramp of the Hollywood freeway.

I must have passed out again, because when I opened my eyes, we were in the desert and it was the middle of the night. There were a million stars. It made my eyes ache to look at all of them. My face was hot and I was slumped in the seat with my head lolling toward Lupe.

"We're about thirty-five miles south of Indio," she told me. "We should hit Mexicali about one-thirty."

It was cold and black beyond the Fiat's headlights. Had the man from Casa Guatemala who went to meet Cathy Vega actually waited for her? I wondered as we sped through the dark. Was it true she failed to show up? Or did the person from Casa Guatemala see her and return to LA with a phony story for the others? Maybe they had quarreled. Emma Garcia could have been the one who had gone. She had reason enough to hate Cathy. Cathy Vega stole her man.

Lupe slowed the car as we approached the steel kiosks and concrete bridges that formed the international border. The air was thick with diesel fuel and the smell of beef cooking from hundreds of pushcart kitchens. "What if we can't find anyone who saw her?" she asked, breaking the long silence between us.

I rubbed my eyes. "Then we're still in the soup."

"*Sopa.* You must learn to speak Spanish."

A short line of cars waited ahead of us at the border. When it was our turn, they waved us through. Mexicali was just like Tijuana—plenty of auto body shops, upholsterers, bars, discos. Kids rushing the car, trying to sell unattractive mass-produced pottery. A horde of tourists surging down the main street because the bars never close.

El Nido, at the far end of the main drag, was a concrete motel painted shocking pink and set back slightly from the highway. It was nearly two in the morning when Lupe pulled off the road and into the motel's gravel parking lot edged by a few weepy-looking palms. Stretching, I started to open the car door.

"Wait here," Lupe ordered. "I know what I'm doing." She shimmied off with the hip-swinging walk. The girl was beautiful.

Through a plate-glass window I saw her talking with a bleary-eyed desk clerk. He was young, with carefully oiled hair and an old black suit. The clerk looked out the window at me, shrugged, then turned to get a key from the rack behind him. He dropped the key on the counter.

I got out of the car. I felt sicker than a dog when I was vertical but I didn't want Lupe to see that. Fixing my hair, pulling in my stomach, I threw my head back and walked grandly into the office.

"We can pay in dollars," Lupe announced as the door closed behind me.

I only had fifteen bucks with me, but before I could worry more about that, Lupe extracted her wallet from her navy Chanel style purse. The desk clerk, draped intently over a black and white Mexican photo magazine, pushed a registration card toward Lupe without bothering to look up.

"This is a nice place," I said. On the countertop was a terracotta pot with pink plastic carnations stuck in it. Behind the desk hung a glossy calendar with the traditional Aztec prince and princess humping each other and pretending to be mountains. "A friend of ours stayed here a couple of weeks ago. She said it was nice."

He glanced at me without much interest. Behind him a television set was tuned to "Dynasty" in English, the volume very low.

"Cathy Vega," Lupe said.

"Carmen Luzano," I corrected.

"Sign here." He took the money from Lupe.

"She's about this tall." I held my hand parallel to the ground, level with my nose.

Lupe shoved her hand between me and the desk clerk. "This tall," she said, her hand vertical. "Don't do it like that," she hissed at me. "That's the way they measure animals in Mexico."

The desk clerk didn't seem to notice. "You have any suitcases?"

"No."

He leered. First at me, then with real lip-smacking zeal at Lupe while he gave her the once-over again. "I don't remember your friend. We get a lot of people. We have here very much privacy."

"She's very pretty," Lupe cooed in the Marilyn voice. "She's an actress. Famous. I'm surprised you don't remember her. She's on television all the time."

Cocking his head to one side, the desk clerk wrinkled his forehead for a moment as he searched his memory.

I wondered if it was going to cost me more money for him to remember. I was afraid to spend what I had left with me. Who knew what other problems might be in store before the night ended? Suddenly a new idea came to me. I realized how effortlessly Lupe and I had arrived in a foreign country. "Another friend was here also. A tall gringo with red hair."

Frowning, Lupe shot me a perplexed look. She shifted uncomfortably in her high heels.

"Tall, with red hair," I repeated.

"*Sí, sí, una barba roja.* " She nodded, her face relaxing into a grin. She must have understood what I guessed.

Tommy Hutchings.

It had to be Tommy Hutchings who had been sent by Casa Guatemala to meet Cathy. A latina and an anglo. Just as Lupe and I had been waved through the border, they would have been briefly questioned on their return about whether they had bought anything, then a quick look at the backseat of the automobile by *la migra* and the two would be headed back toward LA. If Tommy Hutchings was going to cross by himself, Immigration wouldn't spend much time with him. They were looking for undocumented workers in trunks of cars. He would buy a few cheap souvenirs and a bottle of rum, placing them on the passenger seat as evidence of his time spent in Mexicali.

If she had any drugs on her, Cathy Vega wouldn't risk traveling with a U.S. passport. She had, according to my calculations, been gone long enough so that she would need it and probably a tourist card. She must have been traveling in Mexico with a phony passport. In LA a fake Social Security card is thirty-five dollars. A green card, about two hundred.

Cathy Vega never planned on crossing any border legally. She was tired of structures, of institutions, of rules, of being told no. She was using a Guatemalan passport, undoubtedly fraudulent, bearing the name of Carmen Luzano. Carmen Luzano would sneak across the border, ditching the Guatemalan passport. Maybe selling it to another illegal. There would never be any record that one Cathy Vega, U.S. citizen, had crossed the fragile boundary between Mexico and the U.S. of A. It seemed so melodramatic. The use of the passport as a prop. So unnecessary for bringing the video into the country. Overly dramatic, but she was an actress.

"I might remember a red beard," said the desk clerk, now alert, pressing his fingertips together as he tried to look helpful. "Was he a tall man?"

"That's him!" Lupe exclaimed, leaning toward the desk. "Wasn't he with a woman?"

The desk clerk leered again. "You say he was looking for a woman?"

"I asked if he found one," I interrupted, stepping closer to the desk and putting my hand on the counter between Lupe and the desk clerk.

He turned sour. "Is not my job. I don't find women, and I don't remember if other people find them. I write things down in the book—that's how I remember." He leaned protectively across the guest register.

I pulled ten dollars out of Lupe's hand and put it in front of him. Examining the picture of Alexander Hamilton, he made a big deal out of smoothing the crumpled bill before shoving the register toward me.

How good were the odds Tommy Hutchings had used his real name or written it in red ink so I'd be sure to find it? I was tired of spending money. I was tired of talking to people like I was in a late night movie. I was tired of having a headache. I wrestled another five out of Lupe's fist.

"Hey, buddy, how about a bottle of tequila?"

He whistled, and a teenage boy only a few years younger than himself appeared, rubbing his eyes. He growled at the kid, who disappeared through the back door. Then the desk clerk sat back down to his magazine.

I turned the register pages to the middle of July. An unusual number of people named Mr. and Mrs. John Doe liked to stay at the El Nido. They came from places like San Bernardino and Riverside. To buy cheap leather goods, get laid in whorehouses, take quack cancer cures at the clinics dotting the border, run away from home to get married, get tattoos, raise hell, drive off-road vehicles, destroy the environment and smuggle drugs. Feeling increasingly morose, I studied the John Does and thought about unpaid for Oldsmobiles with bad mufflers, fat men drinking White Russians, underage girls getting drunk and fingerbanged by eighteen year old sailors from the nearby Salton Sea naval test area.

I didn't see Tommy Hutchings's name but someone in a crabbed handwriting and calling himself Che Guevara had stayed there the night before Cathy Vega was killed.

"Is this the guy with the red beard?" I asked, pointing to the signature in the register.

The desk clerk didn't say anything, but I could tell from his eyes and the way he quickly looked away as though he were disinterested that it was.

I was right. It was Tommy Hutchings they'd sent to meet Cathy Vega. Tommy Hutchings was to pick up the video. What was his relation to Cathy? He had been the one who brought her to the organization. Did he know she was one of the sources of tension between Emma Garcia and Tony Guerrero? What did he think of that? Maybe he didn't think at all. Maybe he just did what he was told. But who was he taking directions from?

The kid couldn't have gone far, because he was back already with a bottle of Cuervo and a white saucer with a mound of salt and some sliced lemons. Closing the register, I followed Lupe down the hall to our room, which fronted on the highway. A pale wood dresser with an aqua ceramic lamp and mirror stood opposite the queen size bed. I lay down and put a pillow carefully behind my head. A panel of white moved across the curtains as a car went by with a whooshing sound. Lupe fluffed the other pil-

low, folded it in half and plopped down with it behind her head. I smelled
the rose perfume as she settled near me. She cracked the seal on the tequila and took a drink before handing it to me.

"What did you think of Tommy Hutchings?" I asked, staring at the ceiling, tequila dribbling down my chin.

She shrugged and kicked off her shoes. "He's no ladies' man. Too big, too
awkward. Intense. The kind who looks but hangs back." She licked the
back of her hand, put salt on it and sucked a lemon before taking another
slug of tequila. "Probably whacks off while reading Marx," she said, passing the bottle back to me as I stared at her, amazed she knew anything
about the Big Man.

It tasted like lighter fluid, but I didn't care. I fixed the salt and lemon as
I'd seen her do. I took another drink and another. It made me stop think-
ing about my throbbing head. The bottle was nearly a third empty before
I remembered to offer it to her again. She waved it away.

Cactus juice flowing in me, feeling hollow to the core, feeling light-head-
ed, I wanted to tell Lupe everything I could remember. I told her about
Monica Fullbright's apartment, I told her about Rudy Sancerre, the agency,
the acting coach. I told her about the thousand dollars. The flowers that
grew in the backyard of my house in Virginia. The cocker spaniel I had
owned. I told her about my father. I kept drinking tequila while she
watched me in silence. I think I told her about the girl from the University of Maryland.

The saucer of salt spilled onto the pink chenille bedspread between us.

CHAPTER SEVENTEEN

"Lupe?"

I sat up. Sunlight was already streaming through a crack in the curtains. Reflected in the mirror, I saw myself: tan, hair bleached nearly platinum by the sun in a frizzy halo around my head, blue eyes, a badly wrinkled white linen skirt.

"Lupe?"

I swung my feet to the apricot-colored carpeting. My head hurt. I stood up carefully, feeling a sudden wave of nausea and vertigo. Lupe's clothes were not on the wooden dresser. The door to the bathroom was partially closed. I knocked.

"Lupe?"

The scent of roses hung in the air. I pushed the door open. A tiny bar of pink soap lay still wet on its white wrapper. A towel was crumpled in the corner near the shower. I splashed some water on my face, examined the faint purple line above my jaw and hurried into my clothes. My strand of pearls was gone.

I ran out. The corridor from our room to the front desk was empty. From elsewhere, another corridor, I heard the whine of a vacuum cleaner. She had ripped me off.

She was probably back in LA having a good laugh. I was surprised she hadn't lifted my wallet as well; she must have seen how little money I had in it. How was I going to get back to LA? Did they have a car rental in Mexicali? Would I have to take the bus? The desk clerk, the same one we'd talked to when we checked in, didn't remember who I was. He was reading a movie magazine and had forgotten how to speak English.

The Fiat was still out front. A sigh of relief escaped my lips. Then I saw Lupe leaning against it, laughing and animated, her face tilted up toward the stupid and pimply countenance of the boy who had brought the tequila the night before. He was talking and she was nodding at him. The bitch. She was probably going to take every *peso* he had for a blowjob. She was wearing my pearls.

"Let's go," I said without looking at the boy, fixing her with a black look.

"Whitney, Carlos. Carlos, *mi hermana* Whitney."

Blushing, the boy stuck his hand out to me.

"Come on, let's go, you thief," I said, ignoring his hand, unable to contain the anger in my voice. "And give me my pearls." I advanced toward her, ready to snatch the necklace from her throat.

She didn't move. She acted as if she hadn't heard this, instead smiling again at the boy. "Carlos was telling me that another man was also here looking for Cathy Vega."

"What? When?" I demanded.

Lupe nodded toward the boy's hand, which was now dangling at his side. I took it in mine and pumped it enthusiastically a few times. "Who was the man? What did he look like?" I asked him.

The boy dropped my hand and turned back to Lupe, eager only to please her. Lazily she arched her neck so the sun caressed her hair, which cascaded down her back, and her breasts jutted slightly forward. I thought I heard the boy sigh.

"He says the man was old. Maybe sixty or more. Glasses. A Cuban. "

"How did he know the man was a Cuban?" I thought about the Cuban photographer I'd met at Rudy's, the men in the restaurant across from Casa Guatemala.

Lupe shook her head as though discouraged with me. "By his accent," she explained gently, as though to a slow child. "All of the different countries have distinctive accents, just like in the different parts of the United States the people have different accents." "Y'all know what I mean?" she drawled in perfect Southern,

The morning was already hot. I looked around the parking lot, but there was no shade. I leaned against the Fiat. "When was the Cuban here?"

Lupe asked the boy something and he responded, then she translated for me. "The same day the woman was talking to the red-haired man. He says there was a hell of a fight between the woman and the Cuban, then the Cuban left."

"Did he hear what they were saying?"

"No, but he saw the woman slap the Cuban. Then the Cuban got in his car and drove away."

"What kind of car?"

"Trans Am," said the boy, obviously proud of his English. "Big engine *pero viejo. Negro y muy sucio.*"

"A dirty black Trans Am," Lupe added. *"Bueno, ya nos vamos."* She pressed a five-dollar bill into the boy's hand. Was she giving him back his money? I had interrupted the flow of commerce. He tried to shrug it away but she said something else to him in Spanish and patted his cheek. The boy blushed again and his hand fell to his side with the money clutched tightly in it. I could almost feel his heart pounding as he watched Lupe turn and walk away with her hips swinging.

She got into the Fiat and adjusted the mirror to quickly check her makeup as she started the car. Her hand caressed the pearls that lay on her smooth brown neck. "Beautiful pearls," she murmured.

"They should be," I grumbled, getting into the car. "They're real."

"I know." She took them off and tossed them in my lap. Lupe threw the car into reverse and blew the boy a kiss as she roared out of the driveway.

We cleared the border with ease. Then she pushed the old car up to 85, as fast as it would go. It made a suspicious clanking sound at that speed. The Yuma desert was sweltering and barren. Who was the Cuban? How did he know Cathy Vega, and what had they quarreled about? Could it be Armando Diaz, the photographer? We sped through El Centro, past the vast orange and citrus groves, the farm labor camps. We made a quick pit stop in Brawley for gas. Past the sunken Salton Sea with the Chocolate Mountains to the east. I studied the map I found in the glove compartment, checking our route and worrying that the car was going to blow up. It was a good thing, I thought, that I didn't have any court appearances that morning after all. I could feel I was getting close to Cathy Vega's murderer. It was Tony Guerrero I was sure. I just needed some way to prove it. The Cuban, who was he? Another lover of Cathy's? Was he jealous of the red-haired man? I wondered.

"Don't ever pull a scene like that or talk to me like that again." Lupe said, cutting into my thoughts and speaking for the first time since we left Mexicali.

"Like what?" My hair was blowing around my face. I held it back with one hand so I could see her more clearly.

"Jealous."

"Jealous!" I laughed. I let go of my hair, and it whipped wildly in the hot breeze. "You're *loca.*"

"Yes, you are. It just pisses you off that I'm as smart as you and I ain't never been to school. That's why you're always trying to boss me around. That's why you're so fucking uptight. I was just clowning around with your precious fucking pearls that your mommy gave you. Admit it, you're jealous."

"I don't boss you around," I sputtered in objection.

She glanced over at me without smiling. "You don't treat me like I'm equal."

"I do!"

"Then let me in on what you're thinking."

Was she right? Was I better than she was because she'd been on the streets? Or because I was white? All the marches, all the protests, the petitions I had signed—did I think I was better than she was?

Her slender brown arms stiffened slightly against the steering wheel as I hesitated. "Well, are you going to tell me what you're thinking?"

"I was thinking about what the boy at the motel said about the Cuban, Lupe. I met a Cuban recently. He has the photo studio right next door to Rudy Sancerre's. He goes to demonstrations and takes pictures of the people from Casa Guatemala."

The car shimmied across the broken white line, but she pulled it firmly back. "You think this Cuban knew Cathy?" asked Lupe.

"At least by sight. But beyond that, I can't imagine it. It couldn't be the same guy. Doesn't make any sense. He's a lot older, conservative, all the things that she seemed to be against."

"Maybe he was a father figure, a john, a lover."

"A lover?" I flicked my hand dismissively, as if I were an expert on the subject. "What could they have had in common?"

"It's not what lovers have in common, it's what they need from each other."

I turned away to watch the mountains recede in the distance, feeling confused.

We arrived in LA a little before ten. It was another scorcher, and we had been burned to bits by the time Lupe pushed the overheated Fiat into Hollywood and down the Boulevard.

"Drop me off at the office." I peeled myself from the sweat-soaked seat, relieved I was going to be alone again. Now that we were back at home, I started to feel more like myself. I had gotten drunk and talked about myself too much. I realized I had felt off balance and out of my element in Mexico.

"I'm going to go get Joey." Her eyes didn't meet mine as she stopped in front of my building. Did she feel the same relief I did?

I straightened my wrinkled linen skirt and looked away also.

"Yeah. Take care of yourself." Stepping away from the car, I started to lift my hand to wave to her, but I dropped it as she pulled away. I watched until she was out of sight, then turned to the door of the office building. No one was expecting me anywhere.

I went to the gym. It was an upper-body day. I wanted to ask Rodney what to do, but he wasn't there. I decided to bench-press. I watched a guy load a barbell with fifty-pound plates. All of the other benches were occupied, so I repeated my stretching routine while I waited for him to finish. He got up and wiped his sweat off the bench. He glanced at me, then called out to someone across the room and walked away, leaving all the weights on the bar. I broke the bar down, leaving sixty pounds on it.

It was the first time I had ever pressed this weight without a spotter. The bar loomed above me massive and solid as I lay on my back staring up at it. I gripped the bar and thrust the weight upward. I rose from the bench shaken but proud. I moved across the room to do side flyes with dumbbells, then standing dumbbell flyes for the shoulders. The Whitney Logan reflected in the mirror was tall and strong. The weight flowed in my hands, and I saw my muscles ripple. Training is really a question of focus. We create ourselves as we want to be. I still hold to a progressive vision of the future.

Back at the office I checked to see if I had any messages. I would go to see Tommy Hutchings and find out what Cathy Vega had been doing in the days before she was killed.

He had told Lupe he was working at Paramount Studios over on Melrose. I hoped this was true. I went to my office to clean myself up. Harvey had not locked up after me. The door was still open, and books scattered out into the hallway. Picking my way across the books, I climbed over the fallen bookcase. It took me some time to right it and shove it back against the wall. As I shelved the books, I thought alternately about Lupe and Cathy Vega until they began to become one person in my mind. I rearranged the black plastic chairs in front of my desk. I cleared off the top of my desk so I could find the phone. My message machine was flashing red. Dropping into the swivel chair behind the desk, I turned the machine on.

I had a call from the printers again about the bill I owed them. A call early in the morning from the clerk of Division 82 telling me to come right down to Bauchet Street to pick up a case they were holding for me. I couldn't believe it. It was the first time they had called me. All the work I'd gotten from them in the past was stuff I had begged while I was down there. My first foot in the door and I had blown it. As I picked up the phone to call the clerk, the message machine rolled off that familiar voice that had started it all.

Monica Fullbright.

She got right to the point. Someone was trying to kill her. She told me to meet her at four at the northeast corner of Sunset where it hits Hillhurst near Sunset Drive. After everything she had put me through it was as simple as that for her, as simple as calling the hairdresser for an appointment, like ordering a bouquet of flowers for Mother's Day. It pissed me off. Trying to erase from my voice the rage I felt at Monica Fullbright, I called the clerk of Division 82. It was too late, the clerk informed me frostily. I slumped back in the chair, the phone resting against my breast, the breath kicked out of me for a moment, before I called information for the number of Paramount.

It seemed like a long time before I got Tommy Hutchings on the phone. I went through a switchboard and was transferred twice to different sound stages. He seemed surprised to hear from me. Although we hadn't been introduced, I assumed he knew what had happened the night before in the shed behind Casa Guatemala. Where had he been? My hand wandered to the lump on the back of my head. Too easily I got him to agree to meet me during his lunch break, which would begin in about an hour. We hung up at the same time.

I checked my watch again. It would take only fifteen minutes to get there. I swiveled around and looked out the window and down onto the Boulevard. Someone had smashed the plate glass window of the video store across the street and now two men had begun boarding it up with plywood. Someone had wanted videocassettes. Could they properly be called movies if they weren't up on the big screen? I wondered. Didn't putting it on a television set make it a different medium?

The thieves would sell the cassettes out of the backs of vans to people too poor to own two VCRs and pirate the images themselves.

By nightfall the plywood would be thick with graffiti. Inevitably someone would try to rob the store again before the plywood was replaced by glass. I turned back to the desk feeling tired and discouraged with the world. Always the invention of new crimes. Now in the late twentieth century it was the theft of images. I thought of Armando, the Cuban photographer. Why did he go to all the demonstrations and take photos? What did he do with them? The paper usually didn't cover the demonstrations, didn't consider them newsworthy enough unless someone famous was there or unless a vote on aid was coming up in Congress, as it was now. I picked up the phone again and asked information for the number of the *Times*.

Eventually I was connected with a guy in the photo department. I asked him if he could find an article from June about a demonstration in front of the Federal Building. He didn't sound too thrilled about it, but it was his job so he put me on hold for about ten minutes. I looked back out the window while I was waiting. A small crowd had gathered to watch the plywood repair and there was laughing and pushing and shoving.

"Ok, I got a story about a demo on June 18." His voice brought me back to attention. "What do you want to know about it?"

"Did any photos run with it?"

"On the front page. Picture of Johnny Why getting arrested. You know, Johnny Why, the singer."

"Who's got the photo credit on it?"

"Marilyn Navarro."

"What? Are you sure?"

"Sure, I'm sure." He sounded bored and cranky about this kind of minimum wage tedium I was putting him through. "I'm looking right at it. Are you going to need a copy of this?"

I hung up the phone. Why had Armando Diaz lied about selling a picture to the paper? Picking up my purse from the edge of the desk as I was getting ready to go meet Tommy Hutchings, I checked to see if I still had the can of mace in it. What did the Cuban do with the photographs?

When I arrived, he was waiting on the street. Leaning against the wall, he stopped reading a paper when he saw me coming. He folded it and stuffed it in his back pocket. His red hair was pulled back with a bandanna; he wore faded jeans, expensive new black and white Air Nikes and a shrunken white T-shirt. I wondered if he lifted weights. He was a tight machine for a skinny guy.

"You were at the video last night, right? That's where I know you from?" he asked.

I nodded impatiently. He'd already called Casa Guatemala before coming out to meet me. I was certain of that. Still, there was a certain ritual we were going to have to perform, only the lump on my head was making me forget my lines.

"You work in television," I said to center us. We were standing under the marquee of a sitcom about two extraterrestrials who crash land in the San Fernando Valley.

"Yeah, this used to be the RKO lot, then it was Desilu, now it's TV stages...." His voice trailed off. He wanted me to get to the point.

By silent agreement we started to walk north toward Santa Monica Boulevard past the black cast iron Spanish Renaissance gates of the studio. He seemed to be the type who thought better in motion.

I drew closer to him. "I came to talk about Cathy Vega. She was your friend. More than with the others, wasn't she?"

"Hey, I barely knew her. Just saw her around sometimes," he said without looking at me.

"I saw her diary at her apartment," I lied. "She wrote everything down, or didn't you know that? Names, dates. She had lots of good things to say about you."

He turned toward me and studied my face, trying to decide if this could be true. I hoped that he knew as little about women as Lupe seemed to think.

"Yeah?" he dared me, slowing his pace slightly. "What did she have to say about me?"

"Don't embarrass me. Let's just say she kept the diary in the drawer with her diaphragm."

Bingo. He sped up again as though he were uncomfortable. We turned the corner at the end of one of the two white stucco tile-roofed buildings.

I pressed on. "She told me you helped her carry the five thousand dollars."

"Five thousand dollars?" Scowling, he stopped and put his hands on his hips.

"Look, I'm a friend of Cathy's, too. Your other friends seem to think I'm out to cause problems, but it's not me causing the problem, it's the money. Or more specifically, the fact that the money is missing. You know what they say—money is the root of all evil. And five thousand dollars is a fat wad. Even a good leftist can be turned around by money, I bet." I looked suspiciously at his Air Nikes, the $190 kind.

"No," he argued. "The money's for medical aid."

"Then why didn't Emma tell me that last night?"

He didn't answer. Had Cathy told him about the money, or was he playing with me?

"Because it was to buy heroin, right?" I insisted.

"No! Nothing to do with heroin. Medical aid."

"Don't bullshit me. I know the people who gave her the money and who set up the connection. I know the dealer and I know the deal. And the deal's been blown. I know you were with her at El Nido. Now, where does that leave you? The five thousand dollars is gone, the heroin is gone and you're the only person left. When the people I know find out about you, something bad is going to happen." I felt like I was putting a cat in a spin dryer.

He slowed down again. "I don't know anything about heroin. And I don't have the money. Cathy said she was going to use the money for..."

"For? I can see you got money to burn. Two hundred bucks for a pair of tennis shoes." I pointed at his feet and enjoyed the fear that flashed across his face. There are at least two or three deaths related to bad dope deals here in LA every week. We're catching up fast with Washington, D.C.

"I got a good gig going here. Studio electrician. I'm union. I make good money when I'm working."

"Get to the part about Cathy," I said impatiently, looking at my watch. It was nearly one-thirty.

He sighed. "I've known her for about a year. I'm the one who turned her on to Casa Guatemala. When I met her, she was floundering around; she didn't understand what was going on around her. She thought that everything that was wrong was wrong with her. Not getting jobs. Shit, that's what they want you to think. I gave her some books to read, took her to some meetings. She started to understand what's happening, how everything fits together."

I imagined Cathy Vega reading *Das Kapital* like an eager student studying The Method. "Why Guatemala?"

"I work about half a year. I'm laid off half a year. I save my money. I travel. I want to travel. I went to Guatemala for the first time about three years ago. Poorest place I've ever been. We got to make these connections. Working people. Imperialism. Racism. We have to struggle."

I knew where I had heard that before. On the frontlines, the demos, from Vietnam to Central America. Dare to struggle. Dare to win.

¡El pueblo unido jamás será vencido!

I imagined a swelling crowd.

Although I had marched and shouted slogans, these people were actually trying to live it! I knew then what Cathy Vega, the failed actress, was going to do with the money. She was going to use the five thousand dollars to buy weapons! I felt giddy with admiration for her.

She'd planned all along to take Monica Fullbright's money and run with it. I didn't think she was crazy enough to try to buy the arms herself. Either she had gone to Mexico to turn the money over to someone who would buy them or she was running the drugs in an effort to make more money for the revolution. If she was going to turn the drugs herself here in LA, she had to be sure she could get rid of them without Monica Fullbright knowing she was back in town. She would need someone she trusted or someone she could control who'd take the drugs off her and get the money back to her. I didn't think she would go to Rudy Sancerre. He didn't seem smart enough or honest enough, but that might explain why the Cuban had been in Mexicali.

"She was going to buy guns with that money, wasn't she?"

"No!" He looked stunned, as though I had read his mind, as though he had just thought of this himself. "When she asked me to help her, she said it was for medical aid. If it was guns, she was acting on her own."

I slowed my step. "There had to be someone from Casa Guatemala working with her. Like you."

"Then it must be Emma! I should have known it!" he exclaimed, stopping in his tracks. "She's a fucking Trotsky."

I was strangely thrilled that women were taking the dangerous lead in the struggle for justice and the taking up of arms. This must be the conflict, the basis of the fight for leadership between Emma Garcia and Tony Guerrero. Politics does make strange bedfellows. And a lot of animosity when the screwing stops.

"You trying to tell me she was acting out her own script?" I sneered, turning back in the direction from which we had come

"She was a little crazy, a little off balance. She had a deep need to prove herself." He hastened after me.

I didn't disagree with him, but I didn't tell him that. Having seen her agent's office and the nude photos of her, I could well imagine Cathy Vega picking up a gun.

"What are you going to do now?" he asked, nervously shoving his hands into his pockets. Cars whistled by on Melrose.

"I have another appointment. We'll be in touch with you."

He watched me walk away. I hoped I had scared him. I hoped he thought I was on my way to meet with dangerous drug dealers with whom I was on close personal terms. I tried not to hurry. He would, I knew, go inside as soon as I was down the block and call Casa Guatemala to report what had happened. Was he supposed to follow me? If they didn't already know where Monica Fullbright was, they were about to find out unless I was very careful.

Glancing at my watch, I saw it was nearly two. I looked back toward the studio gates before turning the corner to Van Ness, where I had left the car. Tommy Hutchings was gone. I still had time to go to the Cuban's if I hurried. Was he the Cuban who had been in Mexicali? I wondered again. My car had only a quarter tank of gas left, but I didn't want to waste time or be spotted stopping at a filling station. I would use the drive over to the Cuban's to shake anyone who might try to tail me.

"Come on, big boy." I turned the ignition key. "Talk to momma."

The engine purred in return and I headed for Van Ness south to Third. I kept my eyes on the rear view mirror but I didn't see anyone. Grungy apartment buildings rented to Salvadorean and Guatemalan refugees line Van Ness and the air is filled with latin music and the ringing of ice cream truck bells. A market painted blue and white proclaimed *Productos Guatemaltecos focoyos, licoros, guanabanas*. Foods I had never heard of. My stomach rumbled. I wondered if Lupe was a good cook. If she would cook me a Mexican dinner when this was over. Then I remembered something my father had told me: never travel without a Hershey bar in your pocket. This had been good advice for me and my mother. When we took a vacation, he would drive all day and all night without stopping to eat. There was a candy bar in the glove compartment, I remembered. I tore the wrapper open and bit into it hungrily. If my old man could only see me now!

I glanced in the rearview mirror again. When I was a teenager my father used to follow me. While I was in my first year of law school I went to a shrink for a while but left when he suggested that I had only imagined my father followed me. It was true. Sometimes I would go off on a date and, in the rearview mirror of some sweaty-palmed Romeo's Ford Fairlane, catch sight of my father's Cadillac two or three cars back. He would casually cruise up beside us at a stoplight to glare at the boy whose arm dangled around my shoulders as though he had unexpectedly encountered us in traffic. This has given me sharp eyes and a healthy sense of paranoia. I glanced in the rearview mirror. Nothing unusual.

I made a left at Third past a giant palm tree covered with posters announcing a salsa dance at the Hollywood Palladium.

El Gran Combo Charanga 76 CELIA CRUZ—LA REINA DE LA SALSA

I wondered if Lupe was a good dancer. She sure could move.
I looked in the rearview mirror again.

Third between Van Ness and Western is cheap clothing stores with extravagantly flounced red dresses, black gowns with rhinestone straps, strangely colored brown mannequins. *Botánicas. Boticas.* I made a mental note to ask Lupe the difference. When this was all over, I would sign up to take a Spanish class at the high school near me. Shoe stores with black patent stilettos. Fruit stands with melons and papayas overflowing onto the sidewalk. Brilliant orange gladiolas and tiger lilies.

I drove past Rudy Sancerre's Flamingo Photo and past the Cuban's, which I now noticed was named *"Guantanamo,"* to Western, when I hung a right. I drove around the block, getting caught for a moment in traffic on Western. I drove by the front of the two studios again. No sign of life in either one; both with heavy protective paper in the windows. Either there was a shoot going on or no one was there. Based on my prior contacts with the two men, I guessed they didn't have any work and that no one was there. For an instant my eyes caught the heavy movement of an old black Chevy in the rearview mirror. It was surging up behind me, but it didn't come any closer and didn't follow me when I made the turn at Western again.

For an instant I hesitated at the entrance to the parking lot behind the studios. I didn't want my car to be seen, but I didn't want to be far away from it if I needed to make a fast getaway. Deciding it was better to have it close at hand, I pulled into the nearly deserted lot. There was an old ranch wagon by the door of the Mexican beer bar and an almost new BMW by the oriental massage parlor.

"Whoa, boy. Ease 'em up." I cut the motor and eased into a parking space. I heard the car door shut loudly. The metal gate that divided the studios from the parking lot was open. I walked up to Rudy Sancerre's back door and put my ear against it. The leaves of dead plants rustled in the breeze. I didn't hear anything. I tiptoed past it to the Cuban's. It, too, was quiet inside. Pressing against the door for a long moment, I listened intently, wondering what I would say if the door were to suddenly fly open.

Satisfied no one was there, I knocked. No one answered. I knocked again, looking around the lot to see if anyone was watching me. No one. I put my hand on the door and was surprised to find it was not locked. I was disappointed. By now I was an old pro at breaking and entering. I had lost my innocence so quickly. And eagerly. I opened the door hastily and stepped inside.

A parrot in a wrought-iron cage squawked at me.

"Shhh," I growled, but the parrot kept mumbling in a *polyglot* of languages I couldn't understand.

The Cuban's studio was the same size as Rudy's but seemed smaller because it was full of white plastic trellises, gazebos and columns that I

supposed were used to make backdrops for bridal pictures. In one corner
was a pile of red, white and pink plastic roses. A clothing rack held a tuxe-
do and a tired looking wedding dress with a yellowing veil. There was a
small desk with a chair, a phone and a Rolodex. I sat down in the chair and
began flipping through the Rolodex quickly to see if he had the number
for Cathy Vega. Or Carmen Luzano, although I felt sure he had known her
by the name Cathy. Those names weren't there and I didn't recognize any
of the ones I saw. I noticed his business calendar, on which was imprinted
his name and address, had a photograph of a girl in a bathing suit holding
a Cuban flag against a backdrop of palm trees. I picked up the calendar.
Above the palms in an arching black script were the words *"Bahía de Guantanamo—Cuba Libre."* The calendar slipped from my fingers. Could this
have been the backdrop against which the nude pictures of Cathy Vega
had been taken? The words cropped from the top of the picture?

I pulled the desk drawers open, but they contained only broken pencils
and order slips for photographic supplies made out to one Armando Diaz.
The bottom drawer on the right side was locked. I went through the drawers again but couldn't find a key. I picked at the lock for a few moments
with a letter opener I found on top of the desk, but it wouldn't give.

"Que Linda, que Linda," the bird whistled.

I stood up and went over to a workbench that ran along the west wall.
My heart was beating fast and my hands trembled slightly with excitement as I shuffled the contents of the bench. It was littered with negatives,
pots of glue and memo sheets. A red photo album with gold script writing
on the cover exclaiming *Feliz Aniversario* lay among the discarded bridal
and coming-out party pictures.

I opened the album. They were the pictures of various demonstrations
Armando Diaz had photographed. Underneath the pictures in a neat but
cramped block print were the dates. I flipped quickly to the back of the
album, hoping that he had already entered the most recent demonstration,
the one I had been at. He had. I saw a photograph of the protester that
Armando Diaz's friend had nearly been in a fight with. A picture of Emma
Garcia handing out leaflets. A photo of Tommy Hutchings carrying the
placard. Another of Tony Guerrero sneering imperviously back at the camera with his hands on his hips the way a bullfighter who has thrown
down his cape challenges a bull. I looked through the pictures immediately preceding but I couldn't find the one he had taken of me. Excitedly I
turned back to the front of the album and tried to make myself look
through it more slowly for a picture of Cathy Vega.

He had been to a lot of demonstrations. He went to the silent vigils, too.
There were many pictures of the nuns I'd seen demonstrating the first
time I'd gone to the Federal Building to look for Carmen Luzano in Immi-

gration. An old woman with gray hair cut in heavy bangs across her forehead and a rosary in her hand. Armando Diaz had slashed the picture with a red pencil. Under it in his neat printing he had written a word: *PUTA*. I knew that meant whore.

Another nun, a young one, not bad looking but with sensible shoes and baggy trousers, had been slashed with the red pencil. *PUTA*.

I turned more quickly. All of the pictures of the nuns were defaced in this way. Women who were not nuns had a big red X marked across their faces. On some he had drawn huge breasts and colored in masses of pubic hair. I began to recognize the people from Casa Guatemala. At the edge of the crowd I saw Cathy Vega. On the following page was a jagged smear of glue as though a photograph had been hastily removed. It must have been of Cathy Vega.

Who did he think she was? In Mexicali he had behaved like a jealous lover; yet he had seen her with the Casa Guatemala people. How had she explained that to him? Still more slowly, I looked through the rest of the photo album, but I didn't find another picture of Cathy.

I thought I heard something scrape against the floor. I stopped and held my breath, but I didn't hear anything again. I put the album down. The only other room was a bathroom, to which the door was partially closed. I walked toward it, hesitated for a second and pushed it open.

Suddenly I saw myself reflected in the mirror above the sink. My hair looking wild and crazy, my eyes startled. The bathroom was empty except for a soiled white towel, a bar of Palmolive soap and a wastebasket with a piece of flattened cardboard in it. I stooped to pick up the cardboard.

It was part of the packaging for a bottle of insulin.

Armando Diaz was a diabetic. And his medicine cabinet behind the mirror was full of plastic syringes like the one we had found on the floor of the loft next to Cathy Vega's body.

CHAPTER EIGHTEEN

I slammed the medicine cabinet shut. Had Armando Diaz been at the loft with Cathy Vega? Believing she was going to model for a photo shoot, she had gone downtown. To her death. Her agent said a man named Rudy who had an accent asked for her. Rudy had no accent, but Armando Diaz certainly did. I remembered the camera lens I had found on the roof of the building across from Casa Guatemala. At first I had thought the man had been holding a gun.

Closing the bathroom door behind me, I dashed back into the studio.

"Bad girl, bad girl." The parrot started his noisy harangue again.

I took another hurried look around the room. The workbench, the desk, the bridal props. On the opposite side of the room was a closet I had not yet explored. I looked at my watch. It was nearly three-thirty. It felt as if time had stopped. Where was Armando Diaz and when was he coming back? Two dark suits and two white shirts hung in the closet. A chemical pine smell from a room freshener pervaded the air. Stacked on built-in shelves were the tools of his trade: film, several lenses, a leather carrying bag, a box of business cards. I snatched one of the cards, which bore the same picture of the crossed American and Cuban flags as the decal pasted on his front window.

ARMANDO DIAZ fotógrafo Bodas
Quinceañeras
Pasaportes CUBA LIBRE PATRIA

He had two cameras. A big Hasselblad was carefully placed on the middle shelf. I wondered if this was the one Rudy Sancerre had planned to use to do my portraits. The Hasselblad was old but perfectly maintained. On the shelf above it was a Leica. Missing its lens cap. I fumbled in my purse for the lens cap I had found when I chased the man on the roof. It was for a Leica.

Armando Diaz had been the man on the roof.

A car pulled into the parking lot behind the studio. I dropped the lens cap back into my purse and made for the window to see who it was. Tearing the edge of the protective paper covering away from the window, I peeked out. A furtive white businessman parked his luxury sedan, looked around to see if anyone was watching him and slipped into the oriental massage parlor. Breathing a sigh of relief, I hurried out to my car.

Monica Fullbright had said to meet her at four on Sunset Drive behind Sunset Boulevard and near Vermont. Although it took me a while to find the small street, I didn't rush; I wanted her to be waiting for me. It was a moderately oppressed neighborhood of stucco bungalows, tiny front yards and cars that needed bodywork. It was a few blocks from Children's Hospital and a few blocks from the chichi shops on Hillhurst and the trendy nouvelle restaurants that place tiny swirls of pureed raspberry-colored food in the center of your plate and surround it with kiwi slices. I never go to those places. I'm a baroque eater. When I'm going to eat, I want to eat.

I drove around the block another time before I spotted her getting out of an old black Lincoln Continental with a dented grill. She didn't see me. Monica Fullbright wore a red dress and a pair of black high heels. Around her neck she had the same designer scarf she was wearing the first time I met her. Her hair was badly arranged. From where I was, I could see she looked thrown together and tired. I waited till she stepped away from her car and started to pace the corner. Like a hooker.

I eased my foot off the brake so my car crept toward her.

"Get in."

Feigning surprise, gripping her purse in her hands, she climbed into the car. Two of her false nails had come off, exposing broken white nails. The smell of her expensive Joy perfume, its dead roses and threatening jasmine, made me feel sick and l didn't want to look at her.

I made a right, heading north toward the entrance to Griffith Park, but just before hitting Franklin I swung a left across traffic into an alley behind a large and busy restaurant. I pulled the car up behind a trash can and turned off the motor. I didn't say anything. Staring straight ahead, I watched as a woman came out of the back of a store located farther down the alley to walk her dog. Monica Fullbright fidgeted on the seat next to me.

"I'm scared," she announced finally.

"You should be."

"I think I'm in trouble," Monica Fullbright whined, lighting one of her cigarettes.

I snatched it from her and threw it out the window. "You got a hell of a nerve to come to me now!" I exploded. "You set me up!"

"No, I didn't!"

"You want me to help you? Then let's start again, and this time tell me the truth." I gripped the steering wheel to try to control myself. The black plastic was hot in my hands. "Admit it. You set me up."

"I didn't think anything would happen to you," she said with a defiant model-like pout.

"Why me?" I continued, hardly mollified but trying to disguise my anger. "How'd you find me? Tell me right now, or I'll throw you out of this car. To the wolves. Or the pigs. They'll lock your behind up for a long time when I tell them what I know about you."

For the first time since getting in the car, she actually looked me in the face. She hesitated for an instant, trying to decide how to play me. She sat up straighter, as if this was supposed to convey honesty. "I used to know Harvey," she admitted. "When Harvey was a big name, he handled a case for a friend of mine. It was a heroin bust, and my friend could have gone away for a long time."

"You mean your husband, don't you?" With supreme confidence I eased back in my seat to watch her.

Warily, Monica Fullbright nodded. Only Rudy could have told me this, and I could see her wondering how much more he'd spilled to me.

"Yes, my husband. I don't know how Harvey fixed it, but the deal got set up and went down smooth. My husband walked."

I tried to imagine Harvey in court but couldn't. "Harvey!" I hooted.

"Harvey was cool," Monica Fullbright snapped defensively and pulled herself into an even more elegant posture. "When I lost contact with Cathy and thought she'd been picked up, I wanted to get a lawyer. I figured we'd need one. So I decided to see Harvey, but when I got over there and saw him, Jesus, he was too fucked up to do anything. Didn't look like he could find the front door. Then I saw you. I thought I could pay you to find out where Cathy was, see if there was a problem. Then I could get a real lawyer if I needed one."

I watched the woman who had been walking the dog. She leaned over and lifted its tail to wipe its runty butt.

"You set Cathy up, too," I said, angrily jabbing my finger at Monica. "Just like you set me up. You killed her."

Words formed in Monica Fullbright's mouth but were muffled when she started to cry big, racking, insincere sobs. "I didn't know Cathy was dead until you told me and showed me those pictures."

The lady patted the dog on the head.

I glared at Monica Fullbright. "Don't bullshit me and don't try the waterworks on me or I'll rip the rest of your fucking fingernails off your hand."

The sobs shook her body, and she dropped her face into her hands, sniffling. "I didn't know she was dead. I swear it."

I drummed my fingers impatiently on the steering wheel. "Oh yeah, I really believe you. How were you planning to get rid of the heroin? Were you going to get Rudy to unload it?"

"Heroin? Rudy?" she asked with an attempt at surprise, as though she could still pretend I didn't know who he was. Daintily she wiped at her eyes. "Rudy?"

I turned and grabbed the front of her dress, pulling her toward me. "Yeah, Rudy, you bimbo."

"No, not him." She tried to squirm away from me, but I was stronger and I threw her back against the door. "All he did was get me the connection in Mexico. I was going to do it myself." She panted, rubbing her elbow, which had hit the door.

I laughed in her face. "Sure you were. I can see you're a real smooth operator."

"It's true! I know a lot of people. Industry people. It was all going to be very discreet. A quick one-time thing so I could get out of this town. Dogtown." She swore, jerking her head and making ugly with her lips.

"Weren't you afraid Cathy might rip you off?" How had the two of them made this bargain? I must have underrated Cathy Vega's acting abilities.

An obscene smirk worked its way across Monica Fullbright's face. "Cathy was stupid. Sure, I had to give her something, but she was stupid. No way she'd know the full value of what I'd get from the people I could sell to. You understand what I'm saying? The people who buy this stuff don't go on the street for it. They're not going to go down to Sixth and Alvarado to stand on the corner."

"What made you think you could trust Cathy?" I forced myself to continue in the same stony enforcer voice I was using to anchor myself in this conversation.

Monica Fullbright sneered. "Not only was she stupid, she was ambitious. Starstruck. She didn't want to be anywhere else. She had to come back to Hollywood. She knew I knew certain people. If she fucked me over, I'd fix it so she'd never get a job in this town. If she did a good job"—Monica Fullbright smoothed her dress over her bosom and arranged the fold of material at her hips—"I could make certain introductions for her."

Poor Cathy Vega. It sounded like more outcall stuff. Had she believed it? I might never know when Cathy had made the decision to steal the money, but because I had come to like her, I hoped it was from the first moment, that she had been smarter than I and had never believed any of Monica Fullbright's pandering.

"Why'd you finally call me today?" I demanded.

Monica Fullbright placed her hand tentatively and beseechingly on my shoulder, apparently deciding this was a better tack than trying to strongarm me.

I hate to be touched.

"Yesterday I got home and somebody'd ripped my place up," she said. "How did anyone find out about me? Who could Cathy have told? It must have been the dealers from Mexico. It was all weird and Manson family stuff written on the walls...." Her voice trailed off and she seemed suddenly ashamed of her attempt to manipulate me, because she dropped her hand from my shoulder.

"What did it say?" I pretended not to know anything about the ransacked apartment.

She shrugged. "It was in a foreign language."

"If you had control over Cathy, why would she tell them about you?" I challenged.

"Maybe the dealers, they tortured her."

I'd let Monica Fullbright keep thinking that. Maybe it would keep her in line. I knew there weren't any dealers. Cathy had gone to Mexico, but she hadn't scored. She had most probably handed the money over to someone there who would buy guns for Guatemala. Then Cathy got scared at the border and it had to do with the Cuban. Later, back in LA, he had lured her to her death, I speculated. Armando Diaz must also have been the one who rampaged through Monica's apartment, but was it for vengeance or to throw suspicion on Casa Guatemala for Cathy's death? Did Monica know about Armando Diaz's involvement with Cathy?

"Cathy ever tell you about any of her friends? Meet any of them?" I asked. Rudy had told me Monica knew Armando Diaz, but did she know of Cathy's involvement with him?

She shook her head. "It was just a deal, understand?"

"Noticed anyone following you?"

"No! I looked. I kept my eyes open because I was jumpy as a cat when Cathy didn't show up when she was supposed to. Then, after you showed me those photos, I haven't been able to sleep. You think someone's following me?"

To keep her worried, I nodded but didn't say anything.

"Do you need more money?" she asked excitedly. "I'll get more! I'll pay you more."

"You don't have enough money for what you've put me through. You're on your own." I started the motor.

"Wait, wait!" she exclaimed, clutching at my arm again.

I hung a U in the parking lot opposite the restaurant to move back along the alley toward Hillhurst so I could dump her at her car. It was roasting in my car and the air in the alley was stale with garbage and the underlying but heady smell of flowers from the back of a florist. We rolled slowly past the delivery doors of some half a dozen businesses. From behind a brick building a red Chevrolet pulled across the alley, blocking me.

It was Tony Guerrero.

Tommy Hutchings must have called him the minute I set up my meeting with him. Guerrero could have hidden nearby to watch us talk. How had he followed me to Armando Diaz's studio, then picked me up again on my way to Monica without me seeing him? I swore at myself. I threw my car into a fast reverse, burning rubber down the alley.

"Get down!" I screamed at Monica Fullbright, who was clutching the dashboard with her broken fingernails.

On Hillhurst I threw a quick right up to Los Feliz. I cut across two lanes of traffic. The red Chevy pulled into the lane behind me. I looked into the rearview mirror.

Guerrero's eyes were furious. Did he actually think I'd killed Cathy? That I was involved with the Cuban? Did he know who Monica was? I didn't want to get out of the car to talk.

The light changed. I charged into traffic to make a left turn. I hung in the intersection until the light was red and the other cars were coming toward us before I made my turn. I hit the gas and my car chugged gamely ahead, going through two automatic gear shifts. I thought I'd left Guerrero in the intersection, but behind me I heard horns honking. A car swerved to miss Guerrero as he followed me, making his turn through oncoming traffic. I saw him again in the mirror. With my foot to the floor I got into the right lane.

He was still behind me.

Monica Fullbright screamed into her skirt.

I clung to the curb and on beautiful Los Feliz made a sharp turn into the entrance of Griffith Park. On either side the road was full of parked cars. My car droned up the hill. I ripped it into low and it surged forward. The Chevy missed a few beats and I could hear its engine misfiring. It was having trouble making the grade too.

Suddenly a kid ran out in front of me, and I turned the wheel toward the parked cars on the opposite side of the street.

Monica Fullbright screamed again.

Guerrero stuck to me as I pushed my old car up the hill. The trees were tall enough to block the sun. Past illegal families spreading blankets for picnics. Past the glens of Ferndell, where kids fished for crayfish in the polluted water and carved their names into the elderly eucalyptus. The road widened at the Greek Theater and Guerrero had to drop back when a car backed out from the theater's box office area. I sped on through a tunnel, then the road forked in three directions; down to Burbank, left up to the observatory and east. I didn't know where the east road went, but I spun the wheels in that direction.

"He's still back there!" yelled Monica, twisting in her seat to see out the back window.

"Of course he's still back there. What did you think you were going to get for a thousand bucks? James Bond?"

I hit a bend too fast and the back wheels spun in the sandy dirt. Although it was the middle of the afternoon the road was deserted. I swerved over the centerline, pulling myself off the curve.

"Cathy ripped you off," I crowed to Monica. "She spent your money in Mexico. She never planned on seeing you again."

MERCEDES LAMBERT

"I don't believe you!" Monica shouted.

"You don't have to. But that's why that guy's following us."

The road started up again and toward a broad sweep that looked out in the direction of downtown and the court buildings. I threw it into low once more, and the engine sounded as if it were eating itself alive. The road made an S and started to go down. I couldn't see Guerrero at the back of the S.

"Jump out," I said to Monica.

"What?"

"Jump out. When I get to the bottom of the curve, I'm going to swing onto the shoulder."

"You're crazy!"

"I said you're on your own now. The man who's following me, I don't know if he's interested in you or not. You'll have to find out. I'm through being your girl."

The car slid into the downside of the S.

"I can't!" she cried.

Hitting the brakes, I turned and swung at her, connecting with her jaw. Her head snapped back. The car's speed dropped to about twenty-five. I leaned past her, threw open the door, and hit her again with everything I had in my right arm. I don't know if I pushed her or if she jumped. I saw a blur of red tumbling from the car, but I didn't look back.

The road headed west again, making a long loop toward the entrance to the park. When I checked the rearview mirror, I saw Guerrero coming off the tail of the S. Then I saw something else. A car had pulled up tight behind him. We were starting to look like a parade.

It was a dirty black Trans Am—just like the one the kid in Mexicali had said the Cuban drove!

Traffic was building up ahead. I hit the brakes, remembered a prayer I knew when I was a kid and slid into the tightest U-turn I could. For a sick moment the nose of my car headed for the edge of the cliff before I was able to pull it back under control. I heard the crazy honking behind me as new cars entering the park slammed on their brakes. I heard the crash of metal as someone behind me rear-ended someone else. Guerrero sailed past me in the opposite direction followed closely by the Cuban.

It was too late for them to turn around to follow me. They were stuck with following each other. I pulled the passenger door shut. I never for a moment considered going back to look for Monica Fullbright; I wanted to get out of the park as fast as possible, so I took the run down to Burbank. The park lets out near the Golden State freeway. I hopped on it heading for downtown and hit the gas again. I threw my head back and howled like a coyote.

It was a good twenty minutes of sweating, watching the rearview mirror and jumping each time a car from another lane cut in to pass me, before I made downtown. I exited on Hill Street which took me through Chinatown. I still didn't feel safe. That's when I decided to buy a gun.

I thought immediately of Tim Watson, the overweight armed robber Burt Schaefer had me make a couple of court appearances with at the beginning of the year. It was another one of those jobs that I had gotten from Burt's gravy train, and he'd paid me nearly three hundred dollars to do two continuances and an interview of Mr. Watson, who'd made me meet him at a poolhall on the edge of Dogtown. There is a real Dogtown, although there is no sign demarcating it from the rest of the city. It is by the railroad tracks on the side where the SPCA has a big pound, across from Chinatown and in the shadows of the glass house where the county sends its bad boys. It's a light industrial area in which illegal families are living in the backs of stores and in cardboard shacks they have built behind places where diesel trucks are repaired.

I wove through Chinatown trying to remember the name of the poolhall. It was on Cardinal and no one was on the street. Everything is hidden in Dogtown. I parked my car and put on some red lipstick. My right hand was throbbing and beginning to turn dark where I had hit Monica Fullbright.

I have never owned a gun. My father has never owned a gun. I am against the death penalty. I am for gun control. I pushed the door to the poolhall open.

It was black inside with a string of red Christmas lights above the bar. The jukebox was playing Frank Sinatra. A tired hooker with sore feet drooped on the end of the bar, a watery coke in front of her. It was all just as I remembered it. Tim Watson looked up from the pool table where he had just made a triple bankshot—7 and 10 balls in the pockets, cue ball split right, hovering just to the side of the center pocket. He grinned.

"Heard you come in, Whitney," he said and did his dainty fatman walk to where I stood.

In California it takes ten days to get a real gun from a real store. There is a licensing process. There is an investigation. There is recordkeeping. I put my hand out to Tim Watson.

"I need to get a gun," I said to him in a low voice. I have never shot a gun, never seen anyone shoot a gun except on television or movies. I have never seen anyone who has been shot with a gun. Tim Watson's hand was hot.

He smiled. "Miss Whitney Logan, I reckon you ought to get yourself to a store, then. Maybe that I. Magnin or Saks Fifth Avenue. Get yourself a real pretty little one with a pearl handle so it'll go with your dresses. I'm real glad to see you still wearing those pretty dresses and not charging around in pants and bowties like them bull elephants I seen down at the courthouse." He squeezed my hand.

Tim Watson is one of those good old country boys I grew up with in the summers at my Grandaddy Al's in Tennessee—inbred, stupid, slow, meaner than a snake. I smiled back at him. I remembered a story my mother liked to tell about my father. He was a Yankee; she was born in Norfolk, Virginia. After they married, they lived for a year or so in Tennessee in a house belonging to Grandaddy Al. In that part of the country at the end of a visit, the host routinely says as you are leaving, "Y'all come and stay the night." My father did not understand that this meant goodnight and that it was simply a remnant from the time when farms were far apart. My father did not know how to refuse and would spend the night although the host didn't want or expect him to. It was in this way that I understood Tim Watson. I squeezed his hand back before letting go of it.

"I don't want to go to a store, honey. I want to do business with people I know. And who know me. What have you got for me?"

His eyes narrowed and I could see him thinking about how much he could take me for. I let him ruminate, exciting himself with the idea of money.

"Now, a little lady like you—"

"I want it small, light and cheap."

He frowned.

"Look, Tim, I don't have all day. I'm in a hurry. I got cash and if it's not enough I'll give you a freebie the next time you get busted."

"Why, Miss Whitney, I won't be getting busted again. I gone straight."

"Right, Tim, glad to hear it. Two priors. You're looking at Folsom next time."

His face cracked into a big grin and he laughed his big disturbed idiot laugh as he walked toward the rear of the bar and pushed open the back door of the poolhall. "Miss Whitney, you are one all right girl."

The sun was blinding after having been indoors. Tim Watson lurched over to an old Pontiac covered with bumper stickers and Grateful Dead decals. He opened the trunk. Although he stood between me and the open trunk, I saw a black canvas bag inside, which he unzipped and from which he took a gun. He whirled toward me with it pointing right in my face.

"Looks like what I want, Tim. How much?"

He laughed again. As a boy he had probably tortured cats. He handed me the gun. "Little .22 automatic. Just right for a lady. Only $65."

It looked rusty. "Does it have bullets?"

Tim Watson turned back to the black canvas bag and pulled out a small cardboard box. "They're extra."

"Load it for me." I watched as he pulled out the clip and put the bullets one by one into it. He slapped it back into place and looked at me.

I opened my purse and took out my wallet. Folded behind my driver's license was the hundred-dollar bill my father had sent me for my birthday this year. He's always too busy to buy me a gift. It's the same every year, the hundred dollar bill in the birthday card. I handed Tim Watson a hundred dollars. He handed me the gun.

"Keep the change." And I turned away without saying anything else.

CHAPTER NINTEEN

I rushed to the top of the stairs. Harvey's door was closed and there was the usual trickle of smoke from under the door which meant he was in. I knocked.

A muffled, sleepy voice answered me. I went in without understanding what he had said.

Harvey was sitting cross-legged on the floor with an incense burner in front of him and a fat joint on its rim.

"Don't bother to get up," I said.

"I was just working on some wills," he mumbled, turning bleary red eyes on me. He pointed in the direction of his desk.

"You know a Monica Fullbright or Monica Farley?" I asked, dropping into the chair next to his desk. The gun I had just bought was cold and awkward against my hip. I had shoved it into the waistband of my skirt and beneath my pantyhose.

Harvey nodded a few times to show he was thinking about my question. "Is she dead or alive?" he asked finally. "I can't keep track of them anymore."

"Alive. You knew her years ago."

He picked up the joint, pulled on it, then took a plastic lighter out of his pocket. He relit the joint and held his breath for a long while. He repeated her name a few times as if it were a new mantra. "Never heard of her."

"She told me she was a friend of yours. That you did some work for her husband. Smack freak. You kept him out of state prison. She thinks you're a great lawyer."

A faint smile twisted Harvey's lips for a moment, but his mouth was so dry he couldn't complete it. He held the joint out toward me.

"Saxophone player," I added, waving the joint away.

He shook his head again. His hair, which was unbound, fell nearly to the middle of his back.

"Come on, Harvey, goddamn it. Someone's trying to kill me. I need you to get with it and help me." The gun felt strange, hard, but like it was trying to mold itself to my body.

Harvey struggled to his feet. "What do you mean?"

I laid it out for him as fast as I could.

He studied me carefully and with some reserve. "Are you sure you're not being paranoid?"

Angrily I got up and headed for the door. For the first time I noticed Harvey had removed from the wall his framed state bar certificate. His certificates for Federal Court and the one that said he was entitled to practice before the U.S. Supreme Court were also missing.

"To me, the woman's name means nothing," he said to my back. "Whitney, I've done so many cases, so many junkies, hookers, so many pimps, burglars, rapists and robbers. I can't remember anyone's name anymore. They're all the same. All just trying to use you to run their scam."

I reached for the doorknob. I wanted to leave but found myself hesitating. Harvey sounded like my father, who kept trying to reach me with his phone calls in which he said nothing.

"Whitney, wait. I don't like to talk about this, but now I want to tell you so you don't make the same mistake I did."

I turned back. I had never given up hoping that one day my father would tell me he loved me.

"It was back in the mid-seventies. About '76. When I was doing criminal work. I was hot. Italian suits. Custom made monogrammed silk shirts. Five hundred bucks for me just to make an appearance. The world was my oyster. I had so many girls I couldn't keep track of them. Starlets. Swingers. Beautiful girls. That's the way this world is—it tricks you and sucks you in. Whatever you want, it makes you want more of it. Maybe one day a client gives you a line of coke or whatever it is that turns you on. Next time, two lines. Three. Half a gram. You like it. And want it. The rush, the lights, the feeling of power." Harvey sighed, toked again and exhaled a long, sad stream of smoke. "But no matter how tough you are, there's always somebody tougher."

I waited for him to go on. I didn't see the point.

"I did some cases for a guy, but the more I did for him, the more he wanted. The money was good. Made me feel important." Harvey pushed his hair back tiredly. "Finally it came down to a payoff to a witness to buy some perjured testimony. My client told me all about the plan. Said if I didn't go along with it or it went sour, he'd tell the cops it was my idea. I did it. Paid off the guy he told me to. The witness got busted and was on the way out when he dropped dead. Didn't look like murder, but I knew my client had him killed. I got scared."

I looked out the window feeling overwhelmed and flashing on all the dreams people have to leave behind when they come to live in Dogtown. Harvey apparently had believed he could make fast money without getting dirty. Cathy Vega had believed she could be a star if only she could show her talent to the right person. Me, I'd believed that I could overthrow the yoke of my father by moving across the country. And Lupe? What was her dream? To get off the streets? Who was Lupe, really?

"The guy was putting the squeeze on me. Either I could keep going with him or, if I tried to get out, they'd kill me, too."

I picked up one of Harvey's bronze Indian figurines from the bookshelf

and started to fiddle with it. The gun I was carrying gnawed uncomfortably into my flesh.

"I thought about going to the cops myself," Harvey said. "But what for?
The guy I was working for would screw me. I'd go down the tubes. Lose
everything I'd worked for. Whitney, don't you see? We're like trashmen.
We're just taking care of somebody else's dirty business."

"What happened?" I asked impatiently. I didn't like what he'd said about
trashmen and it made me even angrier at Monica Fullbright.

"My name was leaked to the DA. They didn't have enough to bring criminal charges, but I was suspended from the Bar for a year. That's when I
found Mahatma." He looked reverently and happily at the bronze figurine,
which I quickly put back on the shelf.

"See you later, Harvey." This time I did go to the door and open it. Harvey's mistakes were his. I hadn't done anything wrong. At least nothing
anyone could prove.

"You didn't hear a word, did you?" he called after me. "You told me the
woman who hired you lied to you and that she used you. Don't you see?
She wants you to take a fall for her, just like the guy I've been trying to tell
you about wanted me to."

I won't take a fall, I promised myself as I shut the door behind me. No
matter what. I was ahead of the game and knew all the players. I won't end
up like Harvey. I won't end up like my father. I'd rather be dead. Rather be
dead like Cathy Vega. At least she had done something she believed in.

Slowly I walked back to my office to phone Armando Diaz. I would tell him
I wanted to come see him and get my photos from him. No, I would just con-
front him with what I knew about him. He had seen me in the park. He had
been watching me. Perhaps had even seen me leaving his studio and guessed
that I knew all about him now. Cautiously and quietly I moved across the
floor. The hall was empty but shadowy without the overhead lights on.

A dark form sat looking out onto Hollywood Boulevard from the chair
behind my desk. I was tired of being surprised. My hand went to the gun
as I nudged open the door. As I entered, the chair spun toward the door. I
started to draw the gun.

Lupe didn't say anything and she didn't seem to notice the nervous
action of my hand. She looked shaken.

I took my hand off the gun.

"Joey's gone!" She raised her face to me. "My baby's gone."

I stood awkwardly just inside the door. The sun was directly behind her.
"What happened?" I squinted to see her better.

"He's gone, I tell you!" Her voice edged near hysteria. "I drove over to my
house. *Nada.* I called my cousin. She don't have him. My mom's not home.
My brother was there, but he said he don't know where Joey is."

I wanted to comfort her but didn't know how. My family is not very touchy-feely. I walked over to her and patted her arm ineffectually. "Hector must be lying to you. He said he'd—"

Words tumbled from Lupe's mouth. "It's all my fault. It's this fucking life. I'm tired of it. Tired of standing on the *pinchi* streetcorners."

Had someone taken Joey? Who? Why? Armando Diaz? The Guatemalans? Had they found Lupe's house and kidnapped him? It was cold blooded, but, after all, they still believed we killed Cathy Vega. An eye for an eye, a tooth for a tooth? Was it Emma Garcia or Tony Guerrero who would order such a cruel thing? Had they sent Raul to grab Joey? Or had her brother Hector really taken Joey, as he had threatened to do the day he busted into my office? My mind raced with these possibilities. I took her hand in mine. She felt so small.

Lupe's voice was a mixture of rage and anguish. "Why would anyone want to hurt him? He's just a little boy."

"Casa Guatemala—" I hesitated, wondering how much to tell her of my suspicions.

"You think they have him?" Lupe erupted. "They seemed like such good people. I'll kill 'em if—"

"Shhh. Calm down." I didn't want Lupe to feel my uncertainty. I squeezed her hand and knelt beside her on the floor next to my chair where she sat curled up. I don't know how long we stayed like that, me whispering in her ear that there was nothing to worry about.

The phone rang. It must have rung a few times before I really heard it.

"Whitney Logan?" a man's voice barked at me.

"Yeah." Who was it? Some new business? It was a bad time for new business. Like Lupe, I was tired. I let go of her hand and pushed myself to my feet.

"Officer Hale of the LAPD. Got a few questions we'd like to ask you."

Lupe got up from the desk and moved away toward the window. She cracked her knuckles as she looked out over Hollywood Boulevard again.

"Questions about what?" I asked, stalling.

"About a body we found."

The phone felt heavy, unfamiliar in my hand. I felt like I had never used one before. Please, God, let me think fast enough, I prayed. "What body? Why are you calling me?"

Turning toward me with horror on her face, Lupe grabbed my arm, nearly pulling me off balance. She must have thought the call was about Joey. I shook my head at her, and she let go of me but didn't move away.

"We found your card among other things in the purse she had with her."

"Who is it?" I already knew, and my stomach turned over. I had killed Monica Fullbright.

"That's what we want you to tell us. Look, unless you're a psychic instead of a lawyer, you're going to have to come down here to I.D. this lady and we can ask you some questions."

"Doesn't she have any I.D. in her purse?" I countered, nervously rearranging some papers in front of me.

"Driver's license says she's Monica Fullbright."

I couldn't believe that was her real name. "If you got her name, what do you want me for'?"

"Let's just say we found her under some suspicious circumstances and we need you to give us some background."

Turning my back to Lupe so she couldn't see how scared I was, I leaned against the desk to steady myself. Monica Fullbright must have died when she jumped out of my car. Or when I pushed her! I could imagine her with branch marks cutting her face, road dirt on her chest.

"She's a divorce client of mine. I don't think there's much else I can tell you." Giving false information to a police officer. A misdemeanor? Or was I sliding over to felony jeopardy? It was too late to worry about that. "What happened to her?" I asked, although I didn't think he'd tell me.

"Strangled. Silk scarf around the throat."

I hadn't killed her! A loud sigh escaped my lips. But wouldn't the police consider me a suspect when they heard my story? It was rather unbelievable. Monica Fullbright's killer had to be one of the men from the car chase. I remembered the bandanna I'd seen tied around Cathy Vega's neck in the shed behind Casa Guatemala. Guerrero? No, I was sure it was Armando Diaz. But I had to know. Had to know so the cops would believe me. Where's your office? I'll be there in about forty minutes."

I didn't hear what he said. We must have said good-bye. I wasn't listening because I knew I wasn't going.

"What's happening? Where are you going? I gotta find Joey," Lupe said, agitated and pacing. "I don't got time for none of your nicey nicey Audrey Hepburn stuff. Let's go to Casa Guatemala."

I shook my head but didn't answer her as I shuffled through the papers on my desk to find Casa Guatemala's number, which I had scribbled on my desk blotter. Punching the number, I waited impatiently for it to ring. I couldn't move against them to find out if they had killed Monica Fullbright and I couldn't put myself in the clear with the cops until I knew that Joey was somewhere safe and out of the way.

The phone was answered immediately.

"I want to talk with Guerrero. Tell him it's Whitney Logan."

Lupe edged closer and pressed her face next to mine so that her ear was on the receiver.

"Guerrero no here," a heavily accented male voice replied.

"Find him. I want to see him now."

There was some confusion on the other end. I could hear people speaking rapidly in Spanish before a woman's voice came on the line.

"He is not here. This is Emma."

"The woman Cathy got the money from is dead. Guerrero just killed her. Like he killed Cathy." I had to lure Emma out to meet me. I would make her tell me if they had Joey. "You knew he killed Cathy. That makes you an accessory to murder."

"No!"

I stretched the phone cord to straighten it. "That's what I'm going to tell the police. I'm on my way there now."

"Wait! You're wrong. It's not the way you think."

I centered the phone neatly on the desk. "I'm tired of thinking. Your time's up."

"Let me talk to you before you go to the police," she said hurriedly.

"The last time I wanted to talk with you, you stuck a gun in my back. One of your goons kicked me in the head." I started to hang up. She would call me right back, ready to do whatever I wanted.

"I'll come alone," she pleaded. "I'll meet you wherever you say."

That's the way I wanted her. Alone, unsure. Now I was ready to set the trap and tell her where to meet me. I paused to give her just another second of anxiety.

Lupe grabbed the phone from my hand and started talking in Spanish. Her voice was surprisingly cold, flat. I don't know what she said. She mentioned Joey's name only once. When she hung up she grabbed her purse from the desk and rushed toward the door.

"What'd you do that for?" I yelled at her, blocking her way out.

"He's my son. I told you. I don't got time for your fancy way of figuring things out, and I don't much care who you think killed who. I only care about Joey, and I'm gonna find him."

I hadn't had time to tell her what I'd found in Armando Diaz's studio. She didn't know how dangerous the shifting landscape was.

"You'll ruin everything. I've got it all planned how I'll—"

"No. We go together to meet Emma. This time you follow me. You said we were equal. Prove it." She had changed clothes when she went home. She wore a red miniskirt, a skin-tight black halter top with cross straps and black high heels. It was not the wardrobe of a person you take seriously.

"I have to go alone," I argued. "That's the way I've always done everything." The times I ran away from home. The way when I was a little kid I used to stay up all night so I could be awake and strong while my parents slept. The time in the Girl Scouts I cut a deep hole in the palm of my left hand to teach myself pain. I still have a scar nearly the size of a dime by my thumb. Going to law school when I knew my father didn't want me to. I don't know any other way to do things.

"I should have known. You're all talk," she snarled, one hand on her hip. "You do think you're better than me. Smarter. All this stuff about the law and helping people—it's bullshit. You're just out to make yourself big. Well, fuck you."

I stared stupidly back at Lupe. There was nothing about me in her eyes.

"Get outta the way. I told Emma where to meet me. I'm going," she growled, pulling her purse more snugly across her shoulder. "With or without you. You can come with me or you can stay here and jerk off with your precious law books."

I found that I stepped aside as she started again for the door. I have never seen eyes as black and angry as hers. Was she right about me? I followed her down the hall to the stairs, feeling uncertain. Everything I had ever learned was about how to stay in control. Before I knew it, she was halfway down the stairs without looking back.

I took a deep breath and let it all go as though I were diving under an enormous wave. "Where are we going?"

"Don't worry. It's safe. And I'll drive."

Without another word passing between us we got into Lupe's old Fiat and she threw it into first so it sounded like a hair dryer breaking apart. She drove south down Van Ness past all the pink and green Central American businesses and apartment buildings. When she got to Santa Monica Boulevard, she turned west, then left at a street near a Mexican restaurant.

On the left side of the street in the middle of a high adobe wall was a huge black wrought-iron gate that was open. She drove into the driveway created by the gate and onto a dirt road shaded by tall trees.

"Where are we?" I wondered aloud.

CHAPTER TWENTY

"The resting place of some of the greats. Hollywood Cemetery."

A clump of tombstones popped into view as we made the first curve of the road. They were bleached white, buffed by smog and the relentless sun. The grass surrounding them was dry, the few intermittent flowers scattered on graves wilted and desiccated.

"Nice place," I said, staring unhappily at what looked like a marble replica of a rocket ship marking one of the graves.

"Yes," Lupe agreed, slowing the car to a crawl. "Very mellow."

Mellow? Mellow was a word I had certainly never expected to hear Lupe use. I thought the streets were her element and that she liked the fast pace. The cemetery was creepy. I didn't like it. "How did you pick this place?"

"It's quiet. No one can hassle us here. I know all the ways out. I been here a lot of times."

Been here a lot of times? With tricks? I glanced with disgust at the brown grass.

"I come to visit the graves of some of the stars and actresses I love. Rudolph Valentino. Virginia Rappe. Tyrone Power. Norma Talmadge," she said, laughing at what I had been thinking.

Embarrassed, I turned away. "Where are we supposed to meet?"

"The far east end. Called the lake section. By that group of trees." She pointed ahead. Visible through the trees were the tops of several of the tall bank buildings in the center of Hollywood.

A limo with tinted glass passed us in the opposite direction and pulled to the side of the road. An old man and woman climbed slowly and painfully out of the backseat.

"That looked just like Bela Lugosi!" Lupe exclaimed, swerving slightly as she turned back to look at the man.

"He's dead."

"Remarkable what they can do with makeup," murmured Lupe more to herself than to me. "Look, there's Adolph Menjou. Best dressed man in Hollywood."

"He's dead," I said, feeling annoyed. It was hotter than hell despite all the trees.

"Of course he's dead; that's where he's buried. Those Guatemalans might have Joey, but I don't think he killed Monica Fullbright."

Suddenly I remembered being a little kid and driving on a Saturday afternoon with my Grandaddy Al in Tennessee to the local VFW where they sold bootleg and homemade hooch because Cumberland County where he lived was dry. Never go anywhere without your own bottle or your own car, he had told me. Now I understood what he had meant. Why on earth had I agreed to depend on her? "Who are you talking about?" I snapped with irritation.

"Guerrero." She put up her hand to silence me. "*Oye*. None of the *Guatemaltecos* knew about Monica Fullbright and the money. If they did, they would have taken it from Cathy. When they sent her to Mexico, she was only supposed to pick up the video. They were testing her. No way they'd let her hold money for them. That's the way it is on the streets; you gotta prove yourself first."

I nodded at Lupe, some of my anger dissipating. It was good reasoning. Socratic, just like they'd taught us in law school. But still, it overlooked several possibilities. "Wouldn't Guerrero know about the money? After all, he was her lover. Or maybe he wanted to move in a different direction from the rest of the group and thought he could use innocent little Cathy to help him do that. Or, possibly, Guerrero, like Cathy, isn't who he says he is."

She frowned skeptically at me.

"What if Guerrero's a double agent?" I pressed. "CIA? FBI?" I had read about the FBI infiltrating another Central American group. Maybe he'd been watching Armando Diaz. Maybe he had tried to use Cathy as bait.

"A double agent?" she sputtered with laughter. "This isn't TV. This is real life. Don't you think people can do something just 'cause they believe in it? You keep saying that's why you went to law school. It's not Guerrero. It's someone else, isn't it?"

I hadn't had time to tell Lupe about the calendar, needles, camera and defaced photos I had found at Armando Diaz's studio. There would be time to tell her; now I didn't want to. I wanted to test her and hear how she had reasoned it out. "Why do you think it's not Guerrero?"

She shrugged and made a dismissive pout as she jerked her chin up impatiently. "I know men. I can read them. Just like you can read those books in your office. They're all dogs. He didn't love Cathy."

"He just spreads his charm around for fun?" I argued, smoothing my skirt down.

"It don't mean nothin'. It's to grease the wheel. He's like a pimp."

"How would you know?"

Instead of answering me, she stared off in the direction of a rococo carved cross above one of the graves. A frown flashed quickly across her dark face, telling me she felt she had said too much already and that she was angry at herself.

"How do you know?" What was she hiding from me? A searing fear told me the thing was ugly and that she'd lied to me from the very beginning.

She slowed the car even more, refusing to look at me.

"Answer me. How do you know?" I grabbed her by the shoulder and shook her violently. Almost immediately I was stunned by what I had done and drew back my hand, horrified that it was part of me. Until the last few days I had never known I had so much anger and rage in me.

Lupe pulled aside the right strap of her halter top. A raised scar ran near her clavicle. I had noticed it at the motel when she lay down next to me, and I'd asked about it.

"I thought you told me you were in a car accident," I said foolishly and in confusion.

She let go of the material so that the scar was once again hidden from view. "Pimp named Harold James cut me 'cause he thought I was holding out on him."

"You told me you never had a pimp. That you'd only been doing this for a little while."

"I lied."

I punched the dash of the car. I had confided in her and told her things about myself I'd never told anyone else. I had thought I could trust her.

Lupe, a stony look on her face, pressed the accelerator again, and the Fiat jumped forward.

The road wound around a group of marble angels poised and hovering above a tombstone polished like a black mirror. I didn't see any cars up ahead under the clump of weeping willows. I had never seen a weeping willow in Southern California except at Disneyland.

Lupe drove to the far east end of the trees, pulled off the road behind a small mausoleum and turned off the engine.

I got out of the car and stepped on the sunken marker of Bugsy Siegel. Without speaking to me, Lupe hurried ahead of me down a row of monuments to the edge of the trees where they grew next to a muddy artificial lake. There was a great sad gulf between us. She went directly to one of the markers and brushed her hand tenderly across it. Virginia Rappe. One of the actresses Lupe had said she loved. The name was sort of familiar, but I couldn't really hook it with anything. Sounded like a third league player to me. If I asked Lupe who she was, she would probably tell me one of the sappy bubblegum stories like the one about Lana Turner at Schwab's drugstore.

"We can see both entrances and the service road from here," she said, still not looking at me. Lupe sat down on a tombstone to wait. As she watched the roads, I couldn't tell what she was thinking about, Joey or me.

I paced around, kicking up small clouds of dust. It was like being in the fifth fucking ring of Dante's inferno. What else had she lied to me about? What was the con? I felt so betrayed. Small. Naked. I kicked at the dirt some more and the silence continued heavy between us.

Finally a small ancient blue car drove by and parked near the Fiat. The person in the car hesitated a moment before getting out. It was Emma Garcia. She tucked an attaché case or large purse under her arm, then came in our direction without looking back. As I was watching her approach, I saw a black car—a Trans Am, I was sure—cruise by in the distance, but it was too far away for me to see the driver. It decelerated slightly as the driver looked at the parked cars, but it kept going toward the main entrance on Santa Monica Boulevard and I saw it exit the cemetery.

"Where's my boy, Joey?" Lupe called out as she jumped to her feet.

"Who's Joey?" Emma Garcia was slightly out of breath. Lupe advanced with her hands outstretched toward Emma Garcia. "My son. Give him to me." Was she begging or ready to fight? It was the first time I'd seen Lupe look like she might lose it. A loose cannon. I knew I shouldn't have let her act as if she was in charge. She couldn't handle it.

"I don't know what you're talking about. Look, I brought something to show you two," said Emma. "So you'll leave us alone once and for all."

My hand moved down to my waist, where the gun was rubbing against my skin. "No funny business, and you better tell us the truth about her son. I got a gun."

Lupe stared at me in amazement.

"Give your bag to Lupe," I ordered.

Emma Garcia shrugged angrily at my directions but tossed the bag at Lupe. "We don't have your boy. We don't know anything about him."

"What about Guerrero. Does he have him?" I demanded.

"Of course not. I'm the one giving the orders now, not him." She laughed the way a palm tree sways in the breeze.

"If you're lying to me..." Lupe took another step forward and jerked her chin up like a real *chola*.

"Knock it off, Lupe," I barked. "What are we looking for?"

"A letter with a blue envelope." Emma's voice was lilting, tropical.

"Just shake it out on the ground," I snapped at Lupe, still fuming at her admitted deception.

A wallet, some keys and a dirty hairbrush hit the ground. Lupe bent to retrieve the letter. I couldn't help watching the smooth curve of her ass. She brought the letter to her nose as though smelling it for perfume.

"It's from Guerrero," said Emma. "I found it with Cathy on the day she was killed."

"There wasn't anything with Cathy," I argued. "I was there. I would have seen it." I didn't take my hand off the gun. I didn't believe her.

"You didn't check everything," Emma said, smirking. "We went into the loft after you two ran off. We had more time, and we moved her body out of there."

Lupe put the fallen things back into Emma's purse. She dusted the bag off before handing it back to Emma.

"Down the hall was a bathroom. There Raul and I found a makeup bag. This was in it," Emma added insistently.

I asked Lupe what the letter was.

"A love letter."

"*La paloma de tu cara no volará más en mis manos,*" Emma Garcia recited.

"The dove which is your face won't fly in my hands anymore," Lupe said, translating for me.

Why couldn't the guy have a little humility and just plagiarize something good? But Guerrero would be too vain to do that.

Lupe read the rest of the page quickly and silently. "It's signed by Guerrero."

Emma got an ugly look on her face. Bitter. She'd probably read the letter hundreds of times since she found it. She was certain Guerrero had killed Cathy, wanted him to have done it so she could use it to wrest control of Casa Guatemala away from him. Emma knew I was watching her so she quickly replaced her angry expression with something benign.

"Had you ever been to the loft before?" I asked her, reluctant to tell her Guerrero was innocent. "Do you know why Cathy was there?"

Emma Garcia shook her head.

"She went for a modeling job."

"Modeling!" Emma howled. "She said she renounced that."

"A man called her agent and said there was a job for her modeling bathing suits down in the garment district, so she went. Whoever killed her had to know how to arrange it so it would sound legit."

Emma sneered. "Can't be Guerrero, then. He's too stupid. Look, maybe it's true he thought he was in love with her—"

"Thought he was in love with her?" interrupted Lupe. "What does that mean?"

"He was obsessed with her. He had this dream of remaking her, of making her the ideal revolutionary woman. But what he loved was the idea of taking a bourgeois woman who had been corrupted by all the decadence of the media and purifying her."

"The madonna-and-the-whore freak types! Shit, I get them all the time." Lupe nodded at Emma, encouraging her to go on.

"What'd Cathy do?" Lupe asked.

And me, was that what I'd been trying to do with Lupe? Purify her and make her into someone like me? Convince her to get off the streets and become a paralegal or something? I glanced quickly and guiltily at her, but she was looking at Emma Garcia.

"What'd Cathy do?" Lupe repeated.

"At first she was all for it. Cathy wanted to be whatever he wanted. They were sleeping together. Then he started testing her. Making up crazy things for her to do. Dangerous things."

"Like what?" Lupe demanded breathlessly.

I wondered if any of her tricks had ever made her do anything she didn't want to do. The pimp, Harold James—what had he done to her? Had he fucked her every which way before he cut her? I felt a sick lump in my throat as I watched Lupe, but she didn't even seem aware of me. She stood with her hands on her hips, waiting impatiently for Emma to respond.

Emma sighed. "You know the bridge over at First Street?"

Lupe nodded.

"He made her walk across the top of the bridge in the middle of the night once. Another time he took her up to the mountains above San Gabriel and left her there without any provisions for three days to see how she'd survive."

Angrily Lupe shook her head and began to pace.

"Did he order her to make the trip to Mexico?" I asked. Only two reasons why he'd do that, I thought: if he knew she had the money and if he also wanted to buy guns.

Emma hesitated. After all of this—the bad poetry, the betrayals—she was still in love with him. She couldn't decide whether to rescue him or turn him in.

"Tell me everything you know about the trip to Mexico or, like I told you on the phone, I'm going to the police." I didn't want to wait for her to resolve her dilemma.

"No," she said hurriedly and in some confusion. "He didn't tell her to go. We were going to send Tommy down, like we have before. But this time Cathy proposed she go. She insisted. She said she'd leave the group if we didn't let her go."

"You would have liked to get rid of her, wouldn't you?" Lupe goaded, crossing her arms smugly across her chest. "You were trying to get him back. Maybe you wanted to get rid of her for good."

"If I wanted to get him back, I could!" Emma spat, stepping toward Lupe.

I tried to remember the last time I'd seen a really good fight between two women. "Did you give her that fake Guatemalan passport?" I interrupted.

"No! We didn't know about that until you told us. It's crazy! Why would she do that? It was to be so easy for her, a U.S. citizen, to go and come back. I still can't believe she did that."

"You never knew any Carmen Luzano?" I persisted. "You don't know where Cathy got that passport?"

"Admit it," taunted Lupe. "You were trying to get him back."

There was the crunch of gravel. We all looked up to see Tony Guerrero striding toward us. I didn't see any other cars. I wondered where he had left his.

"Where did Cathy get the Guatemalan passport?" I called out to him before he had the chance to say anything.

"I don't know."

"*¡Mentiroso!* Stop lying!" Emma screamed at him. "Where else would she have gotten it except from you. The woman could barely speak Spanish."

Lupe and I gaped at each other in amazement.

"She couldn't speak Spanish!" exclaimed Lupe.

Emma sneered. "Not good. *Pocho* Spanish."

"Not good enough to be mistaken for a Guatemalan?" I asked in disbelief.

"No. She kept studying, but she wasn't very good. No one could possibly have mistaken her for a Guatemalan," Emma said. She looked very pleased by this.

"You bastard!" Lupe yelled at Guerrero. "You must have put her up to this. We heard about the tests you had for her."

I thought Lupe was going to spit at him as he brushed roughly past her and stepped toward me.

"Who was the man following us in the park?" he demanded.

"A Cuban." So he hadn't known about Armando Diaz. Didn't know he had them under surveillance.

Tony Guerrero frowned to cover his uncertainty but couldn't stop himself from looking around for Emma Garcia. She was the real power in Casa Guatemala.

"*¡Un cubano!*" Emma shouted at him. "Now what have you got us involved in? Wasn't it enough that you killed Cathy?"

I pushed myself between them. I was glad she had him on the defensive, but I was going to be the one to take him down. "The woman who was in my car has been killed. You must have killed her."

"I saw the woman..." he stammered, losing his careful shoe salesman composure and addressing himself more to Emma, who was hovering behind me, than to me.

"I'll bet you did," she snapped in his face. "Who was she?"

"I don't know who she was," he whined, making a weak gesture with his hands.

Lupe sniffed in disgust.

"It was the woman who gave money to Cathy to take into Mexico. She thought Cathy was going to buy heroin they could sell here. But Cathy was going to buy guns, wasn't she? Or didn't you know about that?" I poked Guerrero in the chest to make sure he was paying attention to me.

"Our goals are educational only," he said, drawing himself up tall and trying to recapture some of his billboard magnetism. "We have nothing to do with guns."

Emma laughed as she swaggered toward him. "Speak for yourself. You're afraid to take up a gun and fight like a man. If Cathy had told me about the money, I would have known what to do with it."

Cathy Vega, being who she was, would have done something big and risky to prove herself. Making an arms deal would be the ultimate wedding of courage and conviction. Five thousand dollars. It didn't seem like much on the international scene, but the people of Guatemala live in desperate conditions. What could she buy? How many AK-47s? How many submachine guns? But how could she possibly believe she could succeed in such an undertaking? Only if she knew whom to give the money to or if she knew someone who would be able to direct her to an arms dealer. I thought of how easily I had bought the .22 from Tim Watson. It had to be someone as desperate as she was.

Tony Guerrero shuffled from one foot to the other. "I tell you, she never talked to me about no guns."

"What about in bed?" asked Lupe.

"Yeah, what about in bed?" Emma and I echoed together. He looked uncomfortably from one to the other of us.

"She must have told you," I insisted impatiently, my adrenaline pumping like crazy. This was taking too long. I wanted to hit someone again and thought fleetingly of the satisfaction of bench-pressing sixty pounds, the pleasure in the simple relief of physical tension. "She had to travel around with a lot of money, find the right people to give it to and then get back into this country, here to Hollywood, without Monica Fullbright learning what had become of her money. Cathy thought she could disappear from Monica, but that meant she couldn't work as an actress."

Lupe leaned back against a marble tombstone, resting one hand on it. "That explains why she was working at that crummy dime-a-dance place."

"And why she took the modeling job," agreed Emma.

"Cathy thought she could pass as a Guatemalan. Maybe this all sounds a little hard to believe, but apparently she believed it," I continued.

No answer from Tony Guerrero.

I poked him in the chest again. "Hey, did you tell her the names of some gun dealers or not?"

Emma crossed her arms and waited for Guerrero to answer me.

A dark movement in the distance caught my attention, and I glanced away from him. The black car that had not much earlier exited the cemetery drove by again.

"I'll bet he don't know the names of no gun dealers," Lupe argued.

"Cathy must have found her own," I said, nodding in agreement. "And her contact must have been someone right here in LA. I don't know why she bothered to go to Mexico. I don't know if she was actually able to turn the money over to someone who'd buy the arms or if she got ripped off. Maybe you people will find that out someday," I said to Guerrero and Emma Garcia. "I don't know why she went to Mexico. Probably just to feel like she was really playing the part. Maybe we'll never know. But the rest of it I can put together real good."

They all looked at me expectantly. Lupe stopped tracing the carving on the tombstone she was leaning against, and her eyes seemed to challenge me.

"Guerrero was in love with her, or at least he had been for a while. Don't say anything." I put up my hand to stop him from adding anything. "We have one of your letters. But Cathy always wanted something bigger, grander. She wanted to be a star. She got the idea to steal money for guns. At first, Guerrero, I thought you killed her. I thought you knew about the money. That's the kind of thing you're supposed to learn from pillow talk, isn't it? Three A.M. secrets."

Emma watched Guerrero carefully.

"But Cathy didn't tell you, did she?" I scoffed. "You must be a very bad fuck."

The sound of a big engine caused me to look up although I was the only one who noticed it. For an instant I looked away in the direction of the sound. The black car that I had now seen many times parked in the distance. I broke into a cold sweat. The man inside the car sat without looking in our direction.

I heard Tony Guerrero saying, "I swear I didn't know who the woman in the car with you was. I didn't kill her. I don't care if she gave money to Cathy. She wouldn't be the first person who gave Cathy money."

I pushed closer into his face. "Then why'd you follow me this afternoon?"

"To make you tell me who killed her."

Lupe sneered at him. "What do you care?"

"I did love her," he said angrily to her. "I did."

"¡Hijo de puta!" screamed Emma, throwing herself at him. "That's what you used to tell me." She swung her hands wildly, clawing at his face.

"I didn't kill her. I didn't kill anybody!" he shouted back at her. "When you and Raul came back from downtown with her body, I thought you'd killed Cathy. More of your fucking Trotsky politics." Then he was screaming at her in Spanish.

"Stop it. Stop it." Lupe tried to push in between them. Emma scratched her across the face, making it bleed, but Lupe managed to pull her off Guerrero. Emma was sobbing.

"Why'd you care what I thought?" I asked the panting Guerrero. "You must have had some ideas of your own. You knew she knew other men. You could see she'd been killed by a man. Didn't Emma tell you Cathy had been raped?"

Emma shook her head, trying to deny what I had said.

"Yes, of course, Emma would tell you that." I glanced over at her. She'd stopped crying, but she was shaking slightly and her eyes were still wet.

Tony Guerrero tried to straighten his shoulders and look tall. "I knew there were other guys. She knew Tommy. She was with him before she knew me. I knew about the junkie who lived in East LA and wouldn't leave her alone."

"The acting coach," added Lupe.

Tony Guerrero looked defeated.

It was all so small. The fallen ideals of revolutionaries and law students.

I looked over to where the black car was waiting. He wouldn't wait long. "Get out of here," I barked at Guerrero and Emma Garcia. "Get out of here right now and I won't tell the police about you. Cathy's mine now. I knew her better than any of you. Go. Try to remember what you once believed in. Serve the people." I didn't mean to sound bitter, but I'm sure I did.

They looked questioningly at me, then at Lupe and finally at each other. A moment passed, but no questions came to their lips.

"*Vamos,*" Emma Garcia said at last, and they walked separately and awkwardly toward Emma's car. They got in and slowly the car drove past us in a hot cloud of dust back into Hollywood.

I looked back to the black car. It was empty. The man in the car was gone. I knew Armando Diaz had killed Cathy. He had followed me through Griffith Park, where he killed Monica.

Now he wanted me.

CHAPTER TWENTY-ONE

The weeping willow dripped over the lake. Shadows grew between the
tombstones and gravemarkers. It was quiet except for the distant whir of
traffic, which sounded like the wind. Lupe and I stood just a few feet apart,
studying each other.

"Get in your car and go home," I told her. "Look for Joey. I'm sure your
brother or one of your relatives has him."

"No." Did she believe she would learn something about Joey by remaining, or was it something else that compelled her to stay? Perhaps the same
need I had to learn what had happened to Cathy Vega. Her face didn't give
anything away. For the first time, despite her red miniskirt, she looked like
a woman instead of a girl.

I had a sudden flash. My entire life, as they say. I saw the girl from the
drunken party at the fraternity house when I was in college. I knew I had-
n't passed out next to her, like I'd always told myself before. I remembered
burrowing up to her. Just wanting to be close. I've always been afraid to be
close. Afraid to need anybody. I've always fought to be alone because it's
the only way I feel safe. I couldn't think of a single friend I had. "Get out
of here now."

"No. You know something about Cathy, and I'm not leaving till you tell
me."

"This isn't the time for an argument."

She crossed her arms over her chest.

"We're not having fun now, Lupe." This is for real. All of it. Everything.
Whatever happens here.

I thought I heard the sound of a branch cracking or the crunch of gravel. I reached out and grabbed Lupe by the wrist, pulling her toward me. I
didn't know which direction the sound had come from. For an instant I
could feel her heart beating under my fingers. Again I heard, or imagined
I heard, the sound of a branch cracking or the crunch of gravel. I loosened
my grip on her.

Lupe pulled away from me. The wind rustled the hair around her face so
I couldn't see her.

"Do they have people working here after it closes?" I asked, glancing at
my watch, which showed it was already past five.

I heard the gravel crunch sound again and Lupe looked at me. This time
she had heard it also.

"Gravediggers," Lupe whispered. "And they have security to make sure
no one is here after closing."

I shook my head and put my fingers to my lips. "It's the man who killed

Cathy. He killed Monica Fullbright, too. He's been following me. I saw him drive in while Tony and Emma were here."

I said this as quietly as I could and with the least amount of expression. I thought she would panic, but she just looked back at me as though this was what she'd been expecting. Lupe looked around the clearing where we stood and listened intently, a slight frown on her face. There were no longer any sounds except for our own breathing. We were completely alone in the spreading shadows of Dogtown.

"He doesn't know how much you know," Lupe said, pushing her hair back from her face.

"True. He thinks I know more than I do." Did I have enough for a prima facie case in court? Or just enough to be dangerous to myself and others? My education suddenly seemed woefully inadequate.

"Get out of here while you can," I begged. "Go to the police."

"Me? The police? And have them take Joey from me. *Estas loca.* Besides, they're probably looking for you right now. You stood up a guy at Parker Center, remember?"

I was past caring about the law. About formal structures. I couldn't remember why I had gone to law school. They would do what they had to do. I would do what I had to do. "Then go to your mother," I told her.

Angrily, Lupe started to say something but she turned away instead. I watched as she hurried down the path on which we had come. Instead of continuing on to the car, she stepped off the path and disappeared between some monuments. What was she doing? Why didn't she listen to me?

I wanted to run after her, but I made myself stand still and listen for whatever sounds might tell me where Armando Diaz was. I wondered what I was going to do. Talk to him? Counsel him? Volunteer to go with him if he'd surrender? I stood there for a long time, sniffing the air like a dog, uncertain about what to do. The sepulchers and markers stood taller than a man and were jumbled together with scant space between them. I stood still for so long that I thought I heard the sound of rain. It was only the sound of sprinklers somewhere in the distance, but it woke me from my blank reverie.

I felt for the gun at my waist again. My fingers embraced the handle, and I ran my thumb over the safety catch, feeling the tension of the mechanism.

In the clearing I was a target. I slipped behind a gray marble headstone that stood at the edge of the trees near the lake. I wanted to move toward the area closer to Santa Monica Boulevard. I didn't want to be caught or pressed between where I was and the wall that ran along the back of the property. With my left hand I balanced myself against the headstone, pressing close to it and holding my breath. The stone was cold where it had been out of the sun. It felt wet, but that was just my hand sweating against it. It didn't seem possible that the cemetery could get any quieter. Then I heard a quick, sharp scraping sound from somewhere off to my right, somewhere down toward where Lupe's car was. Maybe she had decided to do as I had told her and she was leaving. Praying she was, I ran across the little clearing to a tall marble marker that was in a line with the spot where I had seen the black Trans Am park.

Up ahead I could see the gray primer side of the Fiat but no Lupe moving toward it. With ragged breath I crouched down to make sure I couldn't be seen above the marker. I heard the scraping sound again. It was still to my right, east. It sounded like a heavy foot trying to be light. It dragged slightly across the gravel. I edged toward the next marker, looking at the ground before stepping forward. It was like mountain climbing, looking for the footing, putting the foot down lightly, testing it, then putting weight upon it.

It took a long time to move from one marker to another this way. Heading in the direction of the road from which I thought I had heard the gravel sound, I was about twenty yards from it when I heard a snapping sound like a branch breaking.

He was off the road and he was close.

I pulled back against the headstone that sheltered me.

"Faithful friend, brave companion," it read.

Had Lupe gone for help? What would Lupe tell the police about why we were here? What would she tell them about herself? I caught the toe of my high heel in a vine and stumbled slightly as I pulled myself upright by grabbing at the headstone. The crunch sound I had heard was close; then I heard two of them in rapid succession as though he were moving toward me quickly now. I dodged and threw myself behind the closest headstone. Then I heard a moan, a muffled voice nearly behind me. I moved back a couple of headstones and peered around.

It was Armando Diaz. He wore the black pants and the white *guyabera* shirt in which I had first seen him. He was hunched over and clutching Lupe to him.

"Hey, man, you got the wrong girl." I touched the gun again to make sure it was still there, then I stepped out from behind the carved headstone.

His shoulders tightened as if he was taking a firmer grip on her. He turned awkwardly, pulling her with him. His skin was lighter than Lupe's and his arms below the short sleeves of his shirt glistened against her. He was close to my dad's age: late fifties. He wore sunglasses with thick black frames. His hair had a lot of gray in it. His mustache was all gray. He was an ordinary-looking man.

"We know what you did," I said.

Lupe's eyes were wide; she seemed surprised now by these turns of events. I had tried to send her away ever since the beginning. I knew the kind of monster I was. Desperate and needy. Now she would have to rely on me. I was afraid and my training hadn't prepared me for improvisation.

"Don't make me hurt your friend here," he said. "You are friends, aren't you?" He added a peculiar and nasty lilting emphasis to this. How long had he been following me? Maybe he had seen Lupe stay at my place.

"You're not going to hurt her. You've already got enough trouble. Let go of her. I don't think you can kill both of us."

"I can. And I'm going to." He laughed a loony laugh.

Lupe must have thought this was a strange reaction, because she twisted frantically in his arms and tried to knee him in the nuts. He pulled her tighter, and I heard her catch her breath as if he had hurt her. My hand gripped the butt of the gun, and as I started to step forward, I realized I'd rather have him hurt me than Lupe. Wrenching her to one side so that she was off balance, he withdrew a switchblade. The air buzzed as he flicked it open, and it gleamed dully in the shadows.

The trouble with determinate sentencing is that people know ahead of time how much trouble they're in. He couldn't get any more time for killing Lupe or me. Once they racked him with Cathy's and Monica's deaths, we were a free ride.

I drew the gun from my waist and pointed it at him. Could he see my arm shaking? I could barely hold the gun. "Let her go. Turn yourself in. You'll have a fair chance. They'll give you a public defender." I had a sudden hysterical recollection of a woman PD I knew from Santa Monica who had been assigned to represent a guy she recognized as having burglarized her apartment.

Armando Diaz would have to be crazy to believe me.

"We know you killed Cathy," I continued. "The woman in my car, too. You were on the roof across from Casa Guatemala. I found your photo album. I saw what you did to those pictures of the women. And I saw needles in the medicine cabinet just like the one we found next to Cathy's body."

"You killed her because she didn't love you anymore," interrupted Lupe. "You felt she failed you."

He looked down at her as though he had forgotten for a moment that he had her in his arms. He drew the knife up closer to her throat so that it was only an inch or two from her. "She never loved me."

"She must have. If only for a little while. How'd you meet her?" Lupe chattered with the innocence of a schoolgirl. She looked absolutely sincere. And not afraid. Was it possible she felt sorry for him? Or was it one of her B-girl tricks?

Armando Diaz didn't say anything.

"It was at Rudy's studio when she went to get some photos done. You must have been there using the darkroom like the day I met you there." I guessed.

His silence convinced me I was right.

The gun was heavy in my hand. When I'd bought it from Tim Watson, it had seemed so light. Did Armando Diaz see the erratic flutter of my hand? "What did you think when you saw her at the demonstrations in front of the Federal Building? You knew she wasn't like you, she didn't believe in the things you do."

"Love is mightier than the sword," misquoted Lupe.

"I thought I could change her," he replied carelessly.

I was stunned. Didn't he know about the heroin deal or the arms Cathy had wanted to buy?

"Poor Armando, poor Cathy. Love can be so unhappy," Lupe murmured.

The knife wavered slightly in his hand.

Lupe used this opportunity to push at the arm holding the knife.

"You gave Cathy money," I insisted.

"No! I don't have to pay for sex," he said, exploding at me. He stepped forward slightly. Now Lupe and Armando Diaz looked as if they were dancing. Lupe pushed him off balance so that he nearly stumbled and with a great effort she jerked free of him, falling almost to her knees. Breathlessly she ran the few yards between us.

"Yeah, you gave her money," taunted Lupe, her hands on her hips and still breathing hard from the tussle with him.

"How much?" I added.

He looked down at the gun and smiled. He saw my hand trembling.

I tried to pull back the safety but couldn't. My hand was shaking wildly and I couldn't get my fingers to work.

He took another step toward us, the knife extended. "You won't use that gun. You're no different than Cathy. She was afraid at the end, too. Yeah, I gave her money. Fifteen hundred dollars. She begged for it. Told me she wanted to go to Mexico to have her tits done."

"Her tits!" Lupe and I exclaimed at the same time. Laughing, Lupe sauntered majestically over and stood next to me.

"So that's why you went down to Mexicali. You really did love her," Lupe said.

"She was a beautiful young girl." Armando Diaz looked away sadly for an instant, then his face grew twisted and angry as he remembered. "I thought I'd surprise her, bring her some flowers, but when I got there she was with a red-haired man and she laughed at me. She said she'd sent the money I gave her to Guatemala to make a revolution. Like Castro."

I remembered the story Rudy Sancerre had told me about how Armando Diaz had escaped from Cuba. That his wife and child had been swept away and died in the ocean between Cuba and Florida. Although it happened nearly fifteen years ago, it was clear that Armando Diaz did not spend a day during which he did not think of this. His daughter would have been Cathy Vega's age by now. Or Lupe's. Or mine.

"How'd you do it?" Lupe asked.

He turned his attention to her again, taking his eyes off the gun. He had already made his judgment about me. He didn't seem particularly afraid of me anymore. "I'll tell you. You're not going to be leaving here alive. Film developer. I gave her a shot. She got sick, but I cleaned it up and left things to look like she overdose."

"Except for the bruise on the back of her neck," I reminded him.

"She fought against me." He took another step. We were only a few yards apart now.

"Before or after you fucked her?" I asked.

"It's so sad. I suppose you wanted to love her just one more time," Lupe interrupted in a small quiet voice.

In the shade his face was a mask. "Before."

Lupe looked sick. "She was already dead, wasn't she?"

Armando Diaz shrugged. "Dead or alive, she was a whore."

The willows groaned in the breeze.

Lupe grabbed the gun from me, clasped both of her hands around it, and threw herself into a shooter's stance with her hands out in front of her chest. "Get over there!" she yelled at him, jerking the gun in the direction of the greasy artificial pond and toward a tombstone a few feet away.

He stood looking blankly back at her.

"Move it. Over to that marker. Look at it. Say that name out loud."

I heard the click of the safety being released, then I saw him move slowly to the tombstone Lupe was pointing at.

"What's the name say?" Lupe demanded. "Say it out loud

"Virginia Rappe." He pronounced the name unfamiliarly.

"You know who she was?" prodded Lupe. The breeze fluffed her hair so that it streamed back from her face. "A girl, like me, just a few years older than I am right now. A girl like Cathy Vega, too. She was raped to death. And the guy who did it got off scot-free. But that's not going to happen here."

He smirked at her, not believing her. Crouching, he tossed the knife from one hand to the other and laughed at her.

Lupe looked briefly over her shoulder at me and smiled. "You done good, Sherlock, but you can't take it far enough. I'm not going to lose this *cabron* in your court system to some guy with a five hundred dollar suit who don't know what time it is."

Armando Diaz grinned and raised the knife. "You won't do it, whore."

"That's it, *pendejo*. Come on. *Ven aca.*"

A spear of sunlight shimmered off the knife as he raised his arm from out of the darkness of the shadow of the willow.

"Come on, *pendejo*. Eat my pussy."

The blade of the knife flashed down. The gun exploded, and the air stung with the smell of it.

Armando Diaz fell, a hole in his gut, blood oozing in spurts across the simple white granite headstone of Virginia Rappe.

I stretched my arm out to Lupe, but she didn't see me.

The gun dropped from her hand and she turned away and walked to the edge of the lake that looked back at Dogtown. I heard her crying.

THE END

SOULTOWN
A Whitney Logan Mystery

by Mercedes Lambert

"She went up Noon Street," Pete Anglich said.
"A bad street for a white girl."
            —from Pickup on Noon Street, by Raymond Chandler

CHAPTER ONE

The moon slipped behind the eucalyptus trees. I sat up, stretched. It was nearly three in the morning. I must have knocked off. I'd been waiting and watching in my car for nearly five hours. A breeze began to blow from the west, and it made the leaves of the eucalyptus dance and chatter. From the other side of the trees came the persistent rumble of the 10 Freeway as crazy night riders raced into the dark.

I turned the radio dial. Oldies, black fuck music. Mexican love songs: "I suffer without you, my heart, my soul." I could make out some of the words because I've been studying Spanish at night school. "I suffer, I..."

I turned back to the oldies. It was a night for oldies. For "Earth Angel." For "Stagger Lee." "Only the Lonely." I twisted the rearview mirror. My hair was longer and still light from the summer. Nearly platinum. I'd started to wear makeup, and there was a line of black mascara smudged under my eyes. I swore as I used spit to wipe off the mascara. It would fucking figure I'd nod after waiting all this time.

It had been seven months since I'd seen Lupe.

I was probably the last person she'd want to see tonight.

The last time I'd seen her had been in court in February. For prostitution. And it had been six months before that when she'd vanished. In an instant I remembered everything again from that squalid August I wanted to forget. My office on Hollywood Boulevard. Lupe. My first dead person. Lupe. The gun. Lupe grabbing the gun from my hand. The explosion. Blood. The man on the ground bleeding to death. I'd promised Lupe she was safe, but she hadn't been. I hadn't been able to stop thinking about the enormity of my betrayal of her in Dogtown. She had good reason not to want to see me.

When Lupe disappeared that night at the end of August last year, she didn't come back to work the corner outside my office. She never called me. I looked for her on other blocks where women hustled. I looked on Western. I asked some of the girls I'd seen her talking to where she was, but all I got was a lot of attitude and more exposure to bad clothing.

The last I'd seen of her was in Division 40 in February. Just a few days after my twenty-seventh birthday. A Tuesday. The skies gray and unpredictable. Lupe wore the county blues and a pair of wrecked-looking K Mart brand tennis shoes. She had pulled her hair back into a tight ponytail, and I saw lines around her eyes that I had never noticed before. Her hands were shoved angrily into the pockets of the shapeless jumper that she had belted tightly around her slender waist.

Lupe shook her head almost imperceptibly as I started excitedly toward her in the jury box, where the defendants stand while awaiting arraignment. There are so many in and out of Division 40 that they don't even bother anymore to walk them in front of the judge's bench. She stood at the end of a line of six girls, three latinas and three blacks. The girls looked drained but restless, like they'd been up all night.

By then I had appeared many times in Division 40 on court-appointed burglaries, GTAs, and possession for sales. The bailiffs and clerks knew me. No one would stop me if I walked up to the box. A chicano bailiff stood between the latinas and the blacks per Sheriffs Department memo to keep them separated. The girl next to Lupe shivered and scratched at her arm. Lupe, her eyes rimmed in black liner, gave me the quick once-over.

I was wearing a new Anne Klein II suit, black, with a pale ivory silk blouse, and my pearls. Bally spectators. Black and white. I sat down in the first row with the other lawyers. I smiled at her, but she only stared back impassively. Someone called me by name.

Burt Schaefer, a lawyer I'd done some work for, said in a stage whisper, "A good morning, my little Miss Due Process. Ready to continue your battle for truth and justice today?"

I didn't answer Burt. I watched Lupe. I wanted to tell her how much I'd changed. I had to convince her I'd never tell anyone what had happened that freakish August in Dogtown.

"Très bien," Burt continued. "The PD's declaring unavailable on the broads. We'll all get one today."

I might get Lupe as a client! I nodded in Burt's direction as I continued to study Lupe. She was twenty-three now. Five feet four with long black hair that was curly from a new perm. She'd lost a little weight since I'd last seen her. Her eyes narrowed into hard dark slits as if she was thinking of something she didn't want to think about, but there was no further acknowledgment that she knew me. She turned away from me as the judge, who'd been in a side bar conference, laughed loudly and the City Attorney strutted back to his place at the counsel table, followed by an overweight and overworked looking PD.

"All right, ladies, just stand up when your name is called and we'll appoint a lawyer for you. You'll have time to talk later after we get everyone assigned."

My hands shook as I opened my briefcase on the chair beside me. I busied myself finding a pen so she couldn't see the flush I felt spreading across my face. The judge straightened the papers in front of him. With a flourish he called names. I saw Burt go forward to one of the black girls with Jheri curls and porcelain Wizard of Oz nails which curved at the end and were painted purple.

"Guadalupe Virginia Ramos."

Lupe stood and threw me a quick defiant look.

"Mr. Peralta, please."

Steve Peralta, a skinny weasel I've seen a million times in the court building high fiving with White Fence boys and taking cash from their grandmas, stood up. He walked over to Lupe and slipped her an oily card.

"...Miss Logan, please."

I went forward when the judge called my name. The PD leaned back in his chair and handed me a copy of a complaint and an arrest report on a Velma Roberts. A bloated black woman in her early thirties waited for me. Her hair was bleached nearly the color of mine. I glanced down at the papers. A 647. Solicitation. I nodded at the woman and gave her my card.

"Whitney Logan? What kind of name is that?" With a disappointed sigh, she stuffed the card in her pocket.

I glanced over at Lupe. Up close I saw she had an old bruise on her right cheek.

"You ever done this before?" asked the black woman. "You look like a social worker."

A grin lit up Lupe's face.

"Yes, Ms. Roberts, about a dozen times so far this year. I can take care of business as well as any lawyer here." I tried to erase the hostility I heard in my voice. "Don't worry, I know what to do."

She still looked skeptical.

Lupe dropped her gaze and examined Steve Peralta's card with exaggerated attention.

"All right, everyone, we're going to hear that motion now. Counsel, please get these cases ready. I'd like to resume the arraignments in about half an hour," ordered the judge.

The chicano sheriff and the other bailiff, Harley, a big white boy who likes to work out, took the women out of the jury box back into the lockup.

I asked the clerk to show me Lupe's file. I got my yellow legal pad and uncapped my pen.

Guadalupe Virginia Ramos.

Good. She had told me her real name. I flipped to the back of the papers to check her CII computer printout. No aliases. Good. Had she told me the truth about her record? No. Two prior arrests and convictions for prostitution. One in the end of '89 and the other the middle of last year. She'd lied. She'd said she'd only been arrested once. Third offense. She was looking at a county lid. A year. Ray Charles could see that coming.

I turned to the arrest report. February 17, 10:45 P.M. Approximate location Gardner just south of Sunset. I read quickly. Basically it came down to Lupe soliciting an undercover officer. I handed the file back to the clerk.

At the end of the jury box lounged Steve Peralta telling a loud story to

Harley and the other bailiff. He hadn't looked at Lupe's file yet.

"Hey, Steve," I interrupted. "You think we could trade cases?"

Steve looked at his audience. "They give you one that's too tough for you, Logan? Maybe you want to go back to the office and do a nice little divorce."

The chicano bailiff laughed politely with Steve. Harley looked uncomfortable, divided in his loyalties. Harley has asked me out in the past. He wanted to know if we could go pump iron together sometime. Only Harley seems to be aware of what is under this black Anne Klein II suit.

The hours at Gold's Gym. The repetitions. The cuts across my back that most people can't achieve without steroids. I can run twelve miles now. And do three times a week. Tae Kwon Do three times a week with Master Sun Lee out in North Hollywood. I am never going to be afraid again. That's what I've wanted to tell Lupe. That I will never again have the failure of nerve I had when she grabbed that gun from my hand and had to pull the trigger. That she is safe with me. That I am worthy of her respect. Of her confidence. That I am her friend.

"Fuck you, Steve."

I asked Harley to let me into the lockup. Steve followed, still grinning. Except for the low drone of Burt Schaefer's voice as he read the police report to his client, the holding cell was quiet. The women probably had a dismal sense of déjà vu. The light was yellow and unappetizing. The walls smeared with the bold but graceful *placas* of Sad Eyes, Mousie, and La Donna. I hung back slightly, watching. Steve called Lupe's name.

Lupe rose from the concrete bench, tilted her chin grandly, then cast her magnificent brown eyes in his direction. She strutted forward.

"Save it, sweetheart," sneered Steve. "I'm going to try to fix it so you don't have to put that thing on ice for a long time."

I saw the muscles tighten around Lupe's mouth, but then she formed a slow, beautiful, gracious smile for him. He opened the police report, which he read quickly to himself. He snapped it shut.

"Anyone who can bail you out?" he asked her.

Lupe's eyes flickered toward me.

"*¿La fianza?*" he repeated when she didn't answer. "Five hundred bucks." I started forward.

"Hey, you, Logan, ain't you here to help me?" Velma Roberts lumbered forward to the bars.

Lupe turned toward Steve Peralta and shook her head. She moved so that her back was to me. She said something to him in a voice I couldn't hear.

"I don't got all day," Velma Roberts insisted.

I smiled professionally at her and nodded, trying to overhear what Peralta was telling Lupe.

Velma Roberts banged on the bars. "I got to get out of here. I got two little babies. The county'll take 'em away from me if you don't get me out of here."

I went to work. Velma Roberts was a strawberry. A strung-out pro. She grabbed the bars of the cell impatiently as I did my introductory schmooze, explained the arraignment, and talked about her constitutional right to a jury trial. I mentioned her prior. I glanced quickly toward Lupe again, but her back was still to me as she talked with Steve Peralta. Forcing myself to concentrate on Velma Roberts, I cited statistics and told her I'd find out what kind of deal I could cut with the City Attorney. Velma Robert's eyes were bloodshot. She was fat the way some women are when they're on the pipe. Smoke for two or three days, don't eat or sleep, then crash, come to and eat everything. The stop-me-before-I-kill-again kind of eating.

Steve and Burt were gone by the time I finished. Lupe lounged against the back wall talking with one of the other latinas. I walked down to the end of the cell until I was opposite her. Velma Roberts and the black girls stopped humming. The latina nodded toward me as she asked Lupe a question. Lupe looked at me without replying. She pushed herself away from the wall and strolled toward me.

"You like?" Lupe placed her hands on her hips so the coarse blue dress clung to her. "It's Susan Hayward. *I Want to Live.*"

"I been looking for you, Lupe. For months. I didn't want to see you here." I sighed wearily. "A defendant."

"Citizen accused," she bristled.

"Right, soliciting a vice cop. I thought you were too smart for that."

"Pigs were trippin'. Another one of those fucking sweeps. It's keeping you busy, though, isn't it? New suit?"

"I've been worried about you. I wanted to find you and"—I lowered my voice—"tell you I'd never tell anyone what—"

"I ain't gonna talk about it."

Had she been able to forget Dogtown? "It's just... I thought we were... after everything that happened... friends."

"You still think I'm Myrna Loy? Forget it. I ain't interested in no *Thin Man* shit."

"I can bail you out." I'd never let Lupe know how broke I was. How little work I had. All the money I owed on my credit cards for silk and gabardine suits for work, an Hermès purse, so I'd look as if I was really making it as an attorney. Sometimes I had to use the cards to buy my groceries. I could come up with five hundred bucks for Lupe in a couple of hours—even if it meant asking my folks for the money.

Lupe leaned against the bars so her face was inches from mine. She smelled like cinnamon gum and Chanel No. 5. "My boyfriend'll bail me out."

"Yeah? Which one? One of your tricks? Where is he? Where's your brother, Hector? I don't see them here waving wads of cash."

"I didn't call yet." She snapped her gum like she was bored.

"You're not going to call. Not Hector. I was there when he told you he was going to kick your butt and take your boy Joey from you if you didn't quit prostituting. You're always talking about what a good mother you are—so what happened to Joey last August anyway?"

Lupe stood up straighter and shifted uneasily from one foot to the other.

"He's with my mother."

"That's where he was all along?"

She sighed. "Yeah. When I went home that night after... He was asleep at my mom's. I promised her she'd never have to worry about Joey. Or about me. We was sitting at the kitchen table. She started to cry. Then Hector came in and he told me that if I fucked up again he'd have Joey taken away from me for good." She looked away. Was she going to cry?

"Let me help you. I'll pay your bail."

"¿Qué pasa, Lupe?" called the latina from the back of the cell. "Hay un problema?"

Lupe turned and shook her head. "No, no. Un momento, 'mana. " She leaned toward me again with a hard look on her face. "I'm going to take care of myself. My way. My boyfriend'll bail me out. I'll give Steve Peralta a blowjob. I'm not doing any time. I'm going home, I'll get Joey, and I'll enroll him in Montessori school."

"Yo te ayudo."

"You speak Spanish now?" She looked amused.

I nodded. "LA's forty percent Latino now. A lot of my clients—"

"Sí, sí. Alta California. La tierra de mi raza. "

"Not too fast. I've only had one semester."

"Alta California. The land white people stole from Mexico. That's what's wrong with you. White guilt. That's why you try to hang out with me. I got my own homegirls"—she jerked her thumb toward the chola leaning against the wall—"and I don't want your help. Leave me alone. Forget you ever knew me. And nobody's ever going to take Joey away from me again. Not Hector, not my mother. Not the pinchi Departamento of Social Services. I'll be out of this hole in a couple hours." She let go of the bars and pointed at my Bally spectators as she backed away from me. "Nice kicks. That's one thing I'll say about you. You always got nice kicks." Then she turned to her friend and resumed the conversation I'd interrupted.

I walked to the door that led back into the courtroom and knocked. Behind me I heard Lupe's voice and that of the other woman, tropical and light like breezes stirring the palms. I knocked again. I heard them laugh. Finally Harley opened the door and let me out into Division 40, where this time the jury box was full of men being shuffled through their arraignments.

That was seven months ago. Lupe had drawn a county lid and had done six months good time. She'd gone down a lot faster than Velma Roberts, who held out for a jury trial—a real circus with Velma testifying against my advice. Before the trial I'd been to Sybil Brand Institute for Women to see Velma on a last-ditch effort to get her to cop a plea; while I was there I sent Lupe a visit-request form from the attorney conference room, but she refused to see me. I sent her two letters and they came back unopened. Now Lupe's six months were up.

Was I an idiot to be waiting in my car in the middle of the night for her? I finished wiping the mascara off. I opened y purse for more and for my Chanel Tempting Red lipstick. They were at the bottom of my purse. Under the snub-nosed .38 two-inch detective special I bought in my local shopping mall last fall. I have a license. The gun is legal, but carrying it concealed is not. If I'm ever stopped I will say I'm coming from the range and forgot to put it back in the trunk of my car. I've spent many hours at the range. I can load this .38 in the dark and I can take a man's head off at twenty-five yards. At least on paper targets. Lupe never believed I was competent at anything.

In front of me, drenched in cinematic moonlight, stretched the uninspired and poorly landscaped facade of Sybil Brand Institute for Women. At SBI they like to process the women out after midnight.

I put on more mascara and some lipstick. A gate on the south end of the building began to open. There was activity in the sheriff's office at that entrance. I heard an intercom being activated and voices I couldn't understand. A woman appeared in Sybil's open doorway, then stepped without hesitation into the passage between the jail and the fence separating the two worlds.

It was Lupe. Even thinner than when I saw her arraigned. Dressed in a tight red skirt and a purple spandex bustier. Her red stilettos clicked across the pavement. The moonlight danced between us. A sluggish female sheriff stepped out of the guard box and unlocked the gate for Lupe.

I opened my car door and got out.

Los Angeles was a dream on the other side of the freeway. The damp breeze blew again from the west and Lupe raised her arms above her head triumphantly embracing the sky like Judy Garland striding onto the stage of the Palladium.

"*Nuestra Señora Reina de Los Angeles,* this is your daughter." Lupe threw back her head and laughed.

I walked to the front of the car. Lupe walked toward me.

"Thought you might need a ride." I pointed at my old car.

"You have a hard time minding your own business, don't you?"

"It's impossible to get a cab up here. The buses aren't running for another couple hours."

Lupe shook her head. She had a tiny black tear painted under her left eye. "Every time I see you there's trouble. I don't want any trouble. Today's the first day of the rest of my life."

"Want me to drive you to the bus stop? Down on Eastern? You can wait till the sun comes up."

"Ten days I knew you. Less than ten days," she said angrily. "And two people got killed." Lupe frowned and looked away into the distance. I knew then that she thought about what happened in Dogtown as much as I did.

"That's why I've been chasing after you, to tell you I'll never tell anyone. Why can't you believe that? I think you got busted this last time because you wanted to get caught. You wanted to be punished."

Lupe stared at me in disbelief. "You are a real piece of work, you know that? Wanted to get caught! Fucking pig was wearing a Brooks Brothers suit and a hearing aid."

I got in and started the engine. "Fine. Do whatever makes you happy. Wait for the bus. I'm leaving." I gunned the engine as I switched on the lights.

The headlights illuminated the front of the jail. In front of them Lupe stood cast in dramatic shadows. She kissed her fingertips and blew the kiss into the wind. She took one last look at the jail, then walked over and opened the passenger door. She got into my car. I pulled it in a U and headed out of the parking lot.

"Take me to get something to eat," Lupe said. "Then over to get Joey. My mom don't get up till around six."

I nodded. I would take Lupe to the Pantry on Figueroa and 9th. It's open twenty-four hours. They have giant breakfasts, steak, eggs, and pancakes. She'd like a good meal. Maybe she wouldn't notice it was only a few blocks from the garment district where we had found a dead body that dangerous August.

"Just breakfast. And go get Joey. That's it, ¿entiendes?"

I nodded again. I had wanted her to mention my makeup, to notice how I'd changed, but she stared out the window at the dark hills. I heard her heave a sigh of relief as I pulled onto the freeway.

CHAPTER TWO

The old Pantry restaurant was crowded at four-thirty in the morning. Working men in jeans and construction boots. Drunks speaking loudly above the clatter of silverware falling on the floor. Rockers in black leather. Waiters in long white aprons hurried from the grill to the tables carrying big plates with eggs, ham, and pancakes hanging over the edges. We took a table in the back. Men stared at Lupe as she strolled down the sawdust-covered aisle. She seemed to grow taller under their inspection, but she took a chair so her back was to the room. I pulled out my chair, a bit miffed. I have a better body than Lupe. I work hard on it.

A waiter with a coffeepot appeared at our table as soon as we sat down. These are real waiters. Men who do it for a living. Not the ones who tell you their names. "Hi, my name is Ted. I'll be back with your burger unless my agent calls."

Lupe glanced over her shoulder to inspect the menu written on a black-board attached to the wall "Bacon, extra done, two eggs over easy, rye toast, dry. A large oj. Short stack. This comes with potatoes, doesn't it?"

A girl can work up a real appetite in jail.

The waiter took my order and left. Lupe reached for her coffee. "Man, I'm beat. Been up since five yesterday morning."

I touched Lupe's wrist. "What's this?" The name "Joan" was tattooed on the pale brown skin of her inner wrist.

She put the cup down and laid her arm on the table. Her skin was warm. My fingers jumped away from it.

"Someone you met in jail?" I didn't want to look her in the face. I kept staring at her wrist. I could see the smeared letters were written with black eyeliner pencil.

Lupe's laugh sounded like one of those snooty-talking cats on tv commercials. "Jealous?"

"Why do you want to mark yourself up like that?"

"You got a boyfriend yet?"

I didn't say anything. The last one, if you could call him that, had been the commodities broker nearly two years ago. I guess some people would think two years is a long time to go without a date.

The waiter interrupted with the food.

Lupe spooned fried egg onto toast and smiled smugly. "No one?" She popped the toast into her mouth and chewed noisily. "Tell you what I'm going to do for you. Since you're giving me a ride and all. I'm going to help you get laid. We're going to find you some nice *vato*. Maybe a lawyer."

"I don't like lawyers!"

"Nobody does. But it's someplace to start." She prodded the other egg so the yolk ran.

"So who's Joan?"

Lupe shook her head as if I was hopeless. "Crawford. Of course. *Rain. Above Suspicion. Mildred Pierce.*"

I dumped more tabasco sauce on my scrambled eggs. "Haven't you given that old movie star stuff up yet? Take a look at your life. You're twenty-three years old..."

"Twenty-two."

"...still standing on street corners, three-time loser in the county system." I shook my head. "The old Hollywood. It's just a dream. Always has been."

Lupe shook her head. "Joan? A dream? A star! She never took shit from anyone. And I'm sure she didn't have any trouble getting laid."

I put my fork down with finality. Lots of men look at me. Every day. They'd love it if I'd talk to them. "I don't have any trouble. I can get as many men as I want. Whenever I want."

"It's been at least a year, hasn't it?" Lupe inquired knowingly.

I stood and picked up the check. "Let's go. Your mom'll be up soon."

Lupe checked her makeup and put on dark lipstick before she rose to face the room. I heard the click of her heels behind me and the excited murmuring of stockbrokers and construction workers in her wake.

The sun was just coming up as we pulled in front of the house she shared with her mother on Floral in East LA. It was a small wooden place painted yellow. There were black bars on all the windows, and the wrought-iron screen door looked like something out of a medieval dungeon. Red hibiscus flanked the front door. An ineffectual-looking fence separated the property from the neighboring similarly fortressed residences.

"Where's my car?" Lupe wondered.

I looked up and down the block. Lupe's red Fiat with the primer gray passenger door was nowhere to be seen.

"They're keeping it in the garage for you."

"These houses don't have garages," she snapped impatiently. "If they did, everyone's cousin from Michoacan would be living in them."

"Maybe Hector's driving it," I offered.

She shook her head. "He's got a Camaro. Real cherry."

It didn't look as if anyone was up in Lupe's house. None of the lights was on. I heard radio music coming from the other houses. Juan Gabriel was singing. I'd been listening to his records on the border radio all summer long. A guy walked out of a faded green house across the street and began to water the parched lawn.

"Thanks for the ride." Lupe got out of the car.

"I'll wait to make sure things are ok."

"Of course they are. My mom expects me. I called her from jail yesterday and told her I was getting out. She'll be making *huevos rancheros* for me and hot chocolate. Joey will be there in the kitchen all dressed up for me in a new shirt." Lupe opened the gate to the house. *"Adiós."*

Lupe walked up the sidewalk to the front door. She took a key from her cheap black vinyl purse, opened the door, and went inside without looking back. I sat in the car. Everything I'd wanted to tell her, that I'd been rehearsing for months, and I hadn't been able to say a word. I'd practiced over and over in front of my bathroom mirror. *Lupe, I'm sorry. It was my fault. I should never have gotten you involved. I'll never tell your secret.* That's the way I wanted to tell her. One long breakneck confession and it would be over forever. We would be free. The smell of her drugstore perfume permeated the car.

I turned the ignition on. It was Tuesday. I didn't have any court appearances to do. Although I was getting at least two or three appointments per month from the Superior Court and was still doing some of Burt Schaefer's overflow, I was barely making ends meet. Harvey Kaplan, my office landlord, had raised my rent at the beginning of the summer to $650. Not an unfair price considering the size of the office and the use of Harvey's library, but it was on one of the worst stretches of Hollywood Boulevard, a block and a half west of Western Avenue, Le Sex Shoppe, and a group of video arcades populated by crack dealers and Vietnamese street gangs. The sun was rising. It would be another hot day. I took my sunglasses from the glove compartment. I should go down to the Torrance courthouse and try again to get on their list to pick up some cases. I was aware I was moving slowly.

I looked at Lupe's house again. It was probably built in the forties. That's ancient for Los Angeles. She'd never told me what her mother did. Or anything about her father. Did they own the house or rent? Was there a father? Was he like my father? I pushed that thought out of my head. I do not like to think about my father. Three neatly trimmed rosebushes struggled for recognition at the south end of the building beneath an open window I presumed to be the kitchen. A woman in her early fifties appeared in the window.

It had to be Lupe's mother. I let the car idle. The woman stepped nearly out of view as though retreating from someone. An angry Lupe appeared in the window. She was yelling at her mother in Spanish.

"¿...por qué?"

"Cálmate, hija...," her mother entreated.

They moved away from the window, but the yelling continued. I heard a dish break. I was wondering whether to go up to the house when the front door was flung open and an irate Lupe came flying down the steps with her purse in one hand and a scrap of paper clutched in the other. She threw the gate open, and it slammed shut behind her.

"Hector came a few nights ago and took Joey from my mom! He says I ain't fit to raise him 'cause I was in jail!" Lupe exclaimed angrily as she climbed into my car. "He's got a new girlfriend. Some slant. A waitress. My mom thinks they're in Koreatown. It's a fucking miracle she even knows the name of the dive where this muff works, but the girl gave Hector a crummy calendar to give my mom as a present. Look, it's got the name and address on it." Lupe dangled the torn piece of paper in front of me. "Girl's named Kim. How fucking typical. Kim."

I put the car into drive. "I presume this means you'd like me to take you to Koreatown."

Lupe nodded unhappily. "Hector took my car and gave it to his slutty girlfriend to use."

I grinned to myself. Now I'd have time to tell Lupe everything and let her see how well things were going with me. I drove down her street to Brooklyn Avenue, hung a right and pointed the car toward the Civic Center. I didn't know exactly where Koreatown was, although I'd seen an exit sign for it on the Santa Monica freeway. I had no idea then how big Koreatown was and how crooked the streets.

Lupe fidgeted restlessly next to me as I headed west. We crossed the bridge from East Los to the edge of JTown and then through downtown past the courthouse and up over the hill into *Varrio Loco Nuevo*. She turned on the radio. I had it set to a rock station that spins the same kind of hard-driving bass-heavy hysteria played at Gold's Gym. Good music for working out. Massages the adrenals. It is good music for driving.

"Goddamn it. I hate that noise." Impatiently Lupe switched stations. The soothing soft guitar sounds of some Mexican troubador filled the air and she relaxed slightly. "How could I be friends with someone who listens to that crap? I know you like me, Whitney. I know it would please your commie red heart to be friends with an actual brown person from a lower socioeconomic group, but your shit gives me a headache."

I made another turn and we rolled down to 8th Street. There were no signs for Koreatown. It was all one big Central American refugee camp with dingy laundry hanging out of open apartment windows.

"We can't be friends because we have different taste in music? That seems pretty superficial." Didn't she care about the deeper values I could bring to a friendship? Loyalty, honesty

Lupe nodded. "Gotta draw the line somewhere." She examined the torn piece of paper. "Cafe James Dean."

"Doesn't sound very Korean," I said knowledgeably as I made the turn down to Olympic Boulevard.

Ahead of us stretched the boulevard, waves of heat shimmering and shaking above the blacktop. Lupe shifted restlessly in her seat. The sun, a silent marauding disk of orange and gold, licked at the locked windows of the buildings lining the street.

"5757 Olympic. Hope they're open." She stared out the car window at the changing languages of signs above businesses as we neared Vermont. Spanish. Broken English. Then dense incomprehensible Korean. "What do Koreans eat for breakfast?"

I thought it was a joke and waited for the punch line, but Lupe lapsed into her own thoughts.

This area was once a series of fashionable suburban streets of single-family white upper-middle-class homes built between 1890 and 1910. Now everything was Korean. Hanmi Bank. Amorean Cosmetics. Banners lettered with black square self-contained characters of an imposing secret language. Office buildings, computer stores, dozens of small restaurants, beauty salons with pictures of white women with stiff permanents in the front windows. Small groups of Central American men hung out in front of a building supply store hoping to be hired as day laborers.

Last spring Koreatown was in flames; today only a warm breeze up from the Sea of Cortez whispered through the streets.

"There it is," Lupe announced.

I slowed the car down, but all I saw was a couple of Salvadoran schoolgirls in blue plaid Catholic school uniforms, rolled into miniskirts, at a bus stop.

"Over there," Lupe insisted. In a minimall at the end of the block on the north side of the street, I spotted Cafe James Dean.

Lupe yanked down the sun visor and checked herself in the mirror. She did a quick number again with her dark red lipstick. She tugged the purple spandex bustier up so slightly less cleavage showed.

I pulled into the driveway of the minimall and parked two doors away from the cafe in front of a bakery. There was a CLOSED sign on the restaurant, but the bakery was open.

"Let's go in," I said, indicating the bakery. "We'll buy something. Act like we have some purpose for being here, then we'll look around."

Sullenly Lupe followed me in. Three large glass counters were filled with red, green, and brown things in plastic bags. A Korean woman in a white smock stood behind the counter. A flicker of suspicion flashed in her eyes; she quickly replaced the look with one of attentive but guarded shopkeeper courtesy. I picked up the nearest bag of red things. Honey rice cakes. It was labeled in Korean and English.

"Made out of rice?" I asked.

"Everything made out of rice."

With the bag of red things still in my hand I looked around the bakery. Pale cookies. Ladyfingers. Five-layer wedding cakes decorated with doves and white sugar bells. "Are these sweet?"

A disdainful look flashed across the woman's face. I wondered if she was suspicious because I was white or because Lupe looked Mexican. Maybe she just didn't like having a woman dressed like a hooker in her store. She snatched the bag from me and replaced it with a bag of the brown things. "Three dollar."

I paid. "When does the restaurant next door open?"

The money disappeared into the cash register. "Don't know."

I heard Lupe slam out the door behind me.

"You think this is a goddamn sightseeing tour?" she said angrily when I came out of the bakery. It was nearly eight. The street was full now of cars headed downtown. The door of a video store plastered with posters of martial arts movies opened. A middle-aged man came out to sweep the sidewalk in front of his business. I wanted to point out the posters and tell Lupe I was studying Tae Kwon Do, but she'd already walked away toward the west end of the building. I hurried after her to the entrance of Cafe James Dean.

The front door was red. There were no windows. A red sign above the door spelled out the name in stiff black script. There was no sign about the hours it was open, no menu posted. I tried the door, but it was locked. Lupe rounded the corner of the building. An alley ran behind the businesses.

A fairly new blue Toyota van with more of the ubiquitous black Korean characters painted on the side was parked outside the back door of the restaurant. The van was closed up, but I imagined it was a supplier of some kind of food product. Lupe stepped in front of the van and peered in its illegally tinted window.

The back door of Cafe James Dean was slightly open. Lupe turned from the van to the door. She put one hand on the door.

"Are you sure it's ok?" I asked. "It's awful early."

She gave me the look that said I was hopeless and pushed open the door.

Three men with big knives stared back at us. With fingers wrapped loosely and familiarly around knives flying like flashes of silver lightning, they hacked at a bloody carcass.

"¿Quienes son?" one of the men demanded. Blood dripped from the knife he held in front of him.

Because they were short, deep caramel colored, and Indian looking, I guessed they were Salvadoran or Guatemalan. Boxes of unfamiliar vegetables and roots were piled between them where they sat in the anteroom of the restaurant's kitchen. The other two men stopped their savage chopping, their knives hovering in the air.

"*¿Dónde está la mujer Kim?*" Lupe asked. I glanced at the oozing carcass. Was it a pig?

The boldest of the Salvadorans pointed his knife into the kitchen. A large commercial stove and refrigerator took up one wall and in the center of the room was a large wooden prep counter covered with chickens' feet. A middle-aged Korean man prodded another animal carcass in a huge stainless steel cauldron of boiling water. A white-clad woman, her apron smeared with blood, looked up from the other end of the counter where she was making dumplings.

"I want to see Kim," Lupe announced loudly to the chefs.

"Kim John Oh?" the man asked. They looked questioningly at each other over the cans of food, bottles of oil, jars of spices. A glossy calendar with a generic beautiful Korean woman posed uncomfortably but proudly in front of a painted backdrop of craggy mountains hung on the wall.

"I know she's here," Lupe insisted as the man and woman drew closer to the door that led into the dining area. "Kim. Kim," Lupe yelled.

The dumpling woman started toward Lupe. "You go now!"

The man said something to the woman before turning away to gather a large handful of crushed dried herb, which he threw into the boiling water he tended.

"Kim. Kim," Lupe cried out again.

The door to the dining area swung open, and into the kitchen strode a gorgeous woman in her late twenties. Her black hair was tied loosely back with a shiny gold-colored ornament and fell nearly to her waist. Her complexion was flawless and pale. She had on complete eye makeup although it was early in the day. She had a fine shape, slender but with tits that looked too good to be true. She wore a pair of skintight black Levi 501s, a cheap-looking pair of red high-heeled sandals, and a USC t-shirt. Even in the cheap heels she was only about five feet three.

"You Kim?" Lupe said aggressively. I saw she too was surprised by the woman's beauty. "You with Hector?"

I remembered Lupe's brother, Hector "Manos" Ramos. Bullet head. Punch-drunk. Fucked-up nose from being broken so many times. What would a fox like this be doing with Hector?

The woman folded her arms and nodded her head. "Are you Hector's sister?" Her English was perfect. "Hector said you were in jail and wouldn't be back until the end of the year."

"Jail!" Lupe exclaimed. "I was in the navy. The S.S. *Sybil*. We just docked. I hear you been taking care of my little boy for me, and I came to get him."

"I can't give Joey to anyone except Hector."

"This is my lawyer." Lupe jerked her thumb in my direction. I tried to look professional. "Let's not have any problems."

"You don't have any guardianship papers or anything giving you temporary custody, do you?" I asked. "A power of attorney signed by Ms. Ramos perhaps?"

Kim shook her head.

"I thought not. It is the legally correct thing for you to turn the boy over now. Hector doesn't have any legal claim to him either."

"But Hector said "

"Where's Joey? Is he here?" Lupe pushed open the swinging door into the dining room.

The dining room was paneled with pale pine, and black vinyl booths lined the perimeter. Six tables of the same pale wood were placed in the center of the room. A painted seascape mural of a port giving off to a huge vista of ocean covered one wall. There was no one in the room.

Lupe looked back in anger and confusion. "Where is he?"

Kim stood leaning against one of the booths. "At my godmother's. I go to bed late and get up early." I had a sudden hideous vision of Hector on top of the beautiful Kim. What could she see in him? How had they met? Weren't latinos supposed to have the smallest dicks in the world?

"Let's go get him," I heard myself say. "I'll drive."

Kim hesitated.

"Don't make me call the police. You don't have any papers," said Lupe. "We want to be friends. Particularly if you're my brother's squeeze."

Kim swung open the door to the kitchen again and we followed her. She said something in rapid high-pitched Korean to the man and woman who worked in the kitchen. I wondered if they were relatives of hers. I'd heard the Koreans all worked together in family businesses. The woman sputtered with annoyance as Kim took a navy Chanel purse that looked real down from a shelf and led us out.

Kim looked at my old Datsun with displeasure. She and Lupe stood by the passenger door glaring at each other until Lupe finally opened the door and climbed into the backseat.

"Where to?" I asked.

"My godmother lives nearby, over on San Lorenzo," said Kim.

"Hmm," Lupe snorted from the backseat. "Ever notice the majority of the streets in LA are named after Spanish saints?"

I told Kim I didn't know where it was and I needed directions. She told me to go around the block and back toward Vermont. Past Jack's Liquor, past a Lutheran church, past Raul's Barbershop—"*Se habla español*—We specialize in flattops." Behind the commercial din of Olympic it was all residential. Apartment buildings and small boxy stuccos. This area west of downtown was once a desirable place for middle-class dwellings. Today it is all immigrants. People who have arrived here within the last ten years.

Two or three families in one house. The northern boundary, Wilshire Boulevard—"the Champs-Elysees of Los Angeles" as it was known in the twenties—is just another strip of minimalls.

Bamboo and squatty palms grew in front of the desperate stuccos. Birds of paradise fluttered in yards of dull-looking grass and gravel. A garden was terraced with green and white stones. Some of the trees and shrubs were severely clipped like bonsai.

"That's it," said Kim. "3333. She lives upstairs in the back. Number 4."

It was a streamline "moderne" apartment building of not more than ten units. I parked in front and we all got out of the car. Kim led the way down the sidewalk and into the building. We climbed the stairs. It was quiet, as if everybody had gone off to work.

Lupe touched her hair nervously, trying to rearrange it. It was six months since she'd seen Joey.

We walked to the back of the building. I heard the murmur of a man's voice speaking a language I couldn't make out but assumed was Korean. Kim stopped abruptly outside the door to number four. A woman's voice said something back to the man, shrill, urgent. Kim shook her head as though it would help her to understand. A noise like a piece of furniture being pushed across the floor snuffed out their voices.

"What's going on in there?" Lupe demanded.

Kim quickly unlocked the door. Lupe pushed her aside and stepped into the small foyer. I was right behind her. Two elderly Korean women dressed in long, full, fuchsia-colored skirts and short black jackets were bound together with extension cords in front of a white couch. The younger one had blood running down her cheek from a cut made by the cord's plug. We heard the squeak of another piece of furniture being pushed aside in the next room.

"Godmother!" Kim said in a low voice.

The old woman saw Kim and replied quickly in a whisper.

Kim bit her lip and nodded. She shoved Lupe toward an open door to the left of the foyer. It led into the kitchen.

"What the fuck is this?" Lupe snarled.

I heard soft footsteps coming from the back of the apartment into the living room. Had we been heard? I grabbed Lupe by the arm and pulled her into the kitchen to try to get us out of sight of whoever else was in the apartment. There was another door connecting the kitchen to a dining area that adjoined the living room. The dining area had no windows and was crowded with china cabinets lining the walls. Within the partial shadows I hoped the cabinets blocked us from view. We pressed against the wall and held our breath as we peered into the living room.

A man in a sharp black two-button suit and a black hat, his face hidden by a pink mask painted with black eyes and a garish mouth, dragged a crying boy into the room. It was Joey! The man held a huge ugly 9mm Browning automatic with a silencer on it. He said something angrily to the godmother and jerked the boy by the arm for emphasis.

Lupe edged forward, but I grabbed her around the waist, pulling her back, and clamped my other hand over her mouth. Kim sank silently down against the wall.

"Ahnee, ahnee," cried the other woman, who had been silent. She kicked wildly at the man, trying to get him in the nuts.

The man threw Joey aside so that he hit the floor. Lupe bit into my hand. I saw the man's finger squeeze the trigger. The left side of the crying woman's face exploded and splattered the couch with blood, tissue, and something gray I knew was brain.

CHAPTER THREE

The man pointed the gun at Kim's godmother, who sprawled weeping across the other woman's body. Her face and gown were speckled as though with confetti by the moist but dead remains. I wondered if she was in shock. My stomach swirled. I felt like throwing up. Joey howled. The man asked the godmother a question, then slapped her several times when she didn't answer. Kim clenched her hands together as if she was going to pray. The godmother nodded wearily toward the southeast corner of the room, where a rosewood cabinet with a Sony tv on top of it stood.

The man crossed the room toward the dining area. I tightened my grip on Lupe. The room was still spinning in front of me, and I could taste bile and other dark things in my throat. If he saw us he'd probably kill us too. I needed to get my gun, but it was at the bottom of my purse. I noticed he was wearing Bally loafers. His suit was good gabardine, and he wore an incongruous Brit public-school-type tie that contrasted bizarrely with his hideous mask. For a lunatic instant it made me think of Richard Nixon, and I nearly laughed out loud.

He pulled the cabinet drawers open and messed the contents around noisily with one hand. He was less than fifteen feet from us. Grunting with approval he pulled out a small black-and-gold chest inlaid with mother of pearl. He unfastened the clasp and looked inside with satisfaction.

Kim sighed unhappily. I glanced at her to tell her to shut up. How much longer before he heard us? I had to act before he found us. Another wave of nausea swept through me. Lupe moved impatiently against me. I let go of her waist. My hand brushed against her ass as I opened my black purse. Her hair smelled like gardenias. I forced my hand as quietly as I could to the bottom of my purse. I gripped my .38 and brought it out. Six shots. I could blow him away from where I was. It wouldn't be hard to explain why I'd shot him in the back. Lupe and Kim would verify my story. The man stopped. The gun was in his right hand. He cocked his head and looked around the room.

Kim looked at me curiously. I'd been on the range at least twice a week, sometimes three or four times if I'd had a bad time in court. If some ball-heavy moronic cop lied to me on the stand. If some shithead cut me off on the freeway. My intentions were not always good.

I drew the gun up and aimed. Kim nodded. "Do it," she mouthed. "Kill him." I felt Lupe's hot tears on my left hand, which still clamped her mouth. I knew why she was crying. She didn't think I could make the shot. She thought I'd hit Joey.

Joey howled again, still trying to get to his feet, but the masked man pushed him down as he strode toward the toppled old women. The man spat out a nasty triumphant phrase. The godmother raised her head. She was pale and creased by time, but I saw hatred in her eyes. He stuck the gun in her face so that it was almost up her nose. My heart stopped beating. I steadied my arm against Lupe and had him dead in my sights. I felt the cold edge of steel. Lupe moaned, shaking her head no. I fingered the trigger, ready to pull.

The man put his gun back into a shoulder holster and buttoned his jacket neatly into place. I glanced at Kim, who was crying silently. A bead of sweat rolled down my cheek. I let my finger ease away from the trigger. Clutching the black-and-gold chest, the man bowed condescendingly to the old woman. Kim nudged the kitchen door closed with her foot as the man turned toward the hall and the kitchen. I heard his footsteps pass by us, then the front door open.

I pushed Lupe away and stepped into the foyer in time to see him starting down the steps. I pulled the trigger, but missed him as he turned down the stairs to the landing on the first floor. He spun around. Seeing his hand come up with the gun I threw myself on the floor. A silent shot slammed into the wall behind me. Then he was gone.

Kim ran sobbing from the kitchen to her godmother.

"Joey!" Lupe rushed for her son.

I got up and shakily shoved the gun into the waistband of my jeans. I'd shot at someone! It seemed to me that it had happened fast, without thinking. Like losing your virginity on a clumsy summer night. I always imagined that if I ever had to shoot at a real person I'd feel something large, mysterious, and existential. But all I'd felt was scared and angry. I closed the front door. None of the neighbors had come out to see what was happening. That's how it is now: you hear gunshots and you mind your own business. Turn up the television. I looked to the living room. Kim held her godmother and murmured to her in Korean while struggling with the knots in the extension cords that bound the two old women.

I went over and knelt by the couch. The dead woman was chubby and brightly made up. She looked as if she'd been fun while she was alive. The broken cavity where the left side of her face had been continued to ooze slowly onto the couch. I'd done a voluntary manslaughter case with Burt Schaefer earlier in the year. Some poor dumb chicano in his early thirties from Montebello who'd clubbed in his girlfriend's head with a wrench while he was dead drunk. I'd had to study the autopsy photos and go to the UCLA medical library to look at more pictures of skull injuries, but nothing had prepared me for the pink and gray mess slithering down the dead woman's face and across her black silk bodice. My hands moved as in a dream, flying flying flying like a swarm of swallows across a wretched red sunset as I pulled at the knots.

I untied the women. Kim pulled her godmother away from the dead body and cradled her in her arms. The old woman went limp. She closed her eyes for what seemed like a long time. Kim continued murmuring in Korean. Finally the old woman's eyes fluttered open and she noticed me. She stared into my face for a few seconds before glancing down at my gun.

"You should have killed him."

I stared back at her in surprise. She spoke heavily accented but perfect English.

She struggled to her feet. "I must get a blanket." She motioned toward the body.

"I'll get it, Dorothy," Kim interjected, but the old woman shook her head and shuffled across the room toward a hall leading to her bedroom. Dorothy seemed like a weird name for a Korean. On the floor Lupe hugged the strangely silent Joey, shielding him so he couldn't see the dead body.

"Who's this?" I whispered to Kim across the body between us.

"Come on, Whitney, skip the small talk," Lupe growled. "Let's get the hell out of here."

Kim ignored her. "Jin."

"Jin Oh." The old woman reentered the living room carrying a sky blue coverlet. She started to cry again. "My sister."

"Why'd that guy kill her?" I asked, but the old woman called Dorothy seemed unable to speak anymore.

Joey got up from the floor where Lupe was holding him on her lap. He tried to totter toward the old woman, but Lupe grabbed him and covered his eyes so he wouldn't see the sprawling body beyond Dorothy. I wondered if Joey knew what death was. He was probably too young.

The dead woman's hand twitched violently. The dead don't just drop the way they do in the movies. The muscles keep contorting. Kim's godmother knelt near me on the floor by the couch. She took her sister's hand in both of hers and kissed it before wrapping the quilt around Jin Oh.

Lupe broke the silence. "How long's Joey been here? Did that guy do anything to him?"

The old woman shook her head.

"Just since last night," Kim said. "I already told you that."

The old woman nodded in agreement as she rose to her feet again. "You must be Joey's mother. Kim told me about you. He's a good boy. Jin and I took him to McDonald's last night." Tears ran down her face again.

"Who's that guy? Why'd he kill your sister? You didn't answer my question." Lupe got to her feet clutching Joey, who started to whine.

"What were they saying to each other?" I asked. "Did he kill her because of that box he took?"

Kim's godmother looked quizzically at me, then at Kim.

"I'm Whitney Logan. A friend of Lupe's." I jerked my thumb in the direction of Lupe, who didn't contradict me.

"Why are you carrying a gun?" the old woman wondered.

"Yeah, why are you carrying a gun?" Lupe asked.

I shrugged. "Protection."

"Are you a detective?" asked the old lady.

"Not exactly, but in the past I have helped—"

Lupe shook her head in disbelief. "You're a lawyer. With an office on Hollywood Boulevard."

"Dorothy, I'm going to call the police," Kim announced.

The old woman shook her head angrily. "Didn't you hear what he said? That he'd kill me if I go to the police. Besides, do you think after last spring I trust the police?"

She meant the Uprising last April. She meant Koreatown burning. She meant the police standing by with their thumbs up their butts as the flames roared through the streets. Then the looters came. By the thousands. Mexicans, Central Americans, blacks joined together to rip off tvs, vcrs, cd players, furniture, and clothing as well as Pampers and food. There may have been whites, but I didn't see them on television.

"No. No police. They don't protect. Maybe this woman, Miss Logan, the detective, can help me." The old woman turned away from Kim and toward me. "Will you help me?"

Lupe laughed. "Hey, excuse me, I don't mean to disrespect the dead, but you got it all wrong. She's a lawyer. She does drunk driving cases. Burglaries. She can't help you. Or anyone."

I glared at Lupe. She did think I was a total fuckup. "I found one woman who was missing."

Lupe stared back at me angrily. "That woman got killed. It was a bad scene. *Vamos*, Whitney."

I dropped my gaze. Ashamed of my bravado. "Kim's right. Call the police. You can't just take the law into your own hands."

The old lady looked over at the blue coverlet on the couch. "I can pay you. What do you want? Five hundred dollars a day?"

"Whatever was in the box was so valuable the man killed for it," I mused.

"Yes, that's what Jin said to him. She said, 'This is too important to us. Take something else. We'll give you something else.' " The old woman faltered. "Then he called her a stupid old bitch and he shot her."

"Tell me what was in the box," I said.

"*Kye*," said Dorothy.

"What?" Lupe and I asked in unison.

This time the old woman spoke more slowly. "In our community we have *kye*. A group of friends put their money together and each person has a turn receiving the money."

"Didn't you ever wonder why so many Koreans own liquor stores and minimarts?" said Kim. "There was seventy-five thousand dollars in that chest. Dorothy, my godmother, was responsible for it."

Dorothy cast her eyes down, ashamed. She explained that five women pooled their money together every year. Yesterday she had gone to the bank to withdraw the group's money, and later this evening was to be the party to give away the money.

"Two years ago I received the money," said Dorothy. "I gave most of it to Kim. That's how she was able to buy the restaurant." Kim nodded in agreement and hugged her godmother. Dorothy added that four years ago Jin had received the *kye* money. "She took me to Italy for a month. We stayed in a villa outside of Florence."

I asked her who knew she had the money.

"The people at the bank, the women in our group, our relatives..."

Lupe looked surprised. "You think someone you know did this?" She wouldn't look toward the couch. She kept jiggling Joey, who'd stopped whining and become catatonic.

Dorothy didn't say anything.

"What do you think, Dorothy?" Kim said impatiently.

"Someone from your own family? Your own *barrio* would do this?" Lupe shook her head in disbelief.

I noticed a gold-framed photo of the two old women on the small marble table at the end of the couch. They were smiling on a green hillside. They stood so close together there was no space between them. "You're going to have to notify the police, Dorothy. Just to get her buried. The mortuary's going to ask questions. Some kind of a report will have to be made."

The old woman shook her head stubbornly. "I'll get her buried. Tell me how much money you want. Seven hundred fifty dollars a day?"

I put my hands up to stop her. Wouldn't I be breaking the law? I'm not licensed as an investigator. "No, really. I can't."

"Find this man."

I shook my head. It had to be reported to the police or it would look as if we had something to hide. Could I be disbarred? What exactly was a crime of moral turpitude as defined by the State Bar? What could there be to hide?

"You tried to protect us," insisted the old lady. "You took a shot at him."

Yeah. It's a crime to be firing a gun within the city limits. Let alone taking potshots at someone.

"Maybe he'll be looking for you too now."

I'd take another shot at any SOB who tried to hurt me. Or Lupe.

The old lady grasped my hand. "Just find out who he is. Then I'll go to the police."

How well had he seen me? Would he look for me? He might still be outside. "Is that a promise?" I asked.

The old woman nodded. Kim looked angry.

"Ok. Seven hundred and fifty dollars a day."

"Plus expenses," chimed Lupe.

"If I can't find him by the end of the week, you go to the cops." Everything would be fine. It had happened too fast. He hadn't had a good look at me. The money would pay the rent at my office and get Harvey Kaplan off my back. The premium was due on my malpractice insurance. I extended my hand to the old woman. "Isn't Dorothy an unusual Korean name?"

"When I came to this country I saw *The Wizard of Oz.*"

I remember the movie from when I was a kid. How surprised I'd been to discover the Wizard was just a little man.

"Are you going to cancel the party tonight?" I asked.

"No. They're going to have to be told about the money."

I asked her if she was going to tell them about Jin. My voice trailed off. I am not accustomed to speaking of the dead.

She nodded her head.

"Don't," I said. "We'll wait and see if anyone acts suspiciously. Who asks about her. Who acts worried."

Dorothy crossed the room to a dining alcove next to the kitchen. A mahogany table with four black chairs whose seat cushions were padded with red and gold silk patterned with flying cranes stood under a dusty chandelier. Peaches and nectarines in a fake gold mesh basket were placed on the table. I recognized the old blue-and-gold Wedgwood pattern "Rhapsody" in the china cabinet because one of my mother's friends had the same pattern when I was a kid. How beautiful I'd thought it was, how elegant. Dorothy had a set of five Austrian crystal goblets each in a different gem color displayed proudly on the middle shelf. Five. One for each of the women in the *kye* group? The emerald green would be for Dorothy. The ruby red for the now deceased Jin?

Dorothy motioned for me to sit at the table. She opened a drawer in the china cabinet and from among some assorted silver and silver-plated serving utensils took out a yellow silk scrapbook with a tree and a bridge embroidered on the front.

"I will show you a picture of my *kye* group at the party we had last year." She opened the book to near the back and slid it in front of me. She tapped a photograph with one vermilion painted nail. I recognized Dorothy. Jin in what looked like an Armani suit. The rest of the women I was ashamed to admit all looked alike to me. Dorothy moved her finger around the photo, tapping each face. "Lee Joon, Chu Chu Park, and Nancy Johnson."

I looked questioningly at the last woman in the photo.

"Nancy Johnson. She married U.S. serviceman. Nice man. Pharmacist. He's dead now."

"They'll all be here tonight?" I asked.

Dorothy nodded and sighed sadly. "You come. Meet the ladies. Talk to them. Find out who they told about our *kye* party."

"Won't they wonder who I am and why I'm at the party? I'm not Korean, I don't speak Korean."

Dorothy smiled. "All of us speak English. We like to speak Korean, tell a lot of jokes. But we all know English. And at least one other language." Dorothy explained that Jin had spoken Italian and French. Nancy, German because her husband was stationed in the service there for a while. The other woman, Chu Chu, spoke Spanish. "Korean women have very high level of education. First university for women. Largest university for women in the world. Education's the most important thing for us."

"You told me Chu Chu took Japanese classes once at UCLA," added Kim.

A sour look crossed Dorothy's face. "Chu Chu's an idiot. When the Japanese were in Korea they made us stop speaking Korean, tried to make everyone speak Japanese, write Japanese. Use Japanese names. No reason for anyone to study Japanese." Dorothy waved her hand dismissively, then shifted her attention back to me. "I'll tell them you're a friend of Kim's."

"Maybe you should tell them she's a sociologist or some kind of professor researching a paper," said Lupe, who had walked over to look at the photograph. As Lupe bent over the table, Joey grabbed a fistful of my hair and gurgled happily and wetly. I'd never told Lupe that I don't like kids very much. "Which one speaks Spanish?" she asked. "I heard Koreans don't like Mexicans."

Without replying Dorothy pointed to the one she said was named Chu Chu Park.

"Maybe you should come tonight too, Lupe," I said.

Lupe shot me a poisonous look. "No. This ain't my kind of *fiesta*. I heard about this new multicultural Los Angeles. Read an article about it in the *Times*. But I thought it meant we were all going to get to eat Thai food and listen to *salsa*. I didn't know it meant you were going to end up looking for a guy who bumped some *chinita*."

Kim stepped angrily up to the table. "You're impossible. I know why Hector told me to keep Joey. You're not able to take care of him. You're a drug addict. A whore. You've been in jail."

"Watch your fucking mouth in front of my kid. I'll fucking clock you." Lupe thrust Joey into my arms and stepped toward Kim. "I'm not no drug addict."

"Hmm, that's what I thought," Kim smirked. "You *are* a whore."

Lupe drew back her arm to slap Kim. Dorothy spread her arms in a quick circular motion and then dropped into *choochoom seogi*, horse stance. First position. Master Lee had taught me this. "You know Tae Kwon Do?" I blurted out.

The old lady bowed slightly. "Black belt. Eighty-two-year-old black belt."

I handed Joey back to Lupe. He was a heavy kid. "Tell your friends I'm writing a dissertation on local Korean economics and that I'll be contacting them individually to interview them about *kye*."

"That's a good idea. Pretend to be a scholar," said Kim. "The old ones don't like outsiders very much. And it's very important to give respect to elders. As a scholar you'll be able to approach them in a respectful way."

I asked Dorothy what she was going to tell the other women about Jin and the money.

"I'll say Jin had to go down to Buena Park to see a cousin who's in the hospital. I'll tell them a man robbed me on the street."

"Why not just tell them the truth, Godmother?" sighed Kim. "They won't blame you."

"Money can make anyone an enemy," Dorothy said. "Even someone you've known all your life."

I agreed with the old woman that I'd return at seven in the evening. I wondered to myself how she was going to get Jin's body out of there and how she was going to clean the stain off the couch. Lupe, carrying Joey, and I walked out of the apartment and down to my car. I didn't want to worry her by speculating out loud if the killer was lurking nearby and watching us. There weren't many cars parked on the street. I glanced around, but didn't see anyone.

"I can't believe it!" Lupe exploded as we stood next to my car. "You're a goddamn menace to society. Wherever you go somebody gets blown away. I thought I was going to puke on my shoes."

"Yeah, I never saw anything like it before." I shook my head. I still felt numb.

Lupe jingled her car keys, which she'd taken from Kim. "Seven hundred and fifty dollars a day is a lot of *pesos*."

CHAPTER FOUR

Lupe stood beside her Fiat and examined it critically. The red paint had faded since I'd last seen the car. The gray primer on the passenger door was scratched.

"I can't believe Hector gave that cunt my ride," complained Lupe. "She owns a restaurant. She's got a bunch of people working for her. Doesn't she have her own fucking car?" She readjusted Joey in her arms like a sack of groceries.

I studied Joey, who continued to survey his surroundings with silent alarm. He did not, as the psychologists say, seem bonded to his mother. I wondered exactly how much time Lupe had lived with him. When I'd met her he must have been about a year old. She'd been leaving him with her mother when she was hooking then, and she'd been hooking every day. Time out for jail. I could tell from the uneasy way he was scanning the street he had practically no idea who she was. "Look, Lupe, I don't know what your plans are, where you're going to live or what you're going to do, but I think you better give Joey back to your mom until you figure it out."

A fierce look greeted my suggestion. I remembered that I had once seen a Joan Crawford movie. *Mildred Pierce.* "Oh, so now you're an expert on child rearing," snapped Lupe.

"You know I don't know fuck-all about kids." Or want to. "But let's face facts. You don't know if your mom's going to let you stay at her place after that argument you had with her this morning."

"Well, I'm not going to stay around this place, that's for sure. I can't believe it. Woman gets killed. Right in front of my little boy. By some crazy *chino.*"

"Chinese?"

Lupe nodded her head. "Chinese. Japanese. Whatever. Didn't you see his throat between the stupid clown mask and his shirt? He wasn't black. He wasn't brown. What's left?"

"Yellow?" I wondered if that was a politically correct term.

Lupe shrugged. "I'm gone."

I squinted into the sun, which was behind her. "You don't know if it's safe. You might see Hector..."

"Oh, I'm going to see Hector, all right. Take care of a personal matter. About that whore. Jesus Christ, he talks about me, then he turns around and hooks up with a real mattress-bender." She jerked her thumb back in the direction of the apartment where we'd left Kim. "He thinks he can give my baby to some *cualquiera!*"

"...you don't know where you're going to be working..." I stopped. Was it possible Lupe still thought prostitution was a viable option? Three convictions. AIDS.

"Yeah, I was wondering when we'd be getting around to this. Look, I been thinking of doing something different. Something where I can sit down."

I nodded excitedly. "Great! I'm so glad to hear that. Maybe an office. Sign up with an agency."

Lupe nodded back. "Just what I was thinking. An office."

"Can you type?"

She shook her head. The miniskirt clinging to her ass was smaller than the average desk blotter.

"Shorthand?" I asked doubtfully.

"I was thinking of working for you. Answer the phone. Take messages."

I couldn't prevent myself from laughing. The Anne Klein suit and Bally spectators she'd seen me in must have made her think I was making more money than I could carry to the bank. I'd charged them. I was two months behind with Visa. "I already have someone."

Lupe drew back angrily. Her dramatic range was limited by the weight of the boy in her arms. "You think I'm not smart enough to work for you? Habeas corpus. Writ. Prima facie. You think I just been sitting on my butt in the joint? I bet I know more fucking law than you do."

"I can't afford a full-time secretary. I use a service that charges by the hour." I bit my lip and felt silly. Lupe knew everything about charging by the hour. I didn't want to encourage her and make her think she could talk me into giving her a job.

"Part-time! Perfect. That's exactly the kind of career transition I had in mind. So I could be with my boy." She hugged the overfed kid. It seemed to rouse him from his stupor.

"Doggie! Doggie!" Joey grunted in a thick Mexican accent and pointed at an old yellow tomcat making its way slowly across the yard we stood in front of.

I wondered who Joey's father was. Some homeboy from the Flats where Lupe lived? A trick accident? Someone she'd been in love with? Probably no one who paid child support.

"You still have all those commie posters on the walls in your office?" Lupe asked. "Those tacky pink silk flowers?"

"Haven't changed a thing."

Lupe shook her head as she looked at me with the same critical eye she'd used on the Fiat. "I'll be a real asset. I could redecorate your office. Have you ever thought of German Expressionism? A glass table!"

She had a car. I could let her file papers for me, serve some subpoenas. I tried to quickly calculate what I might be able to pay her. It would mean no more Ballys. No more Walter Steigers. "Ok, a hundred bucks a week."

"One fifty."

I shook my head. "You have to learn to type. A hundred."

She could make that on the street in a couple of hours. She turned away and started to put Joey in the Fiat. "What about the money Dorothy's going to pay you?"

"I'll give you a raise in a month or so if things work out."

"*Mierda,*" she sighed. "At least I'll be able to tell my probation officer I'm working for a lawyer."

I told Lupe I'd bring my old Sperry Remington in for her to use. I explained about subpoenas. Lupe buckled Joey in the passenger seat. I decided it was pointless to tell her it's illegal in California to drive him without an infant seat. They cost sixty or seventy bucks, which she probably didn't have.

"Don't forget to report to your p.o. You've got to do that within twenty-four hours," I said.

Lupe got into the car with a quick, careless wave in my direction. She pointed the Fiat east toward her mother's house, and I got into my old blue Datsun to search for a pay phone to call my office. I wondered what her probation officer would think of Lupe's being at the scene of a murder.

At 8th and Normandie I saw a phone in a busy supermarket parking lot. There was actually nothing super about it. No radicchio, no baby vegetables, no Sonoma goat cheese. This was a stripped-down operation full of heart attack food and a big red sign in the window that said "*Aceptamos Food Stamps.*" Guatemalan women sold mangoes on the corner and grilled corn on the cob on barbecues. The strolling crowds of Mexican, Salvadoran, and Honduran shoppers welled in and out of adjacent cheap clothing stores from which poured latin rhythms. I had thought I was still in Koreatown. I bought an ear of corn from a woman and let her slather it with mayonnaise, lime, and chili powder.

Miraculously, I located one of the 8 percent of public phones in Los Angeles that works. I called my phone answer machine and beeped in my code. This has been a huge change in my life. I went to Circuit City and bought a machine that lets you call in for your messages. It was worth the extra money to participate in the late twentieth century. I had three calls. One from the clerk of Division 40 telling me they had a case for me to pick up if I could get there before 10:30. One from Manny Washington, my process server, asking for an advance on some paper he was supposed to lay. And one from my father, who sounded half bagged again.

"Your mother says... your mother says..." He couldn't remember why he'd called me.

I looked at my watch. It was nearly ten. That would make it nearly one back in Maryland, where he and my mother live. There are two basic kinds of phone calls from my father, Donn. I usually think of him as Donn, the irritating stranger I had to live with while I was growing up, and less often, when I'm feeling vulnerable, as the father I might someday please. Donn either wants to tell me I'm ruining my mother's life because I don't have a husband and child or a regular job with a prestigious law firm, or he wants to rant and rave about the welfare system. I hung up and looked around me at the Central American refugees swarming along the sidewalks.

I called Division 40 and told them I was on my way. I was glad to have something to take my mind off the sickening image of the dead woman. I didn't have time to go back to my office where I keep an old suit in the closet for such last-minute court appearances, so I went into the nearest clothing store. Black iron bars were pushed back from the display window. All the apparel was made of rayon. Hot pink, purple, orange. Tropical colors. The store was run by Koreans.

The woman at the cash register watched me as I ruffled through the cheap dresses. Less than three weeks ago, and not far from here, a Korean liquor store owner had shot and killed a fifteen-year-old Salvadoran boy she believed to be high on drugs and about to steal a quart of milk. Autopsy revealed no drugs in his system and his stomach was empty. I pulled a sleeveless orange dress with a white collar from the rack. Sadly, it was not only cheap looking but matronly, but it was only eleven dollars and I was in a hurry. I told the woman I'd take it, went into the changing area, and put it on. My legs were tan enough to go without stockings and I had an old pair of black Bruno Magli heels in the car.

I sped down Seventh, past the banks and corporate headquarters representing Japanese investments, past demoralized Pershing Square, where the homeless congregate. Beneath them are eight levels of parking. Up the hill at Grand, past the civil courthouse that attempts to be modern, past the Music Center, one of America's least interesting public spaces. The denuded plaza was empty. It is not growing better with age. At Temple I turned right to the criminal courts building at Broadway. It was hot again and the air was sour.

I parked across the street, hid my gun in the trunk, and hurried up the stairs to the fifth floor. I'd never been to court without a suit; at least my arms are tight and well defined. I was benchpressing nearly my own weight now. Division 40 was crowded as usual. It's one of two large arraignment courts. Pimps, gangbangers, public drunks. The court was in recess and there was much talk talk and carrying on. I knew most of the defense attorneys and Public Defenders. George Jackson, a black guy I knew from UCLA law school, detached himself from a small group drinking coffee in the back of the room.

"Yo, Whitney, long time no see." He put his hand out to me. "How about those Bruins?"

I have an adequate sports vocabulary although it bores me, but I do like to bet and I'd be insulted to be excluded from a football pool because I'm a woman. The UCLA football team was playing Tennessee on Saturday. I shook George's hand. "Yeah, those Bruins. Kicking butt and taking names."

We traded a few more banalities before George announced, "You're going to be famous soon. They got a hot case for you. Judge Harrison himself mentioned to the clerk they should call you."

I looked warily toward the clerk, a busy no-nonsense woman I felt I'd never been able to charm. Although there's a list of attorneys signed up to take appointments and the clerk is supposed to go methodically down the list, I knew about half a dozen people were getting the majority of the business. My humble efforts, a box of candy at Christmas, happy chitchat "Hi! Gorgeous weather, isn't it?"—had been met with disinterest. I hadn't decided yet how the judge felt about me.

Behind his back he's called Foxy Grandpa. He is a huge, obese anglo-saxon guy in his late fifties. He's lucky he was able to get a job wearing a robe. It was either that or a tent. His hair is silver and he wears it combed back. Seated on the bench he's an imposing figure, but when he opens his mouth it's a different story. He calls women "girls" and "sweetheart." He's proud to be called a good ol' boy.

I slipped George ten bucks and told him to put it on UCLA for me with a six-point spread. Then I went to find out what Foxy Grandpa had in store for me. Ignoring my greeting, the clerk handed me a complaint.

"Venus Howard. In lockup."

PC 647. I sighed. More prostitution. I had the bailiff let me into the custody area.

It was empty. The only sound I heard was the click of my heels across the concrete. Foxy Grandpa had been yelling at everyone for weeks to get the arraignments done before noon in the interests of judicial economy. I knew it was so he'd be able to get out promptly for lunch. I'd heard that one of his favorite places was the old Langer's Deli on Seventh at the edge of MacArthur Park. I could see him settling his great girth onto one of the red leather booths, surrounded by his sycophants, those fucking sharkskin lawyers who licked his enormous buttocks and made a hundred and forty grand minimum a year from the public trough for chickenshit breaking-and-entering cases. I imagined Foxy Grandpa ordering: "I'll have half a cow and the left side of the menu."

A tall, slender white woman, a redhead with hair flowing past her shoulders, napped face down on the cold gray bench in the cell adjoining Division 40. She was either asleep with her right arm pillowed under her head or she'd frozen to death in the meat-locker cold of the lockup. I shivered, wishing I'd bought a dress with a little jacket. Stretched out, the woman was at least five feet ten. A pair of cheesy gold Frederick's of Hollywood pumps stood next to the bench. Was there nothing new in the world of prostitution?

"Ms. Howard?"

The redhead didn't move. A pale, shapely calf poked out of the baggy blue county overalls.

"Ms. Howard?" I coughed to get her attention.

She still didn't move. Her skin was firm. Her hair was shiny. She couldn't be more than twenty-five. I coughed again. "Ms Howard?"

The pale arm on which her head was cushioned extended out and reached for the opposite wall. She had long nails painted red with silver stripes. I sighed again. Silver looks terrible on redheads. She turned, swung her legs over the bench, and fumbled for her shoes. Her long hair covered her face. She threw it back.

She was on the bad side of fifty. Her face was thin and heavily lined. Her lines had lines. Her face was like one of those horrible dolls made from a dried apple.

"Hail, daughter of Portia. You got a cigarette?" she asked.

I shook my head and introduced myself. "Let me go over this complaint with you, Ms. Howard "

"Venus," she corrected me. "The Great Goddess. Queen of the Shades. Mother of the Venetian tribes of the Adriatic. Goddess of Generation. Also known as Aphrodite..."

I flipped quickly through the complaint. "Excuse me, ma'am, I don't see that name."

"Fuck," she muttered. "I should have known they'd give me some simpleton with no poetry in her soul. I asked for a Woman. Did they tell you that? Only a Woman can understand the mysteries I represent."

"This is the police report. It says here you've been under investigation for the last six months for prostitution, running a house of prostitution—"

"A temple."

"At 1200 N. Bronson? Hollywood?"

She nodded her head. Her red hair danced in the mucky yellow light. "Yes, the Church of the Big Mother. I am the High Priestess."

I fiddled awkwardly with the stupid Peter Pan collar on my new dress. "I don't understand."

"Didn't they have a women's studies program at your school? Come, come, daughter, is it possible you do not know your her-story? Your matriarchal roots?" Venus Howard shoved her feet into the gold shoes as if she was going somewhere.

I read aloud from the police report. "Officers arrived at the aforenamed address, spoke with suspect who stated she would engage in sexual intercourse and oral copulation. Suspect stated 'I will absolve you of all your sins for $25.' Further—"

"Anything I must do for the Great One, I will do." Her eyes were heavily outlined with kohl and she wore green eye shadow. "Sex is the religion of the Big Mother. I am but her humble servant."

"You were going to take money to fuck these two cops?"

Venus Howard folded her garish hands over her heart. "They were guilty men with many sins to be forgiven. It is my duty and that of the Big Mother's other priestesses to absolve the sins of man."

"Wait a sec. Let me get this straight. You want me to go out in the courtroom and say that it's part of your religion to have sex with men and they give you money?"

She bowed her head before looking back up at me. "Donations. For the temple. Excuse me, fair daughter, you have heard of the First Amendment, haven't you?"

I nodded unhappily. Another fucking lunatic. Why couldn't I get a grand theft auto? "It'll be about two grand to bail you out of here. You have anyone you want me to get in contact with?"

"Adonis, my Horned God. Or either of the Vestal Virgins of the Church—Heather and Sarah. They know where I keep the donations."

She gave me directions how to get to the church, a beeper number for Adonis, and told me to stand up straight and be proud of my breasts.

I could barely wait to get out of the courthouse. I sauntered, as grandly as I could, out of Division 40 with the laughter of the DA and all the other defense lawyers ringing in my ears. All I wanted was to go back to the office and talk with Harvey.

West up Sunset Boulevard through the Vietnamese outskirts of downtown, through the Mexican and Central American neighborhoods with *carnicerías*, Pentecostal churches, and brightly colored auto repair shops all painted with images of the Virgin of Guadalupe and the names of dead gang members. I went past the gay bars, the funky laundromats and old movie theaters to the fork in the road that turns into Hollywood Boulevard. My office is at Wilton on a seedy-looking block with Thai restaurants and several of the new backbone of the Los Angeles economy: the ninety-nine-cent store. Everything in the store costs ninety-nine cents and is made in some other country.

Harvey Kaplan, my landlord, was in his office reclining on his couch rereading one of the tedious and incomprehensible books detailing the life of his guru. Harvey wore an old white T-shirt with what looked like a spaghetti sauce stain on the left pec. His long gray hair was pulled into a ponytail held back by a blue Dodgers baseball cap. He had on a pair of jeans that were faded to nearly white and a pair of those terrible religious-fanatic Birkenstocks from which his big naked toes protruded. This is the man I prefer to think of as my real father. Harvey used to be a great crim-inal lawyer. I used to read about him in the paper when he was doing death penalty cases.

I closed Harvey's open door behind me. "Hey, man, you busy?" I sat down on the arm of the couch without waiting for his reply.

Harvey dropped the book on the floor. His eyes were glassy behind the thick Coca-Cola bottles he wears for reading, and I saw he was stoned again.

"You know anything about Koreatown?" I wouldn't tell him why I was asking. To tell Harvey I'd seen a woman murdered and had agreed for the sum of $750 per day to search for her killer would be to invite criticism. He'd tell me to stick to possession and prostitution cases. Harvey believes in karma and hard cash.

"The DMZ that divides the North and South is the most militarized area in the world. The U.S. military and nuclear presence in the South is the greatest obstacle to peace in the region," Harvey mumbled as he scratched his beard lazily. The beard is new. It's nearly all gray and looks like pubic hair. "A people divided against themselves."

"So what's that have to do with Koreatown?"

"Same people who live in Korea live in Koreatown. Except now most of the people who live in Koreatown are Central American."

I got up, nodding my head as if I understood.

"You don't by any chance have any cookies or anything to eat in your office, do you?" Harvey asked.

On my way out I left his door open as I had found it. I checked my mail quickly and tossed the overdue notice from the *Daily Journal* into the trash. I had to go home to figure out what to wear to the *kye* party at Dorothy's house that evening.

I decided on a navy pantsuit with a white silk blouse and a pair of black Ferragamo flats. I looked preppy. Harmless. As if I'd gone to Sweet Briar or one of the other not very difficult women's colleges in the South. To com-plete my soft look I pinned a navy silk flower to my lapel. Before putting it in my purse, I cleaned and loaded my .38.

The sun was in its last slow amber arc in the west as I crested over Mul-holland Drive and zoomed through the leafy green of Laurel Canyon. I turned up the volume on the Bob Marley cassette in my tape player, pushed my old Datsun into a turn, and felt the back wheels swing out into the gravel. This was a hell of a lot more fun than being a lawyer.

I cruised down Fairfax still bopping to the reggae. Orthodox Jews shopped and visited with each other on the street. I wondered why they had to wear wool with long sleeves all year round. It was still over ninety. September and the beginning of October are the hottest months in Los Angeles. The seasons have been stretched beyond definition and you need air-conditioning.

The lights were just coming on in Koreatown when I turned off Olympic Boulevard onto Dorothy's street. I parked. It wasn't until I had walked across the yellow lawn and past the border of birds of paradise in front of her building and started up the stairs that I felt scared. What had I gotten myself into? I glanced at my watch. It was less than eleven hours since I'd first been there and seen Jin murdered.

I knocked on the door of Dorothy's apartment.

It swung open. Kim smiled and bowed. From inside I heard a scratchy old record of Andy Williams singing "Moon River."

Kim stood back, and I saw Lee Joon and Chu Chu Park with Nancy Johnson sitting on the immaculate white couch.

CHAPTER FIVE

Dorothy appeared from the kitchen carrying six drinks in short frosty glasses on a silver tray. Kim closed the door behind me. I couldn't help but remember the killer running down the hallway and out onto the stairs. Shooting at him. Him shooting at me. My stomach turned over again. I made myself take a deep breath and stand up taller. The women on the couch stopped talking and stared at me. I felt my face flush the same unnatural color as the cherry floating on top of the drink Dorothy handed me.

"How wonderful! A Manhattan!" I gushed. It's hard to get one's daily requirement of Red Dye No. 40.

The women's attention shifted momentarily from me to the drinks as Dorothy distributed them. Kim took her drink from her godmother and walked over to stand near the cabinet from which the man earlier in the day had removed the carved box containing the *kye* money. I glanced down at the white carpeting, expecting to see a smudged red trail where Jin would have been dragged from the living room. A colorful throw rug had been tossed down to cover the spot. I wondered what they'd done with her body.

"Yes, I make the best Manhattan in town. We always have Manhattan at our parties, isn't that right, girls?" Dorothy prodded the ancient crones.

I made a quick survey while I waited for someone to reply. They wore bright clothes and unlike Dorothy, who wore her white hair long and straight they had curled their hair into stiff dated 'dos. Clearly Dorothy was the oldest of the group. She was in her eighties. Two of the others were in their mid to late seventies, I judged, but the portly one squeezed in the middle of the couch was a spring chicken, not a day over sixty-five. No one moved. No one spoke. Perhaps their vocal cords had atrophied with age. Perhaps they couldn't speak English as well as Dorothy had indicated. Did they wonder what a white girl was doing at their party? What had Dorothy told them about me?

"Come on, girls, drink up," insisted Dorothy. "Skoal. Let's have a nice toast to welcome Whitney Logan. She's the lawyer I was telling you about who could help us form a limited partnership."

We'd agreed earlier that I was going to tell them I was a scholar. I'd dressed as a grad student. Why was Dorothy changing the story?

"Can we avoid taxes? In case one of us kicks the bucket?" asked the tall woman seated at the end of the couch closest to the kitchen.

Had Dorothy told them before I arrived that Jin was dead? What did they know? They watched me and waited for my answer. My mind raced back to my second year in law school. It had been compulsory to take corporate law. It was on the bar exam. It didn't interest me. I was busy taking "Law and Social Responsibility" and working in the prisoners rights project at the federal pen on Terminal Island.

I glanced over at the flamboyant woman who'd asked the question. I'd thought Lupe's clothes were weird. I made a quick mental note to lay off criticizing Lupe's wardrobe. To accessorize an aqua-and-pink Pucci dress, the Korean woman wore silver Mexican necklaces mixed with strands of gray and white seed pearls, a large not-inexpensive-looking ring with a green stone, and dangling gold Middle Eastern earrings that jingled when she moved. She looked as if she'd dressed in a boutique on a cruise ship.

I didn't remember anything about limited partnerships or taxation.

The youngest of the three old women said something in Korean as I contemplated an answer. She sounded angry.

"Lee, we're all going to speak English here tonight. I told Whitney we all speak English," said Dorothy.

"Why don't we get Korean lawyer? Korean lawyer is best." The woman frowned.

Dorothy placed her serving tray on the mahogany coffee table in front of the couch. "I haven't even introduced everyone yet, Lee, and you're already making snap judgments."

Kim stepped into the circle of women. She was wearing the same dark brown Armani pantsuit Jin Oh wore in the photo Dorothy had shown me of last year's *kye* party. Death is death, but Armani is forever. I wondered if Kim helped cart Jin's body out. Maybe it was in the bedroom. Maybe it was propped up in the shower stall. Maybe they'd driven it somewhere. I felt a bit sick juggling the possibilities. "Auntie Lee, she's a good lawyer. She went to UCLA law school."

I sipped the Manhattan so as not to let surprise register on my face. Kim must have been to the library and looked me up in a Martindale-Hubbell directory to be sure her godmother wasn't throwing money away on bunko services.

"Besides, she's not going to charge very much money," Kim added, smiling in my direction.

"Miss Logan, come here," said Dorothy. "These are my friends. Lee Joon Song..."

The argumentative woman nodded but didn't say anything. She had a thin mouth and deepset eyes in a broad face. Although Lee Joon was the youngest, I doubted she'd ever been a beauty. She was dressed in the same kind of full-length traditional dress Dorothy and Jin had worn earlier in the day. Hers was lime green and topped by a short orange jacket tied on one side by a wide strip of black cloth in a single bowknot. With it she wore a good-looking pair of black Bally pumps.

"...Nancy Johnson..."

I put my hand out to the woman sitting where the bloodstain had been. She tentatively gave me her hand. I shook it. It was scrawny but warm. Later I would learn it was considered bad manners to touch an older person or offer to shake hands.

"I was married to U.S. serviceman. Dr. Bill Johnson. Pharmacist. From Connecticut. He called me Nancy."

I nodded, uncertain where to go with this information. She wore rose-tinted glasses. Her face was heavily lined, more so than Dorothy's and Dorothy was older. Perhaps she'd spent a lot of time in the sun. I'd seen that same aged-football look creeping up on my mother, who spent a lot of time outdoors playing tennis. I wouldn't be caught dead al fresco without SPF 30.

"....and Chu Chu Park."

Chu Chu Park, the dotty-looking one, nodded slightly so her earrings tinkled a tune. She had on a pair of gold Turkish mules, the toes of which curved up into little crescents. "My husband was an obstetrician," she said, looking at me but apparently addressing herself more to Nancy Johnson in an offhand boast. "He's dead now. All of our husbands are dead. We're the 'Black Widows.' "

Kim giggled politely with her hand in front of her mouth.

"All widows. That's why it's so important that we take good care of our money," said Nancy Johnson, giggling in the same formal way with hand over mouth.

Dorothy took this opportunity to sit down in the red easy chair next to the couch. She pulled at the knees of her black silk trousers to adjust them, then leaned forward toward the other women. "Something very bad has happened."

The icy glass in my hand felt heavy, but I didn't want to put it down. Was she going to tell them Jin had been murdered in this room? I'd asked her not to. She'd said she was only going to tell them about the money, but she'd been changing everything else we'd discussed earlier.

The trio looked back expectantly.

Dorothy looked from Lee Joon to Chu Chu Park and then to Nancy Johnson. "A man stole our *kye*."

"What? What? What?" they exploded nearly in unison.

They'd each put in $15,000. Dorothy had explained to me that the money was awarded by lottery at the party. Each woman wrote her name on a piece of paper and the winning name was drawn by one of them from a bowl. Seventy-five thousand dollars plus interest would mean a lot to anyone.

"This morning..." Dorothy tried to explain.

Lee Joon began beating her breast and wailing in a primordial ritual. As if on cue, all the other women set down their drinks and began wailing along with her. They rocked back and forth moaning and weeping.

I looked uncomfortably away and examined a lithograph of craggy mauve mountains on the far wall. I come from a family where little is said about feelings. I'd never cry in front of anyone. I couldn't remember ever having seen my mother cry. The wailing grew louder. I'd seen my father cry once when he was really drunk. It was the summer after my first year in law school and I'd gone back to Maryland to visit them. Donn asked me to go with him to the country club they belong to. Although my mother's an excellent tennis player, she doesn't like to hang around the club the way my father does. Donn and I drank martinis and tried to find things to talk about. Somewhere between martini five and six Donn started to babble about Tina, one of the younger women my mother plays tennis with. He began to cry, and I realized he'd had an affair with her.

The wailing of the Korean women increased to an agitated pitch, then just as suddenly died away. The women dabbed at their faces with cocktail napkins and snuffled their runny noses. They picked up their drinks again.

Lee Joon grunted apprehensively. "Why couldn't you keep the money in the freezer like everyone else does? It was one of those Mexicans, wasn't it? One of the ones who burned Koreatown down last April."

The Pico-Union bordering Koreatown is primarily Mexican and Central American. Even Koreatown seemed to be largely latino now. Someday all of Southern California would return to its rightful owner, Mexico. It was not an invasion but a reabsorption.

"Where's Jin?" Nancy Johnson interrupted, looking worried. "Did something happen to Jin? Is that why she's not here?"

Dorothy shook her head. "No, Jin's fine. She had to go to Buena Park because one of our cousins is in the hospital."

I looked at Dorothy as I bent over my drink again. She was a cool liar.

"Our cousin Charles," added Kim, but no one seemed interested in the story about the hospital.

"What happened to our money?" Chu Chu Park demanded.

Kim held her hand up to stop the old women from talking. "Dorothy was walking home from the bank—"

"Not good to keep *kye* in bank," said Lee Joon.

"Walking?" wailed Nancy Johnson. "Why didn't you call a cab? Why didn't Kim come get you?"

Dorothy leaned forward slightly. "Kim was at work. You know I always walk everywhere. Two miles a day. Every day."

"Yes, yes, we know. Walk everywhere. That's why you are Grandmother Tiger. All the special health foods, the herbs. The tonics," Lee Joon said. She looked as if the herbs and tonics pissed her off, that she'd heard this routine one too many times. "So what happened to the money?"

"I'm trying to tell you. You act like a group of old ladies. Just hold onto your pants." Dorothy paused to make sure she had the floor. "I was walking from the bank, I was on San Marino, near the corner of Western—"

"That's where those Mexicans hang out," Nancy Johnson wailed again. Folding her arms across her orange jacket, Lee Joon nodded knowingly.

I was glad Lupe hadn't come with me. I wouldn't want her to have to hear the racist ramblings of the angry old women.

"I don't know if he was Mexican," Dorothy said. "He had on a mask—"

"A mask! In broad daylight!" exclaimed Chu Chu Park. "I tell you the riots made those people bolder than ever. It's not safe to walk in your own neighborhood! It's unbelievable. Why, you can walk anywhere in London, in Paris, in Madrid, in—"

Kim put her hand on Chu Chu Park's garishly swathed arm. "I know, Auntie, I try to tell her it isn't safe anymore."

"A Chusok festival mask," Dorothy said.

I started to ask what that meant, but Dorothy quickly explained to me that we were only a few days away from Chusok, the festival celebrating the harvest and the autumn moon.

Lupe had called the killer a *chino*. Now Dorothy was saying he was Korean.

Dorothy sat up a bit straighter and looked directly at the women. "I was about to cross the street. It was eleven-thirty in the morning..."

Jin had been killed much earlier. She was stiff as a plank by that time. Why was Dorothy creating this story? Why these details?

"...I had our *kye* money in crisp new thousand dollar bills in the bottom of my bag. The man ran up to me..."

How had the man gotten into Dorothy's apartment? There'd been no sign of forced entry.

"...he must have been hiding behind one of the buildings..."

Had she let him in? Was it someone she knew? Someone whose voice she recognized? Was that why he was wearing the mask?

"...he pushed me off balance and grabbed my purse. It all happened so quickly that's all I remember."

The three women looked stunned. Kim hugged her godmother. Lee Joon recovered most quickly. "Who besides us knew you'd be going for the money today?"

"Just us," Dorothy replied. A somber silence hung heavily in the air.

"One of us must have told someone," said Lee Joon.

"Of course we did," Chu Chu Park retorted. "Everyone we know knows we belong to *kye* group and that we have our lottery party same time every year."

Nancy Johnson sipped at her drink. "That's right. For Chusok."

"It was your idea to put the *kye* in a bank," Chu Chu Park added grumpily.

Every year the party was at a different person's house. The hostess went
to the bank, wrapped the money up in red tissue paper, and prepared a
supper, Kim explained to me.

"Did you report it to the police?" asked Nancy Johnson.

Dorothy shook her head.

The syrupy drink in Nancy Johnson's hand nearly spilled as she gestured
with it. "Didn't report it! You could have walked right over to the Koreatown Police Community Center on 8th and Normandie, since you like to
walk so much," she sputtered.

Lee Joon laughed, but not pleasantly. "Nancy, you think because the
police come around now to Koreatown Civic Association and give us pep
talks that they're gonna take care of us? They didn't during the riots. Our
men did."

I'd seen the live television coverage of armed Korean merchants guarding their businesses during the Uprising. Uzis. Semiautomatics.

Chu Chu Park smacked her empty glass down on the coffee table. "This
isn't time to discuss politics. And we don't want to hear about your volunteer job at the civic association again. We're sick of you bragging about
it. What happened to our *kye?* Someone here knows what happened to our
money."

The old ladies looked at each other as though for the first time. The gold-
and-black enamel clock on the cabinet near where Kim stood ticked loudly in the silence.

"Dorothy, when did you tell her about our money?" asked Lee Joon in a
shrill voice, pointing a bony accusing finger at me.

Could these old bats possibly think that I was involved in the theft of
their money?

"Just yesterday," Dorothy replied calmly. Then she explained that she'd
been thinking about what to do with the money if she was the winner of
the *kye* lottery. She said she'd been thinking for a while of changing her
will, but the lawyer who had originally done it for her had died, so she
called the Los Angeles County Bar Association and asked for referrals.
They gave her my name. She decided my name had a propitious number
of letters in it so she called me, explained the situation, and I'd told her I
could come over for an appointment with her and meet the group to
explain the benefits of a limited partnership for future *kye.*

A propitious number? I quickly counted the letters in my name. Seven
for Whitney. Five for Logan. Twelve! What was the meaning of twelve?
Did Dorothy believe in onomancy, the divination of destinies deciphered

from names? She was more than a little wack, I decided. And where was she coming up with these stories? This multicultural business was tough work. It occurred to me that, in law, a document in the handwriting of one person with the signature in the hand of another is called onomastic. They teach you so little in law school that you can actually use. I studied each of the old women again. I hadn't seen any money except for the $750 Dorothy had given me earlier in the day. All I'd seen was the wooden box.

"That's ridiculous, to think this young woman could have anything to do with it," snapped Dorothy. "You sit around your house too much. You've been watching too much television."

"How about another drink, everyone?" Kim collected the glasses and took the serving tray into the kitchen without waiting for a reply. I heard the reassuring sound of ice clinking in glasses and the burbly burble of booze being poured.

Chu Chu Park shook her jewelry dismissively at her friends. "How could a white woman possibly steal our money in the middle of Koreatown now?"

There, the cat was out of the bag. They all knew I was white.

"It's too ridiculous," repeated Chu Chu, stretching her arms out in front of her. She had a squeaky voice that was probably quite ugly if she got excited. "You know everyone keeps an eye on the *hiyun.*"

"White man," Dorothy whispered so I'd understand.

It had not previously occurred to me that I was a foreigner. My forefathers had been among the very earliest groups of criminals sent to this country by England.

The other women examined me as though I was an exotic but not particularly appealing or clean animal.

"Why do we need her here now if the money's gone?" asked Lee Joon, glaring angrily from me to Dorothy.

Because your friend Jin was murdered in this room. Because Dorothy wants to find out who killed her sister. Because I think Dorothy doesn't really trust you.

Dorothy didn't say anything. I was about to pick up my purse to beat a dignified retreat when Kim reentered the room and handed me another drink.

"I say Miss Logan stays," said Dorothy.

The women looked anxiously back and forth from one to another like kids choosing up competing kickball teams.

"Call me Whitney." I tried to look appealing and clean. I had bills to pay. Lupe's salary.

Dorothy smiled at me. I smiled back. Maybe if they kicked me out she'd let me keep the $750 anyway, for having made the trip over the hill.

"Whitney is going to figure out if we can deduct the loss of our money on our income taxes."

I felt my knees buckle. Now I was a tax expert.

There was an excited murmur of assent from all the seated women except Lee Joon.

Kim finished handing out the round of drinks. She placed a plate of shrimp crackers and another of silvery dried fish on the coffee table. As she bent over, her pants' legs crept up her ankles. I noticed she had a small blue-and-red circle tattooed on her left ankle.

I bowed slightly to the group. "I'm sorry I'm meeting you on an occasion of such loss...."

Dorothy sighed, but none of the others seemed to notice. She must have been thinking of her sister.

"...You must be in shock about the theft of your money."

Nancy Johnson shoved a handful of the tiny dried fish into her mouth and tried to insist the others have something to eat also.

"Nancy." Chu Chu Park waved aside the proffered snacks. "Did you tell your nephew Henry about the money?"

Nancy Johnson chewed deliberately and swallowed. She wiped her fingers carefully with the cocktail napkin. She set it aside with great precision. "Why do you ask that?"

"He was arrested once, wasn't he?"

Kim shook her head. "That was for driving with a suspended license, Auntie. That doesn't count."

"Arrested is arrested. They took him to the police station, didn't they? Nobody in my family's ever been arrested."

"It wasn't Henry," argued Nancy Johnson. "He doesn't need our money. He's in Seoul on business. Our little seventy-five thousand dollars is peanuts to him." Nancy Johnson puffed up and looked very proud of her nephew.

"I always wondered where he got the money to start his business," muttered Chu Chu Park.

"What did you say, Chu Chu?" demanded Nancy Johnson. "How do you go on all those trips? Europe. Mexico. Hong Kong. Didn't you get that ring in Hong Kong?"

"You told us it's an emerald," added Lee Joon.

Chu Chu instinctively twisted the ring on her right hand to display the stone more prominently. "It is an emerald. You're both jealous because I'm the only one who wears nice clothes and looks good all the time."

I couldn't help bending forward slightly to get a better look at the ring. It was a good green rock about half the size of Ireland.

"I save my money," Chu Chu said. "I still have a lot of money my husband left me. He left me a lot of money. I didn't put it in those crazy aero-space industry and movie studio stocks like Lee's brother-in-law talked her into."

Lee Joon clicked her teeth and waved her hand angrily. "My stocks are good stocks. Not government bonds like you have. I'm smart enough to know how to play the market. And commodities. I invest in Korea. Strong Korea. I don't waste my money in bonds. Maybe you stole the money because—"

"Sisters, sisters!" Dorothy clapped her hands, trying to bring order to the room. "It's not going to do any good to fight among ourselves. The money is gone. We can't prove who took it. We don't want to report to the police until we calm down a little so we don't say hasty things that are going to cause us harm. We've known each other a long time. We must give each other respect. We are family."

Did the bickering women consider Dorothy their leader or were they simply being polite because they were in her house? Each of them seemed to have some reason to want the money. How long had they known each other? I thought of Lupe. Would I know her for a long time? I thought again of the $750 a day Dorothy had said she'd pay me to find out who'd killed her sister. I needed it. And I wasn't afraid of old ladies.

"I may have to take some statements from you. I'll need to come and speak with each of you individually."

"Depositions," Nancy Johnson announced importantly but inaccurately. "I've seen that on 'Perry Mason.' " The other women murmured an affir-mation of this.

I took a grateful drink from the glass. I was on solid ground. None of them knew anything about the law except what they'd learned from tele-vision. I would have to remember to use legal terminology with them more often.

CHAPTER SIX

The next day I went to my office early in the morning to wait for Lupe to begin her job as my secretary. I cleaned off the top of my desk and set up the antiquated electric typewriter I'd brought from home. It surged on when I plugged it in and the carriage jumped slightly. Ready to go! I sharpened all the pencils and replaced them in their pink-and-orange Mexican papier-mâché jug shaped like a mermaid that I'd bought on Olvera Street. I put all the books I wasn't using back on the bookshelf. Since Lupe had last been in my office I'd acquired used sets of *Bender's Criminal Defense* and *Witkin on Evidence.* Then I sat down to wait. I read some back issues of the *Daily Journal* and noted in the classifieds that real legal secretaries were making a minimum of $22,500 a year. After an hour of waiting, I went out for a cup of coffee at the Viet restaurant down the block.

The caffeine made me nervous as a bird dog. I raced back up the stairs to my office. From the second floor wafted the moving sounds of the Delfonics. "LaLaLa Means I Love You."

I opened the door.

Lupe stood beside the desk. She had on a gray pinstripe flannel suit with a midcalf-length skirt and a jacket belted at the waist. A plastic cameo was pinned to the lapel. Her shiny black hair was twisted up into a bun. Soft curls framed her face. She wore blood red lipstick and a pair of black pumps with a thick heel from the forties. A steno pad was in one hand, a pencil in the other. "Professional, no?" she said. "Rosalind Russell in *His Girl Friday.*"

"It's perfect. Unfortunately, not a lot of clients come in here. It's ok for you to wear jeans. That'd probably be best since you'll be delivering papers."

"You said I was going to be an executive secretary." Lupe frowned and waved the steno pad at the desk. "Look, I've been typing already."

I walked over to look at the paper in the typewriter. It said LUPE RAMOS LUPE RAMOD LUPE RAMOS.

She leaned past me and peered at the paper. I heard her grunt with displeasure at it.

"*No preocupese,* " I mispronounced. "It's only your first day. You'll get better. You're on your own for right now 'cause I gotta go back to Koreatown. To talk with one of the old ladies I met last night at Kim's godmother's." I intentionally did not mention the dead woman, Jin.

"Did Dorothy pay you yet?"

I shook my head. I quickly explained there were barely constrained tensions among the old women and I needed to learn what those tensions were if I expected to find out who was responsible for the theft of the *kye* and the murder. I was hoping to skirt around the edges so Lupe wouldn't freak out on me again.

"Man, that's so *chingón*. Someone you actually know stealing your *pan*." Lupe tsk'ed in disapproval. "What are you going to ask this *vieja?*"

"I'm gonna find out if she believes Dorothy's story about the robbery for starters. I can't imagine anyone saying anything incriminating to me if she thinks a murder's involved. Snitching off a thief's a different matter. Also, I been wondering why the guy only shot Jin. With determinate sentencing you might as well kill as many people as you want; you get the same punishment. It's like two for the price of one."

"He didn't have to shoot Dorothy. Got her too scared to go to the cops. She's lucky," said Lupe. "I'm glad. She seemed nice to me. Took good care of Joey."

"I guess since she was the older sister she always looked after Jin." I wondered why Dorothy hadn't tried to kick the guy if she knew Tae Kwon Do. Why did she leave that to Jin? I supposed that she was afraid. It's one thing to practice the forms and another thing to spar. One thing to shoot at a paper target. Another thing to shoot at someone. "She must feel awful that she couldn't have done anything to protect her." I waited to see if Lupe would add anything. If she would understand the way I was hinting at our tangled relationship from Dogtown to the present.

"Get her to talk about Jin," suggested Lupe, without indicating she'd understood my allusion. "Find out who was Jin's best friend."

I didn't have a best friend. Always been a loner. It's easier that way. Don't have to explain my father's drinking or any of the wack things he does. Never have to have my mother look down her nose at anyone I might've brought home. I studied Lupe. Did she have a best friend? This might be an appropriate time for a direct personal question. To connect with her. To show her I cared about her life. "What'd your mom say when you got home yesterday with Joey?"

"Nothing." Lupe smoothed her skirt and edged closer to the desk as though there was something she didn't want me to see.

I waited for her to tell me more, but she busied herself shifting a file from one side of the desk to the other. "Are you going to be staying there? I need to know how to get in touch with you. About work."

"Yeah, we'll be staying there till I make enough to get our own place. Things are cool."

Would she laugh at me if I told her I was worried about her? "What about Hector? Where's he?"

"You don't understand English, or what? I don't feel like talking about it. Hector and me, it's not finished, but it don't have nothing to do with you."

She paused. "Doesn't got nothing to do with you," she corrected herself, apparently mindful of her new employment position. She adjusted a gold picture frame with a 5x7 of Joey so I could see it. "Don't get me wrong, I appreciate what you're doing for me and all, but it's none of your business."

"I may run into Hector while—"

She snapped open the steno pad to a fresh, attentive page. "What do you want me to do here today?"

I told her to review all the files, be sure they were alphabetized, and check that all upcoming court cases were recorded both on the calendar I carry and on the desk calendar. This double calendaring is one of the requirements of being insured for malpractice. The insurers don't want to pay out big bucks because some careless lawyer let a statute of limitations or an appeal period run. For a while I didn't carry insurance, but I'd had too many sleepless nights worrying about what would happen if I fucked up someone's case. Most lawyers are conscientious about their work not because they have the deep abiding desire to do good but because they want to avoid judgments being taken against them. The sheriff coming in and ripping your Charles Jourdan shoes out of the closet along with everything else you own. I am ashamed that I, a member of the National Lawyers Guild, think about such things too, but there you have it.

I showed Lupe the message pad I wanted her to use to record phone messages in duplicate. I told her that all the supplies she'd need were in the file cabinet.

"Don't worry about a thing," Lupe assured me. She turned busily away to check the contents of the cabinet. She wore black stockings with seams up the back. Her skirt was slit all the way up to her butt.

I drove west on Hollywood Boulevard so I could go down Vermont and check out how much of the damage from the riots had been repaired. I shoved a Peter Tosh cassette into my tape player. Koreatown was busy with shoppers, both Korean and Central American, that Wednesday morning. In the aftermath of the riots there had been a call for a rainbow coalition. Whites from the Westside had poured into South Central, the Pico-Union, and Koreatown armed with brooms and dustpans to begin cleaning up the city. I still felt guilty I hadn't helped. Sweeping up burned things had seemed an unsatisfactory response to the disaster. I'd picked up a lot of cases in the arraignment courts in the days following the violence. Looting, possession of narcotics, drunk in public, curfew violations. I told myself that this was my contribution to society. Serve the people.

The gutted furniture and clothing stores had been leveled, but the memory of smoke and burning plastics hung in the air. The sky was blue, but greasy with smog. Big dumpsters covered and then re-covered with competing gang graffiti stood on the sidewalks in front of empty businesses. On the eastern edge of Koreatown the *placas* of Salvatrucha began appearing spray-painted on walls. In Salvadoran slang it means something like bad dudes. It's the largest gang in the area.

I found Irolo Street, where I intended to look for Lee Joon. Since she was the most openly hostile to me the night before, I'd decided to start my questioning with her. I had to talk to two telephone operators and then a supervisor before they could find any phone listing or address for a Koreatown Civic Association. I was guessing this was the same place Chu Chu Park was talking about when she'd been ragging on Lee Joon.

The Koreatown Civic Association was a light-brown stone building on the corner of 8th surrounded by the usual crummy dress shops, Salvadoran restaurants, and a video rental store covered with thick black bars. I went around the block and ended up parking on Ardmore in front of an early-twenties bungalow court with an Islamic facade. A sloped and painted driveway led from the street into a narrow entrance. Pairs of small towers adorned each of the two wings of the court. I thought of Chu Chu Park's crazy Middle Eastern slippers. I locked my pull-out radio in the trunk next to my gun.

Some Salvadoran boys leaning on an old dented gold El Dorado yelled and whistled at me as I walked to the Korean civic association. I was wearing the same navy pantsuit and blouse I'd worn the night before. I hoped it would make me look familiar to Lee Joon. I wondered if many whites went to the association.

I opened the door and stepped from the bright sunlight into a small cool room painted ivory. A large Korean flag hung on the wall behind a wooden desk. A fat old man with many liver spots on his face dozed at the desk with his arm resting next to a red leather guest book and a white ballpoint pen. A pile of fliers announced an exhibition of contemporary art. He started awake and mumbled something as I closed the door.

"I'm sorry. I don't speak Korean. Do you speak English?"

"Of course. I'm Korean-American. Eighty-five percent of Koreans are here less than twenty years, but we all speak English. Koreans are good students. Education most important to us," he said with a heavy accent I could barely understand.

I nodded and looked down the hall to my right, where I could see doors to other rooms. Was Lee Joon there?

"Your first time here? You come to see exhibit of paintings?"

I nodded, glad to be able to agree.

He pointed to the flag behind him. In the center of a white background was a circle divided in two parts, the upper part red and the lower blue. In the four corners were black lines, three rows each. "The circle is universe in perfect balance and harmony. These symbols represent heaven, earth, fire, and water." He handed me a flier and gestured to where the gallery was. "Have a nice day."

I looked in the first room. A small group of women sat making green clay bowls and figurines at a long table covered with white butcher paper. They didn't bother to look up. Traditional music of plucked instruments came from a tape player in a corner. Lee Joon wasn't among the women. I moved on to the next room, where five tables of men and women played cards. I stepped into the doorway to get a better look at them. No Lee Joon. The cigarette smoke was heavy, and there was laughter and joking. They all stopped talking when they noticed me.

"Art gallery there," barked a guy who pointed a nicotine-stained finger farther down the hall.

I stepped back into the hall, and the laughter and talking resumed. As I walked away I heard an argument coming from a room at the far end of the hall and on the opposite side of the corridor. A teenage girl's voice was raised in anger. Then a woman's voice snapped in response. I walked past the entrance to the gallery, which was empty, toward the voices.

The door to the room was partially closed. I stood so I could see into it. It was a large kitchen with restaurant-size and -quality appliances. In the center of the room the teenage girl glanced up at me in fierce confusion. She wore a Depeche Mode t-shirt with a pair of skimpy denim cutoffs over a pair of black tights and unlaced Doc Martens. The girl threw a knife coated with peanut butter down on the tile counter next to the sink, grabbed a sandwich from the counter, and rushed past me.

"Old cunt," she snarled at the slight figure who stood between us.

Lee Joon turned and barked something Korean in response at the girl's retreating back. The old woman looked startled to see me standing in the doorway. Had she understood what the girl had said to her? Her timeworn features rearranged themselves, but were unable to completely erase her ire or her surprise.

"She stole food," Lee Joon said. "We only eat at certain times. Everyone pays or has special voucher."

"Perhaps I should have called to make an appointment to see you." I tried to look apologetic but professional.

"Junk food. That's all the young people want nowadays is junk food. Here we fix good food. Real food." She wiped the already clean counter furiously with a damp sponge.

A large pot simmered on the stove. I walked over and looked in at steaming chunks of fish floating plump and white on the bubbling surface. I had never tasted Korean food. A ladle lay nearby. I picked it up. "May I?"

Lee Joon frowned with annoyance but handed me a small styrofoam cup from a cabinet. She took the ladle from me and gave me a minute amount of the boiling broth.

It burned my lips. It was spicy, hot, and complex. I murmured my appreciation.

"*Maeuntang,* " she named it.

"Did you make this? It's wonderful."

She took the paper cup from me without saying anything and threw it in the trash.

"You're a great cook," I offered enthusiastically.

"Yes, I am very good cook." She folded her arms across her chest. "Why do you come here? I got nothing to say to you."

"I'm just trying to help. You must be upset about the *kye.* It'll make you feel better to talk about what happened."

She waved her hand dismissively as if she didn't have any use for touchy-feely bullshit. "Maybe somebody did steal our money. I didn't see money."

I hadn't seen any either. Only the box. Had it really contained the money? The guy who stole it had seemed happy about whatever was in it. I hoped this old lady would tell me more if I treated her right. Being gracious didn't seem to work. That was too bad: I like being gracious. "You've known Dorothy a long time, haven't you?"

"Long enough." With some encouragement Lee Joon said she'd known both sisters since her husband opened a store on Olympic. She said the name of the store as if it was Neiman-Marcus.

"I haven't met Jin yet," I said. "Is she a good friend of yours?"

Lee Joon nodded without answering.

"It must be wonderful to have a friend like Dorothy too," I gushed like a sorority girl at a rush party. "She's beautiful. I can see everyone adores her and looks up to her because she's so wise. She's a natural-born leader."

"Dorothy always try to run the show, all right," exploded Lee Joon. "Tell everyone what to do."

I gazed down at the floor awkwardly as if her anger discomforted me. I held it for a second as if she'd surprised me and embarrassed both of us with her unseemly outburst. It's like fishing. One of the few valuable things I ever learned from my father. You let the fish have the line and you wait and then you play it. When a decent length of time had passed, I looked up. She was slightly flushed. I had embarrassed her. Time to throw some nice. I told her I hadn't understood the name of her husband's store. I apologized and asked her to repeat it for me.

Inspecting me with disdain, she repeated it. "Hangul is most sensible language in the world. Simplest." She shook her head as though I should learn it but I was probably too dumb.

"Is your store still in existence?" The uprising was like an economic holo-

caust for the Korean business community. Nearly 90 percent of the
destroyed businesses hadn't been able to rebuild.

"Best grocery store in town. You bet. My son runs it now."

"Was it damaged in the riots?"

Lee Joon turned away and stirred the soup briskly before turning off the
fire beneath it.

"I'm sorry. I don't mean to pry. I'm just trying to think of all the possible
tax implications. The news said storeowners lost everything, their entire
life savings."

"We have insurance," she insisted.

I wondered if it was true. I'd read that many merchants had not been carrying insurance because of prohibitive costs due to redlining. Even if they
did have coverage, it was unlikely that the companies were making
prompt payment. Seventy-five thousand could come in very handy to a
damaged business. I watched Lee Joon. She'd probably told her son about
the *kye* money. She'd want to help him out. Wouldn't she choose her son
above all others?

"Are you still involved in the store? I imagine you worked with your husband when it got started."

"Of course I helped my husband," she retorted, adding that they'd
worked fifteen-hour days and the store was very successful. "When my
husband died two years ago, I wanted to keep working, keep track of the
books and accounts. But my son said, 'Mom, you take vacation.' "

I nodded. "So now you volunteer your time here."

"I always volunteer here. Many years," she corrected me.

"That's wonderful. If you change your mind and want to talk to me about
the tax situation, give me a call." I handed her one of my business cards.
"Would you show me around before I leave?"

Lee Joon walked past me without responding, turned out the kitchen
light, and started down the hall. I hurried after her. Her lips were set grim-
ly, but then, not without some pride, she barked, "There's art gallery, card
room, room for sculpture and painting."

I let her show me the rooms I'd already seen and asked what was in the
rest of the building. We shuffled silently toward the other hall, past the old
man at the reception desk. He was asleep again, snoring this time, with an
unlit but still stinky cigar perched in a red enamel ashtray.

"Library." Lee Joon opened the door and pointed inside a small empty
room whose walls were covered with shelves laden with both musty books
and shiny magazines. "Meeting room." She opened the door and showed
me a larger room with about fifty metal folding chairs stacked in the rear
corners. At the end of the hall she stopped and opened the last door. "Exercise room." I peered in. The angry teenage girl I'd seen with the sandwich

danced alone while smoking a cigarette. She wore a Sony Walkman, which was turned up full blast. She glanced at us, did an aggressive Roger Rabbit, then continued her solitary hip-hop routine.

"Do many young people come here?" I wondered aloud as Lee Joon started to lead me back out the door. Shouldn't the girl be in school? They were always talking about how important education was.

"We have very nice dances. Boys and girls dress up nice." She sniffed disapprovingly at the lonely dancer. "The Koreatown Civic Association is very popular with the girls and boys. Very popular."

The girl ripped off her headphones before running out of the room. "Are you kidding me! This is the most boring fucking place on earth! I can't wait till the new sports center's finished so there'll be something to do, somewhere to go where you don't have to look like a mummy."

Lee Joon stamped her little foot in its sensible collegiate Bass Weejun. I wondered where she had bought them. I hadn't seen any for years.

"I'm sorry she was rude to you," I said. "You've had an awful day. Her, me, both of us bothering you." I put my hand out toward her to steady her or comfort her.

The old woman ignored my hand. "Sports center! I'm sick of hearing about sports center. Just another place for gangsters and hooligans."

I stopped in my tracks. I was charmed. Hooligans. "What's the sports center?"

"On Normandie. Near Olympic. New center for Mexicans. Salvadorans. Going to have boxing." She shook her head as though she couldn't imagine anyone of any value liking boxing.

"Mexicans? Salvadorans?"

Lee Joon smiled slightly, pleased with my apparent stupidity. She'd be able to tell Dorothy I was an idiot. "When Koreatown was burned down, it wasn't the blacks. Mexicans and Salvadorans burn down Koreatown. Here everybody from Mexico and Central America. Now just a few from Korea."

I gestured in the air as if I didn't understand what she was getting at.

"Korean businessman, Mr. Ko Won Bae, gives money to the community to build this sports center." She looked proud of this civic effort but doubtful of its success. "Get Mexicans and others off the street. They say no more trouble."

I nodded my head. "Great idea! Give kids somewhere to go. Let people from all countries be together, play together."

Lee Joon snorted with disdain. "Place for all criminals to be together. Make more trouble. Look, don'tgetmewrong..."

Had Lee Joon learned English from old gangster movies? George Raft? This would thrill Lupe, all these old biddies talking like B movies. Why do they always talk so fast in those old movies?

"...Ko Won Bae, plenty smart businessman. Makes a lot of money. Gives a lot of money to people of Koreatown. To our association. I support Ko Won, respect Ko Won, but I don't want more Mexicans in Koreatown with their loud music and noisy children. They're the kind of people who throw trash on the streets. Koreatown for Koreans."

Did many of the Koreans feel like Lee Joon? I wondered again where Hector "Manos" Ramos had met Kim and why the Ivory Princess was sleeping with a bullethead like Hector. Lee Joon showed me to the front door. I wondered if I should bow. She opened the door. Blaring *salsa* music and the roar of traffic rushed in. Then the sound of flutes and small drums wafted down the hall of the Koreatown Civic Association. A woman's voice soared in a high-pitched but sweet traditional song. I closed my eyes for a second. I smelled rose incense and oranges. I opened my eyes and once again examined the old woman in front of me. I felt suffused with the lovely mysteries of the Orient and a deep aching to be part of the new multicultural Los Angeles. I bowed.

Lee Joon slammed the door between us.

I got in my car, shoved the Peter Tosh Equal Rights tape in again, adjusted it to full blast, and drove out to North Hollywood. It was hotter than hell in the Valley and everything was pale, sundrenched, bleached of sharp edges. I drove past Universal City, the old lot of Universal Studios that has been turned into an amusement park with a public transportation system more sophisticated than that of the city surrounding it. Above the freeway the three black glass towers of the City loom menacingly on a hill, their smooth surfaces marred by huge horizontal brown travertine marble slabs like the eruptions of some terrifying tropical disease. I drove down the wide boulevard through what were once the immeasurable wheat fields of Isaac Lankershim. The film industry found the Valley photogenic and western. Less hazy at one time than the LA basin.

I drove up Burbank Boulevard past a mile or so of burger stands and Xerox places, then turned left near a Methodist church built in the Spanish Colonial revival style now reserved for taco take-out franchises. I parked in front of a run-down but clean white stucco store next to a vet's. It was the temple of my master.

It was cool and quiet inside the *do jang.* The stucco walls covered with white rice paper, the concrete floor with thick white matting. The room was empty. I took off my high heels and placed them on a wooden rack next to the door. I glanced at my watch. The next class wasn't until four. It was just a little past one. I saw the flicker of candlelight from the end of the hall where Master Kyung Sun Lee, Golden Tiger, maintains his red and gold altar.

As though expecting me, Sun Lee, dressed in his immaculate white *do bak* covered with colorful silk patches of tournaments he has won, stepped from the hallway into the space. With his receding nebbish brown hair clipped short and his Wonder Bread skin, he looks like a computer nerd. He's as anglo as you can get. I suspect his real name is Bob.

I bowed. He bowed in return.

"I hope I'm not disturbing you. There's something I wanted to ask you..." I stopped. I still have trouble calling him Master Tiger. A year ago I had found an ad for his Tae Kwon Do school in my local throwaway paper. Tae Kwon Do, original Korean karate, ancient, sophisticated. I've never really told him why I wanted to learn martial arts. Never told him about my gun, the shooting range. It's well enough if he thinks I want to protect myself from rapists and muggers. Bob is training warriors, yes, but not killers.

"I got a job over in Koreatown. I don't understand the people. They won't talk with me. There are things I need to find out."

Sun Lee turned toward his kitchen to make us some tea. "Every stranger is a stranger. And the mountain is tall."

I shook my head as I followed him silently to the kitchen. Great. Someday fish will fly. Why did I have to come from such a dysfunctional family?

CHAPTER SEVEN

Geologically the Korean peninsula is mostly paleozoic and mesozoic like southern Manchuria, but the southeastern part of the country, like Japan, is more recent. The people of this mountainous island bounded by the Yellow Sea and the Sea of Japan are related to the Mongolian race and can probably be traced back to the fossil men of Tzuyang and Liuchang. The Golden Tiger had spoken in a stilted formal way, as if he was narrating a travelogue.

I didn't pay much attention to the scenery in Laurel Canyon on my way back over the hill to Hollywood. I was trying to digest everything he'd told me because I needed a basis for understanding the old women. One of them had to have been involved in the theft of the *kye*. And the death of a friend. But which one?

As part of our warm-up exercises at the *do jang* I'd learned to count to 100 in Korean while we did sit-ups and push-ups, but I realized I didn't know the slightest thing about Korea or Koreans. Despite my professed desire to sing the Internationale on top of all the barricades across the world wherever human rights were endangered, hadn't I been as guilty as anyone of buying into the stereotype of Koreans in LA as just greedy liquor store owners? Before I met Kim and Dorothy, the only Korean I'd ever spoken to was a guy who ran a minimart with take-out pizza near my apartment.

The Golden Tiger had described ancient competing states to me. Like Big Hazard and *Tres Puntos* in East LA, like South Central and Koreatown, I thought. The founding mythologies of these Korean states were more or less the same: the immigrant leader of a more advanced culture was invariably called the Heavenly Son. He marries a girl of the native people with a less developed culture and founds a royal family. The social system is then a dual organization, an upper class of immigrants and a lower class of native peoples. You can't get away from it, I admonished myself, it's always the story of class struggle. These ancient people made clay figurines. They built huts in a round dugout form. They fished with nets and hunted with spears. They knew how to sew with bone needles, how to select seeds, and how to destroy weeds to protect their crops. They cast bronze trinkets, axes, and arrowheads. They believed all things in nature had powerful spirits, and shamans were their intermediaries with the spirits.

I hugged the curve and downshifted, slowing up behind a ragged old baby blue Cadillac with a bumper sticker that proclaimed: PROSPERITY IS MY CHOICE.

"They worshiped their ancestors," Sun Lee had said. I'd seen that Kim was devoted to Dorothy. Was I a good daughter? Probably not. I moved to Los Angeles to put as much distance as possible between myself and my parents.

I started to feel the old anxiety and guilt in my stomach about my family, so I tried to remember what else the Golden Tiger had told me. That Korean history was the story of these competing local tribes and their efforts to remain free of the Chinese and Japanese, who both wanted to dominate the strategic landbridge. It was the history of a people who wanted to remain isolated. They invented woodblock printing and the first encyclopedia, they printed with metal type two hundred years before Gutenberg. He explained that during much of this century and the last the Japanese had occupied Korea with a military government that tried to eliminate Korean culture. Natural resources were exported, civil rights almost completely wiped out. During World War II, Japan used Korea as a factory and arsenal. Korean citizens were drafted into the Japanese army.

"They had a history before they came here," he reminded me.

He also said that Korean people are typically inclined to possess a self-motivated, self-effacing, extroversive, and sociable character. So why wouldn't they talk with me? I was trying to help them.

I decided I should drive over to central Hollywood to Bronson before I returned to Koreatown. At the south end of Bronson is the Paramount Studio lot with its black iron Spanish Renaissance gate. At the north end, according to my Thomas map guide, is the location of the Church of the Big Mother. I thought I should find out if anyone was going to bail Venus Howard out of jail.

I cruised slowly up the street toward Franklin, looking for the address I had written in her file. A crack dealer stood on a quiet corner blanched by the ferocious September sun. Number 1200 was a white stone Hansel and Gretel cottage probably built in the mid-twenties. It looked like medieval rural England except for two enormous royal palms behind it dancing and swaying in the filthy breeze.

The yard was immaculate emerald grass, and I followed a curving red brick path across it to a heavy dark wood door hinged on the right with two large black triangles of metal. I was unable to hear anything inside. On either side of the door were windows with heavy leaded glass tinted red. I knocked on the door.

When no one answered, I tried the doorknob. Was the church truly a place of worship open to all? The door creaked and swung slowly inward. I stepped inside.

I was in a small white anteroom bathed with red sunlight from the windows. On either side of me stood copper vases nearly as high as my waist.

They were filled with water, and on the surface of each floated a gardenia. In front of me was a narrow arch shaped like a vagina. This entrance was cloaked with many strands of clear crystal beads that hung like a spooky psychedelic hymen, the sunlight breaking and shattering against the beads into red, blue, purple, and yellow all over the innocent walls.

I waited for permission to go farther, but no one appeared. From the next room I heard Pachelbel's unmistakable Canon in D. I paused warily, feeling something was wrong. Disco, yes. Rod Stewart, yes. This I would expect. Perhaps the kinkiest libido might demand Motley Crue or Guns n' Roses. But Pachelbel? I pushed through the beads.

The air was heavy with jasmine and musk incense. At my feet was a red, black, and orange Persian rug, the kind sold outdoors on Highland Avenue down near Sunset for $29.99 by guys who drive old Toyota Celicas. I was flanked by two white marble columns—these sold on La Brea south of Wilshire by black men going "checkitout, checkitout." On each column smoked a bronze incense burner. The walls were white, the ceiling a pale pale blue over which someone had clumsily daubed white paint to indicate clouds.

In front of me stood the goddess Aphrodite.

Made from a mannequin. She wore a sheer red nylon nightie. Her feet were stuffed into a cracked pair of black patent stilettos to which had been added black ribbon winding around her calves like ancient sandals. The flame red wig on her head was crowned with a wreath of bay leaves. Her arms stretched out stiffly to me.

"Step forward. The Mother will receive you," rasped a live voice.

I looked around the room. Off to my right I saw a small dirty kitchen. I stepped toward it and peered in. It was empty except for the usual grimy broken appliances left by people who have moved out in a hurry.

"The Mother is waiting," the voice croaked.

In the flickering shadows, moving deeper into the main room I passed the statue of Aphrodite and nearly tripped on a wooden kneeler stationed in front of a throne covered with black fur and mottled with old come stains. The throne was empty, but flanked by mirrors so that my own image was thrown back at me. Platinum hair blown straight that morning after I washed it and held back from my face now by a narrow black grosgrain ribbon. The careful makeup I had been taught to apply by a nice man at the Chanel counter of I. Magnin. Translucent powder, slight highlights of copper on my cheeks and eyes, black mascara. Tempting Red lipstick. Of course I have good skin and a regular routine. And I always dab a discreet touch of Chanel No. 22 on my wrists.

"Behold the Mother." The voice interrupted my careful appraisal of myself.

A pale slender teenage girl rose silently from where she had been coiled on the red satin sheets of a king-size bed. Directly behind her stood a gold altar with two flickering white candles. Above the altar was a black-and-white poster of Marilyn Monroe with her skirt blown up toward her waist. The girl walked to the edge of the bed and posed above me with her arms stretched out, her long black hair past her waist but not completely covering her nakedness. I stared at her navel in confusion. A small black spider was tattooed on her left pelvic bone.

"I'm here about Venus," I stammered, withdrawing my attention from her shaved private part. I wondered how this was done. Every time I try to shave my bikini area I end up with a rash of small red bumps.

"You want Venus? For the mother-daughter number? A hundred and seventy-five dollars gets you Mom in an apron and a Catholic schoolgirl uniform for yourself. Mom goes down on you or you can go down on Mom. It's two hundred and fifty dollars for 69."

I'd never even seen my mother naked! Who'd want to see their mother naked? I don't want any kind of family activity. Even the conventional visit-the-family-for-Thanksgiving kind of thing. No, thank you. Families, they fuck you up. It had taken me years to get away from mine. Was this neurotic on my part? Other people wanted to be close to their families. Lupe wanted to be with her mother and her son. Kim and Dorothy were a family. I've always been a loner. "No, Venus—"

"Oh, you want the secrets of Venus." She cupped her breast like Botticelli's Venus rising from the sea. "The secrets of love. The secrets of erotic enchantment." A strong blast of mouthwash emanated from her ruby lips.

"Venus sent me—"

"After you give your offering, I will teach you the ancient wisdom." She dropped to her knees on the bed, knocked a *TV Guide* to the floor, and placed a basket of fruit between us. She grabbed a banana. "Watch this. We'll start with blowjobs. Is that gonna be cash or credit card?"

"I'm Venus's lawyer." I explained I'd been told to come here so someone could get the cash to spring the High Priestess from jail. I asked if she was Heather or Sarah.

The girl tossed her hair nonchalantly aside, peeled the banana, and chomped into it. "Sarah," she said with a mouthful of food. "Larry, I mean Adonis, is the only one who can get the money. He's gone. You'll have to come back later." She pushed the rest of the banana into her mouth. "Sure you don't need to know any of the ancient secrets? It's supposed to be forty-five dollars, but if you give me cash, I can show you for thirty. Your husband'll never look at another woman."

"I'm not married."

"Ok, your boyfriend then."

"I don't have a boyfriend. Not for several years."

"Man." She shook her head thoughtfully. Her hair parted, letting one of her small breasts peek out. "Then you're gonna need the whole series. How to meet men. How to dress." She pointed disapprovingly at my navy linen pants. "You can pay it in installments."

I told her I'd get back to her on that and that I had another appointment I had to go to.

Back at my car I hung my navy jacket carefully on the passenger seat so it wouldn't get any more wrinkled. What did I know about men? The last time I had a real boyfriend was four years ago while I was still in law school. Bill Hughes was my age but was behind me in school because he had worked as an engineer for two years after graduating from Stanford. I noticed him the very first day. He was nearly six feet tall and had light brown hair that fell past his shoulder blades. I hung out in the morning on the patio where he drank coffee with other guys from his class, but he never noticed me. After several weeks I followed him down the hall to his torts class and introduced myself. We were together for nearly a year after that.

I started the car. There was no point in going through the whole stupid thing about Bill again. Where I'd gone wrong, the skinny brunette I found out he was fucking every time he wasn't with me. I turned the radio on, punched the stations a few times, then found a Howlin' Wolf tape. I didn't want to think about those things. It was ancient history. The day was growing hotter by the minute, and I had business in Koreatown.

On Vermont I stopped to use a pay phone. I called Dorothy, but no one was there. I called Cafe James Dean and asked for Kim. There was some haggling in Korean in the background before Kim answered. I told her I planned to go talk with Nancy Johnson that afternoon and I wanted to know how to get hold of her. I said it would be best if I could drop in on Nancy Johnson without her knowing I was coming.

"That's a good idea," Kim agreed. "You and I didn't get to talk much last night. I want to be able to fill you in on anything you need to know. Nancy wasn't Jin's best friend, but they did spend some time together." She told me that nearly every Wednesday afternoon Nancy went to the United Korean Methodist Church on New Hampshire to attend a service and then drink tea with the other wizened Methodists.

"You will find out who did this, won't you?" Kim implored. "My god-mother Dorothy's frantic. She's so old, I don't know how much more stress she can take. She hasn't stopped crying over Jin. She's ashamed the money was stolen. For us it's very important not to lose face. We need someone who will help us now, someone good."

I've always had the feeling that no matter what I do it will never be good enough. UCLA law school, cum laude. I will end up a bag lady on the streets of Los Angeles. I promised Kim I'd find out who'd been responsible for the tragedy. I would find out. I would prove myself to them. To Lupe. To Kim. To my father. And all the jerks who ever laughed at me. To Bill Hughes. To Bill's fucking skinny brunette slut. To all the creeps who tried to put me down.

The United Korean Methodist Church was west of the intersection of New Hampshire and 9th and adjacent to the burned-out shell of a former market. I pulled into a lot behind the church and parked next to a Hyundai. Shouldn't Koreans be Buddhists? I made a note to ask the Golden Tiger the next time I went to the *do jang*. I put my suit jacket on and more lipstick. The back door of the church was unlocked and the unilluminated hallway cool. I heard talking and laughing, voices calling out in greeting to one another.

Services had just ended. I hurried toward the departing parishioners. Nancy Johnson straggled out at the end of the group. She was dressed like Pat Nixon in a blue-and-black floral print dress with matching short-sleeve jacket. Her hair was stiff and shiny, as though she had just had it done that morning and then had it frozen. Like cryogenics.

I stepped up to her and said hello. She looked quickly from me to the women she was talking with. A frown flashed across her face as she recognized me, and she spoke hastily in Korean to the other women. They nodded and made their way toward the exit.

"What did you say about me?" I wondered.

"I told them you are life insurance agent," she said, pointing at my crumpled suit. "Come, we'll go sit in the library and drink some tea. You can explain how I'll get tax deduction for theft of the *kye* money."

I followed her into the library. She gestured for me to make myself a cup of tea. I had expected some kind of ceremony with a ceramic teapot and dainty cups without handles, but instead I was handed a chipped mug and a Lipton's tea bag.

"You should have made an appointment so I could have my tax returns with me."

I felt queasy. Tax was the hardest class I ever took. Zero comprehension. I'm good at memorizing things, though, so I learned it like a foreign language for the exams and then forgot it. I took a deep breath and dove in. "It won't be necessary to see the returns at this time since we won't be averaging the loss. We'll be extrapolating from capital gain and then reassessing in the next quarter with a division between "

"Ok, ok. I never understand all that stuff. My husband always took care of it."

I nodded sympathetically. "Yes, you said he was a U.S. soldier. Did you meet him during the Korean War?" I paused awkwardly. Maybe her family had been killed or their house destroyed. Maybe they had been bombed.

She said she'd met him at the end of the war, and he brought her to the United States. "I'm a citizen."

"Did you know Dorothy in Korea?"

She looked at me incredulously. Like I was some Midwesterner asking a person from Hollywood if he knew Charlton Heston. "No. I met Dorothy when she opened her restaurant..."

"In Koreatown?"

She nodded. "Same street where Kim has her restaurant. At that time not so many Koreans here as now. Not so many restaurants. Dorothy made it just like the Shining Pearl, her restaurant in Seoul."

Nancy Johnson was a real chatterbox. Too helpful. It made me wonder if she was telling me the truth. Her story would need double-checking. I'd have to play all the old women against each other to find the essential elements. I asked if she'd gone often to the restaurant in Koreatown.

"Oh, yes. All the time for lunch. My husband want to eat hamburger every day, but I get tired of Bob's Big Boy. I want *saengson chigye*, fish and vegetable stew. Too much trouble to make for just one person."

I wanted to know how tight she was with Dorothy, so I asked her if she had lived in Koreatown since she arrived as a war bride.

"My husband bought us a house in San Fernando Valley, Studio City. In those days you buy good house, with big yard, lemon and orange trees. I am only Korean person, only person not white. They treat me like I'm a little doll, not a real person. I feel bad. All alone. Don't have any children because my husband doesn't want any. He sees I am lonely, don't have any friends, so he teaches me to play poker. We go to other people's houses, they come to ours, but still I don't get close with anyone. Finally he understands how lonely I am. I get him to give me car so I can go over to Koreatown in daytime, talk my language, eat food I like. So I meet Jin."

"I haven't met Jin yet," I said. "Didn't she just come here recently from Korea?"

"No, she came same time as Dorothy in beginning of sixties." Nancy Johnson said the Shining Pearl restaurant made good money for the two sisters in Korea. Seoul, which suffered more destruction during World War II than Berlin, was a very busy place after the war. "They have money, but also have old parents, and parents don't want to leave Seoul so Jin and Dorothy don't move here until their mother and father die. We take care of family."

More of the arcane and tedious familial obligations. I shuddered. "You became a good friend of Jin's?"

"She's like big sister to me. I go to the restaurant every day, see Jin. We talk. I teach Jin to play poker. We laugh. Sometimes drink a little *jinro*."

"Is she as beautiful as Dorothy?"

Nancy Johnson laughed. She told me that although Dorothy and Jin were perfect sisters, Jin was certainly the more beautiful. She said she'd learned in the long afternoons over cards that Jin had been an excellent student but was only able to attend school until she was fifteen because the economic situation under the Japanese occupation of their country was so terrible she needed to get a job to help her family. Jin had wanted to be a teacher and teach at a university but instead had to work in a factory.

"When Jin was just seventeen she marry one of her teachers. He was a lot older than her. They had a son, but he was killed in Korean War. Jin's husband died too, long time ago. She never get married again."

I looked down at the empty mug in my hand. I'd been lost in Nancy Johnson's story and didn't remember drinking the tea. "Last night someone said they thought your nephew Henry stole the *kye* money."

"That's Chu Chu Park. Big talk. Henry owns clothing business. Very rich. Went to Seoul last week to make deal to buy another business. Even though he's gone much of the time, he still remember to send me a little check every month. He's good nephew. Somebody want to find out what happened to our money, they find out about Chu Chu."

"What about Chu Chu?"

Nancy Johnson slumped back in her chair. "This is church. I don't talk bad about another person in church. You ask someone else who Chu Chu owes money to."

I quickly reviewed with myself what I knew. That Nancy Johnson's husband had been a pharmacist. He left her the house when he died, probably insurance and a pension fund. There would be some Social Security. How much would that be? I asked her if she still lived in Studio City. "In case I need to see you again. I want to get back to you as soon as possible with your tax information."

She shook her head. "When my husband died I sold the house and buy other house in Koreatown, near Crenshaw. But now almost all nigger black people there. Like a jungle."

I'd felt bad about her losing her *kye* money until she said that. I stood up. I got Nancy Johnson to tell me the name of her nephew's business, and I wrote down her address and phone number as well. There will be a day when the color of a man's skin is of no more significance than the color of his eyes. The day will come. I believe that. I drove through Koreatown toward my office and thought about the excitement I'd felt watching the televised riots and the disappointment when it was over.

Lupe sat at the desk reading one of my files and drinking a diet Coke.

She glanced up when I came in. "Man, you got some sick dudes. No wonder you don't have much interest in finding a boyfriend. This guy, he had his *pito* out in public. Right in front of a school. How can you defend these sleazebags?"

"It's one of the fundamental rights of the Constitution, equal protection, due process..."

"You only got paid two hundred and fifty dollars for this?" She pointed accusingly at my financial declaration in the file. "You did this for two hundred and fifty dollars? Let this guy go back out on the street so he can shake his wienie at little kids?" She closed the file abruptly and pushed it aside. "I don't know about you. Oh, that reminds me, you got a couple messages from some cretin calls himself Adonis."

I took the slips of paper she handed me. "I been in Koreatown all day. Found out a lot." I told her I talked with Lee Joon, the old woman who'd given me the most attitude. Lee Joon was resentful that her son had stopped her from working. I didn't think she liked Dorothy very much and suspected she envied her independence. She could have taken the *kye* so she'd have something of her own or something to give her son. Nancy Johnson disliked her black neighbors. Maybe she was unable to sell her place in the depressed housing market and took the money to be able to move. There was all throughout Los Angeles a gathering sense of unease and a premonition that *el futuro* would be parched and empty.

"*Oye*, I been thinking about this," Lupe interrupted. "I read your files. You're hardly making any money. Nobody's going to tell you anything about what happened to that *kye*, let alone who killed the old lady. You don't even know if Dorothy's really going to pay you. You should cut your losses now."

Didn't Lupe realize the killer might come back? I intentionally hadn't mentioned it because I didn't want to spook her, but I also couldn't believe she hadn't been thinking of it herself. And no matter what happens or what I have to go through, I will not give up my vision of creating a life for myself here. Under no circumstances. No matter how crazy or dangerous LA, this is the last stop, the last desperate brink before we all drop off the edge of the page.

I picked up the phone and punched in Adonis's number so I could take care of business with him, but it was busy. Probably arranging out-calls for miscreant penitents and other would-be saints.

"So I been thinking about how you could make more money so you could pay me more," Lupe said. "I was reading in the paper about these guys who fake car accidents—"

"Lupe!"

"Well, it was just an idea. I'm only trying to help you. Ok, then, if you're going to go ahead with this, here's what you're going to have to do. It's just like Paul Muni in *The Good Earth*. He had to experiment with makeup until he was able to look Chinese. You know they made all those old movies with white people made up to look Asian." She rummaged excitedly through her purse and triumphantly pulled out a black eyeliner pencil. She pushed me into one of the matching vinyl chairs in front of the desk. "Yeah, this is going to be great. But we're going to have to do something with your hair."

CHAPTER EIGHT

Lupe and I started the night at Yee Mee Loo's on Spring and Ord in Chinatown. It was dark and everything was painted gold and red. Racks of booze formed a pagoda behind the bar. I couldn't believe I'd let her talk me into this. I didn't want to stay because I was afraid we'd run into someone I knew. Who could miss my blond hair? The place was full of downtown artists, off-duty cops, and haggard Public Defenders. They might ask about Lupe or my bizarre black eye makeup.

"Great place to pick up sheriffs near retirement age," Lupe observed. She ordered Mai Tais with extra cherries and orange slices, then began instructing me on how to act Oriental.

"Keep your eyes down when you speak. Giggle at the end of every sentence. Didn't you see *Flower Drum Song?*"

"That was about Chinese, not Koreans," I argued. "What are we doing in Chinatown?"

Lupe shrugged. "It's all basically the same. Watch the women for any pointers you can pick up." She ordered egg rolls and a couple of dishes of little barbecue ribs. The kind that look like they come from dwarf pigs.

Later we went over to a karaoke bar on Beverly Boulevard and had more Mai Tais at a place with a waterfall. Rollicking patrons sang along to Frank Sinatra as the lyrics to "My Blue Heaven" flashed on video monitors bracketed overhead. Lupe pointed out a table with a group of salesmen from Taiwan and pushed me toward them so I could practice my "Orientalness."

"A hundred thousand miracles are happening every day. A hundred thousand miracles," Lupe crooned off-key.

"Knock it off, would you?" I moaned in embarrassment, hoping no one could hear her. I turned away from her barstool. The group she had pointed out stared back at us. Lupe was a little drunk and her voice was getting loud.

One of the men stood up, then came over to the bar. He asked us to sit with them. He told us he'd graduated from the University of Ohio business school. With a greedy look in her eye, Lupe pulled me to the table with her. She smiled and bowed at everyone until she finally chose a chair next to the oldest of the men and drew it up close beside him. The businessmen, who were plenty drunk, ordered another round of drinks for us and kept speaking to each other in Taiwanese and the occasional English phrase.

"Macintosh," shouted one of the men on the opposite side of the table.

"Apple," shouted another in response.

The man next to me leaned close and put his hand on my knee. "I love your eye makeup. It's so European. So French."

I hoped Lupe noticed the heavy cruise the guy was giving me. I'd told her I could get as many men as I wanted. Didn't this prove it? His hand rubbed up toward the inside of my thigh. I picked the hand off my leg and kicked Lupe under the table while the businessmen screamed about computers. The Esperanto of the fin de siècle. We turned back and forth between the arguing men like spectators at a tennis match. I was bored out of my skull, but trying to be polite.

"What kind of watch is that? Does it have different time zones on it?" Lupe asked the old guy next to her. "I always get so confused when I travel. How many hours' difference is there between LA and Hong Kong?"

He told her how many hours' difference there was. His English wasn't as good as the other men's. I tried to catch Lupe's eye to tell her I wanted to leave.

"You must do a lot of traveling in your business. How many time zones does it keep track of?" She touched his hand, which he extended toward her so she could get a better look at the Rolex.

"It's very heavy," Lupe murmured. "Heavy," she repeated in slow breathy English.

He took the watch off and handed it to her. She strapped it on her wrist with a satisfied look. The conversation around us went on in more and more technical terms. It was endless, and I could no longer tell what language they were speaking.

"IBM," shouted one of the partisans.

"Epson!"

Lupe giggled uncontrollably at something the old guy said. Her arms flailed wildly above her head, knocking the tray of drinks out of the hand of the passing cocktail waitress. Ice flew everywhere. Lupe and her gentleman friend were drenched with Mai Tais and grasshoppers. The old guy jumped up, wiping furiously at his green-stained lap, and stalked off to the men's loo. (I made a mental note to find out if this was a Chinese word.)

Lupe got up, apologizing and bowing as she'd instructed me to do earlier. She bowed her way out the front door. I caught up with her by the car. I told her to go back inside and give back the Rolex.

"He said I could have it."

"Lupe, if you want to keep your job at my office, take it right back in there and—"

"He did say I could have it, because I'm so pretty." She shifted slightly so the streetlight caught the right side of her face and cast the left into a shadow.

She was staggeringly beautiful. I've always been intimidated by girls who are prettier than me. "My place is totally legit and if you work there, so are you," I insisted.

"He did give it to me..." I heard her muttering as she went back inside the bar. She was back in a minute and we got into the car.

"Did you give it back?"

"Of course," she pouted.

"Scout's honor?"

She tossed her hair impatiently and buckled her seat belt. "Yes."

We moved on to a Japanese place on Beverly. With geishas. They wore kimonos with vibrant pink and purple silk sashes. A couple of the more contemporary geishas wore Chanel suits. At the door a guy charged us twenty-five dollars admission. It seemed like a lot of money, but Lupe insisted we go in. When we got inside and ordered a drink, the waitress told us it was another twenty-five dollars for the table. Hang on, Visa, it's going to be a bumpy night. We were the only women in the place besides the geishas. Then Lupe insisted we switch to scotch. "More sophisticated," she assured me. They were nearly eight bucks a shot.

"Check this out," Lupe instructed, nodding toward the geishas, her voice filled with admiration. "These are some real pros."

I watched the attentive way the geishas leaned toward the men, the graceful arching of necks, the delicate flutter of white hands.

"They make some real money in one of these clubs. Ten grand a month. And tips," Lupe said. "Man, I hear they get diamond rings, apartments, sometimes a Porsche Targa."

I took a closer look at the geishas. The exquisite ivory skin. The magnificent long red nails. The room was permeated with the gentle smell of costly perfume. The geisha closest to me was wearing a new pair of Manolo Blahnik purple stilettos. Kicky. Fun. Deadly expensive. I'd seen the same pair in *Vogue* magazine. As I admired the shoes, I noticed she had a small black circle tattooed on her ankle. I tried to decide if it ruined the shoes or showed a strong sense of style. Actually, it was cheap looking.

It reminded me of Kim's tattoo.

"Supposedly, these places are run by gangs. Organized crime," Lupe said, nudging me out of my contemplation of the tattoo. "I don't know. Whenever someone who's not white makes a lot of money, somebody says it's organized crime. Looks like a good job to me."

I remember getting my Visa card out of my wallet and in exchange receiving a bill for fifty-seven dollars accompanied by two cellophane-wrapped peppermint candies. Lupe grabbed the receipt and handed it to me. "Expenses."

I dropped Lupe off in front of the office and told her it would be ok if she came in a little late for work. It was already Thursday morning and she'd need to check on Joey and get some sleep. Then I stopped at an all-night coffee shop on Sunset and had a cup of mud. I'd had only one drink at each place, I calculated. Maybe two at Yee Mee Loo's. Or was it more? Two at the geisha bar?

I coasted over the hill. The San Fernando Valley, a million red and white twitching lights, spread before me. Eucalyptus perfumed the balmy night. The car twisted into a curve, but I held it steady. The Beach Boys sang "good, good vibrations." I didn't want to think about Kim's tattoo anymore.

I was legally drunk.

It is not true that alcoholism is genetic. I had only one drink an hour. It occurred to me that Lupe hadn't finished either of her drinks at the last two bars.

I rolled carefully down Coldwater Canyon and turned left onto my street, Dickens. My apartment's the basic two-story stucco box with a flat gravel roof. It shared a common driveway with an identical building that faced it. Both were owned and minimally maintained by an Armenian named Mr. Zarifian. It was the same dump I lived in while I was going to law school.

I was the only person still awake on my block. I turned off my radio and cut the engine as I turned into my driveway. I coasted to the back of the apartment building and into my assigned parking space. It was dark. Fuck. Neither Mr. Zarifian nor his surly, obese wife had fixed the lights above the parking stalls. A passing cloud covered the moon. I got out of the car holding the keys in my right hand.

I began to walk across the asphalt toward my apartment. The click of my high heels resounded in the empty night. I was steady on my feet, but I tightened the grip on my car keys. I'm always aware. Be aware of your surroundings, that's what the Golden Tiger says. I felt good. They could have tested me right there. My blood alcohol might be more than .10, but I could pass the field sobriety test. Walk a straight line. Stand on one foot with my eyes closed. Fuck the police. I whistled the beginning of the goofy song Lupe had sung in the bar.

Something singed the air near my ears.

I heard the dull whoosh of a flying object.

Then I felt something tighten around my shoulders. A rough rope cut into my chest.

My hands flew up to loosen the grip. I stumbled in my black heels. I was wrenched backward toward the shadowy area where the dumpster was pushed against a concrete wall. At that same instant I heard the muffled footsteps of someone in sneakers closing the distance between us.

I worked my left hand desperately between the thick, scratchy rope and my chest. I smelled the musky pine of aftershave. I was jerked off balance as my assailant wrestled for control. I fell back against him.

He began to grope at the front of my silk blouse, ripping off the mother-of-pearl buttons. He shoved his hand into my bra. He grabbed my breast roughly and I heard him breathing hard. I glanced down. His right hand was pretty beat up looking. As if he'd been in more than a few fights. Everything turned black and swam in front of my eyes. My knees buckled. I felt myself start to sink to the ground. I was about to become a rape statistic. Was he going to kill me when he was finished?

"Horse stance. Balance." I heard the Golden Tiger's voice in the back of my mind. I slid my left foot to the side, bent my knees until I resembled a mounted rider; I felt my elbow smash backward into the unprotected stomach of my attacker.

He let out a gasp as I reached between his legs, pounding with my right fist and the car keys dead into his crotch. "Aim for the zipper," the Golden Tiger taught us. The man dropped the rope. He groaned as he stumbled backward.

"Always follow through. Now what do you do?" I'd heard the Golden Tiger urging many times in the *do jang. I* pivoted quickly on my left foot and with my right kicked the black sweatsuited form in the nuts.

He screamed as he fell into Mrs. Zarifian's camellia bushes. I didn't get a good look at him because he had the hood of the sweatsuit over his head.

Pulling the rope off, I ran toward the stairs to my apartment as I'd never run in my life. I hit the stairs like a pro track star and made it to my front door on the second floor. With shaking hands I fumbled the key into the lock. Listening for him following me, I unlocked the door. I was panting out of control. It had all happened in less than twenty seconds.

I locked the door behind me and fell against it. I couldn't catch my breath. The loud ragged sound of my wheezing filled the room. I dropped the rope I still carried onto the floor. I made my way to the window overlooking the parking area.

The man was just climbing to his feet. He kept his head down, but the hood of the sweatshirt had dropped off. It looked as if he had black hair tied back in a ponytail, but it was dark and I couldn't be certain. I couldn't see his face. He limped as he ran down the driveway to the street. He looked crazy, like some B movie werewolf loping into the darkness. He disappeared and shortly thereafter I heard a car start up. With screeching tires it pulled away fast and sped down Dickens Avenue until everything was quiet again.

I saw something lying in the driveway. From the kitchen I took the large, sharp Reed & Barton silver meat carver my mother gave me for Christmas, then I opened the front door and stepped out onto the landing. None of the neighbors had woken up during the fight. I tiptoed down the stairs. The moonlight sparkled on the oil-stained driveway.

I knelt beside the trampled pink mask.

Black eyes. Garish red mouth. It was the same kind of mask the man who killed Jin Oh not two days ago had worn.

I picked it up and got weakly to my feet. How had he found me? I knew he hadn't been following me all night. I would have noticed. Wouldn't I?

I climbed numbly back up the stairs to the safety of my apartment. I turned on the light and sank down onto the couch. I put the meat carver on the floor next to me. I examined the mask more closely. Who knew me? Only Dorothy. Who could find out where I lived? Lee Joon? Nancy Johnson? Chu Chu Park? I wasn't listed in the phone book. I hadn't even been out to talk with Chu Chu Park yet. How could any of them know where I lived? For Christ's sake. They were little old ladies. Did they have enough money left to hire the thug who jumped me?

Would the guy who attacked me try to hurt Lupe? I tossed the mask on the coffee table and tore open my wallet looking for the piece of paper with her home phone number. I glanced at my Timex. It was nearly 4:00 A.M. With shaking hands I dialed her mother's place in East LA.

The phone rang and rang. I imagined the door of their old stucco busted down, the walls riddled with bullet holes, Lupe and her old lady in a pool of blood. Joey, dumb with shock, wandering vacantly between the bodies...

"¿Qué?" the old woman answered groggily.

"Está Lupe? Necesito—"

"I don't understand. What do you want?"

"I'm looking for Lupe "

"She's not here. I don't know where she is." Lupe's mother slammed down the receiver.

I turned off the light and sat in the dark. It didn't do much good to have a gun if you left it locked in the car. But man, my Tae Kwon Do moves! It worked! I saw my rapid-fire punches and kicks like a superspectacular cinerama all action flying fists movie.

Why hadn't he punched me back? In class the Golden Tiger had shown us how to block a kick. We learned defensive moves. If my attacker was Korean, wouldn't he know Tae Kwon Do? Better than I did? Maybe it was just a stereotype for me to think he knew Tae Kwon Do. Not all American men play baseball. Or had he intentionally taken it easy on me? The mask grinned nastily back at me. Eventually I slept.

It was nearly ten when I woke up. I had a headache. While staring at the cottage-cheese ceiling, reviewing all that had happened, I decided to go to Koreatown to see Kim. I took a long hot shower, then put on a sleeveless white silk dress and my brown-and-white Bally spectator pumps. It seemed too difficult to get all of the Chanel makeup on, so I had to settle for lipstick and mascara. There was a faint red mark across my chest where the rope had chafed my skin.

It was nearly ten-thirty. I called the office to leave a message for Lupe.

The phone was answered on the first ring. "Law offices. *A sus ordenes.*" Lupe sounded bright and cheerful.

"How'd you get there so early this morning?" I asked.

"I didn't get home that late."

"Your mom said you weren't there."

"Why are you checking up on me? I already got a probation officer. Who, incidentally, is coming here this afternoon. I wish you'd let me hang some different pictures in here. Monet. Some of those cute water lilies—"

"Lupe, a guy tried to rape me last night."

"*No me jodas.*"

"I'm not joking. When I got home he was hiding in one of the parking spaces and he grabbed me."

"Did he...?"

"No. He just tore my blouse and felt my tit." I felt sick thinking about it again. His hot, clammy hand fondling me. "I'm ok." I felt dirty. I wanted to take another shower. Quickly I explained that the man wore a mask identical to the one worn by Jin Oh's killer.

"It's the same guy!"

"I'm not sure. The mask fell off while I was trying to get away, but I didn't see his face." I wondered if there was more than one of these guys. It had been a strange killing. Professional, but squirrelly.

"That creep could come after me too! Jesus, I feel just like Ava Gardner in *The Killers.*"

"Do you have a gun?"

"Of course not! I'm on probation, *¿recuerdas?*"

"Want me to get one for you?"

Lupe didn't say anything for a long time. "I don't need a gun. What are you gonna do? Take the money for it out of my slave wages, then sell it to me?"

I hung up. Damn. Why did I ever think I wanted to be her friend? She was a cold bitch. Or was she afraid of guns because of what had happened in Dogtown? She hadn't even said she was sorry I got molested.

I took the freeway to Koreatown. I felt a kind of dismal Monday morning of the soul. I didn't notice much when I got off on Vermont. It was all the same. Incomprehensible. Foreign and closed to outsiders. A liquor store. A furniture store. A video store. I passed an aqua and purple building with a yellow FOR LEASE sign. Mexicans and Central American men from El Salvador, Guatemala, Honduras stood on Olympic outside a large building supply store waiting to help rebuild the city in a multicultural kind of a way. I supposed I did have an ugly attitude. I parked in front of Cafe James Dean.

It was lunchtime. Inside I stood for a second by the door next to a Lotto

SOULTOWN

273

machine, checking the place out. Only two of the tables were occupied. At court I'd heard people say there were extortion rackets in all the businesses in the Southeast Asian immigrant communities. Kim herself carried a couple of meals to one of the waiting tables. She wore a yellow silk suit. Her long, thick black hair was pulled back with a black chiffon scarf, and she smiled when she looked up and saw me. She put the food down quickly and hurried over to me. I wondered if she had to pay out to keep her place running. If this was a typical noon crowd, it looked as if she'd have a hard time coming up with the necessary extra cash.

"Did you find out something?" she asked without formality.

"I'd like to have lunch. Something not too fancy."

She apologized for not guessing that I was hungry and put me at a table near the kitchen. She went into the kitchen. There was a small stiff cardboard announcement printed in Korean and English propped up on the table. All the tables had one, I noticed. It asked people to contribute to the new Koreatown Sports Center that would be opening soon. I pushed it aside when Kim reappeared and sat down with me. "I told them to grill you some fish."

"A guy jumped me last night. Wearing a Chusok mask."

Kim gasped. She leaned across the table to grasp my forearm. The color drained out of her face and she looked very white under her face powder.

A Mexican busboy came to the table and placed six small white ceramic dishes with different foods in front of me. Kim waved him away with her free hand. "What happened?"

I told her. "Who do you think he is?"

She shook her head. "I wish I knew. Did he hurt you? Did he...?"

"No, he was just rubbing my breasts and..." I broke down, near tears, and stared at the table.

"It happened to me too," Kim said.

I looked up.

"When I was in college at SC. The year before I graduated."

"I'm sorry, Kim..." Why had I been so hung up on the tattoo on her ankle? Lots of college girls have tattoos nowadays.

She let go of my forearm and looked away before continuing. "I was walking to my car after a class. It was about ten at night. This big black guy jumped out of the bushes. I was too scared to scream. After he left I just lay there in the dirt. I couldn't believe he didn't kill me."

"Oh, Kim..."

She said they wrote about it in the *Trojan*, and later she helped organize student watch groups to walk girls to their cars at night. Kim sighed heavily, then, shrugging off the memory, snapped her fingers. The busboy came running over. "Beer?" she asked me.

I shook my head again. "I'm so sorry, Kim. I was lucky. This scumbag wasn't much taller than me. I kicked him in the nuts. I don't think he's going be using his dick for a while."

"Good for you!" She patted my arm again. "Have something to eat. That's kimchi." She pointed at the dishes, explaining that there were spinach, mung bean sprouts, and pickled taro. She told me kimchi is made in the fall. In the average family they use fifty heads of cabbage per family member. The cabbage is seasoned with salt, ground up with hot red peppers, then mixed with pickled turnips, radishes, cucumbers, or other vegetables. It is left to ferment for several weeks in huge earthenware jars buried up to their necks in the ground.

I watched Kim as she explained this. It was apparent she'd said all she was going to say about the attack upon her, but I knew I'd touched something within her. Maybe she felt the same way, because she seemed less guarded and angry than the first time I'd met her. Granted the first time there had been the issue of Joey and the murky offscreen presence of Lupe's potatohead brother, Hector "Manos" Ramos.

I told Kim I'd talked with Nancy Johnson and Lee Joon.

"Not Chu Chu Park?" asked Kim.

I shook my head. "Is that a real Korean name? Seems pretty unusual."

"That's just my point!" Kim exclaimed. "It's not a real name. It's invented. It would be like someone calling herself La Fifi or The Mimi. I don't know why Jin put up with her. Dorothy can't stand her."

"Dorothy means a lot to you, doesn't she?"

"She's been my godmother since I was born. She raised me.

The busboy brought a large white plate containing a thick fillet of salmon to the table. Kim inspected it quickly. It was perfectly grilled with the requisite crosshatches indicating it had been charbroiled. A delicate fragrant sauce in a small white bowl accompanied the fish. I glanced around the dining room, wondering why it wasn't full. Cafe James Dean was a good restaurant.

Kim also glanced around the room and seemed a bit dissatisfied with what she saw. "Dorothy was a friend of my grandmother. Both my mother and my grandmother are dead. I have no family. Dorothy took me in."

"Dorothy helped you get started with the restaurant? With *kye* money, right?"

Kim nodded. "Yeah, after I graduated from SC. There wasn't much I could do with an anthropology degree. Dorothy's always been generous. She's always given me everything I've ever asked for. Jin was like that too."

The fish was delicious. I realized how hungry I was.

"Look, there's something Dorothy didn't tell you about the box that was stolen," Kim said. "I told her she must tell you everything if she expects you to find out who killed Jin. We had sort of an argument about it, and she said I could go ahead and tell you. I think it's part of the reason why she didn't want to call the police. The old people, and the new ones just off the boat, are reluctant to report crimes to the police. A lot of them are self-conscious about their English and they're unsure of the system. A lot of them come from countries where the cops are crooks."

I'd seen that downtown. I often got appointed to represent Mexicans and Central Americans who were afraid of the system. A few months ago I'd been appointed to represent a woman from El Salvador who'd been battered almost to a pulp by her husband, and she'd been more afraid of the police than of her husband.

"It's kind of nutty" Kim's voice trailed off apologetically "but she insists the box is valuable. She didn't want people knowing she had it because she thought they'd criticize her for keeping it instead of giving it to a museum or maybe that someone would try to steal it from her. She says it belonged to Queen Min."

I put down the chopsticks. "Who?"

"Queen Min. The last Korean queen before the Japanese occupation of Korea. When they took over they killed the royal family. Dragged Queen Min out of the palace and set her on fire."

Was the box what the guy in the Chusok mask had been asking Dorothy and Jin about before he killed Jin? "How'd Dorothy get the box?"

Kim shrugged. "I never paid any attention to Korean history. Jin was the one who loved history, knew all that stuff. I wish I'd listened more to her stories...." Kim looked as if she was going to cry. "Korean people have what's called *han*. That means bitter feelings because of injustices committed by government, the Japanese occupation, even by your family members or friends. The box must be valuable to old people like Jin and Dorothy for *han*—"

Kim's story was interrupted by a dark shadow falling over the table. Hector "Manos" Ramos bent down and kissed Kim on the mouth.

"Hey, ain't you the dyke my sister Lupe hangs out with?" he growled at me.

I saw that my chances for a pleasant lunch were over.

CHAPTER NINE

Hector was heavier than the last time I'd seen him, a year ago. Although I searched the sports page for his name, I never saw it. The fight scene in LA is minimal compared with what they say it was like in the forties and fifties, when there were weekly matches at the Hollywood Legion Hall. All the stars attended. The great gyms were down on Main Street. The action moved to the Olympic Auditorium for a couple of decades. Then the old auditorium was taken over by wrestling mania and punk thrash bands who tore the place apart. Now the fights are limited to the Forum on Monday nights, where beers cost five bucks, or to the smoky confines of a nearly bust night spot like the Diamond Girl Bar in Reseda. No, there'd been no mention of Hector in the papers, and he was ominously over the weight requirements for a light welterweight.

Hector pulled out a chair and plopped down next to Kim. He threw his arm territorially around her shoulder and began squeezing it. Kim flinched slightly, as if it was irritating her. "What's she doing here?" he barked, jerking his chin in my direction.

Kim glanced uncertainly at me. I wondered if Hector had known Jin or Dorothy. Had Kim told him she'd dumped Joey off on them? "She wanted to talk about Joey," Kim lied. Her eyes beseeched me not to contradict her. Was she afraid of him?

"Joey!" exploded Hector, pounding his fist on the table. "Don't get me started on that! You were supposed to be taking care of him for me."

"Come on, honey," Kim cooed. "Calm down. You know I had to give him to your sister when she showed up. We can't keep him without legal papers...."

"That's what I'm here about," I heard myself saying. Lord, forgive me for lying and using small children as currency. "Lupe, your sister Guadalupe Virginia, that is, sent me to enter into negotiations with you about the possible placement of her son Joey with you."

Hector frowned. He knew his sister. He knew she wouldn't give Joey to him.

"Perhaps under a temporary guardianship." Lupe would be pleased if I was able to cajole Hector into giving me the lowdown on his new life. "She's very ashamed of her recent misadventure and incarceration. She knows she has to prove herself to society and to her family." I hoped she never found out what I had to say about her to try to get him to talk.

Hector spread his fat hand on the table and stared at it with thoughtful admiration, as if he usually depended on it to make decisions for him. I was glad I'd put on my lawyer clothes that morning so Hector could take seriously what I was saying. "Just let me take care of it," I said. "I know you and your sister aren't getting along very well right now." I smiled a good white Junior League kind of smile at him, polite and beneficent.

"Ok, that's good then. She's finally coming to her senses." Hector nodded his meaty-looking head at me. "Lupe don't take care of him. In and outta jail. My mother's getting too old for this shit." He gave Kim's shoulder another mauling. "There you go, babydoll, just like I told you. Everything'll work out. We'll be able to get married. Like I promised you."

I shot a quick look at Kim. She looked radiant. Transfixed. It didn't figure. She was attractive. He was not. She was smart. He was dumb. Is it really all about sex? Is the whole meaning of life just the old in/out in/out? Nietzsche, Sartre, Aristotle? Maybe it is all just splayed beaver and pounding dick.

"There are still some very important things we'd have to discuss," I insisted in my best Pasadena matron tone. "I need some information about your residence, your day-care plan. Your income." I wondered how he'd met Kim. What was he doing in Koreatown?

Hector glared at me suspiciously.

"There's a form we have to fill out and file with the court about your income," I continued right in my jurist stride. "To show you're financially capable of assuming the responsibility for your nephew."

He removed his arm from Kim's shoulder and leaned toward me, placing both hands on the table.

I stared at his hands again. They were square and mahogany brown. He was much darker than Lupe. The right hand was larger than the left, the knuckles puffy, as if he'd busted his hand a few times.

"Money won't be a problem," Hector bragged. "I'm the director of the new sports center that's opening here in Koreatown."

I congratulated him and told him I'd heard of it. I pointed at the cardboard announcement on the table touting the sports center. Why had a chicano been hired as director rather than a Korean? I wondered if Hector had experienced any of the racism some of the old Korean ladies expressed to me. I asked him to tell me more about the new job.

Hector sat back in his chair looking expansive. "It's a five-million-dollar dream come true. State of the art. Gvm. Weights. Boxing ring. Sauna. Jacuzzi. It's even got an indoor court for basketball or volleyball. I was specially hired to run it, to start a boxing program..."

Wouldn't it be Tae Kwon Do in Koreatown?

"...help get kids off the street. You know, after the riots and all of that."

I nodded encouragement. "Because you're the best-known boxer in LA." Why Hector? In the last eight years two young guys from East LA had fought in the Olympics. Both had won medals in their weight categories.

Their names were in the papers. If the sports center was really a big deal, wouldn't they have tried to get one of them?

"It's not just a job. It's an opportunity to serve the community," Hector recited. "Bring Koreans and latinos together."

I tilted my head in dumb but appreciative bemusement. "I thought most latinos living in Koreatown were Central American, not chicano like you...."

"Community in the big sense." Hector was on a roll. "It was very visionary of Mr. Ko Won—"

"Who?" I interrupted, although Lee Joon had mentioned him.

"Ko Won Bae," chimed Kim in a singsongy voice.

"Ko Won," Hector said. "He's a big businessman here in Koreatown, isn't that right, Kim, honey? He owns, I don't know, maybe three, four, or five businesses. A big electronics store. One of the only ones in this area that wasn't looted and destroyed by the riots. He put his guys with Uzis right up on the roof. It was, like, you know, 'Fuck this shit!'"

What would a big man in Koreatown want with a has-been like Hector, I wondered, but I nodded and looked impressed. "I saw that on television!"

Hector looked well pleased by his connection to greatness. "Yeah, he's on television all the time. Plus, that's how I met Kim."

Kim nodded. "Mr. Won's a big fight fan."

"That's right," said Hector. "I was fighting an exhibition about three months ago out in Monterey Park, and Ko came to it and brought Kim with him. With his group. A big group. It wasn't like Kim was his girlfriend or nothing. That's the kinda guy he is. Brought ten people, paid for everyone. Guy's got class. Total class.

"Anyhow, I won my match. Stupid duffer *mayate* outta Nickerson Gardens. Ko comes back to the dressing room to tell me how great I was. Kim was with him. He invited me out to dinner with his friends. And that was it! Love at first sight, ain't that right, baby?" He threw his arm back around Kim and gave her another ferocious squeeze.

Kim put her hand on his thigh high up near his groin. "That's right, baby."

"Man, whatta night!" Hector sighed, placing his hand over his heart. As his sleeve pulled up slightly I noticed the blue hem of a tattoo of the Blessed Virgin Mary on his forearm. "Ko took us to Pacific Dining Car. You heard about that? Old place near downtown. Right in the middle of *Varrio* 13. Man, if those homeboys only knew. Steaks cost like thirty bucks each. We were drinking French wine and champagne like there was no tomorrow. He sure knows how to party."

"Fantastic!" I agreed. I imagined Hector puking Chateau Lafite and hastily gobbled filet mignon in the men's room of the Pacific Dining Car, returning to the table to paw Kim some more. "Is that when he offered you the job as director of the sports center?"

"Do you need all this for your papers?" Hector asked with annoyance. "What do you really want? You don't care about my life, so don't try to jerk me off."

"Yes, I have to file all this information with the court, and I'm doing this for Lupe "

"You want to stick your face in her box."

"Don't talk to me like that. You don't know me either, so don't be shooting your mouth off about stuff you don't know anything about. I give you respect, so you give me some. I'm willing to help Lupe, give her a job. You want her out on the streets again? Fine, I'll fire her and tell her to go turn tricks right in front of your sports center. I'll tell her to wear a big sign that says she's your sister. We'll see how long you get to be the big *queso* in Koreatown."

Hector thought about this. Kim nodded at him to assist him with understanding the logic of my proposal. "Ok," he said grumpily. "What else do you need to know? Ko Won hired me 'cause I gave him some real good ideas on programs on how to get the Latino kids involved. That's the idea, you know. Get the Latino kids and the Korean kids involved with each other. Sports instead of bangin' on the streets. All they're gonna think about is gangin', bangin', and slangin' unless the community gets involved to provide them with an alternative."

Hector sounded as if he was reading a press release, but with real unstudied sincerity. Kim motioned for the busboy to clear my dishes away. Hector gave the boy a *vato* handshake: a quick shake, then hand curled into a fist and knocked against the other's knuckles. The busboy flushed with pleasure at this recognition. It was possible that I had been wrong about everything. Maybe Hector was famous all over town. Perhaps he was not the monster Lupe had made him out to be.

"You wouldn't mind if I spoke with Mr. Won, would you?" I asked Hector. "Just to verify the required information for the guardianship forms?"

"Whenever you like. My main man. He'll be glad to do anything for me." Kim nodded in agreement, took Hector's hand in hers, and gave it a squeeze. Hector told me he'd call the next day to get me an appointment. I stood up. I got his assurance he wouldn't talk to Lupe about the guardianship.

"Hey," he chortled across the restaurant as I was leaving. "Remember to keep your hands off Lupe. Or I'll have to kill you."

I drove up Vermont toward the office. I was in a bad mood. I wanted to hurt someone. I tried psychotherapy once. I went to a woman in Westwood with an office decorated in soothing blues and beiges. A waiting room with old issues of *Time*. Like someone who's about to kill himself wants to read about last year's news. Leaving out the parts I considered most damaging, I told her my story. She suggested that my family was dysfunctional. That I was out of contact with my inner child. That I felt victimized. She told me to sit on the floor. She gave me a piece of chalk and asked me to draw a circle around myself. To make a boundary that expressed the amount of intimacy I was comfortable with. It cost me a hundred dollars.

I never went back.

Instead I went to the gym. I built my deltoids and my biceps. Sculpted my abdomen. Made my thighs into steel.

I do not believe in the inner child. The idea of a little Whitney Logan inside of me crying out for a teddy bear—I don't buy it. We are filled with dragons and demons and primordial ooze. At least I am. And so I guessed were Hector and Lupe and the guy who tried to rape me last night. I shoved a Bob Marley tape into the tape player. "Positive vibrations, positive vibrations," sang the great Rasta. Positive vibrations, oh yeah.

Lupe was in the office, wearing the same pinstripe suit she'd had on yesterday.

"Didn't go home last night?" I asked, gesturing at her getup.

She didn't answer. Instead she showed me a stack of newly created index cards she had filled out to make a filing system for my disordered cases. She had small, neat block printing. The product of a Catholic school education, I guessed. I imagined Lupe's mother slaving to pay for school and tried to picture Lupe as a girl in a plaid uniform and one of those boxy blue wool blazers with a sacred bleeding heart of Jesus embroidered on the pocket.

"I just saw Hector," I told her.

"So?" Lupe shrugged without looking up from the cards. She nervously shuffled them into a pile.

"I told him you wanted me to do the papers so he can get guardianship of Joey."

Lupe sprang angrily to her feet. "What the fuck are you talking about? I told you to stay out of my business!"

"Relax. I only told him that so I could get him to cooperate with me." I informed Lupe I'd discovered how her brother knew Kim and that there seemed to be something fishy indeed about it.

"Hector's not much for *sesos*," Lupe agreed after I told her all I'd learned. "I'd love to find out more about this gig he has going in Koreatown. I'm sick of hearing my mother talk about how great Hector is. Hector's important new job. You'd think I never brought home a paycheck," she muttered.

I dropped my purse on the desk. "Your mom sounded pissed when I called last night. Why didn't you go home? What about Joey? You're always talking about him, for Christ's sake. Talk, talk, talk. You don't spend any time with him." I shook my head in disgust.

"My mom won't let me stay there no more. Ok? Got it? You need me to draw a picture? My old lady threw me out and I slept on your stupid fucking *pinchi* floor. You'll probably want to deduct that from my crummy salary too. How can you even call this a job? Look, look what I found here." Lupe stepped behind the desk and jerked the top drawer open. "A number 2 pencil, a couple of ballpoint pens, one of which is out of ink"—Lupe threw the pen angrily into the trash—"a two-for-one coupon for Taco Bell, and this." Lupe pulled open the bottom drawer and pointed at a nearly empty bottle of Southern Comfort. "You are seriously undercapitalized. Even worse than I thought. How can you call yourself a professional? I can't believe I let you talk me into working in this shithole."

I walked across the room and pointed out the window at Hollywood Boulevard. A skinny black hooker in a leopardskin mini and a silver halter top lurked in the shade of the video store across the street. I recognized her. She was about thirty. Last year she'd had a friend, a black woman who wore a blond wig, who'd often worked the same corner. I'd seen them many times talking and sharing a smoke. I heard the blonde died. "Come here. Take a look out there."

Lupe sauntered across the room to the window and glanced out. "Yeah, it's the Boulevard. Same old same old. I've done it before, I can do it again. It's not so bad."

"You don't like it here? Want to go back out there? You want to get AIDS? Go on. The door's open. You don't have to be a secretary." I leaned against the windowsill and wouldn't look at her.

"There's a lot to be said for the street. Meet new people. Be my own boss. Keep all the money. Not have to put up with a lot of bullshit from some white chick thinks she knows everything." I heard the click of Lupe's high heels moving away from me across the old wooden floor. "See ya around, *gringa.*" The door slammed closed.

I looked at the Boulevard again. For the second time that day I was near tears. I turned to go after her.

Lupe stood beside the door grinning. "Want me to stay? Cut me in on half of what that old lady Dorothy's gonna pay you."

"You should stay out of this Koreatown stuff. You got Joey to think about, your probation..." I wrapped my arms around myself without thinking, but when I realized how silly that looked I felt foolish and let go. "I'm sorry you got involved. Sorry you saw Jin killed. I told you what happened to me last night. Almost happened," I corrected myself.

"I'll take my chances. Plus I'm gonna use this opportunity to find out about Hector, and I'm gonna finish him off once and for all so he stays out of my business and leaves me and Joey the fuck alone."

I straightened a book in the bookshelf before looking over at her. She was serious. "Ok, if you help me, I'll give you a third. That's it. No deals, no bargains."

"Fucking lawyers," Lupe mumbled as she walked back across the room to take her seat at the desk. She rearranged the papers on top of the desk to her satisfaction. "I had to order some business cards. I charged them to you." She unfolded a yellow paper and showed me a receipt.

MS. VIRGINIA G. RAMOS
PARALEGAL

"You're not a paralegal! You have to go to school for that. It takes about a year—"

"The printer's only gonna take about three hours, so could you let me have the money now? Tell you what, if I like working here, I'll go to school and make it legit. I was good in school. I ever tell you that? Had a 3.8 at East LA City College. Biology major. Got a B in English or I would've had all A's. I was a cheerleader too. Vice president of the coin collectors club...."

I told Lupe to call Dorothy and find out if she knew Ko Won or the names and locations of his businesses in Koreatown. Lupe and I would go that afternoon to talk with him. As I left to get some tacos I heard Lupe on the speaker phone.

"Dorothy? Ms. Ramos here. Ms. Logan's investigative partner...."

Dorothy knew who Ko Won was. She seemed impressed by his name. "Very important man in the community," I heard her say, but her voice was soft and distant as though she didn't really approve of him.

We were given an address on Olympic in Koreatown, and we drove over in my car. Ko Won's place was an electronics emporium in a large mini-mall about half a mile east of Cafe James Dean. The parking lot was crowded, and while we waited for a space Lupe gave her makeup a quick touch-up—another swoop of crimson across her full lips, then black liner under her lower lashes.

She surveyed herself with pleasure in the mirror of a shiny black compact. "Hmm, I wish I had time to get into the whole beading the eyelashes thing. Like Garbo. By the way, Dorothy doesn't know Kim's already friends with this guy."

I rolled up the window and locked the doors. "How do you know that?"

"What do you think, I'm psychic? I asked her if she and Kim knew him. She said they didn't. Not personally, anyhow. I'll tell you something." She tossed her lipstick into her purse. "I don't like this Ko Won guy already.

He's a pimp." She got out of the car tugging her skintight skirt into place.

"We can't go in there with attitude or we won't find anything out," I argued. "As far as we know he's an outstanding citizen." I wondered why Kim hadn't told her godmother she knew Ko Won.

"Then why'd he fix my *pinchi* brother up with that whore Kim?"

"We don't know if she is or not. She's a wannabe rich girl. Went to USC. Besides, she seems to like Hector. Maybe she should marry him and get him off your back."

"I know a working girl when I see one." Lupe frowned.

"Leave it alone," I warned. Had I made a mistake in telling her she could be my partner? Lupe always had to act as if she knew everything. I didn't want her to blow this.

A couple blocked the door of the store readjusting and securing a color tv in a box on a dolly. Lupe tapped her foot impatiently, waiting for them to get out of our way, then pushed past them into the store. The unavoidable slit in her skirt gaped open as she walked, revealing her shapely brown legs.

Don't be sticking your butt in Mr. Won's face. Please, I begged silently.

The store was crammed from floor to ceiling with every kind of tv, vcr, video camera, cellular phone, and laser disc player made in the Far East. There were many shoppers. We stood in the tv sales area as I looked about for a salesperson who could direct us to Ko Won. Lupe stepped in front of one of the cameras that was hooked up to a monitor. Immediately she appeared on the screen of a big fifty-inch Mitsubishi. She threw back her hair and gave the camera some good profile.

"Give me a whiskey, baby. And don't be stingy," she said in a low, gravelly, not-quite-accurate Swedish accent.

"Would you get over here?" I hissed.

"Lighting's not very good," she muttered, leaning into the camera to examine her eye makeup.

A short, fat, bespectacled, friendly-looking salesman in a black suit bore down on us. I raised my hand, motioning him over.

"You want to see some televisions?" he asked, bowing at both of us. "Best prices in town. That Mitsubishi you were just looking at—and I must say, Miss, haven't I seen you on tv before?"

Lupe shot me a smug glance. "Yes. I'm—"

"We're not here to buy anything," I interrupted. "We're here to see Ko Won Bae. Is he here?"

The man bowed again. "Do you have an appointment?"

"No. I'm from *Esquire* magazine," I lied. I hoped he'd heard of it. Koreans seemed to like big names. While driving through Koreatown I'd noticed a Cafe Van Gogh, a Club Annie Hall, and a noodle shop called the Al Pacino. "We're doing an article, 'Where Now, LA? Six Months After the Rebel-lion'—I mean riots—and we want to meet some prominent members of this community to schedule interviews with. That's why we want to speak with Mr. Ko Won Bae."

The man nodded. "Follow me." He led us down the aisle on the east side of the store to a small office. He opened the door without knocking. An ebony wood desk was nearly buried beneath papers and receipts. Two black lacquer chairs with red silk seats flanked the desk, and he motioned us into them. I sat down. It felt as if the legs of the chair had been sawed down. My knees were nearly in my chest, and I had to look up at the desk. The salesman moved behind the desk and drew the chair out. I glanced down. He was wearing $900 English oxfords of deep buttery rich cordovan leather. Handmade. Right out of the pages of *Town & Country* magazine, which my mother had made me read.

"You're Ko Won Bae!" I exclaimed.

He nodded.

"These chairs are real comfortable," said Lupe. "A lot of times my legs just dangle and I can't touch the floor." She smiled graciously and crossed one leg over the other, hiking her skirt up in the process.

"My photographer, Miss Lopez," I hastened. "The reason I was so interested in meeting you is the sports center. I understand you're the driving force behind it."

He bowed again. All this bowing stuff was getting repetitive. He looked like an accountant. "I couldn't have done it without the support of a lot of people. It's for all the people of the community. Koreans, Pan-Asians..."

"Pan-latinos?" Lupe asked. I couldn't tell if she was putting him on or not.

"How did the sports center idea come into being? It's so wonderful, so necessary, bringing people together ." I faltered. What would the sports center mean to Koreatown? Would it be used by all the people of the area? Could people of all colors come together in utopian games or would it become just a graffiti-covered outpost where people were afraid to use the bathroom? Not everyone had forgotten the Uzis on the roofs yet.

"The community responded to the call, and there's been a tremendous outpouring of public support. It's one hundred percent community funded." Ko Won smiled.

Beware those who brag about their charitable work. When I was a little kid I believed in Santa Claus and the Easter Bunny too. The Easter I was seven, I climbed on top of the kitchen cabinets and found the green plastic grass that would fill my Easter basket and a carton of waxy chocolate eggs. I no longer believed all the stories I was told. "I've heard that some people think you just started the ball rolling so you'll get a huge tax deduction."

"No!" He smacked his hand on the desk. "I don't contribute money, I contribute my heart. I get people together so they can support it, so it can belong to them. Koreatown's given me a lot and I'm proud to be able to give something back to all the people who live here. What you say's the kind of talk that keeps our town divided. Everybody suspicious of everyone who's different from them. Now's the time for everybody to come together. Work together. Play together."

"I hear you hired Hector Ramos to run the program," interrupted Lupe, obviously bored with my line of questioning.

"Yes," Ko Won agreed. "The great welterweight 'Manos' Ramos. And he's a real nice guy. You might want to do a photo of him for your article."

"He's washed up. He hasn't had a big fight since late in eighty-eight." Lupe stopped abruptly, but Ko Won didn't seem to notice.

Ko Won nodded. "You must be a fight fan."

"A real fan. He fought Manny Estrada at the Forum. Got his butt kicked. Six rounds. TKO. I had a hundred and fifty dollars on Estrada and I cleaned up."

I pushed myself out of the tiny chair and to my feet. I wanted to get Lupe out of there. I didn't want Ko Won to guess she was Hector's sister. "We won't keep you. You must be awfully busy. Several businesses. The sports center." I shook my head in admiration. "May I call on you again for an in-depth interview?"

"And the photos," he added agreeably, pointing us to the office door. "I'd love to see one of your articles. Send me a copy of something you've published recently. I'll bet you must be a young lady who knows her way around this town. Would that be a good bet for me to take, Miss Lopez?"

Lupe didn't have much to say on the way back to my office. I saw her chewing her lower lip thoughtfully. She stared out the window at the streets of faltering businesses and dying palms.

"What do you think Ko Won meant when we were leaving?" I finally asked Lupe, interrupting her inspection of the Mexicans, *salvadorenos, guatemaltecos,* and Colombians waiting for buses and milling about the corner of Vermont and Santa Monica Boulevard. This was the northern boundary of Koreatown, and the city seemed to reassert its tropical heat. A car pulled up next to us playing a loud *cumbia.* Lupe nodded her head in time to the music.

"Did you hear me? What did he mean?" I repeated.

Lupe glanced over at me. "He meant he thought you were a smartass. I think he knows Hector's my brother. This Koreatown shit looks like it's going to be a harder roll than I thought." She turned back away from me and listened to her music.

I wondered if she was thinking about Dogtown, where we'd seen a man die. I dropped her in front of the office and headed for downtown.

I parked behind a chain link fence next to a warehouse in the light industrial area south of Little Tokyo. I got my gun out of the trunk of the car and went into the warehouse. It's an indoor shooting range. Guns are illegal in Japan, so this is a favorite destination of Japanese tourists. Ten bucks to rent anything you want: .357 Magnum, Smith & Wesson, Lambretta. Bullets are expensive if you have to buy them at the range. I was glad I'd brought my own. I wanted to stay awhile. I felt edgy.

CHAPTER TEN

The northern edge of Exposition Park, a racetrack in the last century, is a lonely though busy intersection. I left my car at a meter and trekked onto the campus of USC. I imagined Kim walking the same path. I was going to find out as much as I could about her. The tattoo on her ankle looked like the one I'd seen on the geisha. Her restaurant looked dramatically unsuccessful. The lofty campanile of the Colonel Seeley Wintersmith Mudd Memorial Hall of Philosophy was overshadowed by dull high rises in which were being educated greedy assholes who drove BMWs, carried cellular phones, and ate at the Hard Rock Cafe. I made my way through crowds of students dressed predictably in $200 athletic shoes and ripped prefaded Levi 501s. Yuppie fucks. They probably asked Mommy and Daddy for money whenever they wanted it.

I wondered if Kim had had the money to keep up with them. She liked nice things. The real Chanel purse. The disdainful way she'd looked at my old car. When did she get the tattoo? As I continued past Northern Italian Romanesque castles to the administration building, I wondered if she'd felt like an outsider here.

There was no record of Kim's graduating. She'd dropped out after the first semester. The demographics say Asian-Americans are more likely than any other racial group to finish high school and go to college. Why had she made such a big deal of her attendance? Was this simply part of the Asian stereotype that they all went to school and got the best grades? Or should it tell me something about Kim's propensity for telling the truth? I'd watch her, but I wouldn't tell her I'd found out she'd lied to me. I didn't like the story she'd told about having been raped here either.

On the way back to my car I stopped at the school of architecture to use a pay phone to call Chu Chu Park, the only member of the *kye* group I hadn't questioned yet. The other women were suspicious that she traveled so much and bought so many clothes and expensive jewelry. Nancy Johnson said Chu Chu was in debt up to her eyeballs. Were creditors after her? Threatening her? Lawsuits? Did she need $75,000 enough to kill for it? I was living on a little over two grand a month and barely staying alive; $75,000 seemed like enough money to solve a few problems with. Yeah, pay off Visa and the department stores, book a trip to the Bahamas. You could squeeze a few pleasurable moments out of $75,000. Might be worth murdering a friend for. I dropped my last quarter in the phone and dialed. The architecture school had a depressing funereal atmosphere. It looked like a savings and loan.

Chu Chu Park answered the phone after three rings. I reminded her who

I was, but she cut me off and said hurriedly in her heavy accent, "I was just on my way out. I have couple errands, then I go to the bass. You come there at eight-thirty." She quickly gave me an address on Oxford Street near Western and hung up. I wondered what the bass was.

It was nearly six-thirty by the time I ate some Kentucky Fried Chicken and vinegary potato salad in my car on the south end of Figueroa, where an uneasy commercial DMZ separates USC from the black ghetto south of Martin Luther King Boulevard. It was all check-cashing places and fast food. McDonald's and Taco Bell with drive-through service so people wouldn't have to risk getting out of their cars. The sky turned a poisonous amber as the sun set miles away in Pacific Palisades or Malibu, where lawns were green and homeowners secure.

The Thursday evening traffic seemed purposeful, as though everyone but me was fleeing for home before night fell. I drove up to 1st Street and then west over the bridge through Newton Division. "Rootin' tootin' shootin' Newton," a cop on a GTA had told me. Since the Uprising the streets are uneasily quiet, as if people are concentrated on furtive plans like survivalists stocking their spare bedrooms with Spam. But still nothing could stop a warm *pachanga* breeze that blew through the Salvadoran night. A man and a woman stopped in front of a *panaderia* and kissed. They walked on, oblivious to the deepening shadows.

I drove into the lot on Oxford Chu Chu Park had told me about. It was on a side street in a busy commercial part of Koreatown, and many of the nearby stores were still open. I was early, but I wanted to case the joint. I was trying to get into talking like that to myself. I'd said I was a detective. I should try to talk like one, even if it was corny. I never made $750 a day practicing law. My office open over two years, and I had yet to rise above doing lame-ass possession cases. The lot was full of Mercedeses. New Jaguars. I left my shabby old blue Datsun with a parking attendant. I was embarrassed my car was so messy. The interior of my car's like a giant purse. Old lipsticks, Evian bottles, newspapers I'm never going to read.

The sign above the entrance to the building said Baths.

The lobby was fine-veined ivory marble with red velvet easy chairs. A two-story-high rough granite wall stood before me. Water cascaded over the granite and formed a pool separated from the entranceway by a polished brass railing. A mahogany grand piano crowned by a large gold vase filled with orange and crimson cymbidium orchids and sprays of eucalyptus stood to the side of the entrance.

Was Chu Chu Park expecting to meet me in the lobby or was I to go inside? Why, if she thought I was a tax attorney, would she ask me to meet her here? I glanced around. If I went in would I have to take off my clothes? I watched two well-dressed Korean businessmen pay the admission and be directed across the lobby to an elevator. I'd be taking off my clothes with men I'd never met before! The woman at the reception desk watched me with an impatient frown as if I should make up my mind or get out. It was getting close to time to meet Chu Chu Park.

I stepped forward and paid my money. I started for the elevator.

"No! Not for you. You go there." The woman gave me a withering glance and pointed me toward a door on the opposite side of the lobby.

At this entrance a middle-aged woman in a white smock handed me two white towels and a blue-and-white seersucker robe, then pointed toward another door down a corridor. Did Chu Chu Park know Jin was dead? What did she know about me? In a large, empty, mirrored dressing area I was shown by another attendant where to store my clothing. I started to put everything into a locker, but the attendant stopped me and with some disdain showed me a special wooden compartment for my shoes. I stared at myself in the mirror covering the far wall. I was in better shape than I'd ever been in. My arms were carved. My stomach flat.

I put on the robe and went into the baths. It was hot and muggy. The woman at the desk had said it was the only natural hot spring in Los Angeles County. Only a few dim circles of light illuminated the cloudy room. Did Chu Chu Park think that by bringing me into her territory and treating this as a social rather than a business meeting she could throw me off? Naked Korean women lounged by the side of the steaming pool. Women with long wet black hair sprawled carelessly, their legs open. They leaned close to each other whispering. A woman lolled in the water, her pear-shaped breasts half submerged and her eyes closed. Another woman crouched upon a smooth low stone with her arms resting on her knees as still another woman washed her back with jasmine-scented soap.

Dropping the robe I slipped into the water. It was exquisitely hot, and I ached all over from the tension and pain of the last two days. I touched my shoulders and chest where the guy who'd tried to rape me had caught me with the rope. Lassoed me like a damn cow. It made me furious all over again, but I let myself sink into the incredible heat of the healing water. I closed my eyes. I might have fallen asleep, but I couldn't get out of my mind the image of the grinning Chusok mask dropped by my attacker. Who was he? The only thing I'd really seen of him was his hands, but it had been dark. Who told him where to find me? He couldn't have followed me home. Even though I'd been drinking I'd kept an eye on the rearview mirror for cops. He'd been waiting for me. Was he really the same man who killed Jin? Could old ladies be malevolent enough to hire a killer?

I opened my eyes and peered around the room for Chu Chu Park. No one in the bath was as old as Chu Chu. No sagging skin. No extended abdomens, no shrivelly dehydrated bosoms. One of the women caught me staring at her and shot me an angry look. I pulled myself out of the water to explore a room whose entrance I could make out on the far side of the pool.

I walked slowly toward the room through the heavy mist past more silent reclining forms. I heard murmuring I couldn't understand and the splatter of heavy drops of water. A woman shuffled by. For an instant I thought it was Lee Joon, but it was too hard to see. I stumbled over an out-stretched arm.

"Be careful!" someone snapped.

I apologized and continued into the room ahead of me. There on a mas-sage table was Chu Chu being scrubbed and massaged with cucumbers and milk by two women wearing red bikini bottoms. Chu Chu's soft skin barely sagged. She was nearly porcelain. The two attendants turned their backs to me and attacked Chu Chu more vigorously. They rinsed off the cucumbers and milk and began to massage her with golden honey.

Chu Chu must have heard my voice because she opened her eyes and looked at me. "Go wait," she murmured.

I glanced around the room for a chair, but there weren't any.

"In steam room." She sounded annoyed. "You know steam room?"

Yeah, I knew steam room. Did she think I was a barbarian? I'd been in Jacuzzis before too. Naked. With my old boyfriend, Bill Hughes, in the middle of the night at his apartment building in Westwood. We did the wild thing underwater.

I found a plastic bowl, which I filled with icy water from the cold pool. I peered through the hazy light. Now the room was nearly empty, and the remaining women were luminescent topaz skin and finishing their ab-lutions. I carried the bowl of cold water with me into the sauna. It was deserted. I arranged my towels on the lowest of the wooden platforms. I wondered if I should wrap myself in one of the towels to conduct the interview. No. I would meet her bush to bush.

After a few minutes the door opened, cutting into my further rumina-tions about why Kim had lied to me. Chu Chu Park stepped inside. "Why you want to see me? I don't need your help."

"All of your friends, the other women—I've talked with all of them already..." I paused for effect as if I felt uncomfortable with what I had to say. I was going to tell her they'd been badmouthing her and then see whom she put the finger on. "They think you're the one responsible for the theft of the *kye* money."

"Who said that?" she snapped, throwing the towel she carried up onto the wooden platform above me.

I shrugged. "Nancy Johnson..."

"Of course." Chu Chu Park flicked her hand as if she was batting away an ugly bug. "She's always been jealous of me. She even tells people I'm older than she is. She—"

"Lee Joon."

"You're lying!"

I shook my head as I prepared another lie. "Lee Joon said you told her you wanted to take the money out of the bank early this year. Not wait for Chusok."

"That stinking sow! That slack-breasted dried-up ancient mongrel! I never said that. What about Kim?"

I nodded my head. "Her too. Even Dorothy said you'd steal anything that wasn't nailed down."

"Not Kim! She didn't say that. It's Dorothy!" Her face twisted in fury as she leaned toward me. It was a startling, rubbery grimace made even more horrible by the dim lighting. "Don't tell me anything about Dorothy. Bah, Dorothy. I've known Dorothy to tell many lies."

"Like what?"

She looked at me suspiciously, but her anger pushed her forward. "Everything. If it wasn't because of Jin I wouldn't have anything to do with Dorothy and also I act nice because she's Kim's grandmother."

"Grandmother? You're wrong. She's Kim's godmother." I pronounced it slowly so she could hear the difference between the two words. Her English wasn't as good as I'd thought.

Chu Chu Park climbed nimbly onto her towel, then leaned down to put her face in mine again. "That's the tale Dorothy tells, but it's not the true one," she hissed. "I'll tell you the true story so that you see the real Dorothy." Chu Chu Park leaned back resplendent with fury to tell her account.

Dorothy was said to have been a plain-looking young girl with long legs and a willful temperament. She displayed artistic and creative ability at a very early age. She wanted to go to a classical dance academy.

"That was when the Japanese occupied our country," spat Chu Chu.

"Dorothy said you studied Japanese."

"Never! That bitch Dorothy! You see the kind of poison she spreads? Our classical dance was forbidden. A person could be sent to jail for dancing, so the training was secret."

Since Dorothy was unable to be a dancer she went to work in a bar.

"She called it a restaurant, but it was a bar," Chu Chu gloated.

Dorothy was nearly eighteen. It was 1928.

"She never married," continued Chu Chu. "But she had a daughter. A daughter she named Chungmi. Isn't that a beautiful name? It means 'The Shining Pearl.' "

I nodded, puzzled, but wanting her to continue.

"There was a father."

I nodded again.

"This father, he was also a husband."

I nodded, less certain. I wondered where she was going with this. It was as complicated as the bizarre cosmologies my Tae Kwon Do instructor had tried to teach me yesterday afternoon in the *do jang.* "This father, he was also a husband," I repeated, to show my efforts to keep up with the story.

"He was Jin's husband."

Dorothy had a child by her sister's husband!

She never told Jin or their family who the father of her child was. She said only that it was a man who frequented the restaurant where she worked. She said he begged many times to marry her, but that she refused him because he was too old.

"He was old when he married Jin, who had been his student," sniffed Chu Chu Park.

"Wait a sec. You mean Jin knew her husband and her sister had an affair? And a baby?" I asked.

Chu Chu laughed, but her laugh became a mean racking cough. "He, like so many men, was a fool. On his deathbed he confessed to Jin what he'd done."

I wiped at the sweat running down my breasts. "Everyone says Dorothy and Jin were perfect sisters...."

Chu Chu Park nodded her head and looked smug. "Jin never told Dorothy that she knew."

I hugged my knees to me as I considered the enormity of this lie between the two sisters. Chu Chu Park continued the story.

Eventually Dorothy was able to afford to buy a tiny restaurant of her own in Seoul near the East Gate. She named it the Shining Pearl.

"Dorothy's always been able to make money. She's got plenty of it. Now she's probably got seventy-five thousand dollars more," said Chu Chu bitterly. "After the war she bought a bigger restaurant. Then she built onto it, making it even bigger. She never changed the name. Always the Shining Pearl."

"She must have loved her daughter very much." I wondered if my mother would have named anything after me. Although I was an only child, I had not seemed to have figured very prominently in her life. It was always tennis, the country club, bridge. Mostly tennis. I guess I'm lucky she didn't name me Schlazenger after her favorite racket. "Where's Dorothy's daughter?"

Chu Chu Park fell silent and examined her body with satisfaction. "You ask Dorothy about that."

"Is her daughter dead?"

"I don't know. Ask Dorothy." Chu Chu Park gathered her towel around herself as though she was going to get up to leave.

I didn't want her to leave. There was so much more I had to find out. "Let me make sure I understand this. You said Kim was Dorothy's granddaughter...."

"Yes."

"And Jin knew Kim was the daughter of Chungmi?"

Chu Chu Park nodded and tossed her towel down impatiently. "Why do you keep talking about Jin like she was in the past? That's the second time now you do that."

I hadn't realized it. I tried to think quickly whether I should tell Chu Chu Park what I knew. Should I tell her her friend was dead? My intuition said no. I might need this later on.

"I have a bad feeling about Jin," insisted Chu Chu Park. "I feel in my heart she is very far away from me."

"Yeah, Buena Park. Visiting a relative." I repeated Dorothy's original story.

Chu Chu shook her head and looked deep into my face. "Jin is old. I am old. I feel a cold wind in my heart when I say her name. It makes me feel she's already dead. You can do no good in here. Whatever it is that Dorothy's talked you into doing, maybe covering up that she lost our money in bad investments, turn your back on it. Walk away."

I glanced down at my hands. I am only twenty-seven years old. I can't believe my hands will ever be wrinkled and spotted like Chu Chu Park's.

"You think we Korean women all spend our time gambling." Chu Chu grunted. "Or haggling in open air markets. You think because we're old we don't know what's going on. Because we don't speak your language we are stupid. Jin was born the same year Albert Einstein formulated the theory of relativity. We old women are not outside of history. We are history."

Chu Chu paused to catch her breath before telling me more about Jin. Jin was introspective and could be stubborn. She was quiet, but when she spoke she chose her words well. She loved beauty. She was a clotheshorse who knew just the right way to drape an Hermes scarf across an old coat and make it look new. She was a subscriber to the Los Angeles Philharmonic and never missed a Saturday matinee performance. She loved Scriabin's strange, mysterious music.

Yes, Jin sounded like a wonderful old woman, but my attention was starting to wander. None of this explained why she was killed.

"...composed his music while in a trance."

"Excuse me?" I glanced up at Chu Chu Park, wondering if I'd missed something.

"Scriabin composed his music while in a trance. I like Bach myself, but

Jin believed in that kind of stuff. That's how Dorothy held the reins over her."

"What are you trying to tell me?"

"Dorothy's a witch."

I plunged my hands into the plastic bowl of icy water and rinsed my face off. Were all of these little old ladies as mad as hatters? Is this what I had to look forward to? I couldn't imagine being thirty, let alone a million years old with my brain abraded to a smidgen like a worn-down gummy pink eraser on a number 2 pencil.

"You don't believe me?" Chu Chu Park pressed. "I've seen her turn herself into a bird, even a wild dog."

I put my head down on my knees. It was really hot in the sauna. I was starting to feel a bit dizzy.

"She dances in the moonlight wearing nothing but a red cape."

I lifted my head to look at Chu Chu Park.

She smiled knowingly at me. "You don't believe me, do you? You think I'm a crazy old woman."

"No, ma'am. I didn't say that. I was just wondering if this is Korean. Like if there's a shamanic tradition, thousands of years old. An emphasis on nature. Anthropomorphism. Animals that talk, that sort of thing."

Chu Chu Park glared angrily back at me. "Oh, you once took an anthropology class. Splendid. You understand all of our quaint customs, then."

I nodded. "I understand you. So far I figured out you don't like Dorothy much."

Chu Chu Park leaned forward with her hands on her knees. Her breasts dangled toward me. I tried not to stare at her tiny nipples. "She ruins everyone's life. Kim doesn't know Dorothy's her grandmother. And don't you tell her. Kim doesn't remember anything about her mother. Dorothy won't tell her. She doesn't remember anything about Korea, where she was born. That's what Dorothy has done! Stolen Kim's life! Imagine not knowing your own mother or your own country."

The volcanic rocks hissed as Chu Chu Park flung my water on them. They flared, then glowed a brighter red. She stood and looked satisfied as she wrapped the large white towel around herself. She opened the door and went out toward the mineral pool. Almost immediately I lost track of her outline as she moved into the heavy mist.

I lay down on the pine bench with my knees up. They looked far away. I felt my bones turning to liquid. I closed my eyes. Would it be so bad not to know your parents? I thought of my father raging through the house drunk at night, the sound of breaking glass, a door slamming. I tried to push myself farther back into the past. Tried to recall a special blue-and-green dress my mother bought me for Easter one year when I was small.

Tried to imagine playing in the snow with my father at my side. My father placing the snowman's head on top of its icy body. My mother sticking a carrot in the snowman's face to make a nose. We all laugh with delight. I'm pushing it. I don't remember any of this.

I doubt that it ever happened.

I hear my father at the door of my mother's bedroom. I am fifteen. It's about three in the morning.

"...you never want to," my father whines at the locked door.

I pull the pillow over my head so I won't have to listen anymore. What if he comes to my room? I'll pretend I'm asleep. The way he looks at me sometimes gives me the willies. I push the pillow aside. I force myself to listen for what will happen next. He stands outside my mother's room for a while. I hear him turn toward my door. I clutch my pillow. I am barely breathing. Finally he shuffles back toward his bedroom. Then the water runs in the bathroom sink and I know he is taking more Miltown.

I opened my eyes in the steam room. I pushed myself up to a sitting position and blotted my face. It had to be at least 120 degrees. I'd lost track of time. My watch was locked safely in the other room. I had to go talk to Dorothy. I had to find out more about her. But what was I going to do? Ask her if she was a witch?

I stood up. I felt wobbly. My head was starting to pound. No wonder they usually have signs that say not to stay in steam rooms more than ten minutes. I wished Chu Chu Park hadn't thrown the cold water out. That was pretty damn inconsiderate. I draped the towel around my waist and walked to the door. I could barely draw a breath in the heavy hot dampness. I put my hand on the door handle and pushed it.

It wouldn't move.

I rattled the handle as hard as I could. It still wouldn't budge. It was getting harder and harder to breathe. "Hey," I yelled. I thought the baths were closing for the night and the attendants had forgotten me.

A shrill hiss of steam spit out at me. Wiping at the fog on the glass in the door I cleared a circle so I could look out. I didn't see anyone. I saw only a thick, blunt board jammed through the handle, making it impossible to open the door from the inside.

"Hey!" I screamed again more loudly and banged on the door.

A smoldering blast of heat filled the small room. It scorched my back. A new wave of steam took over the room. I gasped for air, but the heavy boiling cloud wouldn't let me breathe.

"Help!" I screamed at the top of my lungs.

In response another cloud of burning steam flooded the small space. I dropped to my knees and pulling the towel off, wrapped it around my face. I crawled back to the fake volcanic rocks. I could barely see. I inched my fingers cautiously around the smoldering fixture, looking for the control switch. The hot metal burned me. I nearly bit through my lip in pain. There was no switch. The heat was controlled from outside.

Whoever had intentionally locked me in the sauna while I'd had my eyes closed intended to boil me alive. Chu Chu Park? Had that been Lee Joon I thought I'd seen earlier?

I crawled back toward the door. I slipped once and skidded along the floor into one of the wooden benches, hitting my shoulder hard. I pushed myself back onto my knees. My head hung like a dog's.

Another blast of steam filled the room. I got to the door and knelt before it.

"Holy Mary Mother of God pray for…" I'd never told Lupe my folks sent me for a year to Catholic school. Was Lupe raised as a Catholic or was I stereotyping her?

My eyes began to close again, and I started to pass out. I saw the Golden Tiger in the *do jang* as though he was veiled in mist. He crouched. His white-robed arms spread like a mighty heron and whipped through the air as he demonstrated how to break a board. Then a brick.

I wrapped the towel around my right fist. I hit the glass as hard as I could. The glass shattered. Cool air rushed in. I smashed the glass again and again. I wrenched the wooden bar from the door handle, staggered out of the steam room, and collapsed on the moist granite floor.

CHAPTER ELEVEN

"Lupe?" I whispered into the phone. I thought that she might be afraid to go home to face her mother and that she might still be at the office.

"Where are you?" her sleepy voice answered. *"¿Que horas son?"*

"Midnight."

" 'Bout time you called in. You gotta go right over to the Church of the Big Mother. Venus Howard's pimp's been calling every ten minutes. Just a sec..."

I heard Lupe fumbling with the things on top of the desk. Something crashed to the floor.

"Ok, got it. I wrote down exactly what he told me. 'Significant constitutional issues you chose to ignore. Make immediate application for writ to Appellate Court. Or we sue you. For everything you own.' Says for you to come by no matter how late it is. He's driving me *loca*. It's hard enough to get any shut-eye here. The traffic. Your landlord. I mean, how many times in a row can you listen to 'Like a Rolling Stone'? And now he's got *a chingada* harmonica."

I sat up in bed. "Lupe, I don't have time right now for Venus Howard. Someone—"

"I'm ready to go over to that freaky church myself and show them something about tort action," she exploded.

I looked down at my hands. They were still shaking. "Someone tried to kill me in Koreatown tonight."

"¿Qué" She sounded as if she didn't believe me.

Leaving out the relatively unimportant part about the manager going bonkers over the broken door and threatening to call the cops to have me arrested for vandalism, I quickly filled Lupe in on what had happened to me at the baths after I met Chu Chu Park.

"Chu Chu Park! The first time I saw her I could see she was living grand. She racked that *plata*, for sure."

I looked over at my clothes, which I'd thrown in a pile on the floor when I dragged in about an hour earlier. My mother would be so disappointed. She always told me, "No skirt of mine has ever been on a chair unless I was in it." I examined the empty bottle of Southern Comfort on the night table and drained the last drops. "I'm totally exhausted, Lupe, but I can't sleep. I got to go to Dorothy's. Find out more of what she knows about Chu Chu and the other women." Did Lupe care what happened to me? I felt embarrassed I was so transparent. Sickened with myself. Begging for her attention. "I was just calling to tell you I don't know when I'll come by the office. Finish organizing the files tomorrow."

I hung up and ran my fingers through my hair, which was still slightly damp. I had to go back to Koreatown. Weren't murderers supposed to return to the scene of the crime? I'd be there waiting, ready. Better that than waiting for him to come for me. He knew where I lived. Had he been at the baths or was it Chu Chu Park? Lee Joon? I pushed myself out of bed. At least I didn't need a shower. I was as clean as a boiled chicken. I pulled on an old pair of jeans, a white t-shirt, and my high-tops.

I pulled up in front of Dorothy's place in Koreatown around two and cut the engine. In the dark it looked like a peaceful neighborhood. There were porches with swings; a statue of Buddha stood in a front yard. A diseased-looking dwarf pine tree attested to the desperate desire to establish roots. I got out of the car and walked up the stairs to Dorothy's apartment.

Outside her door I looked around to see if anyone was watching. I put my ear against the door. Soft chanting came from the living room. It was only one voice. Dorothy's. I pressed against the door, trying to hear more of what was happening. The drone repeated over and over. I turned away. The dead deserved their honor. Dorothy was praying.

Back in the car, I turned my radio down real low. It was the blues station from Long Beach. The groove was good. Esther Phillips. I started to relax for the first time since I escaped from the steam bath.

"...got the black-eyed blues...," sang Esther, dead too and buried somewhere in Inglewood.

An hour or more passed while the ebony night smothered the city. I wondered what they'd done with Jin's body. I wondered whether Buddhists believe in heaven. Or would Jin immediately reincarnate? Dorothy had told me Jin's name meant "Star." I looked upward. Off in the distance, where the stars should be, lights on top of a Wilshire high rise blinked.

A car split the silent night, screeching around the corner and roaring fast in my direction. It groaned into an anguished third, popped into a flat-out fourth.

I was right. He was coming back!

The headlights swerved as the car wove across the imaginary center line and raced toward me. In one movement I reached under the seat for my gun then flattened myself across the passenger seat to avoid being spotted.

An old Fiat roared to a stop parallel to my car.

Lupe turned off the motor, which continued to kick and sputter. She stepped out as though unaware of the clatter of her heap. She strolled over to my car and leaned in. Then she pulled a brand-new half pint of Southern Comfort from her purse, unscrewed the top, took a drink. "Here. I thought you might want this. Tastes like fucking cough syrup to me." She handed me the bottle.

"I put a spell on you...," moaned Screamin' Jay Hawkins. How many places in the world can you listen to Screamin' Jay Hawkins in the middle of the night?

I took a drink. It was good.

"Thought I'd drop by and go undercover with you," Lupe said.

"Thanks." I pushed the gun farther back under my seat so she wouldn't see it.

"*De nada.*" Lupe got into the car. "Plus this way I can keep an eye on my money. You're getting seven fifty a day, right? Let's see, a third is two fifty. Plus my expenses. Let's say three hundred, OK?"

"You'd risk your life for that? What about right and wrong? The underlying truth? Unraveling the complexities of the human mind?"

"Complexities! Ayyy, you give me a headache." She shook her head with disgust. "There's plenty of guys who just wanna go boom boom boom and take everything you've ever worked for. I don't have any trouble at all believing some *vato* blew Jin away for seventy-five grand. Where I come from there are guys who'd do a hit for a hundred bucks. Or just to prove they're *macho*."

"So you think it's a jungle out there?"

She nodded. "Absolutely. It's just you. And your family. Fuck everybody else."

I took another drink. What Lupe said made me bluer than the blues. What about community? Friendship? "When I gave you a job, it was supposed to be your chance to go straight, so you could get Joey back. I wanted to help you. You're my only friend."

"Ohhh, get out the violins. What about law school? You must have friends from there. Late-night studying, talking about the lectures as you walk the ivy-covered arcades. The great professors. Like Robert Donat in *Goodbye Mr. Chips.* Everyone wearing tweed..."

"I don't know anyone from school. I didn't really hang out with anyone...."

"*Jesus!* That's it. That's what's wrong with you. You don't know how to hang out. Yeah, I read once in *People* magazine about this famous guy who went up into a bell tower and killed, like, seven nurses. And they were interviewing everyone who knew him and this one guy said, 'Oh, yeah, he was weird, like he didn't even know how to hang out, he didn't hang out anywhere, he didn't even know how to roller-skate.' " Lupe stopped breathlessly to study me.

I stared out the window. I don't know how to roller-skate. I hate adults on roller skates. We both slumped back in our seats listening to the blues. What did I have to do to make her acknowledge the screwed-up situation we were in?

"You think families are so important? So sacred? Well, explain this then.

Last night I found out Dorothy's Kim's grandmother. Not her godmother. And you were right that Kim's probably a pro." I laid out the rest of the facts as I'd been pondering them in the dark. An armed robbery turns into murder. An old lady I don't know, whose language I can't speak, hires me to find the killer of her beloved sister. She lies to me about her family because she had an illegitimate daughter fathered by her sister's husband. She won't go to the police because she's got a righteous grudge against them and she's been threatened by her sister's killer.

Lupe put her hand up to stop me. "Don't make this so difficult. All you have to do is figure out who's responsible, not put 'em in jail. We're not playing 'Gunsmoke.' This is a real gig. With real money."

I slapped the dash in frustration. "Why don't you think that whoever killed Jin couldn't come back to kill us? They've already tried twice to hurt me. It's not just about the money anymore."

"Not just about the money! What do you think I was doing out here with all those guys for twenty-five dollars? Having a Coke and a chat? Getting stock tips? Nah, I've sucked enough dicks for one lifetime. Shit, that's ten blowjobs per day to make what I can get from Dorothy, so don't be telling me what's dangerous and what I ought or ought not be doing—"

I snapped my fingers in front of her face. "Hey, girlfriend! Haven't you heard what I was telling you?"

"So she lied because she had an illegitimate kid. That's not the worst thing in the world. How do you think I felt when I found out I was pregnant with Joey?"

I held my breath and let it out slowly. I didn't want to start yelling at her. "Maybe Dorothy doesn't have any money."

"Then what are we sitting here for?" She reached angrily for the car door handle. "Let's go up there right now and find out. I'm not gonna waste my time and put my tail on the line if there's no money."

From behind Dorothy's building, a car started up, gunned its engine, and then came down the driveway. We both ducked. I glanced at my watch. Nearly five-thirty. Dorothy drove past in a gold Acura. I let her get to the end of the block. She hung a fast right and skidded around the corner. I started my engine and followed her north.

"Would it be racist if I said Orientals are really bad drivers?" Lupe asked as the Acura wove in and out of traffic.

The sun was coming up. It was autumn in Los Angeles. Although the air was balmy it would be staggeringly hot by 11:00 A.M. A bank of clouds moved sluggishly over the mottled green Hollywood Hills. Dorothy swung over to Hoover and up through the Central American streets of orange blossoms, mango stands, and rubber trees towards Wilshire.

"Over there," said Lupe, pointing out my window. "About a block over's the apartment where Kid McCoy killed his girlfriend in the twenties. He was once the welterweight and the middleweight champion of the world. You think I haven't been wondering about my bonehead brother and that Kim? I wouldn't be surprised to find out Hector's up to his neck in this whole thing. He could have gotten one of his homies he was in the pen with to be the shooter."

I glanced over at Lupe. "Hector was in state prison?"

"Sure. I can't believe I never told you that. I must have told you."

I shook my head. "What for?"

"Assault with a deadly weapon. Busted down from manslaughter. Maybe that's part of the reason Hector has trouble getting fights."

I was starting to feel unwell.

"It was at some *ruca's* place in East LA. He was drinking with this broad and screwing around while her husband was at work. The *esposo* came home and caught them. There was a fight. Hector broke the bottle of whiskey and cut the guy bad. That's how he is. He thought this woman belonged to him even though she was married to someone else."

We passed a more benign collection of houses and apartments in the stately Queen Anne style. A pair of apartments modified with classical American colonial revival detailing. Then a jungle of palms appeared before us at the intersection of Wilshire. It was Lafayette Park.

I slowed up to fall behind as Dorothy circled the park looking for a good place to leave her car. Finally she decided on a spot at the far end near Wilshire Boulevard and the old Sheraton-Town House hotel. "Hector did that?"

She nodded. "He's the real McCoy."

We watched as Dorothy, dressed in a pair of baggy black sweats and an oversize black sweatshirt, got out of her car. She headed away from the hotel.

"What's she doing? Is she nuts? This is a dangerous park," muttered Lupe. "I thought she was going to breakfast at the Sheraton." Lupe quickly explained the building was constructed in 1929 as luxury apartments and converted to a hotel by Conrad Hilton in 1942. Howard Hughes rented a suite there for a time. In the fifties the hotel's Zebra Room was one of the city's ritziest nightclubs. "Mae West's last film was shot there."

Dorothy crossed the street and went down a slope into the park. There were several white-haired old ladies and men dressed the same as Dorothy waiting for her. They bowed in greeting to her.

I pulled the car onto the side street and as close as possible to see what was happening.

"What the hell are they doing here?" Lupe wondered.

Dorothy stood before the assembled group. She bowed to them in return. She crouched low to the ground with her hands out before her. The others imitated her to the best of their ability. She was leading them in *kicho il bo,* the first *poomsae* of the stances, blocks, and punches of Tae Kwon Do.

We sat silently in the car watching the old people practicing the defensive techniques.

"You know anything about self-defense?" I asked Lupe.

"No."

"What about when you were out on the streets?"

Lupe sat up proudly. "I never been hurt on the streets by any man. They treated me good."

I wondered who gave her the bruise I'd noticed on her face the day I saw her arraigned in court. "They could try anything once they're alone with you. There are a lot of sickies out here. You said so yourself. I'll teach you some martial arts." I nodded toward Dorothy and her group. "If those dinosaurs can do it, you can do it."

"Nothing's gonna happen to me." Lupe shook her head. "When I walk that walk, I'm the dream come true. They'd die to feel the touch of my hand." She opened her purse and took out her makeup bag. She put on foundation, mascara, a brown blusher, two different purple eyeshadows, and magenta lipstick, then touched her eyebrows with black pencil. She examined her face in the mirror before dropping the makeup bag back in her purse. "Enough of being nice. Let's go find out about our money." She gestured toward the martial arts group concluding its exercise.

We waited until Dorothy and the other old people finished chatting and Dorothy was on her way back to her car alone. The promising pink light of a new day pushed forth as Lupe and I hurried into the park, which was starting to get busy with drug deals. Lupe looked with a combination of pity and disdain at a young strawberry in yellow stretch pants and a filthy floral blouse giving a frantic handjob behind a eucalyptus tree to a ragged Salvadoran too stoned to come.

I looked at Lupe. She'd never told me how she started prostituting. I knew she once worked in a dance hall, dancing for thirty cents a minute with lonely Mexicans and Central Americans on Pico near downtown. What was the turning point, the day, the hour, the slant of the sun, the direction of the moon; what were the forces at play at the moment Lupe became a whore?

"Yo, Mrs. Oh!" Lupe called after Dorothy's retreating figure.

Dorothy turned. If she was surprised to see us there among the flotsam and jetsam of the park, she didn't show it. She stopped and waited until we caught up with her. I stood beside her. She wasn't even winded from her exercise. She was tiny. Smaller than I remembered. Maybe only five feet. She bowed slightly when she saw me. She was less pleased to see Lupe.

"What's this about Kim being your granddaughter?" Lupe asked.

So much for cunning and subtlety. I had wanted to invite her to the Sheraton, sit down for a cup of tea, have some lead-in.

Dorothy looked questioningly at me. I reported what Chu Chu Park had told me.

"My oldest friend!" Dorothy responded with disdain. "Chu Chu Park's a very bitter woman. Don't listen to her." Dorothy started to walk again across the park toward her car, with us tagging along beside her. "Her own children never even spend any time with her."

"Why'd you lie?" I asked. "Why'd you say Kim's not your flesh and blood?"

Dorothy stopped and put her hands on her hips. At that instant she looked ancient. Older than the earth upon which we stood. "I don't know if she is or not."

Dorothy spun away from us and began to walk more quickly. Lupe ran around in front of her, forcing her to a halt. "Why don't you ask your daughter? Where is she?"

With an impatient look Dorothy stepped around Lupe. "I don't know. The last time I saw my daughter she was twelve years old."

I touched Lupe on the arm to get her out of Dorothy's way, but she wouldn't budge. She was going to screw everything up. She pushed her face up close to Dorothy's. "Tell us where she is. We don't got all day."

"Don't talk to me like that," snapped Dorothy. "Whitney's the one helping me."

I nodded soothingly. "That's right. I want to help you, but I need for you to tell me about your daughter. Help me to help you."

"The Japanese took her," Dorothy said.

"What do you mean, took her?" Lupe demanded.

Dorothy stepped back slightly. "During the war. They took her to a comfort camp. To comfort the soldiers." Dorothy saw our lack of comprehension. "For prostitution. At least eighty thousand women. The little girls too."

"¡Jesús y María!" Lupe exploded. "A brothel!"

Dorothy stumbled past Lupe. "After the war she wouldn't come home. She was too ashamed. She was seventeen. She wrote and said she had another life. For me to forget her."

A junkie in stinking jeans and no shirt approached with his hand out. There were open sores on his chest. I pulled a dollar out of my pocket and thrust it at him. He turned to Dorothy, who waved her hands at him to brush him away. She broke away from us and started toward her car, as he lumbered behind us mumbling inarticulately.

"Get the fuck out of here," Lupe screamed at him, pushing him aside. She grabbed Dorothy by the arm, jerking her to a standstill. "What kind of mother are you? Why didn't you go get her? Why didn't you stop her?"

Dorothy shook her head. "She wouldn't even send me her address. All I knew was that she was in Kaesong. Not so far from Seoul, but after our civil war, after our country was divided, it wasn't possible."

Lupe let go of Dorothy's arm. She stared away from us and toward the growing traffic on Wilshire. Beneath her careful makeup I saw under her left eye the tiny black tear tattoo she'd gotten in jail. The first time I'd seen it I assumed she'd drawn it on with eyeliner pencil. Now I realized it was real and a permanent part of her.

"You never saw your daughter again?" I asked Dorothy. I wondered if what I was able to find out about Chungmi would help me understand Lupe.

Dorothy shook her head, and I thought she might cry. "It was a blessing when I finally heard from a minister and his wife in 1977..."

The park was rapidly filling up with Salvatrucha gangbangers, the homeless, and the mentally ill. Dorothy hurried past them as she told us about the minister and his wife who had found Kim when she was only four years old. The couple formally adopted Kim when they arrived back in the U.S.A. I could imagine the whole story in *Life* magazine. The adorable little girl with big dark eyes and black hair hanging in bangs cut neatly and precisely above her eyebrows. The little girl dressed in a sailor suit with a big red bow. The minister and his wife would have been so glad to get away from the menacing Communists on the other side of the 38th Parallel and return to the good old U.S. of A. that there would be some slightly militaristic bent in their selection of clothes for the child. When she was fourteen her adopted parents learned Kim's grandmother lived in Los Angeles and decided to do the right thing: to send Kim to Dorothy so she could know her real family and her real culture.

"How'd they find you?" I wondered.

"The orphanage had records. They spent a lot of time and money looking for me. God bless them."

It was a beautiful and inspiring story. Lupe was hushed and solemn. The sun flooded the street like a bank of klieg lights as we stepped from beneath the trees and exited the park.

I walked next to Dorothy up the hill to the street, not wanting to let on yet how much I knew about Kim. "Tell me again what the man said before he shot Jin. He was speaking Korean, wasn't he?"

Dorothy stopped beside her gold Acura. She pulled up her sweatshirt and fished her car keys out of a neon green fannypack she wore around her waist. "Sort of."

I asked her what she meant.

"He's not a real Korean. Not from Korea."

"Man, I hate that too," Lupe said. "*Pocho* Spanish. All those *chingón* yuppies from the Westside who gotta try to order their food in Spanish in Mexican restaurants. Who say 'boo nos day ass' to their maids—"

"Did he ask if it was the Queen Min box?" I interrupted. I wondered what Lupe thought of my Spanish.

Dorothy shook her head.

Who was this guy if Dorothy didn't think he was Korean? "What's this Queen Min box?" I asked. "I keep hearing people talking about it. How come Kim told me about it and you didn't?"

Dorothy got into her car. "It doesn't concern you...."

I grabbed the door to keep her from shutting it. "What do you mean, it doesn't concern me? Look, I've been trying to be cool, but so far, since I met you, just three days ago, I've been jumped, some guy tried to rape me, and last night when I went to meet Chu Chu Park at the baths she, or someone, maybe Lee Joon, locked me in the steam room and almost burned me to death."

"And don't forget the money," Lupe added. "So far you owe Whitney twenty-two hundred and fifty dollars."

Dorothy fumbled again with the pouch fastened around her waist. She took out a wad of twenties and pushed it toward me. "Here. You want money? You say Chu Chu tried to hurt you at the baths last night. That settles it. That's all I need to know. I knew she was behind this. Thank you. You don't need to do anything more for me."

"I gotta find this guy or I could be killed...."

"So could I." Lupe snatched the money from Dorothy's hand and quickly counted it. "And so could you, Mrs. Oh. Don't overlook that. So could you." She tucked the cash into her black bra. "This'll do for starters. Now what's this about the Queen Min box?"

Dorothy put her head down on the steering wheel for a few seconds. "I feel very tired now," she whispered. I could barely hear her. I leaned toward her. "Old and tired. I need to go home and make some special vitality tea. You come to my house later. Just you, Whitney. Tonight around nine. I'll tell you about Queen Min."

We stood in the street shielding our eyes against the sun and watching the departing gold Acura as it hurried south. A flock of birds filled the sky, headed south also. They were migrating for the winter. It was nearly ninety. A breeze shivered the palm trees on the fringe of the park. It is hard to tell what's happening and read all the signs in the tropics.

CHAPTER TWELVE

The cook at Cafe James Dean told me where Kim was. Lupe and I hurried over to a glass-and-marble mall at the corner of Western and 9th. It was bordered by crumbling, charred apartments of Central American refugees. Inside the Korean mall water cascaded from a jade fountain into a pool the color of tourmaline. There were toy stores, boutiques of women's silk clothing, imported British tweeds for the gentlemen, and a French bakery. Gooey Muzak teased the air as we rode the escalator up through a large atrium filled with palms. Kim was getting her hair done in a black-and-white-tiled beauty salon on the second floor.

Seated in a stylist's chair at the back of the salon, Kim spotted us in the mirror as soon as we approached. The action in the salon stopped. Women stared at us, and I heard their critical, amused whispers as we walked past them. Lupe paused in front of a glass display case to examine some knock-offs of Chanel belts. "How clever," Lupe announced in a dramatic stage whisper. "Totally fake. Like Kim."

I nodded in greeting at Kim, hoping she hadn't heard Lupe.

Kim's hair was in rollers, but she was already made up. I'd never seen her sans the full Earl Scheib paint job. I wondered what she looked like without it. Probably damn good. She had real cheekbones and big sexy lips.

Kim lifted her hand to cover her mouth and giggled as though embarrassed by her pink plastic crown. "I told them to tell you where I was. I was hoping to talk to you today." She gave some curt direction in Korean to the woman doing her hair. "Why don't you wait for me in the bakery, Whitney. They make excellent cappuccino."

The salon fell quiet again as Lupe, in her tawdry gray pinstripe suit, and I turned to leave. I had no doubt they were in shock at Lupe's skirt slit high up the rear. Fuck them. What did they know? They'd probably never heard of Lana Turner or Ava Gardner. I smiled encouragingly at Lupe as we ran the silent gauntlet.

"Jesus Christ," sighed Lupe once we were outside. "I wish you'd make more of an effort to dress. Sometimes it's really embarrassing."

We went down to the bakery we'd seen near the fountain on the first floor. Lupe wanted to use a pay phone, so I waited for her a short distance away in front of a jeweler's, pretending to study the necklaces and bracelets while I strained to hear over the passing shoppers what Lupe was saying.

"Hola, hola, Joey. Soy yo, Mami... Joey? Joey?" She hung the phone up angrily, and I guessed her mother had taken the phone from Joey and hung up on her.

We killed about forty minutes grazing through brioches and almond croissants. I told Lupe I wanted her to be more polite to Kim. "You're acting like you're prejudiced against Koreans," I warned.

Lupe shrugged. "It's a free country. I ain't prejudiced against anybody. I just don't like this broad."

"I'm in a service industry now, so cool it if you expect Dorothy to pay me."

Kim finally showed up with her shiny, fresh-smelling hair artfully combed as though it hadn't been done at all. Although the table was littered with cups and crumbs, she insisted on ordering more of everything for us. The busboy cleared the table for the second round of coffees.

"Ever notice no matter what kind of restaurant it is, the busboys are always Mexican?" Lupe grumbled.

Kim laughed. I wondered how she felt and what she thought while she was fucking Hector Ramos.

"I'm so relieved you came, Whitney," said Kim, pointedly ignoring Lupe. "I haven't been able to stop thinking about everything that's happened. There's something else I thought of to tell you. About Lee Joon." She paused as the waiter deposited cups and carbs in front of us. She tore open a Sweet 'N Low and stirred it into her decaf caffè latte. "About a month ago Lee Joon said she was buying a timeshare in Puerto Vallarta."

"Mexico?" I asked. "I thought Chu Chu was the traveler."

"Lee loves Mexico."

Lupe set down her cup with a roar of loud, mean laughter. "*¡Qué rico!* That explains why everyone's so hot to open the new sports center. Because they love Mexicans."

"She had a little tea party to tell Jin and Dorothy and the other women. They were all planning on going there this Christmas, although the three of us were wondering how Lee was going to pay for the place—"

"You think this Lee Joon lady's the one who stole the money?" Lupe interrupted. She leaned across the table, brushing her dark black hair back from her face with one delicate brown hand as she spoke. Her hair fell in a lush curve onto her breast. "Where would she get the guy with the gun?"

Kim patted her gleaming coiffed hair into place. "Her youngest nephew. He lives in Fresno."

"Fresno?" I said. "How's he figure?"

"He's a gangbanger." Kim tore a scrap of croissant and spread it with jam. "It'd be easy to do. Drive down here, steal the money, turn around and drive back. His family sent him up there. Trying to get him away from bad influences." She paused to push croissant into her rosy painted mouth. "Nobody likes to talk about it, but there are gangs here."

"Even in Koreatown?" Lupe asked with a sneer in her voice.

I flashed her a warning look, but she just smiled. I leaned back in my

chair so Kim wouldn't see I was getting irritated with Lupe. I asked Kim
how she knew it was the gangbanger from Fresno.

"It's been a long time since I've seen him," she admitted. "I'm not even
sure what he looks like now, but his voice was familiar. I know it was him.
This had to be Lee Joon's fault. She couldn't keep her mouth shut in a
swarm of flies."

"But why kill Jin?" I asked. "For the Queen Min box? Is it worth that
much?" Was the box real gold? Or merely gilt? From where I'd been hiding when I saw the man take the box from Dorothy, I couldn't tell. I could-
n't believe it was gold. Why wouldn't Dorothy keep it in a safe deposit box
or a museum if it was real?

Kim sighed. "No. I tried to explain to you. Dorothy's built this box up in
her mind because history's important to the old Koreans, probably because
they'll never really fit in here. Believe me, if it was real Dorothy would
have it locked up in a bank so nobody could touch it."

I told Kim we'd already seen Dorothy that morning and she'd told us
Kim was born in Korea. I wondered why Kim sounded impatient about the
bank when she'd told me how generous Dorothy was.

"You weren't born here," Lupe crowed. "I was. So was my mother."

"I'm an American citizen," Kim snapped.

I grimaced at Lupe, trying to get her to shut up. "You speak English just
like an American," I said to Kim in my most diplomatic tone.

"I don't even remember Korea," Kim said, angrily swiveling to face Lupe.
"I don't think I'd like it. Too sexist. There, in the old days, they had to have
laws to keep men off the streets in the evening so upper-class women
could go visit one another. If you weren't rich, forget it. If you went outside of your house you had to wear *chan'got*—cape—covering your face."

I scooped the fuzz off my cappuccino and scraped it on the saucer. It was
getting increasingly difficult to get a real cup of coffee anywhere in town.
"Dorothy said you left Korea when you were a little girl with some mis-
sionaries who I adopted you...."

Kim broke a chocolate croissant from the basket between us into smaller pieces and smiled. "She told you about the Petersons?"

I nodded. "Yeah. She said they brought you out of North Korea. That your
mom gave you to them..."

"My mother's dead," said Kim.

"I'm sorry," I said. "I didn't know. Dorothy said your mother'd been taken
by the Japanese to..."

"A whorehouse," said Lupe, folding her arms across her chest and staring
coldly at Kim. "You don't even know who your father was."

Kim pushed back her chair and started to stand. I leaned forward and
touched Kim on the arm. "Shut up, Lupe. Say you're sorry."

Lupe turned her mad-dog eyes to me. "First day we met she called me a whore. And her puttin' on airs like she's somebody."

"I don't think she meant it. She was upset. Nearly hysterical. It was right after Jin." I fumbled. "You didn't mean it, did you, Kim?"

Kim sat down in the chair again. She shook her head and wiped at her eyes. "No. I was shook up. Please don't tell Hector. Let's be friends, ok?"

I looked back and forth between the two women, each poised on the edge of her chair as though about to spring.

Instead of answering, Lupe closed her eyes and nodded her head a couple of times as if she was thinking something out.

Can't we all just get along?

I pushed my chair back slightly in case they decided to go for it.

"Yeah, ok. I'm sorry too," Lupe said at last. "I'm sorry about your mother. That's tough not having your mother. Your real mother."

"I don't even have a photograph of her," said Kim.

We all fell silent. Adrift in Los Angeles and far from home. "Lucky for you the Petersons were able to bring you out of North Korea," I said finally.

Kim nodded. "They were the most wonderful people in the world. They're dead now. I don't remember a lot about them. Just little bits and pieces. My mom, Mrs. Peterson, bought me a bright red coat with a little white rabbit collar."

Why couldn't I have been adopted? Some nice working-class family? One with a union maid in its background. A red diaper baby. My mother singing union songs as she rocked me on some barricade, instead of swinging at tennis balls on a grass court in Maryland.

Kim went on to explain that the Petersons had been able to locate Dorothy and Jin, who were believed to have some blood relationship to Kim's mother. "Like distant cousins. That's why I call Dorothy godmother. To give her respect."

Was it possible she didn't know Dorothy was her grandmother? Was Kim lying to us? Why? I flashed a look at Lupe, begging her to keep her mouth shut while I probed some more. "Do you think you'll ever go back? To Korea? To find the rest of your family," I suggested.

Kim shrugged. "What for? This country has given me everything. A family. A good education. Everything I want's right here. My restaurant. Hector."

Lupe burst into laughter. "I can't believe you're serious about my brother. He's an idiot and meaner than a skunk on crank."

Kim put down a couple of tens to pay for our food. "You don't know him like I do. Hector's much smarter than anybody gives him credit for. He just needed the right woman. This job as director of the new multicultural sports center's only the beginning for him." She got up from the table. "And he's a very sexy guy."

I reached uneasily for my water glass. I did not like to think of Hector with a hard-on.

Kim dropped her Louis Vuitton wallet into her Gucci purse. "We're getting married next month. You'll be my maid of honor, Lupe." She turned and walked away, her pert hips moving in a tasteful way under her pale pink silk dress.

Lupe toyed with the crescent tip of an almond croissant, rolling it between her fingers for some time, before declaring, "That broad's *loca.*"

I put on some lipstick. The zen way. No mirror. "Yeah. Let's go talk to Mr. Ko Won again. I don't believe Kim. She's way too good-looking for your brother."

"What do you mean?" snarled Lupe, tossing the mangled croissant on the littered table. "It is possible that someone could be in love with my brother. He may be a shit and an asshole, but he's my brother."

I told Lupe we should meet Ko Won after work that evening and learn more about how Kim happened to accompany him to the fights the night she met Hector. We left the mall as a slobbering string arrangement of "Ain't No Mountain High Enough" tainted the air. "She ain't that good looking," Lupe kept muttering.

I glanced at my watch. I couldn't put off my meeting with Adonis at the Church of the Big Mother any longer. Not if I was serious about keeping my license to practice law. I asked Lupe to drive me there so I'd have a witness if they tried to hassle me again about the way I was handling their case. People only hear what they want to hear, and Venus Howard seemed like the type who'd try to claim I hadn't fully explained things to her. It's a shame but it's true: a lot of time is spent defending yourself from your client.

The small Tudor house looked just as it had the first time I was there, except there was a white stretch limo parked in the driveway.

"*Quelle charmante,* " said Lupe. "The seven dwarves must be here."

We went up the path. From outside the front door we heard a burst of Italian.

"What's that?" Lupe said suspiciously. "Someone in trouble?"

"No, it's opera." I knocked on the door, but no one answered. I tried the door, but it was locked. I knocked again.

It was opened by a middle-aged flabby guy in a navy Brooks Brothers suit and a pair of tortoiseshell glasses. His jacket was open, and although he wore a bow tie he was shirtless. A halter of black leather straps was bound across his chest. His sagging nipples were pierced with silver rings. From the room behind him came the murmur of a small crowd.

I stuck my hand out and introduced myself. "You Adonis?"

He tittered with pleasure as he shook his head. "Just a friend."

"How about Venus? She's here to see Venus," Lupe added, leaning against the doorframe. She sounded bored, as if she was being presented with a not very fresh or colorful sales rack *of minifaldas.* She fingered one of the black leather straps near the man's nipple. "Feels like ya bought it in TJ." She sighed, exhausted by the mediocrity of the material. "Never shop discount for restraints. You're the lowest of the low. Filthy pig," she said with scorn.

The man looked thrilled by her rejection. He stepped back to open the door for us.

I faltered in the open doorway. Lupe didn't do kink. Did she? The gilded light of the small anteroom was smudged with patchouli incense. Lupe parted the shimmering bead curtains and we stepped inside the Royal Hall.

Two clean-cut men crawled naked, except for black leather waist restraints, in a circle on the floor. The two temple maidens, Heather and Sarah, stood over them in stiletto black suede boots. Each held a riding crop. In the center of it all stood Venus Howard elevated above them on a table.

Lupe started forward. *"¡Dios mío!"* she exclaimed.

Venus wore a platinum blonde wig and a white dress. Fans on the floor were aimed up at her so that her dress blew up toward her waist. On the wall behind her, above the altar in the inner sanctuary of the Church of the Big Mother, was the famous poster of Marilyn, her white dress blown up toward her waist.

"Dios," Lupe exclaimed again as though being offered a piece of the Holy Grail. She held her trembling hand out in front of her. "Cotton pique," she mumbled as though saying a rosary. "Just like Marilyn's dress in *The Seven Year Itch.* August 17, 1954, 2:00 A.M., the Trans-Lux Theatre, Manhattan"—Lupe paused, color returning to her face once more as she shook herself from her reverie—"but this frail here's got legs like a moose."

Venus Howard glanced toward us. She pointed with her chin for us to go into the small kitchenette. "Priestesses," she intoned in a baby voice to her foxy minions, "I am most displeased with my servants."

The handmaidens began to prod the crawling men with the riding crops as Venus Howard climbed stiffly down from the table. On her way to the kitchen she kicked one of the guys with her nasty stiletto. He looked as if he'd gone to heaven.

"What'd you want to see me about, Ms. Howard?" I asked, taking a spot in the kitchen where I could keep an eye on the other room. One of the handmaidens had one of the men bent over a chair and was spanking him. His butthole looked like an angry spider. His unattractive aryan balls dangled unevenly.

Venus Howard studied Lupe with distrust.

"My legal secretary, Ms. Ramos. She's here to take notes."

"I don't have to write it down. I have a photographic memory," Lupe said.

Venus Howard turned her attention back my way with a dramatic sweeping hand gesture. "I have a very important offer to accept: my own show on Channel 50! The word must be spread! My trial televised! Have you finished researching the constitutional issues yet?"

Television! And have the world know about the lunatics I was forced to represent? How much worse could my life get? I shook my head. "I haven't had time and I don't think it's—"

"How much are you making for this scene?" Lupe asked, indicating the other room.

"That's it! That's what I'm trying to explain. That's what we must make clear for our television audience." Venus poked me in the arm. "There's no fee. It's a donation to the church. The ancient sacred prostitutes were often known as Charities or Graces because they dealt in a unique combination of beauty and kindness called *charitas*—"

"Five hundred bucks?" guessed Lupe. "You got two girls, overhead... I don't think it could be done, realistically, for less than seven fifty."

Venus shook her head. "In Babylonia the custom compelled every woman of the land once in her life to sit in the temple of love and have intercourse with some stranger. It didn't matter what sum of money was offered, the woman would not refuse because the money of this act was sacred."

"A grand," Lupe insisted.

Venus turned from Lupe to me. "Get all the networks at my trial. Think of what it'll do for your career! Praise the Great Slit."

"You can't be serious, can you?" I stammered. I looked at Lupe for help.

"It's brilliant," said Lupe. "I see a series. T-shirts..."

I glanced back into the temple and saw the handmaiden with long hair yawn as she continued the spanking. "What's the cosmology involved here? The gods, the goddesses?"

"Ishtar, Mylitta, Attar..."

I walked out of the kitchenette and into the altar room. I stood towering over the prostrated man. "Hey, buddy, who's Attar?"

He looked at me blankly, a thin line of spittle oozing out of his excited mouth.

"Ishtar?" I asked.

He continued to look up at me stupidly.

"You're fucked without a cosmology. You're looking at jail time," I called to Venus Howard on my way to the front door. "You get me a pantheon of gods and goddesses before I set foot in front of a jury."

Lupe and I left the Church of the Big Mother to the uncertain chanting of "Attar, Attar, Attar."

I had Lupe drop me off at my car in Koreatown, then I sent her back to the office. I shoved another Bob Marley tape into my cassette player and drove to the Superior Court archives between Hill and Broadway.

Archives is a creepy bomb shelter beneath a not very well conceptualized or maintained minipark, one of those desperate islands of jacaranda and green that passes for public space in the Civic Center. I ordered the docket sheets for adoptions from 1965 to 1968. I wanted to see if Kim's story about being adopted by people named Peterson was true.

Koreatown was less than five miles away. I felt it pressing in on me, taunting me with its blood secrets. Jin was killed by a masked assailant who stole not only the *kye* money but the mysterious box as well. He must have known what he was looking for. Did he know Korean history? Did the other old women know the box's special meaning? Would history provide the clue I needed? Would it explain why Jin was killed? History has never been anything more than blood.

And where was Jin's killer at this moment?

The arrival of the microfiche for the documents I'd requested put an end to my conjectures. I loaded it into a machine as instructed by an obese county employee who could barely wait to get rid of me and return to watching her tiny Japanese television. I scrolled carefully through the film and found several adoptions involving people named Peterson. I ordered those files and waited again while Oprah interviewed recovering anorexics.

The files were finally delivered to me. One was for a Luke and Mary Peterson of North Hollywood who had adopted a four-year-old girl they named Kim. There were no notices to her parents. The court order had dismissed the necessity of notices or due diligences, simply stating, "Unknown in North Korea."

It was nearly five o'clock by the time I finished reading the file. The Petersons had requested the court to set aside their adoption when the girl was fourteen years old. The accompanying court order absolved them of responsibility. I copied down their address. There wouldn't be time to try to locate the Petersons before going to see Ko Won. I'd told Lupe to meet me outside his store at five-thirty. I stopped on Olympic near Normandie at a Korean place and wolfed down a quick bowl of *manduguk,* meatball soup, and a bottle of beer.

Lupe was waiting when I pulled up in front of Ko Won's electronics place. "We should follow him, try to catch him in a more relaxed setting," she said, climbing into my car. She switched the radio station to KLVE and the booming tropical sound of Juan Luis Guerra and his band 440. I pulled onto the side street so we could watch the front of the store and the parking lot behind it. There was a huge, immaculate white Mercedes in the lot, and we agreed it was probably his. About twenty minutes later the Mercedes, driven by Ko Won, pulled out of the lot, passed our street, and headed toward the magenta sunset.

He continued out of Koreatown, past the oak- and palm-lined fringe of Hancock Park, past the tire shops and soul food diners near La Brea, past San Vicente and Midway Hospital, where a guy I knew from law school had died of AIDS. He drove past Beverly Hills, past Rexford Park where men in white pants and shirts were bowling on the emerald grass, past the triangular twin towers of Century City to a southbound ramp of the 405 freeway.

"Where's he going?" Lupe wondered. I could tell she didn't know this part of town.

When he turned onto the Richard M. Nixon freeway I knew he was going to the Marina.

Marina del Rey is the largest man-made marina in the world. It was dredged out of a marsh fronting the Santa Monica Bay. An improbable Italian Renaissance hotel stands next to a place designed to look like a cannery. Condos and luxury apartments in garish architectural ménages of Vegas and the South Seas line the artificially created channels where the boats are moored. Still, it's hard to make water look bad, and I noticed Lupe was looking about eagerly. The last rays of sun struck the masts of the sailboats, gilding them gold. There are nearly a dozen steak and seafood restaurants with busy bars in the Marina. At one time there was a hot singles and pickup scene in those bars. Rumors about airline stewardesses abounded. They got off their flights, came back to the apartments they shared with fifteen other stewardesses, poured themselves into jeans and hot pants, drenched themselves with Fracas from duty free shops, and went out and fucked everyone until it was time to get back on another plane headed east. Now, with the epidemic, I wondered if anyone was still playing those games.

Ko Won drove to Via Dolce, turned onto a eucalyptus-lined street, and then disappeared into an underground garage beneath a condo called the Buccaneer. It was directly across from a restaurant. I pulled into its lot and parked at the far end. I glanced at the sign above the restaurant. The Rusty Wharf. Despite the warm breeze and the inviting dance of the palms that framed it, the restaurant didn't look very busy. There were less than half a dozen other cars in the lot, although they were all jags and Mercedeses and BMWs.

"Are we going to get to eat?" Lupe asked. "I'm hungry."

I shook my head guiltily. We could be in for a long night. Another Mercedes pulled into the lot, and two Korean guys got out. Even from where we were I could see that both of their suits were expensive and the jackets slightly oversize to accommodate guns. They went into the restaurant. Not another five minutes went by but another luxury car pulled up in front of the Rusty Wharf. Three more Korean guys wearing the same kind of dark suits got out and went in. Two of them wore their hair in ponytails.

"Would I be off the mark if I said those guys look like gangsters?" Lupe asked.

Ko Won, in navy boat shoes, white slacks, and a navy cashmere sweater, came out of the condominium and ambled across the street toward the restaurant. I stretched my hand out toward Lupe, motioning her to remain still. Ko Won glanced in our direction. Would he be expecting to see us again? Had Kim told him about us? If Kim was tight with Ko Won, why hadn't she gotten him and his men to take care of Jin's killer? Ko Won walked quickly to the Rusty Wharf without another look in our direction and went inside.

I shook my head. "Shit. What's this nice businessman community leader doing here?"

"Let's get out of here," Lupe whispered. "We can't fuck around with professionals. *Firme* suits and packing rods, are you kidding me? We'll get killed."

"You said you knew what you were getting into." I reached under the seat and took out the .38. I held it out to her.

Lupe looked off into the distance. The only sound was the clanking of metal fittings and ropes against the masts of the sailboats.

"Be careful with this. It's loaded." I laid the gun in her lap. I showed her the safety, but she just kept shaking her head and staring through me. "I'm going in there to talk with him."

"Right, so he'll know you followed him here. That's very smart."

"He thinks I'm a reporter."

"And I'm Little Bo Peep. Don't you think Kim's told him who you are?"

How much could I trust Kim? I knew she'd lied to me about three things. Three is an important number. I adjusted the rearview mirror toward myself and combed my hair. I looked scared. Had Lupe noticed? "Move the car to the opposite end of the street. Then I want you to get into his building, scout out his condo, see what you can learn. We'll meet back at the car in forty minutes." I glanced at my watch. I noticed Lupe wasn't wearing one. I unfastened mine and offered it to her.

Lupe shook her head. She opened her purse and took out a Rolex, which she strapped on her wrist. What were those things worth? $8,000? $15,000? A fucking felony. What else had Lupe been keeping from me, I wondered. She got out of the car and came around to the driver side. "The reporter shtick's not going to work."

I got out of the car and looked at the boats. It was so peaceful. I heard the car start up and Lupe drive away, leaving me alone in the dark. I walked toward the Rusty Wharf. Although I'd learned to sail on the Chesapeake Bay when I was a kid, I hadn't sailed in at least fifteen years. I wondered if I still remembered how. I quit sailing because I got tired of my father yelling at me all the time. "Tack! Draw in the jib! Can't you pay attention?" It had been exhausting being the daughter who couldn't do anything right.

CHAPTER THIRTEEN

The entrance to the bar had a tremendous view of the south channel. The Rusty Wharf was the usual light-pine-furniture and potted-ficus kind of place popular along the beach. The kind of place everyone on earth thinks all of So Cal looks like. Pale buffed wood, big picture windows, salad bar. My favorite is the kind of dark seaside dive with little windows like portholes. When I go out I want to be waited on. I don't want to have to go to a salad bar, stand in line, then haul my own chopped greens back to the table. A hundred-foot yacht was in a slip in front of the restaurant and beyond that a cruising catamaran I guessed to be a Solaris 42.

At the bar were a couple of bleached blondes with permanent tans and guys who looked as if they smoked too much. The women wore the official LA uniform: skintight T-shirts, miniskirts, bare legs, and black cowboy boots. I spotted Ko Won sitting at a large round table near the far wall. He faced the room so he could survey everything. He was talking and laughing and the five dark suits with him looked as if they were having as much fun as possible without actually being relaxed. I hoped Lupe wasn't going to run into any trouble trying to case his condo. Would there be anyone guarding it? What would Ko Won do if he knew who I was and that I wanted to con him into telling me what he knew about Kim? I wished I'd followed Lupe's advice and changed clothes. Something a bit sexy. Exposed flesh. I wanted Ko Won to think I was just like the other bimbettes. Only with better legs.

I went over to the bar and sat down on an empty stool next to a guy in his late fifties. He was about the same age as my father. I smiled at him and ordered a glass of white wine. He was drunk. He smiled back.

I had to keep Ko Won from knowing I'd followed him to the Marina. I nodded at the drunk. I'd prostitute myself for verisimilitude. My smile felt plastered on my face. Lupe would have pulled the barstool close to him and whispered in his ear. She would have managed to bend forward when she spoke so that her exciting cleavage would be in his face. I discreetly unbuttoned the top button of my silk shirt. "I'd like for you to do something for me," I whispered.

His smile turned into a horny, stomach-churning leer. How could Lupe and Venus Howard put up with this?

"There's a guy over there, I'm trying to get a job in his company, and I don't want him to know I came here alone. I don't want him to think I'm that kind of a girl." I swiveled further in his direction to give him a peep down my blouse, but he seemed unaware of the subtlety of my movement. No wonder Lupe wore halter tops so often. I laid my hand on the forearm of the stranger and squeezed it in a way I hoped was suggestive. "Would you just wait right here for me while I go talk to him, sugar? And then you and I'll have some fun."

Ko Won didn't give any sign of recognition when I marched up to his table and stood in front of him. Was it true all of us white people looked alike? Finally he nodded and put his scotch down on the table. The men with him put their drinks on the table too. Next to Ko Won was a hot-looking guy about my age with a ponytail and a midnight black two-button Armani suit. Could he be the man who'd attacked me? He moved his hand quickly but discreetly under his jacket to his gun. Ko Won smiled at me as he shook his head almost imperceptibly at the guy. The other man with a ponytail was a few years older. Could it have been him? He had a black suit too.

"Hi," I bubbled. "I thought that was you. I was just over at the bar having a drink with a friend when I saw you."

Ko Won glanced over at the bar. I wiggled my fingers in a little wave at the drunk at the bar who looked back at me with uncertainty, then lifted his glass in my direction. I saw the other ponytailed man's eyes flicker over me, looking more at my breasts than my face. Ko Won made a slight gesture toward the table with his hand.

The younger of the ponytail guys got up and brought a chair over from another table. He held it out for me, seating me between Ko Won and himself. He was my height, just like my attacker.

The last man I'd been this close to was from one of these bars. A commodities broker I let pick me up during a tequila shooter happy hour at a Mexican restaurant on the main channel a couple of years ago.

Ko Won's man let his hand brush against me as he guided me into the chair. He sat down, drawing his chair close to mine. I glanced quickly at him as he settled into my peripheral vision. He had long black lashes and eyes the color of moss. I wondered if he had contacts. His cheekbones were carved from ice. He was the color of caramel. I felt a little wet. Yes! It was good to know all of my parts were still working. But was he the guy in the Chusok mask?

"I'm glad to see you again," I told Ko Won. I quickly inventoried his casual but expensive clothing and rings. He wore a large blue-white diamond on each hand. Was he really a gangster? I'd never met anyone in organized crime. I knew undocumented workers who got into fights in barrooms in La Puente. Black guys from Inglewood who were picked up for commercial burglaries. I knew the occasional bad-check writer. "There's something I wanted to explain to you." I wished I'd brought my drink over from the bar with me. "When I told you I worked for *Esquire* magazine, that wasn't exactly true. I'm a free-lance writer, and I'm doing an article to sell to them. I sort of exaggerated because I thought it would help me schedule an appointment with you—"

"Have you interviewed anyone else for this article?" he interrupted.

"Korean people?" I stalled. I looked around the table, hoping to catch a friendly eye. The men stared back at me with blank, hard looks. The older ponytailed man picked up his drink, with his left hand rattling the ice cubes as he brought it to his lips. I wasn't able to get a good look at his hand to see if it was the same one which had grabbed my breast.

"We're Korean-Americans," Ko Won said.

I nodded, embarrassed. "Several."

"Who?" he asked.

"Kim Oh." I had to go ahead, move. "To get a woman's perspective on the riots, their aftermath..."

"Kim?" He said her name without inflection or surprise.

I nodded. Had she been Ko Won's squeeze on the night they met Hector? Or was Lupe right about her? That she was just another working girl? The tattoo meant something. Was it like a brand? Did someone own her? Ko Won? "Yeah, she was great. What a role model! A woman business owner. Strong. Dynamic. Your community must be very proud of her."

"You know Kim?" he mused. Had she told him anything about me? What would she have told him? What did he know about Jin's murder? If he didn't know, why hadn't Kim told him? Maybe she didn't tell him everything. Maybe there were things she didn't want him to know. He didn't take his eyes off my face. I felt as if I was playing poker with a viper.

I nodded again. "She said you'd been instrumental in helping her." I was betting that Kim kept secrets from Ko Won and he would wonder what they were.

Ko Won looked thoughtful, and there were a few uneasy beats before he replied. "Well, why didn't you just tell me you knew Kim?" He laughed. "I wondered why your photographer didn't have a camera when you came to my store." He said something in Korean. All the men laughed.

I laughed too. "Yeah, that was crazy. I just graduated with a degree in journalism and I guess I'm still pretty green. That's why it's so important to me to get such a big story. 'The New Los Angeles!' "

Ko Won looked at his scotch as though he'd just rediscovered it. He took a big executive pull on it. They were all smoking Marlboros. There was a lot of masculine energy. I could practically smell testosterone in the air. "I'd be glad to have you interview me. To talk about redevelopment..."

"New businesses!" I cheered.

"...building new relationships with blacks and Hispanics...," he added.

"Brotherhood!"

"...and the sports center," he said.

"Right on!" I wondered why he didn't offer to buy me a drink. My mouth felt dry and my heart was pounding.

"My business associates," he said, indicating the pistol-packing crew at the table. I wondered what business they were in. Drugs? "We were having an informal meeting about some new property developments in Koreatown. Let's you and I meet at Kim's restaurant the night of Chusok festival. Tomorrow," he proposed.

I didn't want Kim to find out I was using Ko Won to check up on her. "I know the article's about connectedness, interrelationship, but I don't want it to look like I'm playing favorites or just relying on a couple of sources. Maybe it would be better if we went somewhere else." That sounded pretty lame to me. I was sweating bullets.

"In Korea we say we don't really know a person until we eat a meal with them," he said.

I was worn out by the inscrutable Oriental business. I was starting to panic. Were they involved in smuggling? Hijacked electronics goodies? A protection racket? "Great. I'd love to try Korean food."

He told me that the food was good at Kim's and that it was all made from her old family recipes. He said it was just like eating in someone's home.

"Soul food," I said.

He looked puzzled.

"Means home-cooked. Family cooking."

Ko Won nodded back at me. "That's the secret of Kim's success! Family." He laughed. "Soul food." He said something in Korean to his cronies who laughed in response.

Out of the corner of my eye I saw the drunk get up from the bar and totter toward Ko Won's table. He bumped into a middle-aged couple dressed in matching nautical sweaters as he bore down upon us.

Although I'd been told several times Dorothy put up the money, I asked Ko Won if he'd helped finance the restaurant.

He nodded and said that in '87, when Kim opened the restaurant, it was hard for women to get loans from banks. "I loaned her money and I cosigned at the bank with her to guarantee another loan."

"I know her godmother owned a restaurant in Seoul, but Kim must only have been a college student. Weren't you worried she didn't know how to run a restaurant?"

"She'd just graduated from SC."

A lie. Or had Kim lied about SC to Ko Won also? What else, how many other things, might she have lied to him about? The sun shuddered as it fell beneath the horizon.

The drunk drew closer to the table. He was wearing boat shoes and a pair of faded khakis that hung below his gut.

Ko Won looked in the direction of the approaching drunk. "Your boyfriend's getting impatient. Tomorrow night we'll have a special dinner. Soul food, right?" Everyone at the table laughed again. He turned to the guy next to me and spoke quickly in Korean. I knew that it was a language that depended on inflection for meaning. Every time he spoke he sounded angry. He turned to me and said he'd told the guy to show me to my car. "And help your friend."

I pushed back my chair and stood up from the table. The guy next to me stood up. I like ponytails on men.

I said good-bye to Ko Won.

The man took my arm. His fingers were warm and firm on my bare tanned biceps. He bowed to Ko Won and started to walk me in the direction of the entrance. "Let's go," he whispered in my ear.

I nodded dumbly. "Your English is good."

"I'm from Bellflower."

The drunk stumbled toward us.

"I don't have my car. I came with my friend." I pointed at the drunk, who'd stopped near the corner of the bar to shoot the breeze with an equally drunk sun-mottled matey in a yachting cap. "Jeez, I see I'm going to have to drive tonight." I prayed the drunk hadn't walked over to the bar from one of the neighboring condos.

I stepped away from my handsome escort, wrapped my arms around the drunk, and gave him a big kiss. He tasted like Tanqueray and tonic. He was surprised, but not too surprised to push his tongue down my throat. I wanted to barf, but I pulled away smiling. "Come on, sugar, let's go. Over to your place. Give me the car keys."

The drunk started to protest, but his pal, giving me a slimy once-over twice, clapped him on the back in approval. Was this what Lupe had to put up with? Bloated old farts who couldn't get hard without an endless jaw-cracking blowjob. I glanced at my watch as I secured my arm more firmly around his waist and started to lead him toward the exit. He handed me the keys. It was nearly an hour since I'd left Lupe. Would she be waiting for me at the corner as I'd told her to?

The Korean stood close by with a slight smirk on his lips. He followed us to the fern-decked foyer.

"Hang on, baby," the drunk slurred, lurching away from me. "Don't go away. I gotta piss like a racehorse." He stumbled into the head.

"I'll wait in the parking lot," I said to his retreating back. Asshole better come back, I thought, or I'm in deep kimchi.

The Korean and I walked outside. It was dark. The sky was full of as many stars as you can see in Los Angeles. Across the water drifted the sound of laughter from a party on a balcony overlooking the channel. He took my arm again, more firmly, and moved me toward the moored boats. He smelled like Karl Lagerfeld cologne.

"Bellflower's a nice place," I said.

He pushed me along quickly to the chain link fence at the edge of the water. I glanced back at him. He was wearing Ferragamo wing tips. The light from the restaurant and the lights from the apartment buildings seemed far away. What had Ko Won told him to do with me? Below us the expensive and beautiful sailboats strained against their moorings. Kill me? I felt pretty certain he was the guy in the Chusok mask, but it had been too dark to really examine his left hand. He was behind me. I remembered a joke.

An old guy at a retirement home asks one of the lady residents to go out boating on the lake with him the following Sunday afternoon.

"Oh, that would be very nice," she says.

They go out to the lake and get into the boat. "Up or down?" he asks her.

She rips off his clothes, rips off her clothes, and makes crazy passionate love to him. He's amazed. But pleased.

I wondered what it would be like to take my clothes off with a guy as good-looking as this Korean.

The following week the old guy asks the woman if she wants to go out to the lake again. She says yes. They go out to the lake. Get in the boat and he asks her, "Up or down?"

She looks at him, puzzled.

"Up or down?" he asks.

I glanced at the guy with the ponytail. What would it be like to have him naked, above me? The ponytail didn't mean anything. Lots of men in Los Angeles have ponytails.

"What are you talking about?" the old lady in the joke says.

"Last week I took you boating. I asked you 'up or down' and you ripped off your clothes, you ripped off my clothes, and made incredible love to me. The best I've ever had."

"Oh," she says. "I didn't have my hearing aid in. I thought you said, 'Fuck or drown.' "

What would I do if he tried to grab me? If he tried to pull me down from behind I'd throw him off balance and chop him in the neck hard enough to mess up his windpipe for a while. Why had I thought I was so smart? That I could mess around with these Korean guys? If he moved to put his other hand on me to try to push me over the fence, I'd twirl and with a roundhouse kick him in the balls. I pulled my arm away from his grasp and turned to face him. "Thanks for everything. I better get going."

He pulled a gun from a holster strapped in his armpit. He held the gun in front of my face. It was big. Even in the dark I could see it was a 9mm

Beretta. It's hard to calculate the stopping power of a handgun bullet. Human reaction to an impacting bullet is complex. You have to calculate permanent crush cavity (PCC) PCC EST. =6.3x(VOLUME) 45.0 and calculate temporary stretch cavity (TSC) TSC EST.- .92x(VOLUME) 56.0, therefore one-shot stopping power equals OSS= (PCC ESTIMATE TSC ESTIMATE) 2. That Beretta could scatter my ashes out to sea.

It was the same kind of gun the guy who killed Jin Oh used. Ko Won could have told him to steal the money. Maybe Kim's position with the gang wasn't as secure as I'd imagined. They'd turned on her and moved against her family. I looked down the barrel of the Beretta. It's also a weapon favored by the police. They cost about $400. If you buy it on the street, $500. Most of the cowboys banging today go for Magnums or semi-automatics they can convert to automatics.

"You playing cops or robbers?" I whispered.

The Beretta disappeared back into its holster. He quickly withdrew a badge from a pocket inside his coat and flashed it at me.

"Show me."

He handed the badge to me. It was LAPD. It said his name was Edward Lu. *Adiós* law career. *Hasta luego* Clarence Darrow. My knees buckled, and I grabbed at the fence to hold myself up. He reached for me as I swayed.

"You're no reporter and you're stepping on an official investigation. I don't want to see you around any of these people again. They're killers. That guy with the ponytail sitting across from you, the one staring at you, he's a convicted rapist. Did time at Folsom." He dropped his arms and studied me. "You have pretty hair."

I didn't want to move away from him or for the moment to end. The moonlight caressed me, and I knew I looked platinum and pearl.

A motor started up nearby, and a boat pulled out of its slip headed south to the main channel and Mexico. I stepped back. I handed him his badge. His hands were small, and the ring finger on his left hand looked as if it had been busted. We looked at each other. I didn't know if he was a cop or not.

We walked back to the front of the restaurant without saying anything more. The drunk was pacing back and forth looking for me. I asked him where his car was. We got into his Lincoln, with a personalized plate that said HOT DDDY, and Edward Lu went back inside the Rusty Wharf.

The drunk leaned across the seat trying to fondle me, but I elbowed him and hit the gas, laying rubber out of the parking lot. We raced beneath the canopy of palms toward the corner where I'd told Lupe to wait. Under a streetlight was the old Fiat. Lupe was listening to loud Mexican rock and roll. I screeched to a halt behind her. The drunk fumbled with his pants, pulling his dick out.

"Chew on it yourself." I bolted from the car.

The Fiat roared to life, and we lickety-splitted out of the Marina.

"Oh, man, you're not going to believe what I found out," Lupe exclaimed as she drove. "That condo. Every bedroom has floor-to-ceiling mirrors. The big corner apartments like Ko Won's all have Jacuzzis in the bathroom...."

"You see his place?"

"No way! You think I'm gonna B and E? I'm on probation! I been talking to some girls who live there. They didn't know him—there's three hundred units in the building—but they told me they see Korean guys coming in and out all the time. They said that joint you went into's like gangster city. The guy who owns it has a rep for not cooperating with the cops."

"I met a cop in there. With Ko Won."

Lupe downshifted to make the turn onto Venice Boulevard. "Right, a cop. Was he wearing a uniform?"

"Undercover, but he showed me his badge. I'm telling you, it's the only time in my life I've ever been glad to see a cop." I didn't say anything about how good-looking he was or that I'd thought I liked it when he held me in his arms.

"He must be narcotics then," said Lupe.

I looked at her.

"Ice."

"Methamphetamine?"

Lupe nodded as she got on the freeway headed back for Koreatown. "You got it, homegirl. This chick I talked to, a pro in a four-hundred-dollar La Perla bathing suit just like I seen in *Vogue* magazine, hanging out by the pool, had a cellular phone. I asked her if she knew where I could score and then she was telling me how the Koreans are big into the ice biz." Lupe turned north toward Dorothy's and continued to chatter excitedly about the fancy call girls, the fancy Marina condos, and the fancy cars. She kept glancing with rapt pride at her stolen Rolex.

I fell silent. We passed hundreds of squalid apartments on the edge of the Pico-Union as we drove up Vermont to Koreatown. The palm trees wept in the moonlight. There were no new jobs. No new schools had been built. I am a member of the National Lawyers Guild. I had believed in equality, fraternity, and the Bill of Rights. What had the Rebellion changed? Now the city was a burned-out Stonehenge of bricks and asbestos.

Was Ko Won involved in drug dealing? It was possible, but stereotypical. So Hollywood. But why else would a narc be with him? The cop from Bellflower, if that's who he was, could have infiltrated Ko Won's group. And Kim? How did she fit in?

"Take me to get my car," I told Lupe. "I got to go talk to Dorothy now. Alone. I get the feeling she doesn't like you."

Lupe shrugged wordlessly away and pumped up the volume of the Mexican rock and roll higher.

Dorothy was in the kitchen making a meat-and-vegetable dish she told me was called *sinsollo*. She gave me a Wedgwood plate, and we carried the food out to the dining table.

I wasn't hungry. I wanted a drink. "You said you'd tell me about the Queen Min box."

"You have to know more about my country." Dorothy pushed her plate of uneaten food away. "We come here as refugees and you expect us to forget our history. For us to metamorphose into something new. No, our memories are in our blood."

She told me the story her mother had told her when she was a child of ten. Her mother, Sae Oh, was born in the late 1800s to a family of poor laborers in the capital city. When Sae was thirteen she became a servant in the royal palace, where she attracted the attention of Queen Min, who made her a chambermaid and, as she grew older, a confidante. When the Japanese invaded the country again, the royal family believed their days were numbered.

"Queen Min gave my mother a rare emerald, as large as a baby's fist, to be hidden in a place of safety until after the occupation."

"Must have been worth a fortune."

Dorothy nodded. Sae left the palace and traveled north up into the mountains as the queen had told her. She buried the emerald in a pouch of leather beneath a pine tree on the edge of a cliff. When Sae returned to the palace the queen gave her a carved box as a reward to commemorate the journey.

"The box is carved with the pictures of pine and mountains. The number of pieces of inlaid mother of pearl are the exact number of miles it took Sae to travel to the mountain."

"The box could be used as a map to find the emerald!"

Dorothy sighed. "Shortly after my mother returned to the palace, the Japanese executed Queen Min."

I didn't say anything. To me it was ancient history, but I could see from the light in Dorothy's eyes it was still a real part of her life.

"It was near this time of year, October."

Dorothy said Sae had been able to flee the palace with the carved box. She returned to her family and later married.

I asked if her mother had ever gone back to the mountains to retrieve the emerald.

Dorothy nodded her head. "She tried. I was only ten years old. My mother, nearly fifty then. She'd been involved for years in the struggle for liberation from the Japanese."

"I didn't know...."

"Decades before Gandhi, the Korean people used non-violence to try to free themselves," Dorothy said impatiently, eager to finish her story. Her mother had traveled back up to the mountain, but the area was controlled by the Japanese. "My mother was captured."

Dorothy got up from the table and went into the kitchen, where I heard her filling a kettle with water.

"Did she come home?"

"Died on the mountain."

I pushed the food around on the plate. How could we remember history if it kept vanishing in front of our eyes? Dorothy's apartment showed no trace that a violent murder had taken place there a couple of days before.

"Is the emerald still buried in Korea?" I asked.

Dorothy reentered the dining area carrying a tray with a ceramic teapot and two cups. She poured me a cup of ginseng tea. "Yes. In the North."

"The mountain's in North Korea?" I could understand that the box was valuable in and of itself. It was wood, carved. It had historical significance, but would someone steal it because it was a map? "How could anybody get in or out of North Korea?"

"My country will be reunited. It's only a matter of time." Dorothy fell silent, her head bent over the cup in front of her. "But not my time. I lived through three wars. Saw Los Angeles in flames. Soon I'll die."

"But you're in perfect health. You do Tae Kwon Do...."

"I don't want to live. Too much pain. My mother, my child, my sister all taken away from me."

"You still have Kim," I argued.

Dorothy looked up at me, but steam clouded her face and I couldn't see her eyes.

CHAPTER FOURTEEN

A blue light was on in the *do jang of* my master, Sun Lee. It was nearly quarter to twelve on Friday night. Less than nineteen hours before I'd face Ko Won again. How was I going to break it to Dorothy that her grand-daughter was tied up with a gangster? Dorothy had had enough disap-pointments. I hesitated for an instant in the dim doorway of the *do jang*. The advanced class of which I'd become a member ended at ten. Although the street was zoned for commercial use only, I knew Sun Lee lived in a room at the back of the *do jang*. I knocked on the door.

There was no reply but the wail of a saxophone and the warped thud of a drum machine. Was he listening to Captain Beefheart?

"It's Whitney Logan," I called.

No answer.

I was surprised that the door was unlocked. Had someone been there? Was there a problem? In the strange blue light the immaculate white walls of the *do jang* glistened like a glacier. I took my high-tops and socks off in a hurry and left them in the carved oak rack next to the front door. I felt the familiar padded floor beneath my feet. I walked down the hallway toward the back of the *do jang*. "Sun Lee?"

At the end of the hall a candle flickered, its yellow flame dancing in the dark.

"Sun Lee?" I walked past the men's dressing room, which was the first room to the left. "Tiger? Golden Tiger?"

A screaming form jumped out at me from the black recesses of the dress-ing room. My arm was twisted up behind my back. I lunged forward as though accepting my attacker's body weight and with a quick movement shoved back. I dropped into fighting position preparing to kick.

"You missed class this evening. First time." My teacher abruptly let go of me and bowed.

"Jesus Christ, Tiger. You scared me. I thought there was someone here."

"You need more discipline." He straightened his shirt. "You should be practicing more for your promotion to red belt."

I nodded, pleased. "I have to talk to you. I know it's late—"

He led me back into his room, which I'd never seen before. He flipped on the overhead light. There was a futon on the floor, a Sony tv, a Sony cd player, and a poster from a competition he'd been in in Long Beach. A teddy bear with one eye sat on the futon. Sun Lee turned off the strange music. I sat on the floor and told him everything that had happened in Koreatown, beginning with the murder of Jin. I ended by telling him about the guys I'd met with Ko Won in the Marina earlier that evening.

"You're involved with a gang, Whitney. Let the police handle it."

"The cops might already be in. I think one of the guys at the bar with Ko Won's a narc."

"He told you that?"

I nodded. "Saw his badge. Name's Edward Lu."

Golden Tiger shook his head. "They're playing with you. No narc's going to tell you who he is. Particularly if he's undercover."

"So where'd he get a badge? You don't get those in a box of Wheaties."

"Made in Hong Kong. Taiwan. Korea." The Golden Tiger grinned at me. "Isn't that why everyone fears the Koreans and the Japanese, because of their ability to make knockoffs of American goods?"

I put my head down, ashamed. A toy badge. How could I not have thought of that? I asked my teacher to tell me what he knew about the Korean gangs.

"There's five gangs. With thousands of members. Primarily in Koreatown, but also the South Bay and Diamond Bar. They're totally different from black gangs or the latinos. They're not territorial. They're influenced by the *yakuza.*"

I'd heard of *yakuza*. They are Japanese gangs, organized, like the Mafia. The Golden Tiger said the Japanese occupation of Korea and the use of Korean laborers in Japan had spread the knowledge of *yakuza*.

"These Korean gangs are mostly business oriented," he said. "They deal in specific crimes—"

"Like stockbrokers?"

He nodded, then went on to tell me that the members take blood oaths. If they break the gang's bylaws they are killed. They use secret handshakes and recite poems to identify themselves. They have special tattoos. When the immigration law changed in '65, the gangs began to grow. The new kids from Korea were quick to assimilate. "The old folks wouldn't use English. The youth want to be Western." The old structure of the family began to crumble.

The gangs started at Uni High, where the Korean kids banded together for protection against the Chinese. The Korean Killers started hanging out around Vermont and Olympic. Soon there were the American Burgers, Rainbow, and the South Bay Killers. I interrupted and asked him who belonged to the gangs.

"Kids. College students. They get recruited, get allowances, credit cards, cars."

The reason Kim dropped out of college! To work with the gang. It was good to imagine they were an equal opportunity employer. A step forward for women. We're never going to be equal until we can all commit the same crimes. "So they're not usually as old as the guys I met today?"

Golden Tiger shrugged. "They can be sixteen, twenty-five, in their mid-fifties, and all be in the same gang. There's tremendous respect for age. The older ones, the big brothers they sponsor the younger guys and use them as eyes and ears and muscle."

"What about ice? How's that fit?"

"The gangs are in business. It might be prostitution. It might be methamphetamine. It costs hundreds of thousands of dollars to get into the ice business."

A guy I'd represented last year told me about ice. Freebase and stay high for twenty-four hours. "How would they sell it?"

"Mostly in bars. The bargirls."

I bet Kim worked in a bar before they set her up in the restaurant. "Ko Won's got a real profitable-looking business selling electronics goodies."

The Golden Tiger resettled himself on the futon, pushing a small red pillow out of his way. "Probably a totally legit business. A guy like that could front the money for the ice—"

"And then resell it for distributions! Or use his store for money laundering!" He could be using Kim's Cafe James Dean for a laundry. "He's a straight-up fucking gangster! I knew he had too many pictures of himself with politicians in his office."

"A dead giveaway," the Golden Tiger agreed. We fell silent and watched the candlelight flicker on the walls. I got up to leave.

He cracked his knuckles. "Even if that guy you met tonight is a cop you can't trust him, especially if he's a member of the Asian Gang Unit. Even other cops don't trust them. If he's real and you get in the way of a take-down..." He shook his head in a sad, thoughtful way.

I stood up and adjusted my purse on my shoulder. For over a year I had relied on Sun Lee to help me grow strong.

"Don't go back to Koreatown," he said.

I shrugged. I'd given my word to Dorothy and Lupe. Courtesy Integrity Perseverance Self-Control Indomitable Spirit. Those were the tenets Sun Lee had taught me in the do jang. "I don't have enough on these people to go to the police. They know my friend Lupe. I got her involved in this mess. I have to go back."

He chewed his lip in silent contemplation for a moment before nodding. "Every circle must be round." He accompanied me to the front door and watched me put on my shoes and socks. The Golden Tiger sank gracefully into fighting stance, stretched his arms in front of him, his hands moving like mad birds, hands moving almost faster than the eye could see, showing me how to remain fluid. Then he drew back and bowed.

He closed the door behind me. I heard him lock it, then the dead bolt slid into place. The street was quiet. It was midnight. Although I wanted to go see the Petersons who had adopted Kim, I didn't think they'd want to meet anyone new this late at night. I headed home to try to catch a few hours' beauty sleep.

With my car's high beams on, I pulled into the parking area behind my apartment. I switched off the lights and the engine and sat studying the blackness surrounding me. I thought again about the guy in the Chusok mask who'd jumped me here. He'd been about my height. Probably weighed thirty or thirty-five pounds more than I did. Black hair in a ponytail, like Edward Lu. I remembered the guy's hands on my breasts and the sound of his disgusting breathing.

The shadows didn't move. There was only the usual lethargic swish of traffic from Dickens Avenue and the sound of people drinking in apartment number 3. I went upstairs. There was a message from Harvey Kaplan reminding me my rent was overdue. I made myself a toasted peanut butter and jelly sandwich and a bourbon and Coke. I checked all the windows to make sure they were locked. I shoved my tatty black couch in front of the apartment door before climbing into the shower, where I stood for a long time with the hot water beating down on me. I set the alarm for six, made another drink, took a couple of Excedrin PMs, and slept with my gun under my pillow.

I started awake, hot and sweaty, before the alarm and dressed in the dark. I doubted the Petersons would still be living at the address that appeared on the adoption forms. No one in LA lives at the same place for more than a year. I pulled on black jeans, a black T-shirt, and tennis shoes. Splashed a drop of Chanel No. 22 on each wrist. I pushed the couch back to its usual place along the wall, grabbed a rotting banana from the kitchen, and hurried out.

The Petersons' address was in North Glendale, called the Rancho San Rafael when the Mexicans owned all the land. It's difficult to find anything left of Glendale's romantic past. After the gringo conquest, the land was subdivided. Its second history began in the early twentieth century when the Pacific Electric Railroad extended its tracks northeast from Central Los Angeles.

The house was a small hacienda plastered with stucco on a tree-lined street in the area between the Glendale City Hall and Forest Lawn Memorial Park. A white station wagon stood in the driveway. Jacaranda blossoms littered the front yard.

I glanced at my watch. It wasn't quite seven yet. From down the block I heard the distant roar of a leaf blower as a Mexican gardener cleared the sidewalk in front of another stucco house. While I was deciding whether to go up to the Petersons' door, an elderly man in a plaid flannel bathrobe came out, looked up and down the street in a proprietary way, then stooped to pick up his LA *Times* from the well-swept driveway.

I went right over to him. "Mr. Peterson?"

He straightened and looked around suspiciously at me. He was tall and thin, like a big man who'd been deflated. He was sallow and had gray eyes. He looked as if he was in poor health.

"Reverend Luke Peterson?" I smiled. I didn't know his correct title. I'd been an Episcopalian. High Church of England. He could be the Grand Pooh-Bah for all I knew about his church, the Assembly of God. I smiled some more. He smiled tentatively. I put my hand out. "I'm Whitney Logan, a lawyer and a friend of Kim's...."

A sour look crossed his face. "I don't know any Kim." He turned back toward his house and started to walk away from me.

I stayed right next to him. "Your daughter."

"I don't have a daughter."

"The girl from Korea you adopted."

He picked up speed, hurrying toward his door.

"When I went to check the Superior Court records, I saw your adoption papers," I said. "Therefore, ipso facto, you're her father."

He stopped and whirled toward me. "I paid a lawyer to set it aside. I have copies!"

I shook my head. "Must be lost then," I lied. "They're not in the file."

A gray-haired woman stuck her head out the front door. "Luke, what's happening?"

"Nothing, Mother. Nothing. Go back inside."

I bounced up to the front door like a friendly puppy. "Hi, Mrs. Peterson. I'm a friend of Kim's."

"Kim?" The gray-haired woman looked staggered.

"Look, I'm sorry I seem to have gotten off on the wrong foot here. I just came to talk to you about Kim "

"She's in trouble again, isn't she?" said the gray-haired woman. She looked as if she was going to cry.

"Could we go inside?" I asked, stepping into the doorway before she could say anything.

"We don't want to have nothing to do with her, young lady, so you just get along now," snapped the reverend.

"Kim's your daughter and God don't make no junk." I'd seen that on a bumper sticker. I wished I knew something biblical to quote. "It wouldn't be Christian to turn me away, would it?"

"Luke." The old lady glared at him. "I want to hear about Kim. You can go have a cup of decaf if you don't want to hear it." She made a tight little thin-lipped smile at me as if she was afraid her dentures would pop out of her mouth. "Yes, dear, you come right in. Don't mind him. He's always grumpy before he has his coffee."

The reverend glared back at her as he showed me rather unceremoniously into the yellow chintz living room. A tedious print of a mythic Southwest crowded with mountains and horses hung above the couch in a gilt frame. Assorted spooky Jesus pictures filled the rest of the walls. On the coffee table a silver-plated bowl held candied orange slices and red-and-white peppermints in individual cellophane wrappers. I sat down on the couch. I smelled coffee in the next room, but they didn't offer me any.

"I didn't mean to upset you," I said quickly. "Kim's not in any trouble; in fact, she's doing very well. She's expanding her business and thought you might want the opportunity to invest...."

The old man put his hands up as if he didn't want to hear any more. "I knew it! I knew one day she'd try to get money out of us!"

"Her business?" gasped the woman. "She's doing well?"

"She owns a restaurant in Koreatown." I did tell the truth as often as possible just to keep things simple for myself.

"Kim owns a restaurant!" Mrs. Peterson shrieked. "Praise the Lord! You hear that, Luke? I been praying for that girl every day. Kim's doing well!"

"Couldn't be better," I agreed.

"'Well,' hell," he snorted. "Tell her she'll never get a red cent out of me." Reverend Peterson stomped out of the room and returned with a photo album. He sat next to me on the couch and opened the album. Breathing in short, ragged breaths as if he was exhausted from so much exercise, he ruffled angrily through the pages to a picture of Kim when she was about five years old. She wore a cowgirl outfit, jeans, a printed shirt with mother-of-pearl snap buttons, red boots, and a miniature Stetson hat perched on her head. Her shiny black hair was cut in a Prince Valiant, and she was grinning broadly.

I chuckled appreciatively over the photo and nodded amiably at Mrs. Peterson.

"That's the only time Kim was doing well. And that's the only good thing I've got to say about her." Reverend Peterson snapped the album shut and stood up impatiently.

"Luke," admonished the Reverend Mrs. with a practiced whine in her voice. "Don't talk like that. She was a precious child of God. We don't know what happened to her before we got her."

"Well, we sure know what happened after we got her, don't we?" he said. "The police calling our home nearly every night, the school principal sending us letters every week "

"Where was her real mother?" I interrupted.

The old lady told me she'd been found near the DMZ by U.S. soldiers. No one knew who her mother was. "They brought her to us at the orphanage run by our church."

"Should have left her there," Reverend Luke snorted again at his wife.

"If we can save one soul, then our lives are blessed and have meaning," snapped her adopted mother. "Kim was a beautiful little girl. Remember when she was in first grade and the teacher wrote us that lovely note and told us she was the most well behaved child in the class?" The woman took the album from her husband and searched through it for the letter. Triumphantly she presented it to me. The faded letter was wrinkled, as though it had been perused many times. After a respectful examination I handed it back to her. I had a hard time imagining Kim as a child. I kept picturing her as I'd seen her the first time at Cafe James Dean in skintight jeans. Or nestling next to Hector Ramos, stroking his groin.

"What a wonderful act of charity on your part," I purred. "You must be very proud of her now."

"Certainly," Mrs. Peterson agreed a bit cautiously, glancing between me and her husband.

Reverend Peterson folded his bony arms across his bony chest. An angry silence enveloped the room, smothering everything except the tick of a brass clock on the mantel above the fireplace.

"She did mention, however, that when she was fourteen you told her to leave," I prodded in a most polite tone.

"She said that? It's a damn lie!" swore Mrs. Peterson, her lips pulled back across her funky dentures so that she looked like an angry dog. "She ran away from home!"

"Tell her why if you're so eager to talk about Kim!" demanded her husband. "I'd been telling you for years that we should have shipped her back to the orphanage, but you wouldn't listen to me."

"It was so long ago, Luke," she mumbled. "It's time to forgive and forget. We won't talk about it any more." A Bible lay open on the coffee table.

"It's your fault she ran away," insisted the old man. "No wonder she ended up on the streets."

"My fault! I came home early from helping at the women's auxiliary meeting one afternoon because I wasn't feeling well..."

"I'm sure you always did your best," I said.

The old man gave me a withering glance before picking up his attack on his wife. "You should have stayed home to look after her instead of gallivanting all around town."

"...I saw a motorcycle up near the front door. I didn't know anyone who had a motorcycle. I went into the house to see what was happening...."

"I told you not to let her hoodlum friends over here!" Reverend Peterson shook with anger. I thought he might pop off in front of me.

"...I heard loud rock and roll music coming from Kim's bedroom. I walked down the hall. I called her name, but she didn't answer. I threw open the door to her bedroom...."

"Go on, Mother! You're the one who always said they were nice kids."

"...Kim was in bed with a man. They were naked. They were..."

"Some man!" sneered the reverend. "He jumped up and put his clothes on and ran right out the door. But Kim..."

"...She just laid there, naked as a jaybird, grinning at me." The old woman shook her head as though trying to clear it of the ugly picture. "I told her there's a name for women who act like that."

"Whore!" spat Reverend Peterson.

"She jumped out of bed."

"That's when she ran away?" I asked.

The old woman looked down at the rug. "I slapped her. In the face." She started to cry, and the reverend put his arm around her. "We couldn't do anything for her. Kim was wilder than a dog. Impure."

"You abandoned her! Shoved her out onto the street where anything could happen to her. She could've been killed."

Kim's adopted mother stopped snuffling long enough to say, "We didn't! We had a photo. It was old and crinkled, wrapped in silk and tied under Kim's clothes the day the soldiers found her. It had Korean writing on the back. It was a picture of a woman and a girl. The writing said the girl was Kim's mother."

"Chungmi!" I exclaimed. "The little girl in the picture was Chungmi."

They looked at me in surprise that I knew this. "Chungmi, the Shining Pearl—that was her mother's name. And the other woman was..." I stopped. I didn't know Dorothy's Korean name, but I was sure the other woman was Dorothy.

The reverend tried to shush his wife, but she struggled to finish her story, as if it was her last confession. "I was so angry that day. I ran to my room and got the photo. We'd never shown it to her before. I threw it in her face and told her to get out of my house."

"You didn't know if Kim had any relatives in LA and you didn't care what happened to her, did you?" I got up and slammed the door on the way out. How did they think she'd survive alone at the age of fourteen? But she had. She had the photo, and she found her way to Koreatown.

I wondered how long she'd been on the streets before she found Dorothy and how she'd managed to locate her grandmother.

I drove to Kim's apartment on San Luis Street in Koreatown, west of Vermont and up near Wilshire. It was nearly nine in the morning when I pulled up in front of her building. It was a renovated Spanish-style place, pink, probably built in the twenties, with a security system. A grocery bag full of used clothes I was going to give to the Salvation Army was in the trunk of the car. I took it out. When I saw a guy going for the door, I hurried toward the building, carrying the bag as if it was heavy. He held the door open for me and I marched in. We got on the elevator together. As soon as the man got off the elevator, I scooted out on the next floor, dumped the bag in the stairwell, and went up the stairs to the sixth floor where Kim lived.

The hall was empty. I knocked on the door. I knocked a couple of times. When no one answered, I took a thin metal file from my purse, got down on my knees, and started to work on the lock. A heavy adrenaline rush hit me. I forced myself to go slowly. I thought I felt the lock turn, so I pushed the file in more carefully as I twisted the doorknob. The door flew open.

"Hector!" The file clattered to the floor. I dropped my purse onto the ground to hide the file. Hector Ramos stared down at me, frowning. I pushed the file under the purse, scooped it up, and stood. Hector moved toward me. I could stab him with the file if I had to.

"What are you doing?" he thundered.

"Tying my shoelace. What are you doing here? Providing maid service?" He was in his underwear and a cheesy-looking black silk robe with a dragon embroidered on it. I tried not to stare at his bikini underwear where the robe gaped open. He'd rocketed past light welterweight and was way too fat to be wearing bikinis. "I wanna see Kim."

He glanced down at my high heel pumps *sans* shoelaces. "You don't have no right to be here," he said. "I live here."

"Your name's not on the mailbox. Enjoy it while you can, Hector. Love's a beautiful thing."

He peered out into the hall. "Where's my slut sister? *La puta.*"

I juggled the purse carefully to get a better grip on the file. "At my office."

Hector howled with laughter. "Yeah, right. She's probably flat on her back on your desk right now screwing all the *mojados* she can pull off the street." He noticed his robe and tied the belt around his lumpy middle. "You here about the legal papers so I can get Joey?"

I shook my head. "Give it a rest with Joey. You think any Superior Court's gonna approve guardianship to someone who has known gang affiliations?"

Hector crossed his arms across his big chest. "I don't gangbang."

I shrugged. "I'm talking about Kim. Your bride-to-be."

"Shut your fucking mouth. You think everybody who's not white is in a gang?" He advanced toward me with his right hand forming a fist.

"Kim's not here," I guessed as I held my ground.

"I told you to shut the fuck up."

The file was about five inches long, sharpened into a point. "Where is she? Left you?"

"She went to get coffee."

"Great, then I'll come in. I could use a cup. Got business to talk to her about."

"What kind of business?"

"Girl stuff. She told me to come over."

Hector stood uncertainly in the doorway.

I pushed past him into the living room, my hand with the hidden file just inches from his gut. A dozen tall cans of Budweiser languished on the coffee table in front of the couch. "She didn't come home last night, did she?"

He didn't answer.

"There's a lot Kim hasn't told you."

He trooped into the living room and dropped onto the couch, where he'd been watching cartoons. There weren't any chairs in the living room. For a love nest it was sparsely and uncomfortably furnished.

"You're not the only man in her life. Has she told you about her thing with Ko Won?" I asked, wanting him to tell me how long she'd been gone so I could figure out where she was.

"You're full of shit! If you're going to wait here, then you keep your big mouth shut." Hector moved restlessly, as if he was thinking of getting up. "He's just a friend." I

Hector looked a bit like Lupe. His eyes were wide set just like hers. "Then she must have told you he's the one who gave her the money for the restaurant," I said.

He settled back into the couch and waved his hand at me as if he was sure I didn't know my ass from a hole in the ground. "Her godmother Dorothy gave it to her!"

"Is that what Kim told you?" I grinned. "I wonder why she'd keep that a secret from you? Ko Won's your friend now too, isn't he?" I paused to see if Hector was following me.

Hector sat up and pulled the robe around himself. "I'm not gonna tell you to shut up again "

"Dorothy's her grandmother, not her godmother. She said the people who adopted her and brought her from North Korea were dead. I saw them less than an hour ago. That she graduated from USC, but I found out by checking at the school that she never did. She told me that while she was at USC she got raped by a guy who was terrorizing the campus. She wasn't even a student there at the time...."

"Maybe she got the date wrong. I'm not so good at dates myself." Hector picked up one of the Budweiser cans and shook it to see if it was empty.

"You're no good at telling time, Hector. You don't know what f-ing time it is." I ran my fingers across the dust on the coffee table. "Kim's got another crib somewhere. This isn't her home. And you're not her man." I pointed around the forlorn room. "Where are you getting the money for this pad, for Christ's sake, Hector?" I exploded. "Use your noodle."

"From my salary."

"Right! Don't you think it's a little weird that you're getting a salary for a job that doesn't exist? The sports center hasn't even begun construction yet!"

"I do PR!"

I turned and walked toward the bedroom. The bed hadn't been slept in. I flung open the closet doors. There was a black suit belonging to Hector. A pair of jeans. A dress and a skirt and blouse. Two pairs of high heels.

"Look at this, Hector. Two pairs of shoes! No woman owns only two pairs of shoes. Can't you figure it out?"

Hector stared from me to the closet and back again.

CHAPTER FIFTEEN

Hundreds of people were on the surrounding streets although it was only ten when I split from Hector. He told me he hadn't seen Kim since Thursday, two days ago. He didn't have any idea where she was, but I did.

It was a warm and brilliant morning. A Santa Ana blew in from the desert, burning the benevolent and blank blue sky. Hanging silk banners and washing down sidewalks, the citizens of Koreatown worked in hurried preparation for the noontime parade kicking off the celebration of Chusok. It was time for the harvest. The moon would be full at night. In some kinder, gentler time in a place where the leaves of the trees would change color and fall to the ground, the people would bring in their crops. The police were barricading the streets that ran perpendicular to Olympic.

I drove around an unmanned wooden sawhorse blocking San Marino Street and parked in front of the same blighted apartments where I'd parked the first time I'd gone to the Koreatown Civic Association. The same *salvadoreno* whistied languidly at me as I locked up my car. I hurried past him toward the community association. I was afraid it might be closed for the holiday. Here, the center of Koreatown, was the last place to check up on all the stories I'd been told about Kim before I went to find her. That meant I had to see Lee Joon again. She didn't like me. I was the foreigner.

Children's voices in high-pitched song rang out from the association building as I hurried toward it. Inside, the hall was full of kids, from toddlers to those in their teens, dressed in splendid costumes of red, cobalt blue, and emerald green silk. They wore satin caps and sashes of the most radiant yellow. Converse high-tops and blue jeans peeked from beneath their floor-length robes. Some of the older teens tried to get the excited little kids into a line based upon height. I recognized one of the organizers as the sulky dancer I'd seen at my first visit. She was stunning in a crimson robe with long gold sleeves. Her damaged skin was covered nicely with makeup, and she wore thick black eyeliner to highlight her delicate almond eyes.

"Hey, Roger Rabbit. Gonna be in the parade?" I asked.

The girl recognized me and nodded, flushed with pride. "Today I do a traditional dance. I'm the one who taught the little kids."

I asked her where Lee Joon was.

She pointed down the hall toward the art gallery. "There. With the old ones."

The art gallery was hung with sheets dyed a brilliant saffron. Draped in black robes that covered them completely, the silent old ones wore the strange pink Chusok masks identical to the one worn by the guy who'd attacked me. I knew I wouldn't be able to leave Koreatown without seeing him again.

Dozens of yellow and gold chrysanthemums were scattered across the shiny black floor. The old people trod barefoot across them so that their ancient yellow feet were caked with pollen and petals. They turned their backs to me, gathered into a circle, and began to dance. I stood inside the door. I was a pale fleck at the edge of the tapestry they were weaving. The room filled with their chorus of piercing shrill Mongolian cries. I couldn't understand a thing. I couldn't tell which one was Lee Joon or whether they were men or women. They moved gracefully, weightless, like ghosts. The leering, mocking masks turned again and again to inspect me as the circle wove slowly past me.

The music faded away, and the dancers spun to a slow arrhythmic conclusion. One of the figures broke away from the group and clapped its hands above its head. The group broke out in excited and well-pleased laughter, removing their masks and calling noisily to each other in Hangul. Lee Joon rushed up to me with her mask in her hand.

"What are you doing here? I don't think you come because you're a fan of Korean music and dance," she said. She looked annoyed to see me again.

"I have to talk to you. A few questions about Kim."

"I'm busy. Parade start soon. We dance in parade." She turned to rejoin her group.

"It'll just take a minute."

With her hands on her hips Lee Joon glared at me. "This is a special day for us. Don't try to push in here."

I told Lee Joon that Dorothy had sent me.

Lee Joon shook her hands dismissively at me. "She could have told you everything you want to know about Kim." Lee Joon looked impatiently around toward the other dancers, who were beginning to straggle out of the room. "Why should I help Dorothy? I never liked her. What's she to me?"

"The sister of your best friend, Jin." I took a few steps in the direction of the door. "I'll leave if you don't want to know what happened to Jin. I was the last person who saw her."

Lee Joon looked stunned for a moment, then she moved me to the far side of the gallery. The old ones finished hanging their masks on the saffron-covered walls and went out into the hall with the children. I heard the old people singing, then above them the voices of the children joining in.

"What do you know about Jin?" Lee Joon asked in a worried whisper. "Tell me!"

"Not so fast. I need answers to some questions first." I told her I thought she'd locked me in the steam room at the baths. "It's not too late for me to report it to the police." I shoved my forearm in her face and showed her where I'd been burned.

"That explains why Kim was there!" exclaimed Lee Joon after a quick inspection of my pink flesh. "She never goes in evening. Says she's too busy at the restaurant."

"Kim!" Of course. She'd known about the Queen Min box. The *kye* money. She kept Hector hooked up with the sports center to provide some multicultural brown camouflage for whatever bunko crime or phony scam she and Ko Won were running. Lee Joon watched me expectantly. I felt mean, jerked around. "Jin's dead. Killed last Tuesday."

"Ahnee, ahnee! No, no!" Lee Joon screamed as she swayed, starting to collapse. I reached for her. She hit me in the chest with both of her tiny balled-up fists. I grabbed her wrists with my right hand and put my other arm around her, pulling her toward me. I hoped no one had heard her. I'd hate to have anyone find me like this. What would they think I was doing? I made shushing noises.

"You lie!" She tried to wriggle out of my grasp.

"No. Ahnee." I shook her roughly. Too rough for an old lady. "You know it's true. You said so yourself."

She went limp in my arms, nodding miserably and mumbling Jin's name. She began to sob, so I held her next to me and felt her trembling body. They'd known each other for nearly half their lives. They'd been friends for longer than I'd been alive. I thought of Lupe. How long would she be my friend?

"What happened?" Lee Joon cried.

I whispered in her ear that I'd seen a man in a mask steal the *kye* money and then shoot Jin. Lee Joon moaned as she shoved me away. Her face was streaked with mascara, and wet, dark liner seeped into the maze of wrinkles around her eyes. "That's why you ask questions about Kim. Kim in this somehow, isn't she? She's no good."

"You know who Chungmi is?"

"Kim's mother." Lee Joon wiped her eyes with the sleeve of her costume. "Oh, Jin, my poor Jin," she kept repeating.

"And you know who Chungmi's mother was?"

She stepped back, erect with trembling dignity. "Why not just ask who told me?" Her face brightened with cruel pleasure. She must have known this story for a long time. "Nancy Johnson. Jin told her years ago when they played cards every day. Stupid to tell Nancy Johnson anything. She tell everyone. Even Chu Chu Park."

"Everyone's always known?" I groaned. I ran my fingers nervously through my hair. I knew Kim had been lying to me, but Dorothy?

"We never told Jin or Dorothy or Kim that we knew. Best to give some respect to their family."

I stared at the Chusok masks hanging on the walls. They stared back blankly at me. Damn, I'd liked Dorothy. I'd thought she was the kind of little old lady I'd like to be one day. I asked Lee Joon if she knew how Kim had found Dorothy in Koreatown. I repeated what the minister and his wife had told me about kicking Kim out of their home.

Lee Joon nodded. "She came here, the civic association, when she was fourteen. I was volunteer at the front desk. She couldn't speak any Hangul. Only English. She was a skinny girl, but already had a bosom. Said she was hungry. That her mother was dead. She said some church had brought her here, but they treat her bad so she ran away."

"Did you try to find the people she'd lived with? Or call the authorities to help her?"

Lee Joon shrugged. "Best for Korean girl to live in Koreatown. Then she showed me the picture she had. It was Dorothy!"

"You knew Dorothy?"

"In those days everyone knew everyone. Not like now." Lee Joon told me she took Kim over to the apartment building where Dorothy and Jin lived and Kim stayed there with them, sometimes with Dorothy and sometimes with Jin, until she was nearly eighteen years old.

I asked her what Kim had been like after she left her grandmother and great-aunt.

"Like every other bargirl." Lee Joon seemed delighted to dog Kim. "Work three or four years at bar on Olympic."

I took my hand out of my coat pocket. I'd been told by a juror after my first jury trial that it made me look insincere. I almost got the guy I represented convicted on solicitation because I'd addressed the jury with my hand in my suit pocket the whole time and they didn't like that. "Dorothy told me Kim had always worked in the restaurant before she became the owner. Why would she lie to me?"

Lee Joon examined the mask in her hands before answering. "You don't understand how important family is. Maybe you don't have one...."

Yeah, I have one. If you want to call it that. Two parents, never divorced. One child. Three bedrooms. Three baths. Living room, den, formal dining room. We move among the rooms without speaking.

"Worst thing in the world to bring shame upon your family," Lee Joon was saying. "No one's going to say Kim's a bargirl. Even though everybody knows it. Knows she sleeps with a lot of men. Take their money. Be big shot with gangsters."

Lee Joon put on the Chusok mask. "Go home. Leave Koreatown for Koreans." She walked out into the hall and disappeared among the clouds of yellow silk.

I ran out of the building to get my car but saw it would be impossible to drive to Dorothy's. Thousands of people waiting for the parade to begin lined the curbs and clogged the streets. I called the office to find out where

Lupe was, to warn her in case Hector decided to go take his beat-up *macho* shit out on her. She didn't answer. I pushed in the code for the message machine.

"Whitney." It was the Golden Tiger. "There's no Edward Lu with the LAPD. I called a buddy of mine who's a hacker, able to bust into practically any computer system...."

I slammed the phone down and jogged north across Olympic toward Dorothy's apartment. I was mad as hell. She'd known all along about Kim but couldn't admit her own flesh stole from her. Or would kill for what she wanted. Dorothy had almost gotten me killed because she wanted to preserve the fiction of her family.

Lupe's Fiat was parked in front of Dorothy's apartment building. What was she doing here? I took the stairs two at a time and ran down the landing. I pounded on the door. Did Lupe believe there was something more for her here in Koreatown? What could it be? I leaned against the wall catching my breath as I waited for one of them to answer. I felt sick all the way through. What had been driving me all along was the shame that Lupe had seen my cowardice in Dogtown. Now I'd put her in another fucked-up situation.

Lupe opened the door with a cup of steaming chrysanthemum tea in her hand. She handed it to me, then stood aside. The radio was playing "Autumn Leaves," and I saw Dorothy dressed in a white suit and sitting on the couch.

"What are you doing here?" I gasped at her.

Lupe went back into the living room without saying anything. She sat down on the couch next to Dorothy and put her arm around her. Dorothy clutched a white handkerchief in one hand and waved it feebly at me. She'd been crying. I glanced at Lupe with alarm. What had she been up to?

"I wear white today because I am mourning Jin...." Dorothy's voice trailed off, and I thought she was going to cry again.

I put the tea down on the dining table, too angry to feel sorry for her. "Stop it. You could have saved us all a lot of grief if you'd told the truth about Kim from the beginning."

"I'm sorry," mumbled Dorothy. She twisted the handkerchief and looked down at her lap.

"Sorry! I've been chased, beaten up, almost raped..."

"Leave her alone, Whitney, she's an old lady. She's worn out," Lupe growled. "Whatever she did, she did to try to keep her family together."

"Keep her family together! What a load of bullshit! Jin was family too. She was killed, right here in this room. It wouldn't have happened if you'd faced the facts about Kim a long time ago, Dorothy."

"Kim didn't have anything to do with it!" exclaimed Dorothy.

"Don't lie to me. Stop lying to yourself. You'll never get your daughter back," I yelled. "You don't even know for certain that Kim's your blood. She was a failure in school, a liar, a bargirl, a whore..."

Dorothy's eyes begged me to stop saying ugly things about her grand-daughter.

"Everything was there in the open for everyone in town to see." I smacked the table. "I was the only one who couldn't see what was going on. Did she ask you for money? The Queen Min box?"

"I told her she'd get the box after Jin and I died...." Dorothy put her head into her hands.

"Go on," I said. "All of it. You owe it to me now."

"She knew the box was part of our family, our history. I tried to give her whatever she wanted. Jin said I spoiled her. Kim heard Jin tell me not to give her the box and to stop giving her money. Kim said I didn't love her. She said I left her mother to die in a whorehouse," Dorothy cried. "I told Kim that if Jin died before I did, she could have the box."

"Jesus fucking Christ, this is your idea of family?" I moaned.

Lupe put her arm more protectively around Dorothy. "Shut up! Stop being such a moron, Whitney. If anything ever happened to your parents, you'd do the same thing."

I heard myself laugh in a loud, ugly explosion. "Place the lives of other people in danger? Have someone killed?"

Lupe let go of Dorothy and stared up at me defiantly. "If anything happened to Joey, I'd do whatever was necessary. Lie, cheat, steal. Why do you think I worked the streets?"

"Because you didn't finish school," I snapped. "Because you're poor. You never heard of deferred gratification. Because—"

"You act like you were raised by wolves," Lupe said angrily. "Your family's the most important thing in the world. To be with your family, to support your family."

I imagined my mother and father sitting in the living room back in Maryland, not speaking to each other. It was almost two and a half years since I'd been back there.

Dorothy sat up. A bit of color returned to her cheeks. She took Lupe's hand and I saw her squeeze it. "I stopped wanting to live after I realized Kim had planned it all. When the man spoke to Jin, I knew he wasn't Korean. He had to be one of Kim's friends."

Lupe nodded her head at Dorothy in understanding. "My grandmother's the same way. Only speaks Spanish. Doesn't know anybody who's not Mexican."

I dropped down in the chair next to the couch and looked Dorothy in the face. "I can't believe it. You knew from the moment you hired me. You were afraid if you called the police they'd be able to figure it out. I was supposed to screw things up so none of your friends would know what happened."

Dorothy took a sip of tea. "I had to. She's my family. Lupe understands what that means."

Lupe squeezed Dorothy's hand.

We all sat there without saying anything. I remembered an afternoon when I was a freshman in college. I'd been invited to dinner at the house of one of my sorority sisters. As she drove me down an oak-lined street I glanced into the living room of a large brick house. A beautiful blond little girl about eight years old sat in a red velvet chair. Her legs dangled over the edge of the chair without touching the ground. She held a large picture book, and on either side of her stood her parents, Mom and Dad, who leaned over her with rapt attention and boundless love as she read aloud from the book. I began to cry and turned away so the girl driving the car wouldn't see. How I wanted my family to be just like that. At dinner my sorority sister's mother served me crab cakes, roast chicken with fresh peas, and strawberry shortcake. I thought they were a perfect family too. Her father never made it home, and later I heard my "sister" and her mother arguing in the kitchen about money. The little girl in the red velvet chair? She was probably being fucked by her father.

Dorothy disengaged herself from Lupe and poured herself more tea. "There is something you can do that the police can't."

Snatching my purse from the floor where I'd tossed it next to the chair, I stood up, shaking my head angrily. "Let's go, Lupe."

"Bring my granddaughter home to me."

"That's a laugh. Why should I do anything else for you?"

Dorothy smoothed the white silk jacket she wore. "Lupe's told me about you. You want to make the world a better place. Deep down you believe people are good. Find Kim. Tell her I forgive her. No matter what she'd done or how far away she tries to go, she is still the daughter of my daughter."

"That really pulls my heartstrings," I said. "I'm outta here. Come on, Lupe."

Lupe glanced at Dorothy but didn't move.

I hesitated. "Lupe?"

I must be a bonehead. It was all so tender. The warm connection between Lupe and Dorothy. A swelling crescendo of violins. I stood in stupid contemplation of Lupe's dogged love for her family. I felt subhuman because I didn't love my family.

Dorothy turned from Lupe to me. "I'm giving your friend Lupe five thousand dollars for her son, Joey. Half now, half when you find Kim and convince her to come home."

I glanced at Lupe. Her eyes were bright with excitement and hunger. If I didn't agree, she'd try to find Kim herself. She'd get killed. "We want cash."

Dorothy nodded.

Lupe got up. "Don't worry, Dorothy. We'll bring her back to you."

I stomped out of Dorothy's apartment with Lupe following. The sound of a marching band came from over on Olympic. I glanced at my watch. It was just past noon. The Chusok parade had begun.

"I just wanted to get the fuck out of Koreatown," I raged. "I can't believe you'd cut a deal with her behind my back."

"Go back to the office, then. I'll handle things myself. I shoulda known it. You're just a *gabacha*. No *alma*. Emotionally constipated. You hate being white and you don't got no soul."

"*Chingate,* homegirl. I got my feet on the street. And no matter what kind of sissy you think I am, I'm not letting that old lady or you screw me out of the money. I've earned it. I put my ass on the line for her. And I've helped you plenty, so don't be giving me any bullshit now about white and brown, or black and yellow. Let's just talk about the green."

"What an honest moral revelation," said Lupe. "You're gonna go for the dough. You're not just a goody-two-shoes crusader after all."

Did she know I was doing this for her? "Yeah, I feel like a whole person. Indignant and greedy."

Lupe nodded at me. "Great. I want to see how you pull this off, O great white liberal, fixer of all that is wrong. Shouldn't be too hard. We just find Kim and tell her Dorothy wants her to come home. And I can't wait to see Hector! Tell him his *amorcito's* a murderer. That's hot! That must be a real turn on, sleeping with the criminally insane. I'll give you a third of it, just like you were gonna give me."

"From now on we're fifty-fifty on everything."

"Sixty-forty," said Lupe. "Dorothy gave the money to me. I've got a kid." She stared defiantly at me, waiting to see if I was going to give her a bad time about Joey. I didn't. I told her Ko Won was using Kim's restaurant for some kind of money laundering. "That guy I told you about from the bar in the Marina, the one who said he's a cop—"

"Your new boyfriend!" crowed Lupe. "Whitney's in love! With a pig. Maybe we can knock this thing off by dinnertime and you can go out to sup *con to novio*—"

"I'm pretty certain I recognized his hands."

"His hands?" Lupe howled. "You been jacking off thinking about what he can do to you with his hands? You do jack off, don't you?"

I shook my head impatiently. "I think he's the guy who tried to rape me.

Since I've been studying Tae Kwon Do I got into looking at people's hands. His are a bit small, ring finger on his left hand's crooked like it's been broken. The first two knuckles of his right hand are calloused like he always tries to lead a punch with them. He's the guy who killed Jin."

"Holy shit," gasped Lupe. "Why didn't you say so sooner? Let's wrap this up. We'll tell Kim she better go make peace with her grandmother because the cops are closing in on Ko Won's gang. Then we're gone. *Adiós* Koreatown."

"Fifty-fifty. I got a gun."

Lupe turned toward Olympic as the sound of the parade drew closer. The Santa Ana blasted the street, and the rough wind pulled at Lupe's long black hair. She smoothed it back from her face and stared off into the distance. Finally she nodded, "Ok, girl, you got a deal. *Vámonos.*" She shuffled impatiently from one foot to the other, eager for us to be on our way.

I grabbed her by the arm. "I wanted to tell you. You've been a real inspiration to me, Lupe. These strong family values. I never told you this, but I come from a dysfunctional family. There, I feel good sharing that with you." I let go of her. "And I'd feel even better if you'd give me my share of the money now."

Lupe frowned for an instant, not knowing if I was serious. Then she opened her purse, flashed $2,500 in hundred dollar bills, and slapped half of them into my hand. "I suggest you use yours for some psychotherapy. I'm gonna buy Joey some clothes and get me a real Chanel belt." She grinned. I wondered if there was more money that she hadn't told me about.

I said we should go to Ko Won's store. Although he was probably riding a big float in the parade, someone there would know where he was. I was pretty sure Kim would be with him. We could give his office a quick toss while he was gone. I told Lupe I'd already been to see Hector that morning, and Kim hadn't been with him. "Come on, we gotta walk."

Lupe looked at me as though I had proposed something truly insane, totally revolutionary. Bananas. Walking in Los Angeles.

The street was busy with stragglers rushing to catch the parade. The closer we got to Olympic the louder became the sound of music and clashing drums. At Olympic the crowd was four and five deep lining the boulevard. It was nearly all Korean with a sprinkling of Salvadorans and Mexicans, who clumped in their own small groups, pretending to be oblivious to the Koreans standing next to them. The latinos had probably looted some of the very merchants who were paying for the bands and floats in the parade. Lupe and I ran across Olympic between a group of dancing children and a marching drum band. We pushed our way through the crowd and down the block to Ko Won's store.

The store was open. A clerk at the front counter was conducting a busy sale of video cassettes and film to tardy parade-goers in straw hats and paper visors imprinted with the name of Ko Won's store. Lupe and I slipped down one of the aisles while the clerk was busy. We went back to the office where we'd first met Ko Won. The door was locked, but I knocked insistently on it.

Ko Won's voice asked something in Korean.

"I'm looking for Kim," I said.

I heard an office chair rolling across the floor, then footsteps. Ko Won opened the door. Kim sat in his office in a tailored black suit with no blouse under the jacket, strands of pearls covering her breasts. She smoked indulgently while holding a vcr remote control in her other hand. She glanced away from the video screen she was watching and looked over at us.

"Your grandmother told us to bring you home," I announced.

Kim laughed, then said something in Korean to Ko Won. He laughed. "Relax," he said to us. "It's a holiday. We were just giving thanks for how good the year's been and remembering those who've been so helpful to us."

"Come here," Kim said to us. "I think you'll enjoy the video we're watching."

Lupe looked questioningly at me. I wished I'd gone back to the car for my gun. I looked at Ko Won in his elegant tapered suit. If he was wearing a gun I couldn't see it. He moved back over to his desk and leaned protectively against it. That told me he had one in the top drawer.

I walked over to stand beside Kim. I looked at the video.

On the screen Kim, in a black merry widow and black thigh-high vinyl boots with stiletto heels, faced the camera as she stood straddling a fat man who lay on his back on the floor of a crummy room. Her exquisite butt was toward his face. The faceless man pulled at his penis.

Kim touched the remote control so sound filled the room. We heard the man's moaning and panting. I glanced quickly over at Ko Won and wondered if he was the man in the video. He looked as if he was enjoying the show very much. I stared back at Kim in the video. She crouched and moved back as if she was going to sit on the man's face, but before she got down she swirled her pelvis up and away from him. He moaned more. Next to me, Kim touched the remote so the sound went up louder.

Lupe walked over, stood beside me, and studied the video. I didn't look at her, but I could feel her next to me as she shifted restlessly. Did Lupe do scenes like this? She'd never actually told me what she did on the street. I'd guessed from her knowledgeability of the S&M happenings at the Church of the Big Mother that she did. It was, I supposed, all pretty standard. High heels, soft little whips, pretend spankings.

In the video Kim turned to face the man. The camera zoomed in on her as she squatted over the prostrate man. She spread her vagina with her fingers. Her muff was dark black, the hair straight and silky. Her labia were nearly crimson. A stream of urine ran out and down onto the face of the man below her.

Lupe shook her head as though she was disgusted but not surprised by Kim. "Figures," Lupe said. "I knew she was a real skeezer."

The man's ragged breathing on the video soundtrack sounded as if he'd been pushed over the edge into ecstasy. He began to babble, to talk fast and crazy, incoherent words. I couldn't make out anything he was saying. He sounded as if he was loaded.

The camera pulled back to reveal his face.

It was Hector Ramos!

Kim burst into laughter.

"You filthy fucking whore," Lupe swore. She jumped at Kim. *"Pinchi puta, hija de perra, con tu culo viejo..."*

Kim bolted from her chair. Lupe swung at her. Kim's right arm came up fast, blocking the punch. Ko Won shoved his chair away from the desk, where he'd taken a seat. Lupe stepped in closer to Kim, trying to grab her by the neck. Kim slapped Lupe as hard as she could. Lupe staggered backward into the desk. Blood trickled from the corner of her mouth. She pushed herself up and threw herself at Kim, ripping at the pearls around Kim's neck. One of the strands broke, and pearls rained across the floor. Lupe clung to her, digging her fingers into Kim's throat. Kim grabbed Lupe's arm with both hands and smashed it down on the edge of the desk. Lupe screamed, grabbing her arm to her chest and doubling over in pain.

Ko Won stood up from the desk.

I leapt toward Kim, planted myself solidly on my left foot and with a roundhouse kicked harder than I'd ever kicked the training bag at the *do jang*. I caught her in the ribs, and I heard something crack and give way beneath my foot.

Ko Won ripped open the top drawer of the desk. He pulled out a gun. I picked up the chair Kim had been sitting in and swung it in his direction. It didn't sail easily over the desk the way you'd expect it to in a movie, but it hit him and threw him off balance. Lupe flung herself against the wall, grabbing for the light switch near the door. The overhead light went out. The evil video flickered in the dark. A shot went off. Kim shoved Lupe aside and bolted from the room.

I ran for the door too, but tripped over the upended trash can and went sprawling. As I got to my feet I saw Kim running down the main aisle of the store and out onto the street.

CHAPTER SIXTEEN

I ran out the front door. A float fashioned of red carnations rolled down Olympic Boulevard. Cheers and applause greeted the princesses on it. They were dressed in long gold-and-pink silk dresses like the ones Jin and Dorothy had been wearing the morning I first came to Koreatown. Old women and children watching from the sidewalk waved flags in the air.

Lupe came careening out the door right behind me. "That fucking bitch. Where'd she go?"

I looked up and down the crowded sidewalk. Had I lost Kim in the swelling crowd? Ko Won emerged from the store talking angrily into a cellular phone and scanning the swarming street. A drunk and lost-looking *salvadoreno* bumped into Ko Won, who shoved him angrily away with his free hand. Then Ko Won spotted us. He barked into the phone.

Lupe grabbed my arm. She shoved me toward the street and started to run.

Was Ko Won calling some of his men? Fifty yards away I saw Kim running east through the crowd. I jerked free of Lupe and sprinted after Kim.

A marching drum corps of black kids from Watts pranced ahead of the float. They stopped, quickstepped, broke and danced while the drums pounded. The Koreans stared at them in silence. I pushed past Mexican families with teenage kids in Guns n' Roses T-shirts; past Korean women in navy tailored pantsuits and sensible jewelry; past Salvadorans with their princess daughters in bright lacy dresses, which stood out stiffly from their thin brown legs; past an old Buddhist nun with a long gray robe and a shaved head.

I ran the way I do on the track at the high school near my apartment. Shoulders loose, hands curled in soft fists, my breathing easy and regular. Kim was forty yards in front of me, running as fast as she could, as I closed the distance between us. I was nearly behind her. She'd kicked off her shoes and she must have been completely hyped on adrenaline, because I knew I'd hurt her when I kicked her. She wove through the crowd, cutting to the right then to the left. Over the pounding drums I thought I could hear Lupe's labored breathing as she struggled to keep up with me. I quickly glanced around at her. Her hair flew wildly and her face was etched with pain.

I slammed into a young Korean guy in black jeans and a yellow polo shirt and we both went down. Apologizing, he tried to help me up, but I was already on my feet and running after Kim again. People clustered around carts selling dolls and food. All along the street many people wore Chusok masks, and thousands more of the weird pink masks swung from poles

carried by vendors. Lupe was caught in the crowd far behind me, losing
ground, and I left her to struggle through for herself.

Kim glanced back over her shoulder. I was less than ninety feet behind
her. Kim burst into a sprint, angling for the end of the block where a Tae
Kwon Do team was putting on a demonstration in the middle of the intersection. Everyone on the team wore white uniforms sashed with colorful
belts denoting his or her individual rank in their school. A select corps of
black belts were in hand to hand combat while the less experienced belts
moved back and forth in a choreography of advance and retreat punctuated by loud fierce cries. Kim looked toward the intersection. I jumped
toward the curb, thinking she was going to try to run across Olympic
between the battling martial arts students.

Kim veered instead to the right at the end of the block and sprinted
through the crowd toward a side street. I hurdled over an ice chest and
sent a family scattering as I raced after her. They jumped up, yelling at me.
Kim disappeared down the side street and into a two-story building hung
with a scarlet-and-yellow banner with writing in Hangul, English, and
Spanish.

—Welcome to Korea town—
—Korea—Land of the Morning Calm—
—Bienvenidos a Koreatown—

I charged after her into the building. Inside there was a glass-domed atrium full of people in both regular clothes and traditional robes. The center
of the atrium was open, and a wooden stage had been erected there. On
the empty stage was a long table covered with white paper and oranges,
bananas, apples, peaches. Half a watermelon wrapped in cellophane lay
next to a sheaf of green leaves. A microphone stood at the edge of the stage.
I searched the milling crowd quickly from where I stood near the entrance.
I didn't see Kim.

I made my way into the happy swarm as a guy in a green t-shirt walked
up to the mike and tapped it. The tapping sound echoed through the atrium. People stopped talking and drew closer to the stage. After a moment
a line of women dressed in identical sky blue gowns marched up onto the
stage carrying drums and a wooden musical instrument that looked like a
Balinese gamalong. The women sat down on the stage and began to play.
The crowd, many of them carrying Panasonic video equipment, surged
closer to tape the ceremony.

I searched through the crowd again. I saw Lupe come in the door, stop
and look around. She gave the room her defiant once-over. She saw me and
began to move through the revelers toward me. There were several hun-

dred people, mostly Korean, but also some latinos and a few whites and blacks. The Koreans were dressed up in good suits and party dresses. I spotted Kim at the far end of the stage breathing hard and with her hand on her ribs where I'd kicked her. She was sweating and wiping at her face with her other hand. She wasn't looking in my direction.

I slipped farther back to the edge of the crowd where the atrium was bounded by bamboo trees with yellowing leaves and began to move slowly toward her. Lupe tried to get through the mass to follow me.

Three more Korean women in the blue robes came through a path that cleared for them in the crowd. They carried a long knotted white cloth above their heads. They were heavily made up with thick foundation powdered with white rice powder. They had painted their eyebrows black, arching up to their temples, and their eyes were also lined with black. Their mouths were crimson. They passed near me. I turned away so Kim wouldn't see me if she was watching their entrance. Cymbals crashed.

An old man in a white gown and a black high hat and blue shoes marched behind the women. He carried a maroon-colored umbrella over his head. A series of frightening bird cries tore through the air. One of the old women put down her drum and whirled to the center of the stage. I realized the cries were coming from her. The dancers on stage swayed with their eyes closed. I moved toward Kim. A Korean guy in a dark suit danced toward the stage waving dollar bills in each hand. He quickly put the money on the stage, which I now understood was an altar.

I edged closer to where Kim stared transfixed at the altar. I wondered what meaning, if any, the old ceremonies had for her. Hadn't she wanted to leave her culture and ties to the past behind? Was she amused by what she saw now? Disgusted? The lowest class, the *ch'onmin*, had been butchers, monks, slaves, serfs, actors, and shamans. This spiritual circus was taking place in a mall. Kim's face was flushed but radiant, almost peaceful. Her right hand moved slowly up to caress the remaining strand of pearls she wore. She closed her eyes and bowed her head for a moment, her lips forming silent words. Then Kim opened her eyes and darted forward and tossed her strand of pearls on the altar.

I pushed toward her.

Glasses of drink passed among the musicians. Another dancer got to her feet and began to twirl around and around in place. She made a dizzying number of revolutions, then dropped to her knees and bowed her head to the floor twice. A third female shaman jumped up, grabbed the microphone from the edge of the stage, and began exhorting the unknown with guttural cries.

A white woman in the audience began to dance in place to the beat of the drums. The Koreans surrounding her pointed at her and laughed. The musicians offered each other more booze. A woman from the audience rushed forward carrying a bottle of Cutty Sark and waved it around before setting it on the stage. The singer sang with vibrato increasing in tempo and urgency.

I crept to within yards of Kim. She looked away from the stage, still flushed and mesmerized, and over in my direction. Her face was a serene island in the excited crowd. I'd never seen her look so gentle or innocent. I stepped toward her. She seemed surprised to see me, as though she'd forgotten where she was. An old woman handed a girl a hundred dollar bill to put on the platform for her. The horde shoved forward, many with cash in their hands.

I crouched behind a couple headed to the stage with their money and ran around the bamboo trees. Kim stepped back from the altar. I saw her looking in wild confusion around the atrium for me. Another woman shaman with a red bandanna tied around her head got up and began to dance. Her blue robe twirled around her legs. She lifted her bare foot slowly, her arms extended outward. The drummers joined together in feverish syncopation to carry the dancer on her journey.

I came from behind the trees and toward Kim. She ran for a flight of stairs at the far end of the hall.

I was nearly close enough to reach out and grab her when she twisted away, hurtling into a dimly lit hall that led toward the back of the building. She'd been here before. She shoved open the back door, and for an instant I saw the immaculate blue sky off to the east. Then she was gone. The door slammed shut.

I opened the door.

In the large parking lot behind the building a village had been constructed of plywood painted the color of clay. Roofs colored like tiles of many intricate designs topped the houses. It looked like a movie set. I didn't see Kim. I stood panting among the artificial houses.

In front of me hundreds of cobalt blue tiles raised diagonally against each other formed a gate in front of the largest house. I went through it and into the house. Sliding walls made of heavy ivory-colored paper divided the house into two rooms. The first room was furnished with the simplest essentials: a couple of small tables and some chests for clothing and bedding.

I went into the second room.

Kim stood facing the wall. She was holding her side. Her breathing was so ragged I was sure I'd cracked her rib.

"This house, this is a re-creation of a Korean village from the last century," she wheezed painfully. "This is my history. This is where I come from. Tonight there'll be a party here for Chusok. Food. Dancing "

I put my hand up to stop her. I wasn't interested in the *National Geographic* tour. "Dorothy asked me to come get you."

"Whitney!" I heard Lupe yell. I could tell from the sound of her voice that she was just outside. "Where are you?"

Kim glanced at the door. We both heard Lupe's high heels as she came through the open portal and through the empty first room.

"In these old houses they built fires under the wooden floors, pipes carried the heated smoke from the fires and heated the whole house." Kim looked around the room as though trying to memorize it. Then her eyes traveled slowly over me. She was sizing me up, measuring the distance between us. "Always watch your opponent's eyes," the Golden Tiger says. "In your opponent's eyes you can see every move he's going to make." There wasn't anywhere left for Kim to run.

I took a step toward her. "She wants you to come home."

"*Ondol*. The heating was called *ondol*."

Lupe shoved open the partially closed rice-paper door and stepped into the room with us. Her white silk blouse had come untucked, and her skirt was ripped from trying to run in it.

"We slept on the floors of our houses," Kim whispered.

Lupe struggled to catch her breath. "You got the bitch!" she crowed to me.

As she wheeled to face Lupe, Kim's features rearranged themselves into a mocking mask. She looked more like herself now. Cunning and quick. "Love your outfit," Kim sneered at her. "Loved it every time I've seen it on you. You must make a fortune when you wear that on the streets."

Lupe ripped off the jacket of her gray flannel suit and threw it down on the floor. She put her hands on her hips, vogued and jerked her chin up at Kim. "Try looking this good, whore-dog."

"Any day, sweetheart. Any day." Tossing back her long velvet hair Kim pursed her lips and blew a kiss at Lupe as she strutted toward her.

"I was born sexy," Lupe purred. "You had to learn it from your whore mother."

I stepped in between them, trying to separate them.

Kim leaned forward quickly, grabbed me by the shoulders, and kissed me. She pushed her tongue into my mouth and guided my hand down onto her breast. "I can take care of your girlfriend here better than you can," she taunted Lupe.

I shoved her away. I spit on the floor and wiped my mouth with the back of my hand.

"That figures. She tastes as rotten as she looks," Lupe said as she moved away, tucking her blouse in. "Yeah, Whitney, you're right. I don't have to compete with a piece of shit like her." Wiping at her sweating face Lupe wouldn't look at me, but she glared at Kim. "She knows you sent the guy who killed Jin. And she wants you to come home anyway."

"Dorothy?" For a split second Kim's eyes shifted away from us and toward the far wall.

I followed her gaze, but didn't say anything. There was a sliding panel there. An escape route? The room was dead silent except for our uneven breathing.

"Dorothy thinks I had something to do with Auntie Jin getting killed!" Kim's voice wavered toward theatrical hysteria.

"She's known all along," said Lupe.

"She's crazy! She's always thought I was trying to take advantage of her."

"Weren't you, Kim? I come from a pretty fucked-up family, but I can't imagine killing any of them. You stole seventy-five thousand dollars from her, but why did Jin have to die? I'm sure Dorothy would have given you the money. Why didn't you just ask her for it?"

"I did." Kim waved her hand angrily as if this was all Dorothy's fault, as if Dorothy deserved whatever happened for being stubborn.

Lupe shook her head. "Why didn't you ask your friend Ko Won for it? Guess your worn-out *caja* just ain't worth it.

Kim folded her arms across her chest. The top button of her jacket had come undone, and her ivory breasts glistened with sweat.

"What's it about, Kim? Money laundering?" I prodded. "I think the restaurant was opened with money from Ko and you gave him the *kye* money to put into a drug lab 'cause you couldn't go into that kind of business on your own. He makes money from ice or whatever the fuck it is and pushes cash through your restaurant. I bet he's not kicking back to you like he promised."

"Yeah," said Lupe, laughing. "You're probably making less than when you were a bargirl."

Kim moved closer to me. "Cafe James Dean's a real restaurant."

"And I'm Ivana Trump," I said. "You should go home and make your peace with Dorothy before you get busted. The cops are right behind us."

"You're a lot of laughs, blondie," Kim hooted.

Lupe picked her jacket up off the floor and dusted it off. "I'll wait for you outside. It stinks in here. I need some fresh air."

I nodded, "Yeah. We'll be out in a sec. I'm sure when I explain things to Kim she'll want to come with us."

"Your grandmother paid us to find you," Lupe said. "A nice pile of real cash. Now I got the money and you can kiss my ass." She tossed her jacket over her shoulder and, with one last poisonous look at Kim, strode out.

Kim and I stared at each other. Her eyes flashed resentment at me.

"What happened to the Queen Min box?" I asked. I could feel that my face was still red, my lips slimy and venomous where she'd touched me.

Kim waved her hand dismissively at me. "That piece of junk."

"It's a map to a treasure."

"Bullshit. The old stories don't mean anything anymore."

I'd never know if the box was real or not. Kim could have sold it to a collector or thrown it out. History has always been negotiable. "Dorothy's not gonna press charges against you, but I saw Ko Won out at the Marina the other night. A cop was there," I said. "Undercover."

Kim smirked. "Oh, really? What'd he look like?"

"Long black hair in a ponytail. Green eyes. Good-looking."

Kim turned toward the sliding paper wall. "Good-looking. You hear that, Eddie?"

The wall panel slid open.

Edward Lu stepped into the room.

I looked back and forth between them. Ko Won must have called him from his cellular telephone as Lupe and I raced out of the electronics store. Kim knew where she was going when she ran out of Ko Won's. To meet Eddie. They were all in the same gang, but I didn't have much time to savor the satisfaction of being right.

Eddie looked me up and down. He was in the same sharp black suit I'd seen him in at the bar. He was packing. Why hadn't I brought the frigging gun? That's what it's for, isn't it?

"Meet my old man, Eddie. Actually, you've met him before."

I looked at Eddie. "Yeah, at the Rusty Wharf in the Marina."

Kim laughed. "Before that."

I nodded my head in sick confirmation of what I'd suspected, but I couldn't speak.

"At your place," Kim prodded.

He *was* the guy in the Chusok mask! Anger rushed from the pit of my stomach to my head. I wanted to throw myself on him. I wanted to kill him. "You tried to rape me!"

"Where do you suppose I got that idea?" smiled Eddie. If he'd been the slightest bit wary of me when I fought back against him outside my apartment building, he didn't show it now. It must have been a fluke that I'd been able to deck him. Or had he let me hurt him to make me overconfident and foolish?

I turned and stared at Kim with dumb animal hatred. "You rotten cunt!"

Eddie snickered.

"Shut up, Eddie," snapped Kim.

"Why'd you tell him to do that?"

Kim shrugged. "Thought it would scare you off."

"Maybe you'd like it," Eddie suggested.

I glanced toward the door. How would I get out of here? The Golden Tiger says there's no shame in running away from a fight. "Does your boyfriend here know about Hector? That you're doing the nasty with him?"

"Who do you think shot that video?" laughed Eddie. He seemed like a guy who had fun wherever he went.

"Hey, Eddie." I looked from Kim to Eddie. He dressed good. He was handsome. "How much of the old ladies' seventy-five grand did you get?"

I watched him watch Kim. Maybe he was in love with her. I shouldn't forget the romantic angle. Maybe Kim did have a pussy that was better than any other on earth.

"The whole thing?" I asked. "I think if you're going to kill someone, you should get the whole thing."

"You told me it was twenty-five thousand," he said to Kim.

"It was." Kim moved closer to him. "She's lying!"

"You must have taken out fifty after Dorothy brought the money home from the bank," I said to Kim. "She told you to kill her auntie Jin too, didn't she? Bet she gave you a key so you could just walk into the old ladies' apartment."

Kim shot a wild look over at me. "I never told him to kill her! You think I would have taken you there if I'd known that's what he was going to do? I didn't even know he was going to be there then!" She whirled toward Eddie again. "Asshole, you were only supposed to scare them!"

"You stupid bitch!" Eddie snarled. "You know I'm gonna waste anybody gets in my way."

"Nobody's gonna buy that I told someone to kill my auntie."

How nice it would have been to believe her that she didn't want Jin dead, but I knew it was true. I grinned reassuringly at her. "That's right, Kim. You're gonna put on a pink dress, cry in front of the jury, and you're gonna walk right out of that courtroom as innocent as the day you were born.

"Murder," I said, shaking my head at Eddie. "While in the commission of a felony. That's special circumstances. You're looking at the death penalty. That's so cool: you fry, and Kim goes shopping. Right on, sister." I gave her a thumbs-up. "And you, Eddie, trying to impersonate a cop. Man, that's so old."

"Fuck you. I was a cop," Eddie said rather petulantly.

"Sure. Let me guess. Asian Gang Unit." I laughed. "In your dreams. I've checked on it. LAPD personnel never heard of you."

"Internal Affairs busted me on some chickenshit charge. That's why my name doesn't show up." He picked a piece of lint off his immaculate suit. "Pure chickenshit."

"Right." I yawned. "I'm sure lots of your fellow officers will come forward to testify as to your fine character. They'll be pushing each other out of the way to get to the witness stand."

Eddie shook his finger in my face. "You wanna do the job right, you gotta go shake hands with people IAD say are dirty. Then they say you're part of organized crime."

"Weren't you?"

Eddie moved away, now restless and angry. "They think we're all gooks. Who do you think the chiefs are? All white, all fucking flatheads who were in 'Nam or Korea. We all look alike to them. Just gooks."

Maybe he had been a cop, once upon a time. Going up against Internal Affairs is like being court-martialed. And he could make a lot more money with Ko Won than with the LAPD. Not to mention being presented with such splendid opportunities as stealing *kye* money from a group of old ladies. "Did Kim tell you that while you were busy packing for your trip to Death Row she was fucking Ko Won?"

Eddie looked from me to Kim, but he didn't look very surprised. "Were you?"

"No." Kim tossed her beautiful long black hair. I imagined them together, her hair cascading over him as it had over Hector Ramos in the video.

"You wouldn't lie to me, would you?" he asked. "I wouldn't like that."

Kim put her hand on his arm and smiled. "You know I wouldn't, honey."

"Good." Eddie stroked her hair. He let it run through his caressing fingers. "So where were you last night?"

"You weren't on the job banging Hector," I said. "I went to the apartment. He said you hadn't been home all night." I felt a little sorry for Hector in his lonely love shack. "You must have been with Ko Won."

"Eddie, baby, that's not true."

Eddie took Kim's hand off his arm and grabbed her wrist. "Ko told me. If you're lying about that, you're lying about how much money there was."

I inched away toward the door. "What happened to the Queen Min box? The big Queen Min emerald?"

"Emerald?" Eddie glanced quickly at me.

"She's talking shit, Eddie." Kim whined.

"I wondered why it was so goddamn important to you to keep that piece of junk," Eddie snarled.

"There's a map carved on it," I added. "Tells where the emerald is." I swallowed the hard lump in my throat so I could tell the big lie. "Jin taught Kim how to read the map. Jin was the only one who knew how."

"I been watching you." He grabbed Kim's hair and jerked her face close to his. "Right outside the door while you were sucking Ko's dick last night. You fucking lying bitch. You're history."

Eddie pulled out his gun.

"Come on, Eddie, don't joke around," Kim said, trying to move backward toward the ivory paper wall. "You and me, forever, you said so. We share everything."

I heard the sound of the parade passing by on Olympic. "Yeah, I think this has gone far enough," I said. "Let's all—"

"Shut up," Eddie said. "Down on your knees, white girl."

I crouched into a fighting position, ready to strike out if he got any closer to me.

Eddie turned with a quick roundhouse and kicked me so fast I couldn't block it. I flew backward, but I got back up. Kim tried to run past him toward the door. He grabbed her and threw her sprawling to the ground. He pointed the gun at us. "On the floor, both of you."

I got down on the floor.

"Eddie, baby. What about all our plans?" Kim whimpered.

"Whore. Think you can steal from me. Tell me to kill your auntie. You wanted to be in business, well, this is business." He jerked the gun at her and shoved her toward the wall.

Kim got to her knees. "Eddie..."

He pushed her head down until it was bowing on the floor.

My heart was pounding. He was only inches away from me.

"Eddie...," Kim moaned.

"Business is business." He put the gun to the back of her head. I heard firecrackers exploding outside as the parade passed by. Eddie pulled the trigger, and everything turned red.

He came toward me. Everything started to shimmer around the edges. A dead silence fell about me, and in it I heard the voice not of the Golden Tiger but of my father.

"Whitney?" he whispered. "Whitney?" My bedroom door creaked slowly open. My father walked across the room to my bed. I was afraid to move. Couldn't protect myself. He pulled down the blanket. He bent over me. His hand hovered inches from my vagina....

Then I saw the Golden Tiger appear, his white uniform whipping the air as he kicked and punched, hiding everything in the past from me. "Whitney!" I heard the Golden Tiger shout as his image faded. "Now, Whitney, now!"

I rolled and grabbed Eddie around the knees, knocking him off balance. Falling, he tried to hit me with the gun. I grabbed his wrist, shoving the gun upward and toward his chest. It went off. It clattered to the floor. Eddie fell to the ground.

I lay on the floor trying to catch my breath. Eddie's face was next to mine. He stared at me. There was a bullet hole the size of a tangerine where his cheek had been. His one remaining eye flickered closed. Blood ran from his mouth. I got to my knees, then to both feet. I picked the gun up from the floor. I wiped it off with my t-shirt. I put the gun back in Eddie's hand and closed his fingers around it.

I walked through the open doorway into the larger of the two rooms. An antique chest of walnut lined with cedar and with brass fittings stood in the center of the room. A typed index card explained in English that the chest was called a *jang* and that the etchings on the brass fittings were symbols of long life.

I walked back through the blue gate out into the streets of the paper-and-wood village. Later I would learn from Dorothy that such gates are for good luck. Lupe stood at a corner under a wooden pole that held a lantern. I glanced at my watch. Everything had happened in the paper village in less than ten minutes. *"Vamos."*

"Where's Kim? What happened?"

I wanted a drink. "Well, she's not going to be marrying your brother."

"I heard shots."

"It was only firecrackers. The parade. Come on, let's go."

Lupe started for the house where Kim and Eddie lay.

"She's dead," I said.

"You...?" asked Lupe as she turned back to where I stood.

"One of Ko Won's guys killed her. The one who said he's a cop. He's in there too. They killed each other."

Lupe looked at me, searching my face. I had never lied to her before, but I wasn't going to tell her what I'd done. Had I wanted Eddie to kill Kim? In that instant I had. I felt her minute inspection, and I didn't blink. I made my eyes soft, innocent.

"I guess they didn't trust her anymore," I said. "Too ambitious. Trying to play too many people against each other...." I stopped, looking away from her to the austere and silent parchment houses. "I'm sorry about the money."

Lupe sighed. She studied my face again. Her eyes were dark brown, almost black. Deep as wells. I don't know what she saw in my face at that moment. "Yeah, ok. I guess I'll have to live without a Chanel belt."

She waited to see if I'd say anything more, but I didn't.

"You could still do that tv show with the sex goddess," she offered. "It would be a good way to get your name known. I can help you with your image." She grinned, but looked away as though she understood the solitude I needed to quiet the rage in my soul.

We walked down the artificial street. The paper houses were bleached white by the noon sun and shimmered nascent in the hot light. We walked back through the building and the bamboo atrium in silence.

Other dancers were on the stage. We walked through the happy, noisy crowd of Koreans and Mexicans and Central Americans. We opened the door and stepped out onto the holiday street.

The uneasy truce quiet that had settled over the city in the last months was punctuated by music. I would go tell Dorothy Oh her granddaughter would not be coming home. The Queen Min box was lost. The *kye* money was probably gone, but she would have the Shining Pearl restaurant. There would be people who wanted soul food. They would sit at tables together to eat and laugh and drink.

The Santa Ana wind blasted down the street, tugged at the brilliant banner hanging over the building, and ripped loose one of the ropes holding it. The banner drooped, the words crumpled upon themselves and disappeared.

NO JUSTICE
NO PEACE

THE END

Mercedes Lambert
(Douglas Anne Munson)
1948—2003

Understanding Mercedes Lambert—whose real name was Douglas Anne Munson—is as much a confrontation with mystery as fact.

1989. While awaiting the release of her first book, El Nino, Douglas Anne Munson—an attorney in the Los Angeles Criminal Court system—begins work on a hardboiled mystery called Dogtown. She is writing like there's no tomorrow, like someone stung by the awareness of how short life can be. Two years earlier, she'd been diagnosed with breast cancer. When a lumpectomy successfully removed the growth, she turned seriously to writing. She is 39 years old.

1997. On an island in the Pacific Northwest, Douglas Anne Munson struggles to resurrect her third Whitney Logan mystery, Ghosttown, after its rejection by her publisher—the very same publisher who had only a few years earlier urged her to continue the series based on the critical reception of Dogtown ("WE WANT MORE!"). Her mood sinks under the ceaseless rain, the daily ferry rides to a $5 an hour job, the migraines that have her injecting herself with medication. She is convinced that the "trajectory of downward mobility" she had joked about with co-workers before leaving Los Angeles has become her fate.

Between those two years, stands the literary legacy of Douglas Anne Munson, one that started late and ended much too soon. In approximately eight years, she wrote four books, all well received. One of those books would not be published until four years after her death.

* * *

She was born in Tennessee in 1948 and moved frequently during childhood. Her family finally settled in southern California. She told a newspaper once she felt like she'd been raised by wolves.

Douglas attended college in New Mexico—studying Latin American studies—then lived briefly in Ecuador before attending law school at UCLA.

Most of her legal career was spent working for the Los Angeles County dependency courts. She was part of a team assigned to determine the best interests of children who had suffered abuse, neglect, or abandonment. The job took its toll. She drank heavily, lived on the edge. The cancer turned that around: she started shaping the horrors she witnessed daily—and the demons of her own past—into fiction.

Satisfaction would always elude her, even when praise and recognition validated the talent her father insisted she lacked; she always felt it was a mistake, that she was a fraud. Despite the lack of support or encouragement she received, Douglas dedicated her first book to her mother and father, and also to Maryse—Maryse Holder, whose book Give Sorrow Words was a major influence.

* * *

In Dogtown and Soultown, Douglas/Mercedes delivers the classic noir double-punch: character and milieu. She appropriated the mean streets of Los Angeles from Raymond Chandler and handed them over to a young, naïve attorney barely able to pay the rent who is haunted by the voice of a reproachful father, and a street-wise Chicana prostitute with a young son, a violent brother, and a encyclopedic knowledge of Hollywood's golden age.

The friction between these protagonists reflects the cultural disharmony of a city. She saw Los Angeles as the epicenter of clashing cultures in America. Violent crime draws them into new worlds that exist—often unseen—in the midst of the world we think we know. The more impenetrable these sub-cultures seem to be, the more we begin to recognize common themes: abuse and exploitation of the innocent, the burdens of family, the tyrannical hold of the past, the struggle for autonomy, the corruption of power, the power of corruption, and fickle promise of love.

We are not so far apart after all.

Douglas told a magazine reporter in 1996: "Sometimes, I'll be staring at the blank page and realize that 40 minutes south down the 405, a Vietnamese poet is staring at the blank page, too; to the east, a Jamaican girl makes up a song and the black girls dance; north, an Iranian family prays; and somewhere near Hoover, a very elegant Peruvian gentleman cuts a deck of cards. We will never hear of one another, but together our words are creating the myth that is Los Angeles."

Douglas helped us to hear of one another.

* * *

Douglas never wrote again for publication after the rejection of the third Whitney Logan mystery, Ghosttown. She kept journals, up to the end. They chronicle the final troubled years: transient hotels, junkie-crash pads, periods of homelessness, and finally—a self-imposed exile in the Czech Republic. The cancer that had started her literary career returned in 2001. She died two years later at the age of 55.

In 2007, Ghosttown was finally published, completing the Dogtown trilogy. Now, thanks to Stark House, the first two books in the series are in print once again.

Mercedes Lambert is back.

LUCAS CROWN
2007

Acknowledgements

Many people deserve thanks for their contribution to the reissue of these books. Here are a few:

Charles Ardai, who offered encouragement and suggested Stark House as a possible publisher.

Greg Shepard, who refuses to let great writers be forgotten by publishing lovely reprint editions of classic crime/noir through Stark House. While these books fall outside the normal timeframe of Stark House—the 1940s, 50s, and 60s—Greg found them compelling enough not to be bound by his own rules.

Ken Bruen, one of the finest crime/noir writers at work today, who kindly agreed to contribute an introduction to this edition.

Louis A. Fernandez, for many years of friendship and encouragement; Louis first introduced me to Ken Bruen's work, then suggested I ask him for an introduction.

Amy Crown, my wife, for her indispensable help and support along the way.

LUCAS CROWN
2007